IN FOR A PENNY

CAROLINE FRANK

CONTENTS

Content Warning	ix
Author's Note	xi
Epigraph	xiii
Prologue	1
Chapter 1	13
Chapter 2	20
Chapter 3	38
Chapter 4	47
Chapter 5	63
Chapter 6	76
Chapter 7	90
Chapter 8	98
Chapter 9	106
Chapter 10	120
Chapter 11	129
Chapter 12	137
Chapter 13	142
Chapter 14	147
Chapter 15	153
Chapter 16	167
Chapter 17	176
Chapter 18	182
Chapter 19	188
Chapter 20	198
Chapter 21	202
Chapter 22	205
Chapter 23	206
Chapter 24	220
Chapter 25	233
Chapter 26	252
Chapter 27	259
Chapter 28	265
Chapter 29	271
Chapter 30	287
Chapter 31	293

Chapter 32	302
Epilogue	313
Acknowledgments	319
Also by Caroline Frank	321
About the Author	323

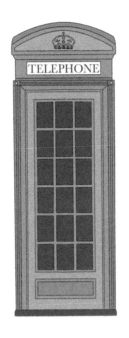

For K, with all my love.

Content Warning

This work of fiction contains graphic and sensitive content pertaining to sex, sexual assault, and eating disorders.

Author's Note

In for a Penny was originally published back in July of 2021. In its second edition, typos have been fixed (my bad for lack of attention to detail).

This book was my debut novel. My baby. Something I wrote as a cathartic experience when I had no intentions of making writing a full-time thing or had any knowledge whatsoever on how the hell to write a full-length book. Up until then, I was mostly a literary fiction short story person.

It's (very) loosely based on events transpired during my years in London. Which is exactly why I'm so protective of it. Though I know I could have made bigger changes to the story—improving character arc or whatever—I didn't want to, in the end. I didn't want to polish the hot mess that is Penny Marquez. I didn't want to make the story more obvious. I didn't want it to follow any "formula" that a writers is "supposed" to when writing a story.

More importantly, I like seeing how far I've come and how much I've grown, and I don't want to hide that.

So, I left Penny as she is—with nicer sentence structure, and a shorter scene, that is.

I think, if you were her at one point, or loved someone like her, you'll be able to understand her. But I'm aware she isn't for everyone. Penny is a complicated mess; but I still think that she's the most realistic and human character I've written to date.

I hope you give her a chance.

XO,

Caroline

It's never too late to be what you
might have been.
-George Eliot

Prologue

THE WARM SUMMER breeze comes through the open door and brushes my face. I close my eyes and take a deep breath, exhaling unsteadily. My heart skips a beat, hoping it isn't him walking through that door. I'm not ready to face him yet. Though, would I ever be?

It's a false alarm—a couple and their two children walk in, smiling expectantly at the hostess.

A restaurant.

I must be insane.

Why would I suggest a restaurant of all places for us to meet? I haven't been able to eat in anticipation of our non-date for the past two days, and I still feel like I am about to hurl. There is no way I will even be able to keep down a glass of water, let alone steak frites.

But it *is* our place. And it had been our place for the three years while we were dating. We used to come here all the time —at least twice a month. And now I'm leaving. Leaving New York and officially leaving him behind, and I had just wanted to say bye one last time before I left the city, if I never came back. If there would be no reason ever to come back. Truthfully, if I would never, ever want to come back.

I haven't physically seen him in a little over a year, but we've foolishly been staying in touch, and it hasn't been easy. To say this has been the most challenging year of my life would be an understatement. I have never felt more unstable or in need to control everything in my entire life.

This dinner is supposed to be *it* until we are ready to come back to each other. Until we can say, "I am my own person and can be with you as equals."

Are we crazy? I don't know. I do know that we needed a breather when we broke up in May of last year. Things were so intense with us. They are still so intense. *So* consuming. We didn't know if it was good or bad, but we knew we wanted to be together in the end, and if that was going to happen, it was important we learn how to be independent of each other. We were way too wrapped up in our relationship.

When we agreed to this separation, it seemed to make sense at the time. Now, I'm struggling to understand how this will truly help.

The breakup was supposed to help with both of our growths, but I have never felt smaller or weaker than I have in the past twelve months.

Is that pathetic? I feel like I'm losing my footing on what my future is supposed to look like. And all for what? Because I needed to enjoy my senior year of college with no emotional ties?

The thing is, I'm already emotionally tied. I will always be emotionally tied to Austin.

He said it would be for the best, but all this separation has done is made me feel anxious. The insecurity has made me miss him more, cry myself to sleep almost every night, sleep with all the wrong boys, and drink way too much—destructive behavior that is starting to take a toll on me.

Maybe this whole thing is a mistake.

I feel like everything in my life is blurring, like everything I thought my life would look like could slip away any second now, despite all that he's said. We were supposed to end up together, but now I'm on my way to grad school on another continent. And I still have no idea how this is supposed to help our relationship.

How are things going to work out in the end?

It's true. I am trying to prove to him that I'm not some inept, overly emotional young girl and that we will be able to do this, have a life together. He will, in the meantime, focus on work and his grad school applications. Austin also has some growing to do in that regard.

We've discussed the separation at length, and he's reassured me several times that he loves me and that he'll wait. Though we discussed being emotionally exclusive, we agreed that we're free to be with other people physically. The plan is to be emotionally unavailable to anyone else but each other. I just can't shake this feeling that something isn't right.

I close my eyes as memories of our last night together flash before my eyes.

"We will come back to each other," he had whispered in my ear as we had made love.

Cringing, I think back to that moment and take a deep breath in and out. I remember every single detail of how Austin's lips had traveled all over my neck and chest, the way our bodies moved together in unison. *"I love you. Forever, I love you,"* he kept whispering in my ear as I moaned in pleasure.

I'm getting dizzy.

"H-hey."

My eyes fly open.

"Oh my God, hey." I laugh awkwardly, feeling my cheeks redden and heat more and more by the second. I'm actually blushing.

Austin smiles sheepishly. "It's so nice to see you again," he says as he stands behind the chair across from me.

Oh God, am I supposed to get up, too?

"Um…" I start to get up from the bench behind the table quite awkwardly. I'm struggling.

He notices this and quickly says, "No, no, please! Don't get up!"

"It's fine." I walk around the table to where he stands and accidentally knock over my water glass.

Jesus Christ, what an idiot.

Everyone in the restaurant starts to look around at the mess and commotion that I've created.

I. Am. Mortified.

We grab napkins from neighboring tables and mop up the spilled drinks.

Way to go. Way to prove what a mature and self-adjusted person you are.

You're a mess, Penny.

Once we successfully mop up most of the water, I stand up straight and look into his blue eyes. He smiles his supermodel smile, and my heart skips another beat. I suddenly begin to realize what a colossal mistake this dinner is. There's definitely no way I'm walking out of this non-date without feeling like we're breaking up all over again.

"Hi," I greet him again with a forced laugh, ignoring the fact that, a minute ago, I was thinking about his lips on me while he moved and made me co—

I snap back to reality.

He opens his arms, and I groan internally. I go in for what I expect to be an awkward, ass-out hug. Instead, he snakes his arms around my waist and presses me close to his chest, kissing the top of my head. I wrap my arms around his neck and lean my head on his shoulder, breathing him in. A combination of Nivea aftershave and Austin's scent hits me like a punch to the gut. It's heady, and I get the sudden urge to bottle it up so I can keep it with me when he goes.

My knees buckle, and I suddenly start feeling very warm.

Fuck. Fucking fuck. I knew this was a mistake.

He cuts the hug short. My breathing is already a little uneven and comes in a little faster. Can he tell? I start panicking but stop once I notice I'm not the only one looking a little hot and bothered.

Well, well, well. Glad to know I'm not the only one affected by the other's presence...

We take our seats on opposite ends of the table and stare at each other for a second.

"So," he starts, "you're moving to London?"

He orders food for us both—our usual—and a bottle of wine. I pass on the alcohol, trying to avoid anything that may increase my chances of experiencing a case of nervous regurgitation.

I notice how easy it is for us to fall back into our regular rhythm. We flirt shamelessly and talk endlessly about all the new things that have happened in our lives since we last saw each other while reminiscing. As we laugh at a Halloween memory, he instinctively reaches out for my hand to hold it. We both stop laughing and stare at each other, his expression intense.

I look away in sad silence.

"*Penny,*" he says quietly.

My hand is still in his, his thumb drawing patterns on my skin.

I close my eyes to keep the tears from running out but, instead, see our naked bodies intertwined.

No.

I quickly open my eyes and am back in the restaurant.

"Penny," he repeats my name with more intent. "I'm sorry."

"For what?" I shrug nonchalantly.

He takes my hand in both of his and lowers his head to meet my gaze.

"For everything. For hurting you, for hurting me. I know this sucks."

Wait. Wait. Does he mean…?

I start to feel hopeful. Is Austin having doubts, too? Does he want to get back together? Is he saying that he's down for a long-distance relationship? This whole thing is ridiculous.

I want to tell him I agree. I want to say that I think it's stupid, too, and that we should work harder on keeping this thing alive because, damn it, it's worth it. We're worth it.

Right?

"But it's the way it has to be," he continues.

Oh.

The wave of disappointment hits me so hard it almost knocks the breath out of me.

"This is going to be fantastic for both of us—you'll see. You're going to be amazing. School is going to be great. You're going to be able to leave your bubble and comfort zone and see what the real world is actually like, away from the comfort of your family and social circle. You need to grow outside of this.

"I want you to experience everything that you can. It's going to be so great for you. And then"—Austin smiles encouragingly—"once you've finished school and I see where I'm at with my MBA, we can see how to proceed."

He still wants to end things. Temporarily, though. A few tears manage to escape from my eyes.

Oh no. Did I remember to wear waterproof mascara?

"Yeah," I mumble out. "Yeah, no, I know," I say unconvincingly. "It's what's best for us. For our relationship."

"Exactly." He smiles encouragingly and says, "Now, let's look at that dessert menu."

I guess he definitely wants this.

He never does let go of my hand after that. Once we finish our crème brûlée and pay the check, he leads me out of the restaurant.

I let go of him and raise my hand in the air for a taxi.

"Stop. Wait—no, don't go." He wraps an arm around my waist and pulls me from the edge of the sidewalk. Austin takes a deep breath. "Not yet please. I'm not ready."

He holds me tight and looks down at me as we hear the squealing of old brakes behind me.

Miss? You need cab? I hear the heavily accented driver ask me, my eyes never leaving his.

I furrow my brow.

"Please," he whispers. "Not yet." He pulls me in closer, his eyes filled with that expression I've gotten to know so well.

I know that look. I know what it means.

His face is so close to mine I can see the gold specks in his blue eyes and can count the freckles on his nose.

I know I need to end the night now. I know I can't bring him back home with me. But I catch another whiff of his aftershave and lose any ounce of self-control left in my body.

"O…kay," I breathe.

I won't sleep with him, though. I'll just let him walk me home.

Must not sleep with him. Must not sleep with him. Inhale through mouth. Avoid sexy man scent.

"We won't be needing a cab. Sorry," Austin says quickly over my shoulder. He breathes a sigh of relief. "Thank you. I'm not ready for this night to be over."

We start walking, hand in hand, toward my apartment, but there's no way he's coming up. I need to be strong, and sleeping together would just tear me apart further.

I feel the heat of the last days of summer hit me as we reach the edge of Central Park. He stops to sit on a bench. We're only a couple of blocks away from my apartment, and this night has to end eventually. He's prolonging it as much as possible.

My heart aches.

I smile and pull out a cigarette. I've been smoking too much lately—a nasty habit.

God, I hate cigarettes.

They are expensive, addictive, the smell is impossible to hide, and—surprise—horrible for you. I take in a drag.

God, I love cigarettes.

I can't help but relish the feeling as the smoke fills my lungs.

He pulls out a vape, and I laugh.

"What?" Austin asks.

"Since when do you vape? I didn't realize that you had made a career move into finance!" I say, alluding to the correlation between Patagucci vest-wearing Wall Street bros and vapes. The city is overflowing with them.

He smiles. "They're better for you than cigarettes!" he laughs, grabs my hand, and pulls me down to sit next to him. "But you're right—it's not the same." He takes the cigarette from my hand and takes a drag.

We've shared many cigarettes over the course of our relationship—proof that we hadn't exactly been the best influences on each other. Sharing one with Austin now brings me back to nights on his balcony where we smoked many of them post-coital.

I flash back to a particular night where we weren't able to make it back into the apartment in time, and he took me there, against the balcony door, for the world to see. Thankfully, it was around three am, and there was not much movement around his neighborhood.

A car stops at the stoplight, blaring my favorite merengue song, and he smiles knowingly, getting up. He quickly puts the cigarette out and throws it in the trash can. Suddenly, he's twirling me and pulling me into his arms. He knows I love to dance—I can't help my Colombian heritage. He knows it's my weakness.

Another memory of us at my favorite Latin club flashes when I close my eyes and feel his chest on my back as he rolls me into him. I had asked him to learn how to dance for me, and he had definitely delivered on that promise. The thought of him doing this with anyone else makes my heart ache.

He rolls me out and into him once more, his arms wrapped around me, burying his face into my hair, breathing me in. The humid end-of-summer air suddenly feels cold on my hot skin. Austin doesn't play fair.

God, I hate him for making me feel this way.

"God, Penny, maybe…"

I stop quickly and pull away from him as the car drives away, taking the sultry song with it. "No. Stop. Please. I feel like you're flip-flopping here."

He looks sad and defeated. "You're just so young. I can't do this. This is why we need this separation."

"Then why do you do stuff like this to me?" I raise my voice, referring to our impromptu dance. Suddenly, I realize that we are not alone on Fifth Avenue and have amassed somewhat of a crowd due to our dancing. I don't blame the onlookers—I really am a good dancer, and he is excellent at leading.

"I don't know! I-I can't think straight when I'm with you! How are we supposed to have a life together when we go from being all gooey with each other to battling it out like this? We need separation! You need time to grow up some more and enjoy other things in life before committing to something more serious!"

I am seething with anger. "Yes, you have made your opinion about my maturity abundantly clear, Austin. To be honest, I think you need this too! You need to grow the fuck up."

He sighs, looking exasperated. "Of course I do. That's the whole point! We are way too serious about each other for where we are in life."

Don't cry, don't cry, don't cry.

"Goodbye, Austin. I can't do this anymore," I say as I start to walk quickly away. He catches up with me easily.

Damn these stilettos.

"Penny, please." I keep walking as quickly as my shoes allow, wanting to run. "Penny! I love you, Penny! Please stop!"

I stop and whip around. "Don't say it if you don't mean it!" There's venom in my voice. I sound like I've had enough, but I'm trying my hardest not to beg him to take me back.

"I do mean it." He pulls me into his arms again. "Please, I don't want to end things this way. Please. I'm sorry. It's just... It's just so fucking hard to think clearly around you! God," he sighs loudly, "all I've been able to think all night during dinner is being with you, thinking about you naked in my bed, telling you how much I love you, and... *fuck*."

He stares intently at me with wary eyes, measuring my reaction.

"Breathe, Penny."

I suddenly realize that I have, in fact, stopped breathing.

"Austin...this is just too hard. If we love each other so much, why do we even need to do this?"

"You have to go, Penny. You need to carve your own path, and so do I. I think we'll resent each other if we start making all these professional decisions based on each other.

"Go to London, go to grad school truly on your own, and then come back to me if you'll still have me."

"I'll always want you. Forever."

Pathetic, Penny. So pathetic. Ever heard of playing hard to get? Who would ever want someone as needy as you?

But he smiles. Austin doesn't think it's pathetic.

"I have to do the same thing, Penny. I have to decide where I am going to do my MBA and focus on my job. And if we stay together, I won't have the strength to do what's best for my career and us." He pauses. "Let me get settled in life. Let me figure my shit out so we can fit neatly together after and then I can give you the world. We both know we want to be together, but we have so much growing up to do first."

I don't realize I'm crying until I find myself sniffling.

Fuck. I don't want to cry.

"Yes," I say. "Just take me home, please."

We stop outside my building, having not spoken since our confession in Central Park.

"When do you leave?" he asks.

"Two weeks," I reply quietly.

He nods and hands me an envelope. "Here. Take this. Read it when you need it." He starts to walk away, head down.

"Austin?" I call out to him.

"Yes?"

"Please don't fuck any of my friends." I smile weakly.

He chuckles. "No worries, babe. I'm not *that* big of a dick." I watch him walk away from the front door of my building until he's out of sight.

Looking up, I stare around at the buildings in my neighborhood, thinking of everything I'll be leaving behind. I think about not having authentic New York City bagels with cream cheese and lox for breakfast. I even think about every crazy experience I've had on the subway and the interesting people I see on a daily basis. I think about all the museums and theaters and everything this city has to offer every damn day—that one place in Morningside Heights that makes the giant pizzas, the way the orange light sunshine hits the fall leaves in Central Park, Chelsea Market, the shuffleboard place with the food truck in Williamsburg, and how fucking beautiful the city looks at night.

People say that New York is overrated, but I think it's because they never got to live it the right way.

Although I do ache at the thought of leaving this city behind, I agree that a change might be what my life needs now, whether I like it or not. There's so much more to look forward to on the horizon—or at least that's what I'm telling myself. I'm not too happy with my (hopefully) temporary breakup, but a move to London might not be the worst thing in the world.

I breathe in the muggy summer air and take in the city night. I'll be saying bye to it soon.

New York, I love you.

One

"OVER THE COURSE of one year, you will have to take six compulsory modules and four elective modules," the program director drones on.

I've been sitting in this damn orientation for the past two hours and slowly losing my mind. I wonder idly how much left of these intros I have to endure before I'm able to go get myself some food. Or air.

"We have modified the structure of the program differently from what it was when you applied, we know. But we believe you will come out stronger in the end, more prepared to take on the policy-making world."

I roll my eyes and sigh, a bit depressed. As I sit in my uncomfortable chair under fluorescent lighting, I surprise myself by feeling a sense of disappointment. Deep down, I *was* excited to continue to learn. I guess I'm only realizing now that coming to London was just about running away from heart-break to whole other continent.

Ugh. Running away was stupid; definitely not my proudest moment.

Though the curriculum change is a huge bummer, I can't deny that I'm super excited about living in London, so at least there's that. I've only been here for a couple of days, and I already feel myself falling in love with it. From my limited travel experience, I'd say that London is the only city in Europe that truly resembles New York.

I still need to get used to the differences, though. Like the fact that it isn't exactly as 24-hour friendly as it claims to be. I mean, where are your 24-hour pharmacies and bodegas, London?

On my first night here, I was dying for Oreos at three am, but couldn't find a single place open near me. Even the subway —or rather, the tube—was shut down. So it's not like I could easily get around (unless I wanted to take the bus in the middle of the night, which, thanks, but no thanks—I've heard enough horror stories about late-night London transport to scare me half to death).

It sounds dumb, and a little spoiled, but I'm from New York City. I'm used to getting whatever I want whenever I want delivered to my house at any time of the day.

Aside from London's inability to provide one with whatever they want whenever they want, it's still a pretty amazing city.

No bagels, though. Sigh.

God, I'd murder someone for a good bagel right now.

I'm so hungry I'm about two seconds away from chewing my arm off. Longingly, I eye the table at the back of the room where some waiters are setting up some drinks and finger sandwiches. I make a mental note to beeline it right over there as soon as the department director wraps it up.

Just as I turn back toward the front, though, I notice a pale, dirty-blond guy staring at me. I furrow my brow inquisitively at him, and he smiles and turns back to the director.

How long has he been staring at me?

His hair is messy and unbrushed, and he's wearing a gray North Face hoodie, plaid shorts, and flip-flops. He doesn't seem to have put a lot of thought into what he's wearing today, even though this was supposed to be a formal orientation.

He looks like he was plucked straight out of a California tourism ad.

For a split second, I feel self-conscious and over-dressed in my black lace dress and stiletto heels, my honey-blonde hair up in a high bun. I thought this could be smart casual if need be, but I guess I'm a little more dressed up than I thought.

When I take a look around the room, though, I can tell there were mixed messages on what the dress code was. Some men came in suits, others in jeans. Some women dressed up while others, to my envy, are just wearing leggings. One woman is wearing shorts so small, it can barely be considered as wearing any clothes at all.

Ugh, I groan. *I'm acting like a total bitch today.*

I need to relax. Be happy. So many people would love to be here and have this opportunity, and I'm acting like it's an inconvenience.

"Hey there," I hear a husky voice behind me at the buffet table. I turn around. "Mind if I slip by you? Need some milk for my tea."

I turn to face a tall, broad-shouldered guy in a three-piece suit and huge Union Jack cufflinks on his sleeves. The image of this large man with a tiny teacup in his hands is laughable—he looks like a gentle giant.

Brits and their tea, I think to myself.

"Sure," I say, smiling as best I can. Quickly grabbing my embarrassingly full plate of piled-up finger sandwiches, I move to the side and give the man enough room so he can serve himself some milk.

He smiles back and gives me a not-so-subtle once-over.

Really?

His brown hair is cut short, with dark chocolate eyes that shine with mischief. He's handsome, that's for sure, but definitely not a Greek god—even though he seems to have the confidence of one.

"American?" He smiles, lifting an eyebrow.

"New Yorker," I reply without elaborating—no need to go into family background or history, thank you very much. Genuinely wanting to be left alone to my own bitter devices, I do my best not to engage in conversation and turn away as I shamefully add another sandwich to my plate.

He pours a splash of milk into his tea and turns to face me.

"Oliver James," he says, sticking out his right hand. I reach out and shake it.

Never trust a man with two first names.

"Penélope Márquez. Or Penny, for short."

"That doesn't sound American." He frowns, confused.

"That's because it's not. It's Spanish." I don't feel like explaining further.

I walk away, wanting to maul the embarrassing number of sandwiches on my plate, leaving him standing alone by the drinks and food table.

Jeez, I am in such a shit mood.

I try to shake this feeling off. I mean, I know Oliver was looking me over like a piece of meat, but he *was* being nice, and I *am* supposed to be networking here. I also need to be making friends in general, right?

I'll try and make a friend after I finish my sandwiches.

I slump down in a chair with my plate of food and take a glass of cheap wine being passed around by waiters. Stuffing a sandwich in my mouth (egg salad—*sweet!*), I close my eyes and take a deep breath.

"So, what's your story?" I jump in my seat at Oliver's voice, startled, interrupting my thoughts on the most amazing egg salad sandwich I've ever had.

"*Jesus!*"

He takes a seat beside me and sips his tea with grace. "Why

do you sound American, say you're from New York, but are Spanish?"

"Aren't English people supposed to be reserved and private? Why the hell do you care?"

PENNY, STOP BEING A BITCH.

He chuckles, and I sigh, surprised he hasn't left me sitting alone at the table at this point. I've been so rude—I definitely deserve it.

"Sorry." I close my eyes and shake my head, sighing. "I don't mean to be rude. You didn't deserve that." I put my head in my hands. *Open yourself up more, Penny. Give this place a shot.* "If you're actually curious, I was born in Colombia and moved to New York when I was younger. *Technically*, I'm American but not sure I always identify as such."

I look over at him, embarrassed at my outburst and my even more embarrassingly unnecessary explanation of my family history. Oliver raises a brow at me, a small smile tugging at his lips.

"I'm in a horrible mood," I sigh, running my fingers through my hair.

"Why? Not excited about 'this new step' in life we're taking, as the program director called it?" he asks.

"Um, sure. Super pumped. Just… nervous," I lie.

"Maybe I can help with that. Help you relax. Colombians are hot." He gives me a lascivious look.

Is this guy for real? Ballsy.

I laugh once in disbelief. "Seriously? Just like that? You've known me all of two seconds."

"Why not?" he answers, setting his now empty teacup on the table. "I find you very attractive."

I laugh at the ridiculousness of this situation. Is he seriously propositioning me at our orientation? I haven't even known him for two minutes. "What's your name again?" I ask, trying to knock his ego down a peg or two.

"Oliver." He smiles confidently, completely unfazed.

I take him in and smile back. His forwardness is bordering on creepy, but there's something about his confidence and humor that make me realize that this approach usually works for him.

"Oliver," I start, "normally, given your attitude and general body language, I think I would loathe you." He snorts, leaning back in his chair with a grin. "But no one has made me laugh like this in a while, so if you'll pardon my forwardness..." I bite my lip, leaning closer to him, looking him in the eye seductively.

"Yes?" he says, intrigued, his chest rising and falling faster.

"I would love it if..." I whisper.

He looks at my lips. "Yes?"

"...we could be friends," I say with a laugh.

Oliver's face falls a bit, disappointed. But, as I expected, he quickly recovers, a broad grin spreading across his face. "You *are* a tease. But I like you. Yes, let's be friends."

"Awesome," I say, shaking my head with a laugh.

"That way, maybe one day, I'll get to fuck you."

"Jesus Christ," I roll my eyes again at his brazenness. Though I have to say, despite his forwardness, he instantly reminds me of a teddy bear. Just a weirdly horny and upfront one.

"Not likely, but okay. Why don't we leave it at just friends?" I ask, sticking my hand out to him.

He takes my hand and shakes it. "Deal. Come on," he says. "I'll introduce you to some people I already know from the program. I went to uni with some of them." He stands and sticks out his hand, helping me get up, staring at my legs up and down.

"You know, you really do have fantastic legs."

I laugh and shake my head. After playing games for three years, and sleeping with all the wrong guys for the past twelve months or so since the breakup, at least this guy makes me feel comfortable by giving it to me straight.

"Leave your sandwiches on the table, and let's go."

I get to my feet and shoot a longing glance at my plate as he quite literally pulls me in the opposite direction.

I never even got to try the tuna salad one!

Two

AFTER THE ORIENTATION cocktails die down a bit, a group of us—led by my new obnoxious friend, Oliver—decide to go to the pub down the street to get to know each other better. Though I was a bit apprehensive at first, I am happy to report that the group of students from my class are pretty amazing. Oliver introduced me to a couple of people he went to university with, and invited them and other students with whom we clicked to the pub across the street.

I think I'm going to like it here. Unlike most of the people from the group of friends I left behind, no one seems to be interested in talking about parties, drugs, or money. It's refreshing. I can see myself creating a friendly support group with what seem like well-adjusted individuals. They're warm and welcoming.

I'm in the middle of what I *think* is a conversation on British royals with one of Oliver's university friends, Chloe, but I'm having serious trouble understanding a word she's saying. It could be because she has a heavy Northern England accent—which I had never heard before tonight—or it could be the fact that I've had three vodka sodas and two beers on top of the two glasses of wine I had at orientation.

What can I say? We're going pretty hard.

Though I'm feeling the effects of the alcohol—*understatement of the century*—most of my classmates seem to be fairing quite well. I'm pretty sure that I'm going to need to train my liver and build up my tolerance in order to survive the year here.

God, what did Chloe just say about school? I didn't understand a word she just said.

My class seems less competitive than what I imagined an American grad school class would be. From what I've heard, pretty much everyone in U.S. schools competes for the best internships and jobs, making the whole experience very cutthroat. So far, my classmates seem genuine and open. It's nice.

Are they real humans? Who was I surrounding myself with before London? Are people actually nice like this? Is this real?

No one has made a single passive-aggressive or snarky comment all afternoon. Granted, I've just met these guys, so there's still a chance that they'll end up being massive assholes, but they seem like better individuals than my so-called friends.

The night *is* young, though. And so is this whole experience.

Back in New York, my social circle sure had loved talking about my breakup and the drama surrounding it—as they did with any piece of new gossip.

It was exhausting. So many passive-aggressive comments. So much pressure to be perfect and bounce back as if nothing happened, but careful not to move on too fast at the risk of being called a whore.

Additionally, so much of my world was about who your family was and what they did. Meeting someone new within our social circle was like going to the doctor for the first time. They focused a lot on your family history first and then looked at you as a whole, second.

Not that there was anything wrong with my family, but I didn't appreciate the social pressures of living in a society where stuff like that mattered. Plus, I'm an immigrant, which put even more pressure on me to act perfect and in accordance with The Rules.

Which is why London is my fresh start.

I feel like I can finally breathe.

After another round, my stomach growls and my head

spins. The need for some pub food hits me like a blow to the face, making me dizzy.

With a wave of my hand, I flag down the closest waiter. "Can I get some chicken nuggets or something?" I ask, slurring my words a little.

Though I'm pretty sure chicken nuggets are a universal concept, the waiter stares at me like I've just spoken gibberish. "Miss, we only have chicken goujons?"

My *hangry* side decides to make a sudden and unwelcome appearance: "What *the fuck* are chicken goujons?" I gasp and cover my mouth, embarrassed. "I'm so sorry," I say, apologizing for my Dr. Jekyll and Mr. Hyde moment. "I didn't mean it to sound that way. I'm not usually this rude, I promise. It's the vodka. And the beer. And the wine."

My new friends laugh at me, not unkindly.

I just want food, dude.

"Would you please bring the lady some chicken goujons?" Oliver asks. "Thanks, mate."

The waiter rolls his eyes and walks away.

"Chicken goujons are like chicken tenders. Don't worry. I've got you, babe."

I groan. "Please don't call me 'babe,'" I beg, wondering idly how long his interest in me will last. "And it's your fault I haven't eaten. You didn't let me finish my sandwiches, so I guess you do owe me."

He laughs, and our table joins in on the fun. I've suddenly become the butt of every joke for the time being, but it's not in an unfriendly way. Our group just seems to be automatically comfortable with each other, and it is so goddamn refreshing.

I look at the people around me and sigh happily, taking them all in.

Chloe Graham, one of Oliver's university friends, is a year older than me. She's short, wears large square glasses, and seems like a nice girl with a quick wit—from what little I've been able to understand. It's easy to tell, just from my short interaction with her so far, that she can be an incredibly loyal friend.

Michael, the guy sitting to my right, is handsome and so sweet he almost makes me teeth ache. With his adorable German accent—which I never thought would sound sexy, but I happily stand corrected—I can tell he has serious rebound potential. My eyes follow his hands as he runs them though his curly brown hair, his hazel eyes shining behind round hipster tortoise glasses.

Down, girl.

North Face Guy's real name turned out to be Josh Fox. And I was right. He is from California—Palo Alto, to be precise. Josh and I share a similar background—both Political Science majors from small liberal arts schools, interned in D.C., and recently uncoupled—which might be why we instantly bonded (pathetic, I know). I don't know much about his breakup, but he seems as beat up about it as I feel.

The sweetest-looking of the bunch, he looks like the type of person that would dedicate his life to his significant other—make them his everything.

Intense.

Then there's Jane, a sarcastic and wild girl around my age from Manchester. She has long blonde hair down her back and the brightest blue eyes I've ever seen. Oliver was definitely into her as well, but his advances were deterred once he found out two things. The first, Jane is in a long-distance relationship. Second, she is a black belt in jiu-jitsu and could easily kick his ass if she needed to. We became friends instantly.

As I stare around at the new friends I've met, I feel a large smile spread across my face. New people and a change in scenery might be exactly what I need.

Though, I consider myself a die-hard New Yorker, through and through, I can easily see the London appeal, even if it's only been a couple of days.

I can do this. I can make it work here. I can restart my life here and figure shit out. It's my time to enjoy whatever life throws at me!

I sigh.

Jesus Christ. I better make this work.

"Darling, are you tired?" Oliver asks in a mocking tone. I realize that I have unconsciously leaned my head on Oliver's shoulder. I can't blame my drunk ass for doing it since he smells nice and his broad shoulders looked comfy.

Spoiler alert: they are.

"Oops, I'm sorry." I yawn.

"Not boring you, am I?" he asks.

"Nope, not you, sorry. Just exhausted with the move and all," I say, fighting back another yawn. I crack my neck, and twist in my chair, stretching my spine. "Honestly, I'm just a little overwhelmed by everything I have to do before classes start." I still need to finish buying apartment necessities.

"Want to have a sleepover? I know several ways I could help relax you right now." He smiles his lascivious smile.

I laugh softly. "Nah, Oliver. Thanks for the offer—again." I roll my eyes. I don't think it would be possible to be his friend and go one day without rolling my eyes at him. I'm legitimately scared they're going to remain permanently stuck in that position.

He chuckles. "I'll get to you one day, babe. Until then, you know you—" He stops as he notices his phone vibrate on the table. "One sec—it's my girlfriend," he says calmly as he stands from the table to take his call.

My jaw drops all the way to China—or at least it feels that way. Chloe, a witness to our conversation, starts to laugh.

"Is he fucking kidding me right now?" I say, pointing

throwing a thumb in Oliver's direction. "He's been hitting on Jane and me all day and night, and he has a *girlfriend*?!" Chloe erupts into a fit of giggles. "Chloe! This is not cool! As a woman, you should—"

"Penny," she says, catching her breath. "Penny, love, they're in a very, *very* much open relationship."

"Huh? People seriously do that?" I am baffled.

"Yes, babe," I hear Oliver say from behind me. I look over as he returns to his seat and faces me. "You jealous?" He kisses me on the cheek, and I swat at him.

I sigh in frustration. "You *would* think that, wouldn't you?"

"Sorry—how in the hell did you manage that?" Josh asks, smirking. "I don't think I have *ever* heard of a successful open relationship before."

"*Manage* that?" Oliver scoffs. "She was the one who demanded it!"

I laugh once incredulously.

"Surely she did it so you wouldn't leave her, and it makes her feel uncomfortable? Maybe she felt pressured? No woman would be one-hundred percent okay with it." I would die. I would not be able to handle myself in a relationship like that. There is no way I would be secure enough to handle that arrangement.

"Dude..." Josh says with a stunned look in his eyes, "are you dating a unicorn?"

"A *what*?" Jane asks, shocked.

"A unicorn. A goddamn unicorn!" Josh exclaims, excited. He looks like he's about ready to jump from his seat. "An attractive woman who provides all the emotional support and benefits of a girlfriend and gives you the freedom to sleep with other girls without any jealousy or fighting. Dude, *please* tell me you're dating a unicorn," he says, clasping his hands in front of him in a begging motion.

Oliver pats Josh on the shoulder once with a smirk. "That I am, my boy," he replies proudly. "That. I. Am."

"Why are they called unicorns?" Jane asks. "Wait!" she holds up her hands. "No, don't tell me! Because they're mythical creatures?"

The boys nod and start laughing.

"Huh," I say more clearly. "That's wild. I don't think I could ever do something like that."

"You don't seem to be the type of girl who would, Penny," Oliver says calmly.

Understatement of the century.

"No," I reply. "I most certainly am not." I can confidently admit that I am too insecure for an open relationship.

But, no, not possible. No woman I know would be okay with that type of situation, would they?

Is this a normal thing people do? Maybe it's just me. Maybe I'm fucking boring. Maybe I'm just not mature enough or experienced enough to understand. Is that why Austin left me? Is that why we're in this bullshit breakup? Because finding things like open relationships impossible is something someone *immature* would do? I wince at my new trigger word.

Do all men really want this? Is that why it's so hard to accept?

Everyone goes back to making conversation while I stare at my hands on the table. I catch Oliver looking at me, and he grimaces.

"What are you thinking?" he asks quietly. Everyone else has moved on to another subject, not paying attention to us.

"Oliver, I'm not judging—not at all," I say as I see the hesitancy on his face. "I feel like there are different ways of being in a relationship. Personally, I don't think I would ever be able to be in an open relationship. I would be freaking out the entire time. But maybe things would be different with—" I clear my throat. "Things would be different for me if I were just a little more chill sometimes. If I were more relaxed and less controlling... I don't know." I shrug. I don't know why I'm saying this to him. "I don't know. Maybe I am a little naive. Some people"

—*AKA Austin*— "have told me that I live in a bubble. That I'm too sheltered, too immature. I guess coming here is a way to prove that I can truly live on my own in a new city. Be a grown-up." I shrug.

He turns in his seat to better look at me and holds my gaze without saying anything. Oliver studies me closely, while I grow uncomfortable in my seat.

The air grows thick, and I feel the familiar tension spreading from my neck, to the rest of my body. I need out. To absolutely no one in particular, I mutter, "I'm going outside for a smoke."

Oliver's the only one who acknowledges my mumbling and watches as I almost jog out of the damned pub. I think about how I should've played it a little bit more cool, but thinking about Austin and our relationship makes it impossible to breathe sometimes. I feel the pressure in my chest constrict, the pain spreading to my limbs.

"You left your cigarettes on the table." I spin quickly around at the sound of Oliver's voice. "I figured if you're about to have a breakdown outside like you seem to be about to, you better have the props to back up your excuse to leave the pub for a bit, mate." He half-smirks sympathetically. Oliver hands me my pack of cigarettes and pink lighter with a smile.

"You know those are bad for you, right?"

"I had no idea," I deadpan.

We both lean against the outside wall of the bar and quietly gaze at the drunks singing what I can only assume by the lyrics is an Arsenal team song, neither of us saying anything for a few minutes.

"So, how recent was your breakup?" he asks finally.

"How did you—"

He holds up a hand. "I can smell heartbreak a mile away— one of my talents for when I'm looking for women on the rebound." Oliver smiles half-heartedly. "I'm just joking—a little." After a beat, "So, who was he?"

I take a deep breath. "Someone who was quite possibly the

love of my life and who ripped my heart out and tore it to shreds."

Oliver snorts, and I physically recoil, anger coursing through me.

"Excuse me?"

"*The love of your life?*" he asks incredulously. "*God*, if you wanted to make me vomit, you could have fed me some of your horrible-looking chicken goujons. How old even are you?"

"I'm twenty-two, but that doesn't invalidate how we felt about each other," I say defensively. "Plus, he was six years older than me."

Oliver smiles patronizingly at me. "You really think you found the love of your life at twenty-two?"

"Excuse me, but I didn't invite you out here to talk about this. I came out here to be alone. So if you're going to ask and pretend like you care, at least be nice and friendly about it. If you don't give a fuck, then why bother even getting involved?"

Oliver's quiet; waits until I calm down and my breathing slows. He can tell that I'm not playing around and am upset.

"You're right. Your *feelings...*" he grimaces, "they're valid. I'm sorry," he says seriously now, all humor gone from his eyes. "Tell me about it. About him."

I look away and sigh.

"He was *supposed* to be the love of my life, I guess. I don't even know what happened. It seems like for the longest time we had agreed we were a done deal. A *forever and ever and ever* type of thing. And then suddenly I was *too young*. Even though I was older than I was when we started?" I shake my head in confusion, so many things that didn't make sense flooding my head. "And suddenly we both had to experience more things in life that we couldn't do together, apparently. And though we had talked about it in the past, about us making decisions regarding grad school and jobs and stuff together, suddenly it was like our relationship was... in the way of what he expected his 'real life' to be, you know?" I take a breath to steady myself, playing with the light in my hand, flicking it on. "I don't know how the hell he managed it—whether it was even conscious or not—but I think… I think I'm starting to realize that I was basically tricked into thinking that this whole break-up-so-we-can-pursue-our-dreams-and-grow-individually-to-come-back-together-later thing was *my* idea. Or that I was at least okay with it. When in reality I *never* wanted that.

"The fact is, lately I've been thinking… Well, wouldn't you do anything to stay with the person you love and make it work? Wouldn't you try and say, 'Hey, I think this place is right for me right now, but I love you, so let's find a way to stay together even if it means doing long-distance for a bit'? Half the people in our class are doing long-distance with their partners. Not saying that they'll all survive the time apart, but why wouldn't he give us a chance? I mean, look at you and your relationship! Even *you* can make it work!" I throw my hands in the air in frustration. "No offense," I add quickly.

"None taken," he says with a single laugh. "And I hate to say you're right, but you are. Lucy and I love each other—so much so that we didn't want to hurt the other by cheating. We knew the likelihood of us being monogamous was very low while living in different cities. But we didn't want to break up. We love each other, so we agreed to an open relationship. It works for us. We make it work."

"That's exactly my point! You found a way to make it work, in your own way. You *wanted* to make it work, to stay with her, so you created your own set of rules and boundaries! But Austin… Did he—Did he just think I wouldn't be able to handle the distance or an alternative solution, or was it really about the whole 'find your own way' thing or…or…"

I take a deep breath.

"Or?" he asks.

I look over at Oliver and am relieved to find compassion instead of pity in his eyes.

"Or was it all an excuse?" I say, my voice breaking. I'm

trying to hold it together, but I feel the tears start to fall down my cheeks. "Was he just a *fucking coward* and just used that all as an excuse to break up with me? Was I somehow mind-fucked into thinking he was going to wait, that this was all okay, when all this time he just used it as a way to let me down easy?"

I start sobbing at the monumental deceit that I just realized I have been put through, not caring about the fact that I am breaking down in front of a virtual stranger.

"Men…" Oliver sighs, "Men often like to keep their foot in the door."

I snort, and nod my head, realizing finally that's what it is. Austin tricked me into thinking that it was a mutual choice and that I had agreed to it. I believed all of it—every single last word—of him wanting to get back together after we "grow and experience new things"—whatever the hell that means. In reality, he just wanted to keep his foot in the door in case he changed his mind.

Fuck him.

I lean my head against the brick wall again and shut my eyes tight, taking a deep breath. Suddenly, I feel Oliver wrap his arms around me, my head against his chest. At first, I freeze. I mean, who is this guy? But then I realize just how much I need it and lean into him. It feels nice.

"Shh…" he says. "It'll be alright."

Oliver doesn't say anything as he waits for my tears to stop, and I sniffle.

"I feel like I've lost my footing on everything."

"Penny." He shakes his head and takes a deep breath. "I can sense that you think you consider yourself to be fragile or weak, but I am an exceptional people-reader, and let me tell you that what I see is a soon-to-be force to be reckoned with going through a shit time. You've just got to keep going." He pauses, frowning a little. "And maybe quit smoking, because you smell like utter shit."

I snort, wiping my snotty nose with the back of my hand. "Oliver?"

"Yes?"

"Thank you for this. Thank you for listening. You haven't even known me for twenty-four hours, and you're already acting more supportive than some friends I've known for years." I smile up at him. "It's been a while since someone has shown me this type of kindness—even if it is out of pity."

"I'm just trying to fuck you, remember?" he says with renewed lightness. "No kindness or feelings of pity here." His grin is wide as he squeezes me tighter.

"Ha! Yes, I forgot about that, offering me comfort just so you can sleep with me later," I laugh.

"Absolutely. I'm glad we cleared that up." He smiles wickedly. "Come here, idiot. I think you and I are going to be great friends." He pulls me into his side and starts dragging me into the pub.

"Insta-friendship," I murmur.

"What are you going on about?"

"Insta-friendship. You know how in romance novels there's insta-love and insta-lust? Well, I feel like we've had an insta-friendship."

He smiles. "Oh no, there was *definitely* some insta-lust. You just haven't been able to admit it to yourself yet, babe."

I open my mouth to protest, but he cuts me off. "Go to the loo and clean yourself up. You look like *utter* shit," and pushes me in the opposite direction toward the bathrooms. "And smell like it, too. You should stop smoking."

"And here I was thinking we just shared a nice moment," I say with a laugh.

I do as Mr. Sensitivity says and go clean myself up, because he's right—I probably do look like utter shit.

The commute home is long but not tragically endless. Forty minutes by DLR from the main campus, and I'm back at my apartment. I'm buzzed and feel kind of anxious—being a drunk girl in sexy heels, alone, late at night does not make me feel particularly safe.

I should have taken an Uber...

I walk home quickly from the station to my building and crash into my roommate as she tries to make her way out of the elevator.

"Oomph!"

A wave of coconut scent hits me as Allie and I collide. Her dark, long hair is curled and shiny, hanging down her back. She's wearing my favorite going-out top—I'll have to talk to her about borrowing my clothes without permission later—and her signature berry-colored lipstick tints her lips. I look down and realize that the contents of my purse have spilled all over the floor.

Fuck this night.

"Oops! Sorry, girl!" She helps to pick up my wallet, keys, and Chapstick quickly. "Going out tonight to meet up with some friends. I'm so late! Don't wait up!" Allie says. She kisses me quickly on the cheek and runs out to meet a car.

Allie and I met in high school. We were part of the same friend group but never super tight. It wasn't until I decided to move to London that we started talking more. She had been here two years already, so she was trying to give me tips on where to live, which realtors to use, etc. Having spent four years of college in the middle of nowhere in disgusting dorms, I refused to live in any type of school housing again.

Unfortunately, I couldn't afford an apartment by myself in the city. I would have had to live in Zone 3 or even 4, which was a long way from campus. As my start date for school grew closer, she also had to find new living arrangements, which turned out to be great for me. The decision to move in together was a no-brainer.

In just a couple of weeks, she found a relatively affordable two-bedroom apartment with an in-unit washer for us, which I was insane psyched about. In New York, having a washer in your apartment is how you know you've made it, so I was very impressed, even if we're barely in Zone 2. Our East London apartment is ten minutes away from Canary Wharf, one of the UK's most expensive neighborhoods, and fifteen minutes away from one of its poorest.

I'm excited to live in this new building with Allie. She's someone familiar, so we can be open about many things but not too tight that things can turn into passive-aggressive roommate wars.

Once I make it upstairs, I throw my purse and jacket on the couch, noticing how Allie has been cleaning and organizing since this morning—*again*. She's either a stress cleaner or a neat freak.

Please let organizing be her coping mechanism, and it not be a habit.

I don't know if I'll be able to make it a year with a neat freak, when I am a know mess.

With a heavy sigh, I pick up my jacket and purse and toss them on top of my bedroom vanity. Messes in my room don't count, right? Allie cannot make a big deal about my room. She isn't even supposed to be in here. But as I pull out my PJs from my dresser, I notice my clothes have been neatly refolded in the Marie Kondo method.

What. The. Fuck.

I walk over to my closet and open it. All of my clothes have been organized and divided up into categories, my shoes nicely lined up at the bottom of my closet.

"Whoa," I whisper under my breath. Is this Allie's way of

thanking me for just taking my top? Or did she find the top she was wearing tonight while she was organizing my closet and decided to borrow it as a thank you to herself? I don't know how I feel about this.

This will be interesting.

I sigh and quickly slip into my PJs, washing off my makeup and brushing my teeth—completing my nighttime ritual. I've never really been one for a seven-step skincare routine.

An hour later and I'm still wide awake, thinking about my conversation with Oliver. It was the first time I ever admitted out loud that I thought Austin was lying to me and using the waiting game as an excuse.

But it all seemed so real.

I feel like my mind is about to explode, like I've lost a grip on reality. I was so sure about the strength of our love and our relationship that I never really questioned him until recently. Have I really been that obtuse?

I groan.

This is so embarrassing. I can't believe I bought it!

I sit up quickly and turn on my light, pulling open my bedside drawer. I stick my hand in there and dig through it for a while until I find a worn-out envelope. It takes a bit to locate—I guess Allie hasn't tackled this drawer yet.

"Read it when you need it most."

I need to read this now. I need to read this now, feeling how I feel at this exact moment in time, but what am I looking for? Reassurance? Or maybe closure would be so much better. I can let go. But what if he doesn't want me to let go? What if I let go and then hurt him and end up missing out on the love of my life?

I.

AM.

PATHETIC.

I open the envelope and take out the letter, ready to read it with this new perspective that I have accepted tonight.

. . .

Penny,

I've been trying to write this letter for quite some time now—ever since I found out you were leaving the country and starting a new life in London. Every time I would begin to put pen to paper, though, nothing would come out. The words never seemed to be right.

I don't know how to adequately express how I'm feeling or how to say goodbye, but I'm out of time—tonight's the last time I'll be seeing you for a while. I'm not a writer, Penny. So please don't take offense if this isn't the most romantic thing you've ever read. I'm trying.

Penny, I love you. First and foremost, I should say that. I. Love. You. Please always remember that.

Second, I want you to know that I am so incredibly proud of you, Penny. You're doing it. You're going on your own to another country where you don't know anyone, and you will be entirely out of your comfort zone. I don't know if this is something you would have done if we had stayed together, but it's something you need, babe. Something we need. And you're going to be fantastic.

Third, and I think most importantly, please don't be sad or try to miss me too much. Don't get wrapped up in us and our separation too much that you can't grow from this and experience new things. I love you, and I want you to succeed in this new chapter of life.

You need this time to mature, and I need this time to organize myself and figure out how to grow professionally so I can take care of us and our future.

Enjoy London and school, and take care of yourself.

Love,

Austin

I refold the letter and stuff it in its envelope.

I've read this letter for what feels like a million times and have always found it incredibly romantic. And now? Viewing it with this new lens of doubt? I feel like it's empty. This is not a romantic, 'See you soon.' This is a regurgitation of the alleged reasons for why he broke up with me. And it sucks. One thing that he wanted me to take with me, and he gives me *this*? I feel like crumpling up the whole thing and throwing it out my window.

I feel embarrassed and ashamed. I've been holding on to this man and imaginary future for over a year, but none of it was real. It was all one-sided. I've come all the way to London to prove to him that I can be a grownup. That I am mature enough to be on my own. That I'm building something for our future and my career. I'm doing all this for us when he is essentially sending me away but trying to keep a foot in the door if he changes his mind. And I'm the love-sick idiot who fell for it.

I start bawling. The feeling of shame and regret is monumental, and I can barely stomach it. I feel used and abused. I feel tricked into believing that I meant more to him. I feel like our entire relationship was meaningless to him when it had become everything to me. I would have done anything to save it, and even agreed to his bullshit plan to do it.

Suddenly, all my plans start crumbling down like buildings in an earthquake, shattered and unrecognizable. What am I supposed to do now? Where am I going? What does my future look like now?

For the longest time, my future looked like Austin and me working in New York, living in Westchester with three kids like a goddamn Stepford wife cliché. I'd probably work at a foundation or other philanthropic society while he ran his father's business. All those late-night talks in bed where we had planned what our lives would look like make me feel like such an idiot that I want to laugh for days and cry for months. I feel like all we talked about was our future together, and I knew exactly what it looked like. And now, for the first time ever, I find myself absolutely lost.

Pathetic. Absolutely pathetic.

My chest tightens, heart racing as I begin to hyperventilate.

Relieved that Allie isn't here to witness this Defcon 1 break-down, I get in the shower, hoping the steam from the hot water will help open my airways, the heat helping to calm my suddenly tense muscles. To be honest, I can't handle a Friend Pep Talk right now, anyway. I just need to feel it. Feel the pain. I need to let all of this sink in.

Once I'm out of the shower, I feel a bit better. I put my hair up in a towel and tie my robe around myself. I don't bother putting on pajamas again. I slip into bed just like that and cry myself to sleep.

What am I supposed to do now?

Three

THE NEXT DAY, I wake with a start, determined not to let this get me down. Today is my first day of class, and I'll be damned if that fucker, Austin, ruins this for me too.

Though it's mid-September, the temperature outside is already starting to drop, so I dress in jeans, a black long-sleeved t-shirt, with a faux-fur vest. I feel grungy and angry, so I add a heavy black cat-eye, a messy bun, and some combat boots. On the outside, I look like I could kill someone today; on the inside... I'm hurt and angry—and could also probably kill someone.

Shit! I'm running late! No time for breakfast.

I make it to my Strategic Management class just in time, right before the professor closes the door to the classroom. He narrows his eyes at me, menacingly, and I clumsily take a seat in the closest available chair, right next to Josh, the guy from California.

"Hey," he whispers. "You made it just in time." Josh's hair is messy, and he's wearing his North Face hoodie again.

He shoots me a smile, and I force one back at him as I try to regulate my breathing. I just had to climb three flights of stairs since the elevators were taking forever and now I'm dying. But no big deal. It doesn't matter that I'm sweaty and gross for my first day of class, or that I didn't have time to eat breakfast.

The professor begins his lecture, and, as if on cue, my stomach growls embarrassingly loud.

Oh my God, kill me. Please, please, please, PLEASE, let no one have heard that.

But it was pretty loud, and I am *positive* that there is no way in hell Josh did not hear that. I shift awkwardly in my seat, trying to pass the sound off as movement in the chair. My actions are transparent, though, as I see his lips quirk up from the corner of my eye.

Josh reaches into his backpack, never removing his gaze from the professor at the front of the class, and pulls out a granola bar. He places it on my desk, still not looking at me, but I can tell he's suppressing a smile. I groan silently, embarrassed, but tear open the bar, because even though I'm incredibly embarrassed, I'm just as hungry.

The granola bar never stood a chance—I devour the thing in under ten seconds.

If I suspected Josh was smiling before, there is no doubt now. He looks down and pretends to concentrate on his notes, but I can tell he's doing his damnedest not to burst out laughing while the professor drones on about how we will be studying successful policy implementation.

The situation is so awkward, having had this near-stranger hear my growling stomach, that I can't help but bite down on my lower lip to keep from smiling as well. I open my notebook and write Josh a note:

OMG, THANK YOU. I'm sorry you had to hear that—how embarrassing. You are a lifesaver.

I turn my notebook and poke him in the arm to get his attention. He leans over and reads it with a smile, reaching out to reply just under where I had written to him.

Josh:

My pleasure. I just couldn't hear the lecture over the sound of your stomach growling.

He smirks at me, and I can't help but chuckle a little.
Me:

Jerk.

He looks over at me and chuckles but tries to cover it with a cough when a blonde girl in obscenely short shorts turns around to glare at us.

Chill out, Short Shorts. He's just going over the syllabus!
Josh:

You owe me a granola bar.

Me:

How about a drink? I think we're all going to the Student Union pub after the last class this afternoon. You down?

I look up to see the professor glaring at us. Josh shifts in his seat, and I straighten myself up in my chair and stare back at the professor, pretending to be enraptured by his lecture. Once he seems satisfied that we are paying attention, he turns back to the board. This feels like high school.

Blah, blah, strategic implementation, blah, blah, catastrophe...

I clear my throat to remind him to read the reply I wrote in my notebook.

He leans over and frowns as he reads it. I'm confused. Why would that make him frown? Oh crap, does he feel left out for no one having invited him earlier? Are his feelings hurt? After a few seconds, he pulls my notebook to him and writes back.

Josh:

Sure. Let's do it.

Smiling at him, I shoot him two thumbs up and go back to pretending to pay attention to our lecture, wondering idly what that look was about. He seems like a friendly guy, someone I could be friends with, and the whole granola bar thing was so sweet. I need a friend like that in my life right now.

Once our class is over and I gather my things, Josh turns toward me and opens his mouth to say something but quickly shuts it, glancing at someone over my shoulder. I turn to see Oliver walking toward us.

"Hello, darling." He smiles at us both. "Hello to you, too, Penny," he jokes.

"Ha-ha." Josh rolls his eyes at Oliver.

"Are you both joining the group tonight at the Student Union?" Oliver asks.

"Penny and I were just planning on heading there this afternoon. What time are you guys planning on going?" he says as he shoves his notebook and pen into his backpack.

Am I imagining the whole "Penny and I" thing sounding a bit possessive? Hmm…not a fan.

"I was planning on going after my afternoon workshop. I'm in section A," I say, ignoring the weird new feeling in the pit of my stomach.

"Brilliant!" Oliver says. "I'm in the same one! I'll see you there then, and we can walk over together."

Josh furrows his brow. "Okay, cool. So, when are you guys out?"

"Around five-thirty, I think. I'll text you! Gimme your number," I demand.

Josh smiles when I pull out my phone and hand it to him so he can save his number to it.

"Cool, see you guys then! I have a break right now and am in urgent need of some coffee," I say as I start heading out.

"Ah, I'll go with you, love. I don't have class for another hour," Oliver says, putting his arm around my shoulders.

We walk out of the classroom and into the hallway. Josh heads left to his next class with a half-hearted wave, and Oliver and I head out to the cafe.

"You know he has a crush on you," he says matter-of-factly.

"Ha, doubtful. I barely even know Josh—or you, for that matter," I say, pushing Oliver's arm off me.

"Duh, crushes are about attraction and first impressions. It's when you get to know someone that crushes turn into feelings," Oliver replies.

"Stop saying wise things, Oliver, or I might start thinking that you're smart."

"You know I'm fucking brilliant, love. I work for a Member of Parliament and have a very long political career ahead of me." His chest puffs proudly as we enter the cafe and find a seat at a table.

"You're not really helping your case," I smile and tease him. "Politicians are rarely considered smart individuals. Only a handful of them are what I would consider admirable."

"Says the other idiot studying to become one," he laughs and pulls out a chair for me. I take it and scooch in.

"Not necessarily." Sighing, I run my fingers through my hair. "I don't know, Oliver. I honestly don't know what to do with my life right now. I've worked in politics and electoral campaigns, helping lobbyists since basically high school. But you know what happens if and when you lose a campaign? It's the biggest type of heartbreak. You fight so long and hard for something you think will change lives—or at the very least, yours—but nothing comes of it. Because when you let people decide, they make the wrong choices. It's hard to empathize with people when sometimes it seems like they don't even want to be helped—or just make stupid choices." I sigh. "Democracy sucks."

"That's your first mistake right there, mate. Politics isn't about helping people. It's about power," he says seriously.

No truer words have ever been spoken. Oliver might just be the most brilliant idiot I've ever met.

I smile. "I know, but come on. Sometimes I feel like people would be better off with a benevolent dictator," I say, joking —*kind of.*

"You'd be a fucking fantastic dictator," he teases.

"Hell yeah, I would!" I shove him.

As I think about my professional future, I notice now how much of it ended up being tied to my relationship plans with Austin. I make a mental note to find out what it is that I really want to do or who I even want to be. It's been quite a while since I've asked myself that question. For so long, I imagined what a perfect life should look like and worked toward that, but I never gave a second thought to whether it was the ideal life *for me.*

Not noticing my brief exit from this conversation, Oliver orders us both teas, ignoring my request for a cappuccino.

"You need to stop drinking that shit," he says when I start to complain. "Tea is better for you."

Between criticizing my cigarettes (which okay, I know they're bad for you and everything, but still) and wanting to change my beverage order, it seems like *he's* the one who wants to be the benevolent dictator.

The Student Union Pub is a bar right inside the main campus building where you can get a pint of beer for three pounds and a burger for five—a fucking *Godsend* for a struggling student with a conversion rate that is massacring her budget.

It's only five on a Monday, and the place is already packed.

Oliver and I quickly head to the bar to order a beer while my eyes roam around the crowd, looking for our new friends. I find Jane and Josh sitting at a corner booth, laughing. I try and wave to get their attention, but they seem engrossed in their conversation.

"What type of beer do you want?" Oliver asks.

"Um...I'll have whatever you want. I don't care."

We take our beers over to the booth and see that Chloe and Michael have joined the group along with someone else I haven't met who introduces herself as Eloise. She's a gorgeous tiny brunette with a cute bob, blue eyes, and a bright-red lip. She and Josh seem to be hitting it off.

Oliver's smile broadens as he sees Eloise, and I'm sure he's adding her to his *To-Do List*.

"Guys, we were just talking about a group outing," Jane says excitedly. "My boyfriend's band is coming to London to play at a place in Shoreditch next month, and I can get us in without a cover. Are you interested in coming with us?"

Oliver turns to Eloise. "Will *you* be there?" He smiles lasciviously. Eloise doesn't back down, her resting bitch face game strong; she doesn't get that he's harmless and half-joking.

"Not sure yet. I might have plans with some old university friends," she says, pressing her lips together.

"Oh, Eloise"—Oliver leans closer toward her as she backs away—"you can't just run off with your old friends when you're still just making new ones! We haven't gotten to know each other properly."

The whole table laughs at Eloise's expression of disgust, very clearly not into his jokes or advances. She ignores Oliver and looks over at Josh with a smile. "Are you going? Because I could tell my friends I'll see them another time."

Whoa! Eloise is a bold one. Good for her. And definitely good for Josh.

Oliver looks over at me with a knowing look. I roll my eyes at him and snort. "Jealous?" he whispers low in my ear.

"Not a chance," I whisper back. "I am his *friend*. Friends do not get jealous."

He laughs. "Sure, sure."

We're several rounds in, and I'm definitely starting to feel the alcohol hit me. I'm exhausted and leaning my head on Oliver's shoulder again. His broad, solid shoulder. Why hadn't I noticed that before? He jokingly pats my head and wraps an arm around me.

"So, Josh," Eloise says. "Tell me about yourself. You have a girlfriend, by any chance?"

Sorry, did I say bold before? I meant obvious.

"Uh…" He leans back a little bit, surprised by her forwardness. "I'm just getting out of a three-year relationship."

"I'm so sorry, Josh." I frown. I can obviously relate. He had briefly mentioned it at the pub after orientation but never really expanded on it. "When did you break up?"

He sighs. "I mean, it's been a year, so not really recent. But it's been rough. I planned on proposing and had been ring shopping that week, and then suddenly—*WHAM!* —it was over."

"Three years is a long time. That sucks." I frown.

Eloise sighs and raises her hand as she looks down sadly at the table. "Same. I broke up two months ago after two years of being together." I feel somewhat bad for her now, especially now that I'm seeing two of her—

How many beers have I had?

I raise my hand and join in on the pathetic fun. "Three years, broke up a year ago, saw him about a month ago at dinner where we said goodbye. High five!"

They both high-five me.

"We're the bloody Lonely Hearts Club here," Eloise says bitterly, with a laugh.

Josh stares at me intensely for a bit, his green eyes never breaking eye contact. "Fuck this," he says, slamming his hands on the table. "I won't be part of this club any longer. How about you guys? Can we leave the club?"

I smile.

"*Hell. Yes.* To new beginnings!"

Jane is laughing at us. "The three of you are killing me. Perhaps you should skip a few rounds."

Four

I OPEN my eyes the next morning, wishing that the sun came with a dimmer. I'm hungover. Again. *Jesus*, I'm going to have to build up my tolerance if I am going to survive a minimum of a year living here in London—at least while I'm in this program. But, I mean, how else am I going to make friends here? Drinking at pubs seems to be the student body's main hobby. Which is definitely a problem, given that I didn't get home until midnight last night and have an early morning class, which—*oh shit!*—I realize I'm late for.

I really need to avoid turning this into a habit.

I run to the bathroom and take the quickest shower known to man, dressing in the first couple of things I see, shoving my makeup bag in my purse to do on the tube. It's a risk, but it won't be the first time I've had to do my makeup in a moving vehicle.

Flying out of the house, I realize I am starving, but there is no time to go back and get a granola bar or even a water bottle.

Oh my God, I'm so hungover. Kill me. Kill me now.

Class has just started when I sneak in, taking a seat in the last row, right next to Josh. He laughs quietly as I clumsily pull my notebooks out, dropping my pens on the ground. I can't even imagine the state I'm in now—a mess, I'm sure. Josh, on the other hand, looks put together. For the first time since I've met him, his hair is brushed, and I'm seeing him without his signature hoodie. It's all about a San Francisco brewery t-shirt today.

"You good, kid?" he asks, never removing his gaze from the board. I nod and sigh. I can't believe this is happening again. "You look a little hungover..." I nod again. He leans down and pulls a water bottle and granola bar from his backpack, placing them quietly on my desk.

"I can't keep taking your food!" I whisper at him, ashamed.

"I packed an extra bar this morning for you. Thought you might need it after what I witnessed last night." My heart warms a little, and I smile. Trying to push away the memories of Oliver, Jane, and me drunkenly singing "Yellow Submarine" completely off-key at our booth, I thank him.

"You're a good friend."

Josh frowns briefly at me and turns to the board.

"You good, kid?" I ask him, using his nickname back at him.

He smiles briefly, pats my hand patronizingly, and points to the board as if to say, *I'm paying attention. Leave me alone.*

Whoa, okay.

I spend the remaining two hours of class distracted, chugging all of Josh's water until it's gone and eating the granola bar in two bites. By the end, the professor announces that we will be splitting up into teams and presenting a case study group project to the class as our final.

Not really looking forward to working with people I don't know, a wave of relief falls over me when the professor pairs me with Josh. He doesn't look like someone who will let me do all the work by myself or take over the whole project—some people never outgrow that type of group-work behavior.

Once class is over, I turn to him, wanting to schedule our first meeting for the project, as he gathers his things and says, "You forgot to do your eyeliner on your left eye."

"Huh?" I say, reaching to touch my eye.

"It seems, in your hangover, you only put makeup on half your face."

I laugh awkwardly, covering my left eye with my hand,

mortified because, *of course.* I keep making a fool out of myself with this guy.

"Thanks for the heads up. Only a good friend would tell you something like that." I smile. A dark cloud passes over his face, but he quickly recovers. He seems off this morning. Maybe he's stressed about school? "I'm used to embarrassing myself, though. It comes with the territory of being a hot mess."

"I like it," he says with a shrug. "It's cute." I feel my cheeks redden, and he chuckles. "You going to lunch?"

Clearing my throat, I reply, "Yeah, you? Wanna join me? Was thinking of just getting a sandwich and then eating it at the library. It's only, like, the second day of school, and I'm already behind on my reading."

"Cool, yeah, let's do that. But we should also talk about the project."

"Gimme a sec to redo my makeup," I say sheepishly, pointing toward the women's bathroom. Josh smiles broadly and shoots me a thumbs up. He leans against the wall across from the bathroom doors, where he remains until I come back out.

"Ugh, so in conclusion, the case study assigned to us is *ancient* and absolutely useless for us to use in real life. Really? How is this relevant for modern-day policymaking? Like, I get it. It's important history. Planes, World Wars, death, et cetera, et cetera," I say crassly, waving my hand dismissively. "But that's not what this class is supposed to be about," I whine, frustrated once more—another disappointment. If I am going to stick with this politics route, I might as well do it well, and it sure as hell doesn't feel like this degree is going to get me anywhere.

Patience, Penny. Patience.

We're in one of the group-study pods in the Waterloo campus library, where we can talk and work on our group assignment. I'm having a hard time concentrating, though. I'm grumpy and hangry and tired—a deadly combo. In an effort to pretend to be a normal and healthy human being, I ordered a salad for lunch—a massive mistake as I am about an hour away before I start imagining people as cartoon cheeseburgers like on *Tom & Jerry.*

"I don't even know what I'm doing here anymore, Josh. I mean, as soon as I got here, I started questioning why I even chose to come and do this program. I know it's only the first week, but ever since orientation, it hasn't felt right." I sigh.

"What do you mean?"

"It's complicated, but I applied here because I thought it was the next step to get to where I want to in life." *Personally and professionally, but he doesn't need to know that.* "But now that I don't know what I even want or where I want to go, it's like what's the point of even being here? I thought maybe I could just ride it out since I actually *like* the topics we would've been studying, but they changed the whole program structure. It's not even the same curriculum we applied to! It's like false advertising."

I'm not going lie. I'm stressed and freaking out. We were told at orientation that the program had changed, but were promised the change was not substantial. It seems pretty substantial to me, though. There is much less flexibility on what classes we can take, the core curriculum has changed, and the readings and topics are focused mainly on British history, despite the fact that over eighty percent of the student body are non-UK citizens.

And I don't know..." I say, shaking my head. "I'm just scared I've made the wrong choice here."

Josh stares quietly at me, brows furrowed.

I get it. I think you just need to give yourself more time to figure it out. Maybe you're too hung up on the fact that your life and this program have changed and you're not focusing enough on how that change can be a positive thing for your life," he says with a gentle smile. "I think maybe you should just give this a little more time."

I sigh. Josh is right. I need to give this a shot. I can't just quit because I'm scared. Maybe I should just give this a try, at least for one semester, and see how the course progresses.

"You're right," I say after we're quiet for some time. "But this class is still stupid, and I hate it."

Josh runs a hand through his sandy-blond hair, laughing. "Dude. Calm down. Haven't you ever heard about learning from history so that it doesn't repeat itself?" He chuckles at my annoyed expression. "Here, look at it this way. Obviously, you would prefer to work on something within this century, but I think if we talk it out, you'll get the *why*."

He scoots closer, pushing the reading material to me, and I catch a whiff of a combination of a manly fruity scent and the comforting smell of what I think is Head & Shoulders. I take another deep breath and confirm that, yep, he uses Head & Shoulders.

Okay, calm down, weirdo.

"They probably want us to look at how the development of the TSR2 aircraft exemplified the processes of bureaucratic politics, okay? We just need to make a case for or against the development."

I stare at him, wide-eyed. "How the hell did you get that?" I ask.

"It's on the syllabus, dummy."

I snort. "Ooh, look at you, reading the syllabus, being all practical," I say, shoving Josh lightly on the shoulder.

"Yeah, it definitely helps with schoolwork if you check what the hell you're supposed to be doing with the material they give you. Makes things easier," he says sarcastically, laughing at me.

"I wish there were a syllabus for life to prepare you for the stuff it throws at you, you know?" I sigh involuntarily. "Like,

'Years zero to ten: blissfully happy, and you don't know it. Years eleven to twelve: awkward tweenage years, puberty. Years thirteen to eighteen: bullies and mean girls. Years eighteen and onwards: general disappointment in humanity and lowering of expectations.'"

"Wow." He leans back. "Cynic, much? You don't really believe that, do you?"

I laugh bitterly. I fold my arms across my chest. "I mean, kinda—yeah. It's hard to trust people when they keep letting you down. Like, *constantly*. At a certain point, you just gotta cut your losses and come to terms with the fact that people are flawed, and you just need to protect yourself because most of them suck."

"Huh. Is this cynicism brought on by a certain person in particular? A recent event, perhaps?" He narrows his eyes at me.

I know what he's getting at. I know what I sound like—a bitter, self-righteous bitch who has been wronged.

If the shoe fits...

"Maybe." I purse my lips, looking away.

He isn't wrong. Lately, I've been getting a sneaking suspicion, a sixth sense, that Austin has been seeing someone new— or at least dating around. He's been much more active on social media—both on his accounts and other people's. People I don't know are commenting on his photos and showing up on his stories. New people in his life could mean a new group from someone he's dating? I've tried not to overthink it, tried not to be a jealous weirdo, but it's proven to be a bit more difficult than usual.

I've seen a couple of my old girlfriends pop up in the comments section, so hopefully, they're keeping tabs. They would let me know if he's started seeing anyone seriously. But still.

Although, to be fair, it isn't all Austin's fault. There are other people and experiences that have added to my cynicism.

"Listen..." Josh takes a deep breath. "No one gets disappointment better than I do, okay? But not *everyone* in life is going to disappoint you. You can't set people in your life into that default mode. It's not fair for anyone. Everyone has flaws. No one is perfect. Not even you." He smirks at the last part. "You have to cut people some slack."

"I don't *have* to do anything, but I get what you're saying," I say. "I would still much rather be pleasantly surprised than be let down by one more person. You get it, right? You recently went through a breakup and didn't even see it coming."

He nods. "I get where you're coming from, but you're absolutely wrong. My breakup with Kat was even worse than you know, but I'm still hopeful. I still think that there's someone out there for me. And I don't automatically cringe at the idea of getting close to someone else again like you seem to do." He points at me, calling out my body language. I've shifted away from him, scooting my chair to the other side of the generic laminate table without me even noticing.

I look away, embarrassed. I feel uncomfortable and transparent, like he's able to pinpoint directly what I'm feeling and thinking with ease. He's figured me out without trouble, and I don't like how he reads me so easily. So I try to change the topic of conversation to focus on him: "What made your breakup even worse than what you told us that other night?"

He narrows his eyes at me, not falling for my deflection. Mercifully, though, Josh shakes his head and plays along, understanding that we are shutting the door on my feelings for now, thank you very much.

"We were living together in Portland—I moved there for her after college, by the way—and I had to fly back home to Palo Alto because my grandfather was dying and didn't have much time left. I already told you I had been ring shopping before, and I meant it. We had a friend's wedding that weekend, and I was planning to propose right after, but given the circumstances, I was going to have to wait, obviously. I thought she would come with me to California, but she decided to go to our friend's wedding instead. She had already paid for the tickets and hotel and didn't want them to go to waste because the spa was, and I quote, 'Sick as shit, babe.'" He closes his eyes and shakes his head in disgust.

"That's horrible," I say.

"Anyway," he goes on, "I get to California Saturday night, the night of the wedding, and I get a drunk call from her. She started saying stuff like she didn't know what was happening, but she wasn't feeling it anymore and that maybe it wasn't a good idea to be together and that we should sit down and talk about what our next steps were once I got back from the funeral."

Josh stops to take a deep breath. "I mean, he wasn't even dead yet! And she was already planning our breakup conversation *over the phone* after four years of being together for 'after the funeral,'" he air-quotes. "I mean, where was her sympathy, you know?"

I shake my head in disgust. "She sounds like a serial killer," I say, trying to add some levity to the situation. He scoffs, laughing bitterly.

"So, what happened next?" I ask.

Josh runs his hand through his hair again and looks up to the ceiling, swallowing hard, his Adam's apple bobbing. "He died the next morning," he says quietly. "And she knew. She knew how close he and I were. She knew how hard it was for me. And she didn't care." He shakes his head softly, pausing, pain evident in his eyes. I suddenly feel this urge to get up and wrap my arms around him, but I quickly stop myself.

Boundaries, Penny.

"I went back to Portland, not knowing what to expect. I was angry, but at the same time, I was scared she would leave me."

I raise an eyebrow. "What do you mean *you were scared she would leave you*? I would've kicked her out or left or whatever."

Josh scoffs. "I know what you mean, but I was vulnerable and grieving, and I didn't want to be alone.

"When I got back, I knew tough times were ahead with her, but I figured that, after four years of being together and three years of friendship before that, she would put aside her shit and be there for me after my grandfather's death. That we would try to work things out like adults. But no. The day I returned to Portland after the funeral, she broke up with me there in our kitchen, and I just fucking lost it."

Josh exhales and runs his hand through his hair, leaning back in his chair. He looks exhausted and lost, much like how I've been feeling the past year, and it makes me feel for him. Losing a family member and a lover in the same week? That's gotta be tough.

"I remember just sitting on the couch, begging her to stay with me, not understanding what went wrong. I asked her how she could do this to me at such a horrible moment in my life, and she just said that she couldn't keep putting it off just because she felt bad for me." He scoffs, and I wince in response feeling an ache in my chest. "I mean, seriously? She couldn't hack it out at least a little while longer while I got a little more emotionally stable?"

"She sounds like an awful person," I say bluntly. "Good riddance. And I'm so sorry for how you broke up. It sounds awful." I say, meaning every word.

"Is any break-up *not* awful, though? Really?"

I shrug quietly, and shake my head.

I can't believe how terrible this girl was to Josh—the sweetest guy I've ever met. I don't know him that well yet, but he seems like the type of man who is as loyal as a fucking German Shepherd. Just by how Josh had fed my hungover ass twice already, I could tell that he is the type of guy who would be there for you and protect you no matter what. He looks like the kind of man who loves deeply and devotedly. Definitely not some random fuckboy looking to sleep with you and get out.

My heart aches for him, for people like Josh who often get screwed over and taken advantage of. They just assume everyone is as lovely as they are, but are met, instead, with a world of disappointment—and it's so infuriating. Hearing how Josh's ex broke his heart makes me feel enraged for his sake—especially after hearing how he asked her not to go. A wave of protectiveness courses through my body for this man, this new friend.

I don't understand why he's telling me this story, though. Josh is proving my point that the majority of people suck. Kat had sucked, and she didn't deserve him.

She was a fucking idiot for letting him go.

"Yeah, I'm not done, though," he says, grimacing.

"Oh, no."

"Oh, yeah. There's more," Josh laughs sheepishly at my expression and sighs, shaking his head before continuing. "We had a vacation planned for two weeks after the funeral with my parents—something we had already scheduled before my grandfather had died. She said she could go with me, and we could pretend to be together so it wouldn't be awkward *for me.* In reality, I'm pretty sure she just didn't want to come off to people like the *asshole* that broke up with me right after my grandfather's funeral."

"Excuse me, where was this vacation?" I ask, tilting my head toward him.

"It was a week in the Bahamas, why?"

I laugh once. "No, Josh. She didn't want to save face or spare you the embarrassment of the breakup with your family. She wanted the free vacation. Are you kidding me? An all-expenses-paid vacation to the Bahamas with potential wild break-up sex?" I say, shaking my head. "I hate to burst your bubble, buddy, but it had nothing to do with you."

He stares wide-eyed at me for a second before turning away, revisiting old memories, viewing them now from a different angle.

"Holy shit, Penny. I think you're right."

"I *know* I'm right. People suck." I pause. "So, did you take her or what?"

He shakes his head. "Nah. I went alone with my family and proceeded to get shit-faced twenty-four-seven for eight days. I don't remember a minute of the vacation. It was great." He smiles bitterly at the memory (*or lack thereof?*).

"I don't understand the point of this story, Josh. You're proving me right. Proving that all people suck, and love sucks, and we would all just be better off if we did not expect anything from absolutely anyone."

I'm a ray of fucking sunshine, I know. Everyone slap some SPF on.

"Okay, calm down, Crazy. The point is, you asked me what made my breakup worse than I led on," Josh says.

"Are you gonna give me a little uplifting speech at the end of your story about how, despite all the hurt, you're still an optimist and people are good and nice and stuff?" I ask with a raised eyebrow.

He presses his lips together, trying not to laugh. "Maybe."

I sigh. "Go on. Although I genuinely do not understand how this story could possibly get any worse."

Josh laughs at my dejectedness and says, "I found out she cheated on me with my best friend."

"She's such a cliché." I *tsk* disapprovingly, shaking my head.

"And gave me chlamydia."

I uncross my arms and slam my hands on the table in front of us. "SHUT THE FUCK UP."

I can't help myself—I burst out laughing, gasping for air.

Now everything about this story is tragic. It's a long-term relationship with what turned out to be a heartless, STD-riddled, free-loader that came to an abrupt halt. I don't think I've ever heard a more comical/sad end to a relationship.

"Shh! We're still in the fucking library, Penny! This room isn't soundproof!" He's trying not to laugh, but I can tell from the amused expression on his face that he's seconds away from joining in.

"I'm so sorry," I say quickly, sobering up. "It's not funny, I know. I didn't mean to laugh at your misfortune. It's just...*Jesus*. The story just got worse and worse, you know? Who even *was* this person? How did you end up with her?" I laugh again, not being able to help myself.

I can tell he's trying to contain his amusement, pressing his lips together again, pretending to be serious and offended by my reaction.

"I'm sorry, I'm sorry. I'll stop." I sit up straight.

"You done?" he asks with a smile.

I nod and bite my bottom lip, trying my hardest not to smile, but I can't contain it. I start laughing again at the series of regrettable and heartbreaking events Josh has just laid out in front of me. It's just so wild. Like a ten-car pile-up in the middle of the freeway. What else could have gone wrong?

He breaks his expression and starts laughing with me. "I mean, she cheated on you and was dumb enough *not* to use a condom? Who is this chick? And with your friend!" I gasp between chortles. "I can't, Josh. It's too stupid. They're just so stupid. I mean, honestly."

He smiles as we both sober up. "Yeah, I guess it is pretty fucking ridiculous."

"But see? You just further proved my point! You weren't just betrayed by one person you loved, but by *two*. Your girlfriend and best friend. What a joke. I told you."

He shakes his head. "Yes, they are *awful, shitty* people, but don't you get it? It was a *good* thing this all happened."

I snort. "How is getting chlamydia from your cheating girlfriend a good thing?"

"*So* many reasons. First"—Josh holds up his index finger, counting off—"it helped push me out of what I now realize was a super toxic and unhealthy relationship I didn't deserve and probably would have never left. Second," he continues counting off, "it showed me what I want in a romantic relationship and friendship. Third, I would have never pursued my master's degree. And fourth, I sure as shit would not have gone to London to do it. I wouldn't have met you or Oliver or Jane—all people who are much cooler than those two idiots. Every bad experience with people should teach you who *not* to surround yourself with, and that's *exactly* what it taught me. Am I hurt? Do I carry some serious emotional baggage? Maybe. But I think I can definitely do better than them, and I will."

"How do you know I'm cooler than Kat or your ex-best friend? I could be a serial killer. Or be super into Nickelback."

He laughs and shakes his head. "I don't think you're either —*thank God*."

I take a deep breath and a good look at him. He looks serene. The sadness I used to be able to catch in his eyes sometimes has gone. I see clearly now what he means. Moving to London has probably helped him as much as it has helped me—and we haven't even been here that long. Like Josh, I also realize that I possibly wasn't surrounding myself with the best people. Of course, his realization came from an actual, tangible event, whereas mine was just a series of tiny cuts that, overall, I found could be equally as painful as getting an STD? Although, I can't say with certainty, given that I've never had one.

Yes, I had been hurt by the person I thought I loved the most and my social circle soon after, but I suppose Josh is right in a way. Though he had not disproved my theory that, in general, most human beings are shitty to their core and good ones are rare gems, he did make a good point. Getting hurt by horrible people can sometimes push you in the direction of something better.

The difference between Josh and I, though, is that where he continues his search for better people, using the knowledge acquired from previous negative experiences, I have just given up and decided not even to try. Why waste time searching for the right person anymore? The risk is too high and not worth it.

"So anyway," he starts, looking down nervously at his hands. "In light of this conversation, I thought that maybe we could—"

"Hello, friends!" Oliver bursts into our study room with arms wide open, smiling from ear to ear with Jane in tow. "I was hoping you would still be here."

Josh audibly sighs and hangs his head.

"Hey, you made it!" I say to them both.

"You told him where we were?" Josh asks, brow furrowed.

"And Jane. Yeah, he said he needed to study, too. I thought we could all work on our Organizational Management homework together since we're all in the same class."

Oliver takes the seat next to me and pulls out a sandwich from his backpack while Jane dramatically throws herself on the couch with an exasperated sigh.

"School is shit," she states, answering our unasked question.

Girl, I feel you.

Oliver ignores her angst and puts an arm around me as he takes another massive bite. "So, what have you two been working on?"

I peel his heavy arm off me, casually noticing his muscles flexing. He's not wearing his signature three-piece suit today, which means his broad shoulders and muscular arms are on display. I wonder idly what his workout routine must be like. Does he ever skip leg day? I mean, he has to—his arms and chest are perfect.

"No work today?" I ask. "How did your country fair without one of its premier MP aids? Who will walk around Parliament in ridiculously tight three-piece suits and ridiculous cufflinks?" I smirk at him. "I particularly enjoy the ones you wore the other day. You know the ones I'm talking about, with your family's crest?"

"Are you making fun of me?" He reaches for my hand, and I pull it away from him immediately.

"Absolutely not," I deadpan. "The state of this lovely

country concerns me if you're not at the forefront of its management."

He sighs and rolls his eyes at me.

"Can we do something fun this weekend?" Jane asks. "Unfortunately, I'm a bit broke at the moment, so I don't think I can go out drinking or partying until my next paycheck."

Relief courses through me. I'm a little burnt out with regards to pubs at the moment, so I'm ecstatic at the idea of something new. A brilliant idea pops into my head.

"Do you know what *Risk* is?" I ask them.

"*Oh, shit,*" Josh says with a knowing smirk. "You wanna play *Risk*?"

His expression lets me know that he knows *exactly* what *Risk* is and how to play it *well*.

Fuck yeah. I knew we were going to be good friends.

"Why do you look like you just got invited to a hedonism party?" Oliver smirks. *Ew.* "Isn't *Risk* just a board game?" He asks.

I scoff. "*Risk* isn't *just* a board game!" How dare he? "*Risk* is a relationship-crushing, strategy game where you use diplomacy and manipulation to utterly destroy your opponents."

"It ruins friendships," Josh says excitedly with a huge smile.

"Oh, yeah," Jane says, smiling. "I used to love playing it as a child."

"Um, excuse me, but *Risk* is not a child's game. *Shit. Gets. Real,*" Josh clarifies.

Thank God someone here gets it.

"I know! Oh my God! Let's do a *Risk* night at my house! Beer, snacks, pizza, destruction, betrayal! All the makings of a fun night," I say. Oliver and Jane look at me like I'm crazy, but Josh is totally here for it.

"Yes!" he says.

"Who else do we invite? We should make it an even six."

"Sorry, do I get a say on whether I want to come or not?" Oliver asks.

"No," Josh and I say in unison. We look at each other and grin. I'm so pumped.

Oliver takes another bite of his sandwich. "Fine," he says with his mouth full, "we'll just go to a pub after we finish."

Josh and I exchange looks. We know exactly what the other is thinking. *Risk* is the single best and most brutal board game out there, and Oliver has no idea that a good game of *Risk* can take *hours*. It was my shit growing up. My brothers and I used to play with our cousins every time we would get together, and it was absolute savagery. It requires a huge amount of tolerance of emotional terrorism, amazing powers of manipulation, and immense diplomatic talents.

"I'll Amazon Prime a set so we have it by Friday," I tell Josh. "I'll find a fifth person, and you bring a sixth, deal?"

"Deal." We shake on it.

"East Coast versus West Coast, baby," I say.

"Oh, it's *on*."

Five

EVERYTHING'S SET for game night. I bought a brand-new board game online since I hadn't thought to bring my *Risk* set from New York. We were lucky enough that it got to my house just in time this morning.

I completely spaced on asking someone to be the sixth member, but I'm not worried about it. It means less people at my house until the wee hours of the morning. Plus, I know Josh is bringing a fifth, so we're good.

Since things can get rowdy during these games, I had warned Allie about my plan to invite my friends over for a battle royale. Needless to say, she quickly made arrangements to stay the night with the guy she's currently seeing—someone she met on Tinder who is wrapped around her little finger. The guy is so gone for her he even invited her on a getaway to Paris and they haven't even been dating for a month!

What a glamorous life I lead. My roommate goes away for the weekend to France, while I host a boardgames night at my house on a Saturday night.

I'm in the middle of setting up the board, claiming the yellow troops for myself in a pile, when I hear the obnoxious buzzer.

"It's me!" I hear Josh say on the other end. I buzz him up and unlock the door so he can let himself in while I finish setting things up.

"Hey," I hear him behind me. "I see you got things organized. I'm so freaking excited, you have no idea."

"I'm glad to hear that! Let's set up the drinks on my TV stand. I'll go get the glasses."

I go to the kitchen and start pulling plates and glasses from the cupboards and the cutlery from the drawers. "How can I help?" he asks in the doorway.

"Here, help me take all this stuff into the living room."

"Alright," he says, taking the items from my hands with a broad smile. His fingers accidentally graze against mine, and I shiver, pulling my hands away as quickly as possible, trying not to drop anything.

Weird.

"Um, I'm just gonna..." Frowning slightly, he walks back into the living room with a stack of plates in one hand and two glasses in another. I carry the rest into the room and set it next to the drinks, offering him one.

"No, I'm okay, thanks. I think I'll wait for the beers."

"Oh, that's fine, then. I'm just gonna have a Coke while we wait for everyone else and order Domino's. Sit with me and help me pick?"

We sit on the couch side by side, and I catch another whiff of his signature scent. I've known Josh for less than a month, but already it feels familiar, comforting, *safe.*

"Have you had Domino's since being in London?" he asks.

I almost want to burst out laughing. After shoes, pizza is my absolute favorite thing in the whole wide world. "Have I had Domino's since being in London?" I scoff. "Um, are you kidding me? I have absolutely had it. And it's *so* much better than American Domino's. They have these amazing—"

"The chocolate chip cookies?" he asks excitedly. "They're incredible. Literally the best cookies I've had in my life. They're all gooey and warm and perfect. Just perfect."

"Yes!" I smile broadly at him.

I know it seems sad that we're this excited over pizza, but honestly, whenever I can talk about food like this, I consider it a win. I used to torture myself with diets and purges and hated my body, so moments like these are proof that I've come a long way in life with my body image issues. Have there been moments where I want to relapse? *Abso-fucking-lutely.* Especially in the past twelve months. But being able to enjoy food is a relatively new thing for me, and I love that I am no longer one of those people who just eat to survive.

"Can we get some of those too?" he asks enthusiastically.

"Duh!" I say excitedly, adding two orders to the cart. "This should be enough for five people. It's five people, right?" I ask. "I know you said you were bringing someone, but I forgot to confirm with you, and I completely forgot to ask someone else."

"Oh, yeah." He smiles. "I asked Eloise. She was so cool when we met her that other night, don't you think?"

Eloise? Cool? Really? Huh.

"Uh, sure. Yeah, I don't really know her too well, but if you think she's cool, then okay."

He smiles, nodding.

I feel like I've been gut-punched. I don't like that he invited her to my apartment. I didn't particularly think she was a riot the other day at the Student Union. She has absolutely no sense of humor and was just so...intense and forward.

"Eloise is going through a breakup, too, so I wanted to be nice and invite her, you know?" he says, kneeling in front of the coffee table by the board, claiming the gray troops.

"I mean, it's not like she doesn't have any other friends in London, Josh," I say, trying to keep my voice level. I finish adding the pizzas to my order, enter my payment info, and click submit, all while trying to remain calm. "She said it herself. But if you think she's cool, then great. Can't wait to get to know her better." But I can hear the tone in my voice, and it is less than enthused.

When would he have had the time to get to know her better? He is almost always with me or Oliver and Jane while we're at school. Is he seeing her outside of class?

"Wait," he says nervously. "Do you not like her? Should I not have invited her?"

Um, NO YOU SHOULD NOT HAVE INVITED HER. She doesn't seem nice at all.

"I just wish you would've asked. I don't really know her. I thought you were going to invite Michael or Chloe, you know? This was supposed to be a friendly-but-unfriendly game of *Risk*. I can't be mean to her during the game now, because I don't know her." I smile a little. "I didn't know you were bringing a *date*." I quickly turn around so he can't see my face.

Fuck. I didn't mean it that way.

I make myself busy by straightening out the glasses and the plates, placing the cutlery on the napkins. God, I just made myself sound so petty.

"Date? She's not my date," he says, concern in his voice. I can't turn to look at him. The jealous girlfriend act really doesn't suit me, especially since I don't even like this guy! I guess I feel like I could become good friends with him, and I don't want to lose him before I even have him.

I slap a fake smile on my face and look at him. "It's fine, Josh. If you like her, she must be great. Can't wait to get to know her better."

"Penny—"

But he's thankfully interrupted by the loud sound of the buzzer. For the first time since I moved here, I thank my lucky stars for such an obnoxious sound.

I run to the door and press the answer button. "Yes?"

"Mr. Oliver James and Miss Jane Green have arrived!" I hear Oliver on the other end. With a laugh, I buzz them up.

"Oliver and Jane are here!" I yell to Josh as I unlock the door for them, waiting until they get off the elevator.

"Oh," I hear Josh from the living room. He reaches the front door, scratching his head. "Listen, I didn't know you felt that way about Eloise. I honestly just thought it would be good to get to know her in solidarity and all. I'm just gonna text her to tell her we had to cancel the game night last minute, and I'll go meet her somewhere else." Contrite and embarrassed, Josh moves to the front door. And I know that I'm overreacting a bit, but the thought of him leaving my house on *my* game night to meet some other girl annoys me even more. This is *our* plan. We're supposed to battle it out at *Risk* and massacre the noobs before destroying each other. Where is the *East Coast versus West Coast* of it all? And why did he invite her? I know he said it was in solidarity, but Eloise doesn't strike me as the type of person who would love to play Risk *at all*. Oliver and Jane, on the other hand, I can see vividly getting into it.

Maybe he sees something in her that I just can't.

"Don't be ridiculous," I say. "If you say she's nice, then she must be." I don't want to bring up the fact that perhaps he doesn't have a great track record on being the best judge of character, given his dating history, because that's just mean.

"Are you sure?" he asks, grimacing.

"Stay." I put a hand on his chest, and he holds my gaze a second too long before our eye contact is broken by the sound of the elevator doors opening. I drop my hand quickly, hiding it behind my back like there would be some evidence of what had just happened visible on my fingertips. "East Coast versus West Coast, remember?"

"Hello, friends!" Jane runs up. "Are we ready to ruin friend-ships tonight?"

"How did we even let this happen?" I ask, shocked to the core. I feel sick to my stomach, and it's not from the pizza, cookies, chips, and dip that I've been gorging myself on for the past hour.

"I don't know. It's all a blur, to be honest," Josh says,

shaking his head in disbelief. "I can't remember how we got to this point."

Half an hour into the game, Josh and I had been defeated by three *Risk* novices.

No. Not defeated—*massacred*.

We both started off strong the first two turns. But then it got ugly.

Somehow, Oliver was able to take over all of Asia in two turns, killing most of Josh off, leaving his remaining territories to be taken over by the rest of us. Most of my territories were split between Europe and South America, but I was done when Eloise took me out in the former and Jane in the latter. My last territory had been in Indonesia, and Oliver got rid of my final troop in one roll of the die with a, "AND THE BRITISH EMPIRE HAS BEEN AVENGED!"

There hadn't even been any time to emotionally manipulate anyone during the game. I hadn't even been able to form an alliance against anyone!

"I'm so disappointed in us," I say with a disbelieving laugh.

Josh and I move onto the couch with a couple of beers so we can talk and watch the remaining three Brits duke it out for world domination (we decided to skip Mission Cards). To be fair, it seems like all three of them are naturals. Jane and Oliver are extremely competitive, and—not to sound catty or anything —but Eloise looks like a little manipulative, so she of course excelled here.

"I'm glad we got to do this, though," Josh says. "I gotta say, I've been feeling kind of homesick, and this helped. I used to play this a lot with my brother and our friends." He flashes me a thankful smile.

"Me too! It's definitely a Marquez family tradition," I smile excitedly. "I remember one time my brothers got into such a big argument over a European takeover that they didn't speak for days," I say with a pang of homesickness. My dad banned us from playing it for *months*.

"Can I tell you something without you making fun of me?" he asks.

"I make no promises," I say, taking a swig of my beer.

He rolls his eyes at me. "And here I thought we were having a moment." He moves as if to get up from the couch, but I grab him by the arm with my free hand, laughing.

"Come on, I'm sorry. What were you gonna tell me?"

He looks over at the table to make sure they're not paying attention, and then his gaze lands back on my face. "Nah, never mind," he says with a mysterious smile. "I think you're gonna have to earn that piece of info."

I snort, trying to look like I don't care. "Okay," I say, but we're interrupted by a very loud groan.

"We had a fucking *alliance*, Jane. An alliance! HAVE YOU NO RESPECT FOR DIPLOMATIC AGREEMENTS?!" Oliver yells frantically. He's struggling to hold Asia and looks like he's about ready to lose his mind.

"Agreements are made to be broken, Oliver," Jane says, shaking the die in her hands. "Pick up your die; let's keep going," her eyes like daggers.

Savage.

I'm so proud of her.

"Okay, I'll make you a deal. If you stop attacking me for two rounds, I promise not to hit on you for a week."

Jane considers this. "Not good enough," she responds and goes back to shaking the die in her hands, preparing to roll.

"Okay! Okay! One month! I'll leave you alone for one whole month." He's a desperate man. "No sexual innuendos, no jokes, nothing."

Josh and I laugh and turn back to each other. "And to think they thought this was a child's game."

"If I promise not to attack you from now on, will you leave me alone forever?" Eloise asks.

I roll my eyes at her, but luckily, no one sees.

Absolutely no sense of humor.

It's two am, and Jane and Oliver are still at it. Eloise "had to leave" and hour ago, thank God. She looked more than relieved when she was killed off by Jane, as if she couldn't stand being here a second longer.

Ugh.

Josh walked her downstairs all the way to her Uber. I casually peeked through the windows to check whether he kissed her goodnight, whether he was lying about it not being a date. I didn't see anything happen from where I stood, but that didn't mean anything. They could have kissed in the elevator.

Who cares, though. I don't.

Once he makes it back, we hang out quietly on the couch until Jane wipes the floor with Oliver and wins the game. I'm so happy I could cry. I just want to go to sleep at this point, and the night has been a roller coaster of emotions with this damn game. A triumphant Jane and a sulking Oliver share an Uber ride home, both extremely drunk, while Josh stays behind to help pick up.

"You really don't have to," I say as I grab a trash bag from under the sink.

He smiles an exhausted smile and starts picking up beer bottles. "It's definitely not my favorite thing, but I'm not going to let you clean this up all by yourself."

"Thanks for the honesty," I chuckle. "I really appreciate the help, though. My roommate is kind of…intense about order and cleanliness."

"Uh, yeah." He laughs. "I was looking for a bar of soap under your sink to wash my hands and saw her Monica-level organizational skills. I've never seen so many different labeled and color-coded boxes in such a small space. And that inventory list taped to the inside of the door! Genius." I laugh at poor

Allie. She can't help it. "I didn't realize there were so many different ways of codifying soap." I'm all about control, but, funnily enough, I'm not an organized person.

"Yeah, she cleans when she's stressed."

"What do *you* do when you're stressed?" he asks. He doesn't mean it in a suggestive way, but the hour and the exhaustion add an extra heaviness and load to his words, twisting their meaning and adding an innuendo in my head.

My mind takes a turn down a weird path, and my stomach does a weird flip-punch thing, and I lose focus. "Uh…what?" I ask, trying to recover.

"I asked what you do when you're stressed—to relieve tension, I mean," he asks genuinely, double-bagging all the beer bottles. "For example, I like to run."

"Oh." I laugh awkwardly, tying off the bag in my hand full of stale chips and containers of dip. "I eat. I stress eat. Which in the end just makes me feel worse, to be honest."

And then it happens. Then I start thinking about it. About what I did.

"Ah, but at least it's tasty!" He laughs, and I decide to take a break, sitting on the edge of the couch. "You okay?" he asks.

I'm tired and tipsy and vulnerable. I just ate three slices of pizza, immeasurable amounts of chips and dip, cookies, beer, and soda.

I start doing the math.

Coke: 140 calories

Two chocolate chip cookies: 190 calories

Artichoke dip: 200 calories

No, no, no, no. STOP.

"I want to throw up," I mutter under my breath, shaking my head, trying to throw my mind off the path I know it wants to go down now.

Three slices of pepperoni pizza: 700 calories

Doritos, two servings: 300 calories

Three beers: 420 calories

I put my head in my hands and try not to think about it. I try not to add the total, but it's right there, I can do it in my head. It's almost two thousand calories.

Two-fucking-thousand.

The numbers don't matter. The numbers don't matter. Breathe.

I take a deep breath in through my nose and exhale through my mouth. I repeat this process five times with my eyes closed, trying to push the reality of everything I just ate out of my head.

How much of it have I digested already? If I throw up now, can I get rid of most of it?

"Oh God." Josh drops his bag and kneels by me. "I didn't realize you had had that much to drink. Here," he says, sliding my arm over his shoulder, trying to lift me from the couch. "Let's get you to the bathroom."

I push him off gently and sigh. "Josh, I'm not drunk. I'm just…" I shake my head. "I'm just having a moment, okay?" He doesn't say anything, doesn't ask any questions. He just stands there and looks at me with an inquisitive expression in his eyes. "Don't let me throw up, okay? No matter what I say."

It takes him a moment, but he seems to realize what I mean when he catches the expression of disgust on my face as I glance at my near-empty plate with three pizza crusts on it. I went from mauling the pepperoni pizza to wanting it to burn a slow and painful death.

Adrenaline courses through my body, my heart beating out of my chest.

"Ah," he says quietly, taking a seat next to me on the couch. "I see."

"It's fine. I don't want to talk about it. I love food now, but sometimes the feelings and urges come back, you know what I mean?" There's silence. "Well. I guess not."

He's careful when he speaks, managing to not come off as nervous or patronizing, which is not always an easy task when finding out someone you know has a history of an eating disorder. "Are you in recovery now, then?"

I nod. "Kind of." I take a deep breath, still not making eye contact. I'm a little ashamed. "It's been a few years, though I had a brief relapse last year. My life was such a mess, and I guess I needed the sense of control it gave me."

He must be regretting befriending someone like me. Who else would want to be friends with someone so dramatic? I mean, first it was the whole *I-hate-school-and-regret-coming-here* thing, then the bitterness, then how petty I acted when he brought Eloise, and now this?

He must think I'm insane.

Josh takes a deep breath like he's about to say something but stops himself.

"What?" I ask.

He shakes his head with eyes closed. "You look like you're embarrassed about it or something. And you shouldn't be." He smiles sympathetically. "Don't take this the wrong way, but it's unfortunately very common. And it happens. It's not nice, but it happens. It's a disease, just like any other. You can't help it, but it looks like you've committed to getting better, and that's a big deal."

"It has been," I say, a bit in a trance.

"Listen, it's clear you don't like to be babied, and I know you're strong and all of that. But if you ever need to talk, you know I'm here, right? I can't pretend to understand one hundred percent what you're going through, but I'm a pretty good listener." He nudges me in the side with his elbow. "Anything you need."

I chuckle, a weird feeling building in my stomach. The word *bulimia* is never said out loud, but, as per usual, Josh needs little explanation in order to gain understanding of the situation.

"Can I ask you for a favor?" I smile.

"Anything," he says seriously, turning to face me head-on.

"Can you make me some ginger tea?" I ask in a small voice. It will help with the nerves-induced nausea that I suddenly seem to be experiencing.

Josh gets up quickly from the couch. "Of course. I'll bring it right out," he says and heads into the kitchen, leaving me alone in the living room.

I sit and stare absentmindedly out the window. It's dark and quiet outside, the street empty of cars and passersby. I put my head in my hands and take a deep breath. The last thing I want is a relapse. But I can feel the monster breathing down my neck, wanting to take over, wanting to take control.

To give me control.

I remind myself that I'm living a different life now, though, and I don't need the monster on my back. I never did, of course, but least of all now. I'm away from the judgmental eyes of my past life. I am free and clear of any passive-aggressive remarks of my weight or what I look like. I can be and do whatever I want for the first time in my life.

I can find control in other ways now. Healthier ways. I think. I'm not the most easygoing person in the world, I know, but I'm better than who I was before.

I hear Josh open and close the cupboards in the kitchen, pulling out a mug, I assume.

Josh.

Such a sweet guy—the only other American in the program besides that weird guy in the Air Force that we all think is secretly a spy.

I'm so glad I met Josh. He's so easy and friendly and nice. I've known him for such a short amount of time, but it doesn't seem so little when you spend most of your days with someone. He's so easy to talk to.

But although that's always great to have in a friend, the *"easy to talk to"* thing doesn't always suit me. The more he knows about me, the more power I feel he—or anyone, for that matter—has over me, and I'm no fan of that. It's all part of the control thing.

I like regulating who knows what about me. I'm often known as an "oversharer," but no one has ever thought that I overshare certain things to cover for the fact that I hide more than I reveal. Only one person has ever called me out on it, and that's my brother. I asked him once, as a joke, if he'd like me if we weren't siblings, and he said he couldn't answer that question because he wasn't sure which Penny I would show him.

That answer felt like a punch to the face.

But things are different now. I'm trying to make a conscious effort to explore who I am and not hide it from people here. There is an obvious relief in not having to constantly be on guard.

"Here." Josh walks back into the living room, holding two mugs with steaming hot ginger. "I added some lemon I found in your fridge, by the way. I hope that's okay."

Still, hiding and controlling what people can and cannot know about me has always been comforting, so revealing this piece of information to Josh feels big.

I smile at him. "Don't tell anyone." Josh knows I'm not talking about the lemon.

"Never." He blows on his tea.

Coming here is beginning to feel like the dividing line of my life: *Before London* and *After London*. *Pretend Penny* and *Real Penny*.

Six

THE NEXT COUPLE of weeks blend into one another in a routine of *school, library, pub, school, library, pub.*

Despite feeling unsure I made the right decision to pursue this career path, I've been very responsible about schoolwork—which honestly surprised even me. I figure I'm here now, so I may as well make the best of it.

Our Strategic Management final project is starting to take shape, and we're barely even halfway through the term, which is fantastic. Josh has proven to be a great partner. We've divided the assignment and then easily blended it together; nothing in our paper shows that it was written by two different people. In the short time that we've known each other, I feel like Josh and I have become best friends, and it's *lovely*—most of the time.

Since game night, Josh has become even more attentive and present in my life, but in doing so, he's developed a talent for breaking down my walls, making me feel like water, spilling out in front of him.

I've never felt more vulnerable.

It sounds horrible, but the worst part about him being so connected and in tune with what I'm feeling is how supportive and understanding he is. Sometimes, the support and comfort he provides is overwhelming. I'm never sure how to react, and it makes me nervous and anxious, makes it hard for me to breathe—like an elephant is sitting on my chest. His optimism is overpowering and a bit overwhelming.

Am I so messed up that I can't appreciate when someone is so positive and supportive?

He hasn't brought up what we discussed that night in my apartment after game night, which I am extremely thankful for. More importantly, he hasn't, for one second, treated me differently. Sometimes, after someone finds out, they overcompensate or pay more attention to what I'm eating, how *much* I'm eating, and how often. It's annoying.

But Josh isn't annoying. Josh *gets it*.

Oliver and Jane have also become a massive part of my life. Most days, the three of us hang out together in between and after classes, whether it's at the pub or the library. Oliver keeps making jokes about us hooking up, and I would find it annoying if he weren't so hilarious—but I can't ever let him know that. His ego is big enough as it is.

Last week, when we all met up at the pub, he showed up with a daisy for me. When I asked him what the occasion was, he replied, "I thought maybe I would switch up my strategy from flirty to romantic. Maybe that will get me somewhere with you?"

I laughed at him, taking the flower from his hand and brushing off his advance by changing the subject. In all honesty, it's not like I haven't considered hooking up with him. As I said, he isn't insanely attractive, but every day I notice his body more and more, wondering what it would feel like under my hands, and he really could be charming if he wanted to.

The problem is that, for all his come-ons, Oliver has turned into a confidant and a pretty big part of my life. Josh tries to turn my bad days into good ones, but Oliver seems to relish my cynical and more honest ones. He seems to get my dark humor better than anyone and never pushes me into seeing the silver lining of any situation, which I highly appreciate on darker days. He is an excellent listener and an even better conversationalist. Oliver doesn't just accept what I consider to be my realism (some would call it cynicism), but he embraces and shares it, too.

I don't want to risk ruining this new friendship.

Also, his hook-up history just since meeting him reads more like a roster than anything else. Would I really be okay with sleeping with someone whose hobby is to add more women of as many backgrounds as possible to his list? I mean, it's his business, but when you sleep with someone, you end up sleeping with everyone else the other person has, right? At least that's what people say, and I'm not sure I want to risk that. I need a rebound, for sure, but a good one.

Meanwhile, my potential German rebound Michael has proven to be a bust. All hopes of hooking up with him crashed and burned when I found out he had a girlfriend back home. And with regards to the other guys in my program, they are sadly not as inspiring, if you know what I mean. I need to expand my horizons if I really want to start putting myself out there and start dating. Since my arrival, I've downloaded a few apps but am too much of a coward to go on any dates, fearing with my luck that one of them would end up being a serial killer and I'd wash up dead in the Thames after a week.

Although my dating life is a bit stunted at the moment, I've been trying to open myself up to new experiences and people. Though I've remained a bit careful and guarded—a hard habit to break—I do notice myself opening up and exploring other parts of myself that I usually wouldn't have in my old environment. I can see how I have evolved in every aspect of life, from small things like my fashion sense, to exploring new and exciting experiences and opportunities. I've always craved independence and felt a hunger to be able to discover who I truly am, and I've finally been given the opportunity to do so in a new and safe environment, free from the constraints of my old life.

I think moving to London may have saved my sanity.

Surrounding myself with people like Jane, Allie, Josh—and

even Oliver!—has been an unexpected wake-up call. I'm happy to have been able to find and develop friendships with intelligent people who might not share the same opinions as me all the time but can respect my own and have thoughtful discussions. I haven't felt the need to filter what I say or do once. Even my sense of style has changed to reflect who I am inside. It sounds trite, I know, but I've never felt less afraid to be myself, and it showed.

My social life has consisted chiefly of pub nights after school with my friends, which means I have to admit that alcohol has become a much more significant part of my life than expected, and I'm not truly sure I feel great about it. Pub nights are so frequent that I've had to switch from drinking beer to harder spirits, like vodka. The bloating and extra calories are just not worth it.

Despite the significant increase in alcohol consumption, I have actually managed to quit smoking. Do I feel like crawling out of my skin every time someone with a cigarette walks by me or I get tipsy? Um, yeah. Fucking definitely. But I've also stopped feeling like I'm dying every time I have to climb two flights of stairs at the DLR station every damn day.

Though I am having a blast, the food is killing me. Pub food is a nightmare, and groceries are expensive, and I have no time to cook. I'm living off *Pret-a-Manger* salads and sandwiches and the occasional *Wagamama* chicken curry. I am dying for a proper home-cooked meal.

My saving grace is Saturday afternoons when Allie works at a Korean barbecue food stall in Notting Hill Gate and hooks me up with literally the best banh mi I've ever tried. It's not a home-cooked meal, but man, is it good. I don't know what the hell is in that marinade, but the pork in those sandwiches is the best thing I have ever tasted. That little place in Chelsea Market in New York that used to be my favorite has nothing on this.

When I'm not hitting up Allie for a free lunch at her side hustle, my Saturdays and Sundays consist of walking around

Covent Garden and Carnaby Street. When I'm homesick or sad, I head out to Bond street to window shop or go into Harrod's shoe department and try on dozens of shoes I will never be able to afford.

Manolo Blahnik + Penny Márquez 4Eva

Minus the food, London has been very good to me. Very good, indeed.

It's been great, but something has been missing from this whole experience. When I made the decision to come to grad school in London, the thing I was most excited about was the idea that I would be able to travel all across Europe. It turns out, however, that I am much more broke than I thought I was. Yes, it's true—you *can* travel through Europe on a very tight budget. I read several articles and blog posts on how to do it and where to stay, but do you want to know the truth? Hostels are gross and filled with pickpockets. Also, cheap flights? Cheap for a reason. Uncomfortable, unsafe, and filled with hidden fees. Trains? Incredibly expensive. My budget? Much smaller than I projected (*thanks, inflation*). It's made it impossible to go anywhere outside the M25, the motorway encircling Greater London. Despite the fact that London is one of the largest cities in the world, I'm starting to feel super claustrophobic.

Sharing a similar frustration, Josh comes up with a plan for all of us to visit Salisbury and Stonehenge. Total cost: seventy-two pounds (*including travel*). When he presented the opportunity to leave the city to us, I jumped right on it. I didn't care what the destination was. It could have been to the circus in the middle of fucking nowhere for all I cared, and I still would have been riding shotgun! I was ready to go and go anywhere, which is why I currently find myself alone in Waterloo station, looking around for anyone from my program, with my ticket in hand.

"Hey," I hear a voice behind me and jump.

Josh stands in front of me wearing his uniform of jeans and a t-shirt with disheveled, just-showered hair. His smile is broad and welcoming, his green eyes gleaming with excitement. I get a weird feeling in my stomach at his practically glowing smile. I'm not sure whether that has anything to do with how much time he's currently been spending with Eloise—which I've noticed is a lot more than usual—or whether it's because we've all become much more comfortable around each other.

Regardless, I think I'm just as happy to see him as he is me. Despite the alarming amount of positivity he provides in my day-to-day, he has been like a lighthouse while I navigate this new stage in my life.

"I'm excited to go to Stonehenge!" I jump in place a few times like an excited toddler. "Where is everyone? Doesn't the train leave in, like, ten minutes?" I stand on my tiptoes, looking around the station for any familiar faces.

"Um, actually," he says, scratching the back of his head, grimacing a little. "Pretty much everyone else canceled."

"What does *'pretty much everyone else'* mean?" I ask with a raised eyebrow.

"Um, everyone? You were the only one who didn't cancel. But you were so excited, and I was organizing it, so I felt bad canceling, too."

Record scratch sound

"So…it's just you and me? Alone? Together? Going alone on this day trip together alone?" I ask nervously, unsure exactly why I feel this sudden panic. I'm sure I sound like an idiot.

Josh tilts his head at me, looking at me like I've gone crazy, which I pretty much always have been, so not sure why this would be a surprise for him. "I mean, yes? Is that a problem?"

YES. Yes, it's definitely a problem because, lately, it's been a bit hard to breathe around you, and you've gotten to know me too well and anticipate my needs and be too supportive. I don't think I can handle the amount of intimacy and positivity that you provide in my life. We tend to talk about serious and profound issues, and I don't feel like spending an entire day alone with you, because I know you will be able to break me down emotionally, and then I'll bond with you, and you'll leave me. So yes, this is a problem.

"No, it's cool," I say with a shrug, padding in the direction of the platform.

Neither of us says anything on the two-hour train ride to Salisbury, our first stop on our way to Stonehenge. Once we arrive, we decide to walk around and tour the town before visiting the ancient monument, stretching our legs. Nervous for a reason I don't truly understand, words seem to fail me—which is why Josh can't help but ask me what's wrong every so often.

I keep replying that I'm fine, just tired—everything's good. But he's not buying it. The truth is, I wouldn't be able to tell him even if I wanted to.

What once used to be one of my favorite parts of our friendship, the ability to spend time together in companionable silence, seems to have left the building for the day. The truth is, this feels way too much like a date—and a bad one at that.

Josh is trying hard to make up for my weirdness by attempting to spark conversation, by commenting on the number of people in the square, or by telling me about the history of the town of Salisbury, and I'm so in my head I can't process anything. I know I'm overreacting, but my mind keeps having this strange reaction to Josh where I want to spend time with him, but I immediately panic at the thought and have no idea why.

I nearly cry from relief as we enter the Salisbury Cathedral and are forced into silence as we roam the sizable medieval church. In here, he won't be able to force conversation. Visitors are requested to keep their voices down and keep conversation limited.

Originally, we came in here to see the Magna Carta, but I'm

suddenly captivated by the Gothic architecture. The cathedral hadn't been on my bucket list of things to see in the U.K. by a long shot, but it has now officially become one of my favorite spots. In the middle of admiring its incredibly tall and narrow nave, I forget about the fact that I seem to be on a faux date with my best friend as I feel him come up behind me.

I smile and turn to face him. My excitement is genuine. I love that we came here. I love that he thought to take me here. I love that he knows me like this.

I hate that he knows me like this.

I catch some of his grapefruit-and-melon scent—fruity but manly and comforting—and stare up into his bright eyes—more gold than green today. My breath hitches a little as I get the sudden urge to be held by him in the middle of the cathedral.

Abort! Abort!

"See?" he says in hushed tones, dragging me away from my reverie. "I'm so glad I didn't cancel the whole trip. I knew you'd love this. That's why I wanted to come in here before heading up to Stonehenge."

I feel like someone has punched me in the gut, so I turn back to look up at the high ceilings, avoiding his gaze. I took art history in high school and college and had always had a thing for Gothic architecture and medieval times. It's not an interest I've shared with him—or anyone, for that matter—so I have no idea how he would be so confident I would enjoy it. But that's the thing about Josh, isn't it? I don't have to share everything about myself for him to *know* me. I have to wonder whether he's psychic, just really intuitive, or whether I've been opening myself up to him more than I realized.

"Come here," he says, wrapping an arm around my shoulders and dragging me in the opposite direction. "Let's go find the Magna Carta and check that baby out." I tense under his arm, and he releases me, frowning a bit.

The scariest thing is that I think I know him that way too.

"It's literally just a bunch of rocks. You know that, right? A *pile o' rocks*." I look at Josh as he pulls out his phone and takes another picture of the Stonehenge monument. "Like, I get the significance of it all; I swear I do. I just don't understand why you insist on taking photos of it from every freaking angle. You're making us look like tourists."

He laughs at me as he continues to snap away. "They're more boulders than rocks, I think. And also, you do realize that everyone here is a tourist? Other than the people who actually work here, we are *all* tourists."

I try to hide my smile and roll my eyes jokingly at him. "Whatever," I say. "You're just giving me hardcore, American-tourist vibes right now, is what I mean. All that's missing is your Teva sandals with socks and a fanny pack."

"I *am* an American tourist." He flashes me a smile and proceeds to snap yet another shot of the prehistoric monument from a different angle. "But I'm definitely not a socks-and-sandals type of guy."

By some holy miracle—which I am attributing to God's divine intervention, given that we had just visited the Salisbury Cathedral—the awkwardness from this morning has all but disappeared. We are back to our teasing and relaxed selves, although I am dangerously close to hangry levels.

I need food—and soon.

"Sorry, I know I'm acting grumpy. I think it might be Penny's lunchtime. I need to be fed soon." I laugh sheepishly.

"Here," he says, pulling something out of his back pocket and tossing it at me. "I don't know if you noticed, but we passed a bunch of really cool food trucks I'm curious to try. Will that hold you over for the next half hour while we wrap it up?"

I look down at what he's handed me—another granola bar.

"I have...so many questions." I stare up at him. "Were you seriously walking around for the past"—I look at my phone to check the time—"*five* hours with a granola bar in your back pocket?"

He laughs at my expression of disgust. "Yes?" he answers hesitantly.

"And you expect me to eat this squashed bar that has been essentially right by your ass all morning?"

He guffaws. "I mean, in all fairness, the bar was meant for me, not you. I should've anticipated your hangriness, as I usually do at school. I won't make the same mistake twice. I'll make sure to pack a royal picnic for next time," he says sarcastically, snatching the bar from my hands.

I smile, incredibly grateful that things haven't changed and he still feels comfortable enough to tease me about my snacking habits despite everything he knows about my history with food.

He's incredible.

"Come on, Crazypants. Let me take a picture of you in front of the '*pile o' rocks,*' as you call them." He takes my phone from my hand and opens the camera app.

"Yeah, I don't do pictures of myself, sorry," I say.

"Not even for *The Gram*?" he asks mockingly. "I thought it was our generation's duty to record and share absolutely everything that we do and every thought we have on social media."

"Ah," I say, lifting a finger in the air. "But I am an old soul, and I'm full of insecurities, so no. I never post pictures of myself." I try to snatch my phone from his hands, but he puts it behind his back.

"Hey now, come on. Seriously, this is a big deal. Stonehenge is a historic place, and you should have a memory of what you did today. We went to a cathedral that's over *seven hundred and fifty* years old, for fuck's sake. Stonehenge dates back to as early as *three thousand BC*. How often do you see shit like that?"

I take a deep breath, dreaming of fries.

"Stand in front of those '*pile o' rocks*' right now, and let me take a picture of you at least *acting* excited about this." He grabs me by the elbow and pushes me near the edge of the monument boundary line.

I sigh, getting into position. "Remember," Josh says, "I want to see excitement. One...two...three!"

I jump at the exact same time he finishes counting, with my arms in the air, channeling my inner cheerleader, overdelivering on my promise.

"Perfect," he says, smiling down at the phone screen. "You're perfect."

The feeling in the pit of my stomach is back—the gut-punch, the flip—and my previous good mood seems to have evaporated into thin air. I suddenly feel exposed and self-conscious.

I ignore his comment and say, "Alright, I'm done. Take me to the food." It comes out harsher than intended, so I try to numb the sting of my bitterness by ruffling his hair with my fingers. My plan backfires as the physical contact between the two of us causes a jolt of electricity that seems to course through my entire body, and I'm back to that feeling in the pit of my stomach, that flip.

I groan internally.

What is wrong with me???

He's a smart man, that Josh. He said he would feed me, and feed me he did.

I'm glad he made me wait until we got back to Salisbury instead of listening to me and feeding me with an overpriced sandwich from the Stonehenge cafe. We went back down to the town square with different food stalls, food trucks, and vendors. It was my salvation. It was more so his salvation, to be honest, since I was about two minutes away from killing someone—him in particular.

We started with bacon cheeseburgers, followed by garlic fries, and finished lunch up nicely with some cider donuts with a caramel dipping sauce. It was heavenly.

Barring the general unease felt on occasion throughout our outing, today has been pretty cool.

We're on our way back to the train station when we walk past a liquor store, and I get an idea.

"Hold on," I say. "Gimme a sec."

I duck into the liquor store and search for a bottle of champagne. I find the cheapest prosecco in the place—seven pounds!—and walk it out to show it proudly to Josh.

"Wow! Look at you, Miss Moneybags!" he jokes, eyeing the bottle in my hands.

"You can't take a trip on a train with friends and not get drunk. It's, like, a rule," I say.

"Is that what New Yorkers do on the Amtrak or Metro-North? Get wasted while they travel? How do you not lose your luggage?"

"*Oh*, believe me, it happens more often than you think. I once made it all the way to D.C. while my bag enjoyed a nice little overnight trip in Penn Station's Lost and Found room."

He laughs and shakes his head at me, taking the bottle from my hands. "Alright. All we need are cups now."

"Good point," I say. Being so open with Josh is already affecting me. The idea of sharing a bottle with him and putting my lips where he puts his physically makes me sick with anxiety. "We need cups."

Definitely.

We end up re-using the Starbucks cups from the coffees we have on hand. Pro-tip: never ever, ever, *ever* use used coffee paper cups to drink warm champagne from.

Despite the nastiness of the coffee-flavored, cheap-tasting sparkling wine, we power through because, *"We're on an adventure!"* as I keep reminding Josh every time he gags or winces as he swallows down the shitty champagne.

We grow quiet after some time, exhausted from our day's excursions and tipsy from the world's worst-tasting sparkling wine in the history of time. I gaze pensively out the train window, looking out onto the English countryside with the sunset as a backdrop. It takes my breath away.

Damn, I love it here.

I realize I haven't thought of New York City or the life I left behind in ages. I love New York. It's where I grew up and fell in love and where most of my life seems to be. Lately, however, I've started to feel a stronger pull to what I've slowly been building here. My life in London isn't perfect, but it's also not riddled with bad memories of heartbreak and questionable loyalties.

When I look toward my future, I'm not sure where I'll be professionally, but I shock myself when I realize that I'm starting to see London as a place to set roots. My dreams of owning and living in a brownstone on the Upper East Side in Manhattan or a house in upstate New York have been replaced by one of living in an apartment in West London.

The life I previously imagined for myself does not exist and will never exist, and I think I've come to terms with it. It's time I carved out a new path for myself, even though I have no idea what it looks like from here. But I am not worried about it anymore—I refuse to continue to feel powerless over my emotions or future. I'm over feeling anxious about not knowing what comes next for me in life, and have decided to instead embrace the unknown.

I feel like a huge weight has been lifted from my shoulders

as I make peace with that decision. I take a deep breath and exhale slowly, regulating my racing heart. Josh looks over at me with a curious look in his eyes.

"I'm done being sad," I tell him with finality.

Josh smiles at me and needs no further explanation than that —he knows exactly what I mean.

Seven

THE NEXT DAY, I invite Oliver to come with me to visit Allie at work and get my weekly banh mi fix. I wasn't able to get it yesterday because of my trip with Josh, and I wasn't about to wait another week to enjoy it.

Hanging out with Oliver is always a blast, and we haven't been able to see much of each other this past week outside of classes, so we planned on some "bonding time." When he isn't a pain in the ass, which is a lot of the time, Oliver is great company.

Together, we walk up toward Notting Hill Gate, taking our time going in and out of local shops, people watching. Oliver is a surprisingly good shopping partner, patiently waiting while I go in and out of vintage clothing vendors, never complaining. You can tell a girlfriend has trained him, since I'm sure any other guy would have lost it by now, but he hasn't so much as grumbled once.

I'm in the middle of buttoning up a *gorgeous* vintage cashmere Burberry coat (that is obscenely out of my budget) when Oliver comes up behind me in the mirror and asks, "How was Stonehenge yesterday? Did you have fun?"

I shrug. "It was cool," I say. *If you like your ancient history tourism charged with whatever uncomfortable tension was felt most of the trip.* I pull my hair from under the coat and adjust the garment on my body.

"You know, you could've told me you couldn't make it. It just ended up being me and Josh on the trip."

"Oh?" he asks coolly, avoiding my gaze.

"Mmhmm. Chloe and Jane canceled as well. Even Michael and his French friend, Guillaume. I mean, *one* of you could have at least communicated to me that you weren't going." I think about this for a second. It *had* been bizarre that no one had texted me to let me know that they were passing. I mean, it's common courtesy, right? I would have probably canceled too if I had known no one else was able to join us. We could have rescheduled and gone as a group as planned.

"Josh had planned the whole thing for us to go as a group. It was really rude of you just to cancel and not let me know." I sniff, caring more about how *I* felt about them bailing than how Josh must have felt.

"Yeah, um, sorry. I should've—*we* should have texted you as well and not just Josh. You're right. But you had fun, right? On your date?"

I turn quickly around to look him straight in the eye. "What do you mean *'date'*?" I ask accusingly. Oliver's eyes widen with concern. "Did Josh say it was a date? Because it wasn't a date. Oh my God, was it a date? Did *he* think it was a date?"

"Oh, wow, okay," he says, backing up a step and raising his hands as if I were about to shoot. "Would you take a fucking breath? I haven't even spoken to him about yesterday."

I raise an eyebrow menacingly at him.

Looking back on what had happened yesterday, my biggest fear is that I had given Josh the wrong impression of what we are to each other, which is nothing more than friends. Yes, we went on a day trip, just the two of us, but that was only a conse-quence of everyone else's flakiness and inability to stick to a plan, not because I was interested in anything other than a friendship.

"Glad to know you're completely relaxed and calm about this, though." He says sarcastically and laughs. "Jesus, you can be so uptight sometimes, you know that? You need to relax a little bit. Lose some control from time to time. Might be good for you."

I ignore him and continue to stare at myself in the mirror. I'm so tired of Oliver telling me I need to relax and "lose control." I can't even begin to imagine what losing control to him even means. To me, it means getting drunk more than three nights in the same week (which is close to becoming the norm at this point, if I'm being honest). He's probably referring to hedonism parties.

"So, it wasn't a romantic trip, then? Nothing happened between the two of you?" he asks, genuinely curious. "There was no handholding or romantic viewing of the sunset together?" he asks with a smirk.

Confused about his line of questioning, I turn back to the mirror to knot the coat belt tightly around my waist. I look at myself sideways and put my hands in the coat pockets, sighing wistfully at how cozy and stylish this Burberry is.

I need this in my life.

I'm having a moment, wishing I had enough cash to take this home with me right now.

Mostly, to be honest, I'm stalling. I don't want to talk about yesterday.

The truth is that, even if the trip was not romantic or a date, it *had* felt weird at times. We weren't dating, that much was obvious, but it was like we had crossed some strange obscure line yesterday that needed to be redrawn or redefined. The charged moments of silence, the way he just knew who I was and what I needed, left me reeling. I haven't had enough time to break it down myself, so I know I am definitely not ready for a full download of information right now. Things are weird, and I still need to process and analyze what went down on our trip.

I turn to look up at him. "I can't afford this," I say, trying to deflect. "I don't want to take it off, though. I can't bring myself to do it."

He grinned. "Let *me* help." He reaches out for my belt, and we both stare into each other's eyes as he slowly unties the knot without breaking eye contact.

Oh, shit.

I can feel myself blushing, my skin blazing—and not from the warmth from the coat.

That was kind of hot.

It's been a while since someone has tried to undress me, if you know what I mean. My mind starts to go to mush, but I snap myself out of it before I let it wander anywhere stupid. I slap Oliver's hands off the coat belt, and he laughs, dragging a hand down his face in frustration.

I frown and remove the coat as quickly as possible, placing it back on its hanger and rack. The need to move on from what just happened is so intense that I make the mistake of switching back to the Josh topic.

"Nothing happened between the two of us. We just toured around Salisbury, went up to Stonehenge, and then back to town to have lunch—which you would know if you had been able to make it," I say haughtily. "What happened to you? Why did you cancel?"

He shrugs, casually browsing through the men's racks. "Busy."

I raise an eyebrow. "'Busy'?" I parrot in a mocking tone. "Seriously? That's your answer?"

"I just had a lot of things to do yesterday. School, work, laundry," he says, avoiding my eyes.

I stop and stare at him. "You're acting suspicious."

"Am not! I swear. I'm a busy man, Penny. You know this. I'm in high demand." He smiles, trying to joke, but it doesn't reach his eyes. He's hiding something.

"Hmm," I say, unconvinced. Oliver usually does not have a filter, and he's never really tried to hide something, but he looks mighty cagey now. "Let's go. I can't afford anything in here, and I'm hungry."

We walk out of the small store, waving to the bored salesperson on our way out. I'm sure he could tell as soon as I had walked in that nothing in his store was in my budget.

I chew on the inside of my cheek. I have this gnawing feeling that I'm not getting the whole truth about why he nor anyone else had shown up to our group trip. We had planned this over a week in advance, had a group chat going. Chloe, basically the mom of the group, had even volunteered to bring snacks. So, what happened?

We continue climbing the road up toward Notting Hill Gate while I lose myself in my thoughts. Oliver and I text several times a day, and he never once thought to warn me or let me know that he wouldn't be going? I had been so focused on breaking down and analyzing the events from yesterday that I hadn't even begun to think about why everyone else had conveniently canceled.

I smell a rat.

"It's so weird that everyone else canceled as well, right?" I say as casually as possible, looking at him from the corner of my eye. "And that, instead of announcing they weren't going in the group chat, they all just reached out to Josh individually?"

Oh my god, did Josh set this whole thing up?

Oliver looks nervously at me. He takes a pamphlet from someone passing them around, looking overly riveted by the information in his hand. The flyer is a guide to find Jesus, something I'd bet my life on Oliver has no interest in doing.

"Actually," he says, scratching his head.

He's about to crack—a horrible liar.

"I might have told Michael not to go. You know, since I wasn't going. So, I just, uh, you know... I just told Josh myself that Michael and his mate from uni weren't up for it."

I stop dead in my tracks to look up at him. Someone crashes right into me from behind, but I ignore their complaints.

"What do you *mean* you *told* them not to go?" I narrow my eyes at him.

"Listen, can we talk about this properly once you've had

some food in you?" Oliver looks anxious. He's not cracking jokes or looking me in the eye. He can sense my ire. "I'll deny I ever said this, but you scare me when you're hungry." He looks around anxiously.

"I don't understand. What is there to talk about?" My voice is cold.

He groans, closing his eyes and shaking his head.

"I just want to preface this by saying that it was done from a place of love. Because your friends care about you. And they want to see you and Josh happy. And it wasn't meant to make things uncomfortable, okay?"

I narrow my eyes at him. "Okay... *What* was done from a place of love?" I raise an eyebrow at him.

He takes a deep breath before speaking. "Jane and I may have...*slightly* sabotaged the trip to Stonehenge."

"What do you mean *slightly* sabotaged the trip, Oliver? What the fuck are you talking about?" I ask through gritted teeth.

Oliver chews the inside of his cheek, considering his words before answering. "Don't get mad, okay? It wasn't meant to hurt you." His words come out desperate, fast. "We just...saw how you two were interacting the other day at the library and that night we played *Risk*—and honestly just any time you two are together—and we thought everyone could see this thing unfolding except for the two of you, so...Jane may have *misled* Chloe into thinking the trip was canceled, and I may have told Michael the same thing." He winces. "We just wanted to push you both in the right direction. See what was there."

I am going to murder them.

"Are you *kidding me*, Oliver?" I grab him by his quilted jacket, not caring that we're in public and people are starting to stare, suppressing the urge to scream in frustration.

"Bloody hell. Let go of me!"

I loosen my grip and drop my hands with a huff. "What you guys did is so manipulative—even for you. Do you have any idea how weird the trip was yesterday? There were times where I swear you could cut the tension with a knife! You could have ruined my relationship with Josh given the amount of unquestionably awkward moments in there during our trip. It's none of your business whether we're together or not. That's a decision *we* would have to make—Josh and me!"

"But see, that's what I'm saying!" he says excitedly. "There *is* a 'Josh and me'—or a Josh and Penny, I mean. He's clearly interested, and you seem to like him as well."

I put my hands on my hips and look down at the ground. I try to steady my breathing before speaking to him, shaking my head in disapproval while I gather my thoughts.

"Oliver," I start. "I get that it came from a good place, but I *need* you to understand that *nothing* is going on between the two of us. I think he might have thought that I was into him, and that's why he was freaking out, because he doesn't like me that way. The problem here is that we are both very close, and maybe he's not used to it. And for me, trusting someone emotionally the way I have been trusting him so soon after my breakup hasn't been easy. So maybe that's what you've seen lately."

Oliver stares down at me with a concerned expression on his face.

"I don't think that's what it is, Penny. I think both of you need to look at what's happening and realize that you have feelings for each other."

I sigh and start walking again, Oliver falling quickly into stride with me.

"No, Oliver. And even if that *were* true, even if we did have feelings for each other—which we don't," I quickly clarify once again, "I am nowhere near close to being emotionally ready to be in a relationship right now. I just want to have fun and relax and for my life to remain uncomplicated."

"Okay..." He takes a deep breath. "Are you going to kill Jane and me?"

I laugh as we continue to weave our way through the crowd, my stomach growling as we near the food stalls and can smell the delicious gastronomical experience that awaits us. (Have I mentioned that I look forward to this sandwich every week?)

"I want to." I take his hand and look up at him. He is pretty tall. "I mean, I *definitely* want to because there were times yesterday on our trip where I would have been able to rank certain moments in the top ten most awkward situations of my life, but no. I get what you guys were doing. It was fucked up and very manipulative, but I get it. It came from a place of love."

"So, nothing is going on with you two?"

"No," I say firmly. I'm honestly not sure *what* is going on between the two of us, but it's nothing that I want to pursue. So for all intents and purposes, no, nothing is going on.

He smiles. "So, I can keep trying to sleep you?"

I roll my eyes at him, laugh-groaning. "Way to ruin a beautiful moment, you ass!"

He smirks at me, and I pull him faster by the hand through the crowds. "Come on, weirdo. I need food now!" I yell over my shoulder, my stomach growling.

Eight

"I LOOK LIKE A WHORE," I say to Allie. I stare at myself in her floor-length mirror, checking myself out after having undergone one of her makeovers.

It's the night of Jane's friend's concert, and I'm wearing a very, very short black leather mini-skirt and a semi-sheer top, which I'm confident is a bit too revealing for where I'm going. One bit of backlight, and I'll be flashing the whole venue. It's also late October and freezing. What is she thinking putting me in this?

Allie laughs and shakes her head. "Nah, man. You look great. Your legs look *amazing* in that mini-skirt, and the heels are killer."

"Allie, I am not going to a club. I'm going to see some random band play at a bar in Shoreditch. This outfit makes me look like I'm desperately trying to get laid or something."

"Um, aren't you?" she asks with a shrug.

"No! I need to bond and solidify friendships with the cool people in this group. I *cannot* wear this. This shirt is essentially see-through."

It's been a couple of weeks since Stonehenge, and I haven't seen Josh as often as I used to. We've met up to work on our Strategic Management project, but we aren't hanging out as much in between or after courses. I think we both feel the awkwardness and are mutually avoiding each other. And though I'm not one hundred percent sure he has feelings for me (or I for him, for that matter), I don't want to risk it.

I know, it's a super mature way of dealing with things.

Allie rolls her eyes at me and starts pulling my leather skirt down a little. "Is this better?"

I sigh, thinking about tonight. The plan is to go over to Chloe's (*in the middle of nowhere*), pregame together, and head out to the venue as a group.

"Listen, I'm tired of hearing you talk about Austin, and I know you talk a big game about having seen a ton of guys post-breakup, but I know for a fact that is utter bull. There were only two men, and both were friends of yours."

"Excuse me, are you saying they were both pity sex or something?" I ask angrily.

Oh my God, am I really that pathetic?

Allie rolls her eyes at me. "Don't be dramatic. I'm sure they were both super happy to get with you, but all I'm saying is that they don't count as '*putting yourself out there*'." She takes a deep breath and looks me in the eye. "You need to *try*, Penny. You're holding yourself back from meeting someone great. Just fucking let go."

Easier said than done.

I look into her eyes in the reflection of the mirror. "I'm not ready to start dating anyone, Allie. I'm a fucking mess. These days, I can't even put my makeup on correctly." I think back to my half-made-up face from last month and how embarrassed I was that I spent the entire class looking like a crazy person. Thank God no one besides Josh noticed, and he told me as soon as we were done with class so I could go and fix it.

I miss Josh.

But I push the thought quickly away.

Allie rolls her eyes at me and starts playing with my hair, experimenting with an updo. I don't even bother with her anymore—I'll be her Barbie doll for the night.

"I'm not telling you to commit to anyone—jeez! If anyone knows what a walking dumpster fire you are right now, it's me. I have to see you every day."

"Wow. Thanks," I mutter.

Allie sighs and turns me around, holding me by the shoulders. "Listen, I'm not saying go find yourself a boyfriend, but I do want you to go out and flirt with some boys *safely*. You need this, Penny. You're beautiful and smart and a good friend, and you don't deserve to be this emotionally bankrupt person anymore. You need to stop waiting for him to come back."

My eyes start to water. Allie is really good at tough love and handing out reality checks. It's what I love/hate the most about her.

Emotionally bankrupt, indeed.

"Don't worry," I say. "I know he's not coming back."

I'd seen a lot of partying activity on his social media and an increase in female comments on his posts. I was verging on stalking, but honestly, who didn't do at least *some* cyberstalking post-breakup? Let he who is free of sin cast the first stone. You know what I'm talking about.

The train ride back into the city the other day had also been eye-opening. I promised myself that, even though I still had a lot of feelings to sort through, it was time I moved on—so I wasn't holding out hope.

Allie sighs, reaching over to hold me in her arms. I inhale her familiar coconut smell and hug her back. I'm so damn lucky to have her here. "If you're not comfortable in this outfit, let's find you something else to wear, but I need you to promise me that you'll *try*. Promise?"

I look her straight in the eye and say, "I promise." And I mean it. I *will* try, and I'm not holding out hope at all.

But it still hurts.

The night already feels a bit shit when I Google Map tube directions to the pregame and realize precisely how long it will take me to get to Chloe's apartment—an hour and forty-five minutes with a total of three tube lines. Desperately, I check to see how much an Uber would cost, but I get a quote for seventy-six pounds.

I never thought I would say this, but despite all of its flaws I've never missed the New York City MTA so much right now.

I sigh and accept defeat, choosing the cheaper, though not necessarily more sensible option, of paying three pounds instead of cutting my time in half by going by car.

This city is so expensive it hurts.

When I arrive to Chloe's apartment, I'm immediately overwhelmed by the amount of people, most of which I recognize from the program but am not necessarily close with. Feeling a slight panic rise in my throat, I look around for the host to say hi and see her in a corner with Josh. With a sigh, I grimace but make my way toward them, sitting on the opposite end of the couch, putting as much room as possible between Josh and me. But after I compliment Chloe for a great turnout, she excuses herself to greet more guests.

"Hey," I mutter awkwardly.

"Hey, yourself," he forces a smile.

Oh god, this is weird.

Just as I plan an escape in my head, about to excuse myself to the bathroom, Jane and Oliver walk over to us.

THANK GOD.

These new random awkward surges going on between us are starting to exhaust me. If this is how it's going to be all night, I'm going to need a strong drink.

Oliver shoots me a drunken grin, falls in the seat next to me, and pulls me into a tight embrace.

"Hello, darling."

Okay, so he's tipsy already.

Jane looks annoyed and frustrated as she takes a seat next to

Josh. "How many people are even here? We can barely fit in this damn flat. I'm going to suffocate!" She says, fanning herself.

"I don't know, but we *need* to go soon because I am already tipsy, and I am not going to make it to the place tonight if we keep drinking." Oliver scoots closer to me on the couch, absent-mindedly wrapping an arm around my shoulders.

I push Oliver's arm away and he pouts.

"I hope Chloe doesn't think I'm getting all her friends in without a cover. This is absolutely ridiculous," Jane says, shaking her head.

I pound back a few vodka shots in a row as we wait for more people to arrive, even though I know it wasn't the best idea. I haven't eaten much all day, which is why, after about a half hour, I start to feel tipsy.

"Can we just go? I'm so overwhelmed by this crowd. Not sure I'm going to want to even go to this place if we don't leave soon," I say.

Josh eyes me skeptically. "You good, kid?"

Is that his damn catchphrase now? I don't need anyone to take care of me.

"Let's get you some water before we leave."

I huff, confused and irritated. I'm not nearly as far gone as most of the people here, but whatever, sure, water is always a good idea when drinking is concerned. I let him get me a glass while Eloise glares at me from the other end of Chloe's flat.

When did she get here? And what is up with her always staring at me like that?

After I'm forced to down a whole glass of room temperature water—because God forbid there be cold water or ice cubes in this country—we rally the troops and push everyone out the door and into a train.

It has become painfully evident that everyone has had a little too much to drink at our pregame when Michael starts pole-dancing in the middle of the moving tube, and we're all hooting.

Oh boy.

Naturally, my friends invite me to make a fool out of myself, and I attempt to pole-dance on the train as well. And Jesus Christ, I must be drunk, because somehow I say yes.

Thanking the Lord that I had the decency to change into jeans before leaving the apartment, I wrap my arm around the pole, push myself off the ground, and attempt to swing around but slip and fall on my ass instead.

Mother Fu—Ow.

Mortified, I get to my feet quickly as I see everyone doubled over in laughter, and to be honest, so am I. I'm embarrassing myself and acting like an idiot, sure, but for the first time in a while, I feel...free. Deciding to make an effort to move forward is already doing wonders to my self-esteem and outlook. I want tonight to be a good night.

I take a seat next to Oliver, noticing a slight discomfort on my ass cheeks. I'm drunk enough that it doesn't bother me that much, but sober enough to know that it will *definitely* hurt more tomorrow.

"So, are you enjoying yourself?" Oliver asks as he sits next to me at the next stop.

"Meh," I say, shrugging. "I am, but I need some music or something. Still need to get more in the mood, I think."

"I can get you in the mood." He smiles.

Frustrated, I say, "Jesus, Oliver! Don't you ever quit?" I say, raising my voice a little too much—enough to make Jane turn around. She frowns, concerned, but I shake my head and give her a look as if to say, *Don't worry, I got this,* and she turns back.

He looks me straight in the eye and says, "No, because you have no idea how great it could be if you just fucking relaxed. I say this for your own good. You're wound too tight. And I'm serious when I say that I can help you."

I scoff. "What? Do you have some magic dick or something? A universal panacea to everything that's wrong with me?"

I stare back at him. I don't doubt his sexual prowess, exactly

—I get the feeling that he's not one of those guys who's over-compensating and talks a big game—but it's more because I just need a fucking friend now. I don't need to sleep with someone. The boys I promised Allie I would flirt with do not include my new school friends.

He shrugs. "I don't know about a magical dick or anything, but I do know that we've become close friends and I know you, Penny. Enough for me to vehemently believe that fucking you will make you feel better."

I roll my eyes. "You mean it will make *you* feel better."

"That too," he says with a wicked smile.

"Sex doesn't cure broken hearts, you know," I say.

"No, but it helps pass the time while they mend. Think about it."

Oliver maintains eye contact, and we don't say anything to each other as we reach our final stop. He closes his eyes and shakes his head with a huff. "You don't even see yourself, do you?" We get up at the same time and walk out of the train, his hand on my lower back, as I realize something with horror: *Fuck. He's piqued my curiosity. Dammit.*

The music is good, and my body is rocking from side to side. Not quite sure what's happening or how many drinks I've had. Everything is kind of a blur. Music is good, good, good.

Thump, thump, thump.

Someone hands me another vodka soda. I think? He looks familiar.

I've had so many drinks…

Thump, thump, thump.

Is that the drummer or my heart?

This vodka soda doesn't taste like anything.

"What is this?" I say to the shadow. He smells good...*mmmm*...like fruit. Manly fruit. Yummy manly fruit.

"Drink it. It's good for you," the man replies.

Thump, thump, thump.

"I think I'm drunk," I say to the shadow, and he laughs.

"Yeah, just a bit."

I smile and close my eyes, sipping the cold drink through the straw, swaying side to side.

I hear the familiar sounds of a guitar, and my eyes fly open eagerly. Jane's boyfriend's band has played a combination of original songs and covers all night, and this one I know. I jump excitedly as the guitar intro starts, and so does the shadow and others around me...

Coming out of my cage
And I've been doing just fine
Gotta gotta be down
Because I want it all....

My drink has spilled all over the floor as I move to my favorite song by The Killers, and I feel an arm snake around my waist, holding me tight.

We move together, swaying side to side, my eyes closed, feeling him feel me. One hand travels down my back, another up my ribcage... I'm breathing faster, and I feel this man's broad shoulders underneath my hands. He feels good. He feels fucking amazing. He smells different than the shadow—citrus.

It started off with a kiss
How did it end up like this?

His lips roam my neck, climbing up toward my jaw, grazing all the way to my mouth...

I turn my face, and his lips are on me.

My hands go in his hair.

His hands travel under my shirt.

It was only a kiss, it was only a kiss...

It is only a kiss, but I feel it all over.

What is happening?

Nine

I'M DEAD. Or dying. One of the two. But I am definitely not feeling alive right now. My mouth is so dry it feels like I've been walking through the desert for weeks. I *desperately* need water.

Where am I?

I can tell it's still dark out, but the streetlight outside peeks through the windows alerting me to the fact that I'm not in my place.

Oh my God. Okay. Don't panic.

I have never, ever blacked out and woken up at another guy's apartment, but by the looks of the rugby memorabilia and dirty men's workout gear in the corner of the room, that's *precisely* where I seem to currently find myself in.

Taking a deep breath, I look over to my right to see who the mystery man is and grimace.

Of course. Oliver.

He's bundled up under the covers into what seems like a ball, looking peaceful in his sleep. His chest is uncovered by the sheet, letting me appreciate his chiseled chest despite the low light.

When a chill passes through me, I realize a bit belatedly that I seem to be wearing less clothing than I was before leaving my apartment. Duh.

This hangover has me stupid.

I shiver once more and lift the comforter to check just how naked I am, thanking god when I see that I'm at least in my underwear. The jeans that I had changed into before leaving the house, though, are on the floor by the bed. My shirt, I notice nervously, is nowhere to be seen.

Suddenly, the shoe drops as I realize that *I am literally in my underwear next to Oliver in his bed.*

I. AM. MORTIFIED.

As embarrassment spreads through me, I think of how I deserve this. This is my life. I make bad choices, so this is what I get.

Goddammit.

One of my closest friends here, and I've gone and messed it up. I won't be able to hang with him anymore. Not when he's seen me naked. Who knows if he'll even want to keep hanging out with me, anyway? What if that was it?

Ugh.

Oliver groans and rolls over onto his stomach in his sleep, the comforter slipping even lower from his upper body, showing off his broad shoulders and back.

I can't help as my bleary eyes widen and take in his muscles, following a trail all the way to where I can see the dimples of his lower back.

In all honestly, I can see why Drunk Penny would want to sleep with him. His upper body is *insane.* How often does this man work out?

His muscles flex, and I shock myself by needing to suppress a groan.

Shit. How did I *not* realize he's actually attractive? Has he always looked like this?

Steeling myself with a deep breath, I lift the comforter to check on his clothing status.

Oh my God, he's naked. He's naked. He is buck-naked under the sheets.

Shit, shit, shit, shit! SHIT. I totally slept with him. You can't fall asleep next to that and not sleep with him.

"Oh god…" I whisper, running my fingers through my hair.

Never, even in my worst post-breakup idiocy, have I ever, *ever* gotten black-out drunk and slept with someone.

Please let me not have slept with him. Please.

I'm not going to deny that I have thought about it. I mean, I've always felt he was attractive, just not *that* attractive. Plus, I'd be lying if I said I hadn't ever considered his... *offers*. But never seriously. Not really. Oliver is an excellent friend, and I've trusted parts of myself to him that I haven't to other people. Risking our friendship over sex was never part of the plan.

God, what an idiot.

I stretch my body a little, checking for any signs whatsoever of whether I had sex last night or not. When I shift my weight in bed, I wince, feeling a sharp ache in my left ass cheek. Grimacing, I remember the monumental mistake that was the group tube pole-dancing extravaganza. What an idiot. If there was any question on the state of my life up until this point, please take this as further evidence that I am a complete and utter mess.

Stupid. Stupid. Stupid Penny.

Rubbing my temples, squeezing my eyes shut, I focus on my breathing to keep from panicking. I need water. I need my shirt. I need to remember. I need to remember. I need to remember what happened last night.

"Oh, *just shut up*," Oliver says into his pillow, interrupting my downward spiral.

At first, I think he's sleep-talking, so I stay silent, hoping he doesn't wake. Honestly, I don't feel ready to face him right now.

"I can almost hear you overthinking this like crazy." Oliver sighs.

Shocked, I wonder how long he's been awake. He doesn't open his eyes, but pulls the comforter up over himself, snuggling deeper into the mattress. "For fuck's sake, it wasn't your fault. I had just drunk a lot. It's more embarrassing for me than it is for you. Can we just never talk about it again?" he mutters.

"I'm so confused," I whisper, but he doesn't seem to hear me.

"Additionally…" He sits up suddenly, and turns to me. The comforter slides off again, and I can't help myself. My eyes flicker down to check out his chest and shoulders out. *Damn.* "We were way too drunk for it to have been smart to do anyways. When I finally do get to have sex with you, I want both of us to remember every second of it."

I look into his eyes, searching for any sort of insight into whatever the hell he's saying. He sighs.

"Listen, please don't take it personally. I think you're fucking gorgeous. It was all me. All my embarrassing fault, all right?" Oliver scratches his head.

I tilt my head at him and gasp, understanding dawning on me.

"Oh my God!" My hand flies to my mouth. "I remember! I say, exploding into a fit of laughter, gasping for breath. But when I notice the hurt in Oliver's eyes, I sober up quickly, struggling to steady my breathing. I watch him grimace and look away in embarrassment, unable to speak.

"*Oh,*" I say stupidly, feeling like an ass. "I wasn't laughing at your inability to…uh…*rise to the occasion.*"

He winces. "Can you not?" He stands up, his back to me, and stretches.

Jesus Christ, his back, his shoulders. His ass.

I horrify myself slightly at the thought of how nice it would feel to have his body on top of me. I mean, this is Oliver we're talking about! But then I realize that's precisely what happened last night. And I vaguely remember it feeling really—*really* good.

"No, seriously," I say quickly. I start to get up until I realize I'm basically naked, so I wrap myself in the comforter, trying to keep myself covered. Oliver, on the other hand, walks around his bedroom stark naked, without an ounce of self-consciousness—though, honestly, he has nothing to feel self-conscious about. "I wasn't laughing at that. I was laughing because, for the past ten minutes, I've been internally freaking out, thinking we slept together. And I must admit, I'm glad we didn't."

He quietly turns around and glares at me. "Swear?"

"Yes," I say seriously. "I would never make fun of you for that, especially now that I remember *why* you took me home. You were just trying to take care of me."

I was wasted last night, it's true. We made out at the bar, it's true. But that was cut short by my inability to stand on my own two feet without any help. I remember Oliver freaking out, his concern for me genuine.

"We need to get her home." he had said.

I remember someone giving me water before while I was dancing. Was it Josh?

"Someone should take her and make sure she doesn't choke on her own vomit," Eloise had said cattily, as if she'd never gotten drunk.

They had all made an embarrassingly big deal out of it.

"Someone get me water right now," Oliver had demanded.

I remember them making me drink it, but honestly, we were all wasted. It was like the blind leading the blind.

"I'm taking you to my flat," he declared.

I remember Josh's face and how unhappy he looked at Oliver's decision. *"Um, are you sure, buddy? I'm a little more sober than you."*

"My flat two blocks away, mate," Oliver replied in confusion, logic clearly on his side. Upon seeing Josh's hesitant reaction, Oliver raised an eyebrow at him, and his voice became sharper as he asked, *"Wait. Are you saying you think I'd hurt her?"*

I had sighed and said, *"I'm fine, guys. I just need to get a cab."*

"No cab. Not like that. You're coming with me."

And you know what, I had been conscious enough to know that he wouldn't do anything weird. I trusted him. The only reason he had ended up naked and I was in my underwear is because I woke up a couple of hours after making it to his place, and I may or may not have launched myself at him.

Okay, I definitely did. I don't know what came over me.

He was just as drunk as I was by then, and I had caught him by surprise. Can't blame him for not being able to...*ahem*...perform.

Oliver narrows his eyes at me. "Okay, I choose to believe you," he says suspiciously, pulling on a pair of black underwear.

Is underwear really necessary? Can he not just stay naked a bit longer? Just for comfort purposes, of course. Not just because he has a fantastic ass. Because he does. Have a fantastic ass, I mean.

Fantastic everything, really. Top notch.

"But let me tell you that this is not a common thing for me. If you're ever interested in pursuing this, I will make it worth your while." He smiles lasciviously.

And just like that, he's back, ladies and gentlemen.

I roll my eyes at him. "Can you just shut up, give me a shirt, and point me in the direction of your bathroom?"

He pulls a t-shirt from his dresser and throws it at my face. I glare at him, pulling it over my head as I walk out toward the bathroom, pulling down the shirt over my ass so as not to give him a nice view of of my black lace panties. I can feel his eyes following me out of the bedroom.

Whatever.

When I reach the bathroom, he woman in the mirror is unrecognizable.

My cat-eye is completely smudged all over my face, my hair is a rat's nest, and my lips are swollen—from kissing Oliver?

God, I cannot believe I made out him him.

I groan again, holding my face in my hands.

At least his shirt smells nice, though—like citrus and sandalwood.

I splash cold water on my face and wipe off any smudged eyeliner. Pulling Oliver's brush through my hair, I think through the possibility of *actually* going through with this, of actually sleeping with him. To be honest, he seems pretty chill about the whole thing. And he *is* a good friend, so I highly doubt Oliver to be the type of guy to stop talking to me after. If it were any other person, I think that things could become weird. I mean, we see each other every day. There is a high probability of it being incredibly uncomfortable, but I don't think it would be with him.

The more I think about it, I just don't get the feeling that Oliver is that kind of guy. There would be no feelings involved, and I don't think I would have another Josh scenario on my hands. It would remain totally casual.

Huh.

"No, no. Too weird," I say to myself out loud, shaking my head.

Even so, I squirt toothpaste on my index finger and attempt to brush my teeth with it. Something is better than nothing, and if my hormones take over, I don't want to be caught off guard by having morning breath and ruining the mood. It *has* been a long time since I've had sex. Three, maybe four months?

Sometimes you just need sex—like cracking your neck.

I quietly head back to his room, tip-toeing the whole way to avoid waking up his roommates.

From the light spilling in through the bedroom windows as I walk back into the room, I can tell the sun is rising, giving me a better view of Oliver as he lies back in bed, hands behind his head, eyes closed. Not sure whether he's awake or asleep, I slip quietly back under the covers.

He opens his eyes and gives me a look. "You look so hot in my shirt," he smirks.

Rolling my eyes, I laugh. "I bet you say that to all the girls."

"Only the hot ones I want to have sex with," he laughs and I shake my head, pressing my lips together to keep from chuckling.

Maybe, maybe, maybe.

"Shut up and go to bed. I've only slept, like, two hours," I tell him.

He huffs and rolls on his side. "Fine. Goodnight."

I roll over, facing the opposite side so I don't have to look at him.

I mean, what would be the worst part? We're both consenting adults, right? We both want this.

And I miss sex. Really miss sex.

Did I mention it's been four months?

"Um...Oliver?" I ask hesitantly.

"Hmm?" He doesn't move or open his eyes.

"So, I was thinking…" I take a deep breath.

"You're not great at thinking, love," he teases.

I ignore his dig and go on. "You know how you're always talking about me being too uptight and needing to lose control a little bit?"

My question intrigues him, I feel his body tense in anticipation.

"*Yeeesssss?*" he says, turning slowly to look at me.

"Well, I was thinking…" my stomach turns, nerves taking over as I feel my palms clam up a little.

"You said that already." He narrows his eyes at me.

"Right. Ha. Yeah, so I was wondering. Does that offer still stand?"

"What offer?" he asks innocently, clearly amused now, the corners of his mouth quirking up.

"Ugh! Forget it." I turn over again in frustration. It's not enough for me to agree to have sex with him. Nope. He needs the added satisfaction of hearing me ask for it.

Dick.

He leans over me. "No, seriously, please do tell me what offer you are talking about—not sure I recall. I'm so generous; I can't keep track of everything I offer people, you know."

Ugh.

He knows this is mortifying me. I won't give him the satisfaction, physical or otherwise. I won't let him win.

God, but that also means that I lose out.

Doesn't matter. Can't let Oliver win this. Do not cave, Penny. No matter how much you miss sex.

"You know what? Don't worry about it. I'm sober now. I'm just gonna go. Thanks for letting me crash."

I move quickly, throwing the covers off and swinging my legs off the bed, reaching for my jeans.

"The hell you are." He jumps out of bed at the speed of light and stands in front of me. "Tell me what you want, Penny." He's not laughing anymore, his eyes darkening. He puts his hands on my hips and walks me backwards until I feel something behind me—his desk.

His breath is minty fresh, and when I spy a box of Altoids on his nightstand, I smile. He must've also hoped I would change my mind, and taken a breath mint in preparation for this moment.

Oliver puts one hand on either side of me on the desk, caging me in, and places a kiss followed by a bite at the base of my throat.

I inhale sharply, feeling an ache build between my legs.

"Well? What is it that you want?"

Jesus Christ, I can't breathe. I can't remember how to speak.

His left hand moves to my waist, gripping it hard. It's unexpected. And hot.

"What. Do. You. Want?" Oliver whispers in my ear.

The way he speaks those words—commanding, determined, confident—sends shivers up and down my spine, causing my eyes slide shut.

What do I want? I want *him*. I want to not think for once; I just want to act.

I can barely get the words out when I say, "I want to lose control."

He moves quickly, taking that as the green light. I feel his lips on mine, his hands sliding down the backs of my thighs, lifting me up and onto the desk, opening my legs wide to stand between them. I'm taken aback by his roughness, and I kind of love it.

He's kissing me with hunger, with abandon, and God knows I want him just as badly. My heart is beating out of my chest, hammering more loudly than a New York City construction zone. He grips me tightly by the hips, sliding me to the edge of the desk, pulling me closer to his body, leaning in, grinding into me. I can't help the moan that escapes my lips.

Oliver is *unquestionably* hard this time around. I can feel every inch of him rubbing against me. Grunting as my hands run through his hair and tug, he groans and holds me tighter to him, fingers digging into me.

Oh, he likes that.

I tug again, harder this time, and he grinds into me with more force. I break away from his lips with a gasp, the sudden jolt of pleasure surprising me.

"Right there?" he asks roughly.

I can only manage a nod. Oliver grins mischievously and grinds into me repeatedly, and I feel him hard and big against me.

I feel it *everywhere.*

I've never felt this type of hunger before, like I can't get close enough fast enough. I had never even felt it with Austin.

I keep pulling Oliver in tighter, digging my nails into his back, making him groan.

I would be embarrassed to admit that I'm moaning a bit too loudly just from some dry humping, but there really is a lot to be said for it, and also, I don't give a fuck right now because IT. FEELS. SO. FUCKING. GOOD.

I pull him back to my mouth and bite his lower lip, holding on tightly to his shoulders. He grunts and pulls me up from the desk, walking me back to his bed, holding onto my ass tightly. We never break contact as he sits on the edge, and I straddle him, riding him a bit longer.

"I'm going to come right now if you keep doing that, and I don't think either one of us wants that yet," he says against my neck. He slides his hands under my shirt as he bites my earlobe, and I feel it all the way down to my core. Oliver divests me of his t-shirt and my bra in the blink of an eye, which reminds me just how experienced this man is. I barely even noticed him touching my bra clasp.

I have no control over my thoughts or decisions anymore. Bye, mind. It was nice knowing you.

Ta-ta. Too busy. About to have sex, thanks.

His breathing is heavy in my ear as I ride him, his underwear still on, hands on my ass.

"Stop moving. I want you on your back first." He pushes me down onto the bed roughly, somehow removing his underwear at the same time.

Who is this man? How many hands does he have?

It feels like he's managed to undress the both of us while never removing a hand from my body. The only thing keeping us separated is my lace panties, and those need to come off ASAP, or I will *lose it.*

I get to admire his body briefly, and dammit if it's not perfect. I hate him a little bit for it. I don't want to give him the satisfaction of knowing I'm that attracted to him. "Are you going to eye-fuck me all day, or are you done?" he asks with a laugh.

I guess the cat's out of the bag, then.

"Shut up," I say, pulling him down roughly to kiss him again.

He kisses down my body, taking his time, his lips gliding over every swell, teeth nipping my skin here and there. His hands slide over my ribs, pausing over my breasts, squeezing them lightly. I arch my back, my heels digging into the bed. He's moving so slowly I think I'm going to die.

"Am I dying? I think I'm dying," I say.

He laughs against my skin. "Nope—definitely not dying."

Oliver continues to kiss down my stomach, biting the hem

of my lace panties, and starts to pull them down with his teeth slowly while maintaining eye contact with me.

Jesus Christ.

I want him to tear off the remaining scrap of clothing between us with his teeth. I want him to stop moving so goddamn slow.

Through the fog, I hear just how ragged my breathing has gotten, but I can barely manage an ounce of embarrassment enough to care.

Tired of waiting around, I take matters into my own hands and try to take off my panties myself. Before I know it, Oliver grabs me by the wrists and pushes my arms up over my head, stopping me from my goal.

His eyes blaze. "What did you say you wanted, Penny?"

My skin feels like it's on fire. Oliver is usually laidback and joking, but this new Oliver, this dominating and controlling Oliver, gets me even more excited. I never expected to feel this thrilled.

"To lose control." I sound pathetically breathy.

"Exactly," he says with hard eyes. "To lose control. So, stop trying to control the situation. *I* am in control." I inhale sharply at his words, gaze locked with his.

"Oliver?" I say as he looks up at me. "I think I'm gonna like this." I cover my face, embarrassed.

He removes my hands from my face and kisses me. "I'll make sure of it."

Oliver's breathing turns just as ragged as mine. After weeks of teasing and—admittedly—a lot of charged sexual tension, it's happening. He pulls down my panties quickly—*finally!* —and reaches toward his nightstand for a condom. Oliver kneels between my legs as I look him up and down.

"*Fuckkkkk.*" I run my fingernails down his chest, leaving a trail of marks on his skin. "Your body is *insane.*" I'm panting now.

"Oh, yeah?" He smiles as he rolls on the condom. He positions himself over me and lifts my left leg over his hip. "What about my cock?" And he thrusts hard into me.

He groans as I moan loudly.

Oh. My. God.

"*Jesus Christ,*" he groans again into my neck. "*Fuuuuckkkk.*"

Words. I forget words.

He pulls out a little, and I gasp as he thrusts into me again, harder this time. He grips my leg tighter, his fingers digging into my thigh, hurting just right, just enough for it to feel amazing. He's hard inside me as I wrap my arms around him. I'm feeling every muscle in his back flex as he moves, digging my nails into his skin. I'm doing my best to hold on here.

He kisses me roughly again and starts up an even rhythm, grunting every so often. I start to wonder why we haven't done this sooner. Why I kept denying him or not believing him when he said how great it would be. I haven't even come yet, and I'm already ranking it high in Penny's Top Ten Sexual Experiences —right there next to that time Austin and I hooked up next to the tennis courts in his dad's house in Connecticut in broad daylight during a family lunch.

I'm getting close, and my breathing speeds. One of Oliver's hands makes its way to my ass again, changing the angle, making me cry out. I have to bite down on his shoulder to keep from getting any louder and waking up his roommates. Although, it's getting more and more difficult by the second to care.

"I'm gonna..." I start to say.

He stops suddenly, pulling me from the brink of orgasm. I'm about to murder him when he flips me roughly onto my stomach and pulls my hips back in one smooth movement, impaling me from behind. I gasp, gripping the sheets.

Holy. Shit.

He groans loudly and stops himself for a minute. He tenses, I can tell he's close, too, and doesn't want it to end. He's gripping my hips tightly, digging into me, and I decide to tease him and push back into him. His own need has thwarted his plan to make this last and stay in control. I love that I can do this to him.

"Stop," he groans. "Stop. You need to stop. Not yet. Stop."

"No. Payback."

He sighs and holds on tighter. "Fine," he says through gritted teeth, thrusting faster now. We're both close, on edge. I can feel it. Suddenly, I cry out in pleasure, barely registering his grunt and final thrust as we both fall onto the bed together.

Ten

WE LIE PANTING on the bed next to each other without saying a word. Suddenly, we burst out laughing. For the second time in under an hour, I can't breathe from sheer laughter.

"That was fun," he says with a final chuckle.

I take a deep breath. "Yeah, good times."

We look over at each other, and he raises his hand, palm up. I high-five him and chuckle again. My skin feels tingly, and a sheen of sweat covers our skin. It feels like every joint in my body has come a little loose, and dammit, if it doesn't feel incredible.

"Did you know you have a *massive* bruise on your ass?" he says while getting up to dispose of the used condom and wrapper. "It almost distracted me from the whole situation. *Almost.*"

"Situation? Sex with me was a '*situation*'?" I snort, unconsciously rubbing my butt cheek, feeling how sore it is. "Ugh, I didn't know it had actually bruised. It's from last night, I guess. I will never attempt to pole-dance ever again—*especially* not on a moving tube."

"I mean, you can pole-dance for me any time you want." He laughs at my expression. Oliver slips back into bed with me.

I raise an eyebrow. "Really? Still? I thought you would calm down if I ever slept with you."

"Never," he says with a smile, putting his hands behind his head.

"Right, well, that was fun, but I'm going back to sleep." I pull up the covers and turn over on my side, ending this conversation. I need a few more hours of sleep, especially after our little tryst. I'm finally comfortable under the comforter in a ball when I feel Oliver's arm snake around my waist. My whole body tenses as I feel the front of his body press up against the back of mine.

"Um, what do you think you're doing?" I ask as nicely as possible, though I'm about five seconds from elbowing him in the balls.

"Um...I don't know. Spooning you?" he answers, confused.

"*Why* are you spooning me, exactly?"

Oliver senses my panic and gets the message, releasing his hold on me. I turn around, half in his arms, to face him and look him straight in the eye.

"Ah," he says, nodding in understanding.

"Spooning is for lovers; for couples. We are not lovers, nor are we a couple. We're friends who happen to find each other attractive and decided to have sex. So please don't ever spoon me ever again," I say as gently as possible. I know that there are no romantic feelings involved here, but I don't want to put either of us in a position that will lead to deeper intimacy. I don't want to set a precedent.

"Noted. No spooning. Ever." He rolls onto his back and stares up at the ceiling. "What about cuddling? I'm a fantastic cuddler," he says with a smile.

Is this man incapable of having a serious conversation? I sigh. I can easily imagine laying my head on his chest and cuddling him—he looks like he would be really comfy, oddly enough. But no—hands down, no. Oliver and I get along all too well, and it would just be playing with fire. He's a man with a million red flags, but you never know—it's easier than we'd like to admit to fall for the wrong ones (please see dreaded ex as example).

Boundaries, boundaries, boundaries.

"Fantastic cuddler or not, it might make things complicated. Who knows?"

"Just from cuddling? Jesus, you are *seriously* fucked up, you know that?" *Duh.* Thank you Captain Obvious. "It *is* possible to have a casual cuddle without it leading to a marriage proposal, you know. And need I remind you that I have a girlfriend?" he adds. "Not that she would be opposed to this little assignation between you and me, but you don't need to worry about me catching *feelings* or anything," he says with mock disgust, making fun of me.

I roll my eyes at him. "It's not just *you* here. It's me. I might be stupid enough to catch feelings for *you*." I snort at the idea. "Also"—I sit up, holding the comforter to cover myself—"why are we even discussing this as though this is not a one-time thing?"

Oliver snorts. "Penny, *please*, you know for a fact that this was not a one-time thing. It was fucking great and will only get better with repetition." He sighs and turns on his side, closing his eyes. "And there will be *lots* more repetition," he adds with a smile on his face.

I love Oliver as a friend, and we've gotten very close in a short time, but right now, his arrogance lights a fire inside, annoyance coursing through me. "You're being a bit presumptuous, aren't you?"

He sighs and sits up again to look me in the eye. "Penny. Answer the following questions for me. Did you have fun?"

I think of the back-bending pleasure that was this morning and the freedom of doing it with someone I trust, but have no romantic feelings for whatsoever. I didn't feel self-conscious ever. I was never concerned about whether I might be bloated from alcohol or anything. It was just fun. Oliver had become a good friend—and a trustworthy one, at that. And... yeah. Sleeping with him had been fun. Something I hadn't really had in a long time with sex.

"Yes," I answer.

"Have I given you any indication that this is something more than it is?" he follows up.

"No." *Thank God.*

"I realize that you are, at present, not emotionally available, and please let me reassure you that neither am I." I realize his tone has evolved into a more formal one. For my sake? "I am in a committed open relationship and have been for several years. So, you shouldn't worry." His expression is serious, official—must be all of his training as a civil servant. I appreciate the effort, as it removes the emotions from the situation—or at least attempts to. I'm trying to remain as emotionally detached as possible.

I pause. "Well, I'm legit freaked out by that. How do I know you're telling the truth and not lying to me about your girl-friend? I realize I probably should have double-checked this before, but how do I know you are in an open relationship, and I'm not this horrible person wronging another woman?"

I don't want to be that girl.

He laughs as if it were the most ridiculous notion and reaches over to his nightstand to get his phone. He opens the messages app to a conversation with someone called Lucy. The last text exchange was *Love, you babe. Have fun tonight.*

"I'll fucking text her right now. She's traveling to visit her parents today, so she must be up early."

OLIVER

> Finally shagged that girl from New York I was telling you about!

Her reply is almost immediate.

LUCY

Congrats, babe! Didn't think you had it in you.

OLIVER

> You're the worst girlfriend ever. :) Love you

"There. Is that enough proof?"

I shake my head. "This is so weird. How is she okay with this?"

He rolls his eyes at me. "Does it matter to you? Every couple is different. Jesus Christ! Stop being so anxious. I told you, you need to relax. If you don't want to do this again, then fine. If you do, then fantastic, because it was a ton of fun. But stop stressing out about it. It's just fucking sex! Lucy would be very happy for me right now." He smirks.

I think about this for a second. I mean, this is the twenty-first century. Modern couples are everywhere, and open relationships are not as big a deal anymore—at least to some people. In a world where polyamory relationships are becoming more common, open relationships sound pretty tame. Even my *grandmother* says monogamy is unrealistic.

And who the fuck am I to judge anyway? To each their own.

"Okay, but let's get back to the fact that you've been telling your girlfriend that you were trying to get me in bed for a second." I raise an eyebrow at him. "I mean, do you guys really talk about this stuff?"

He rolls his eyes at me again. "Are you kidding me? She's been calling me a loser for *weeks* for not being able to get anywhere with you. I'm so happy to be able just to rub it in her pretty face." He laughs.

"So, is that all it was? Proving her wrong?"

"Fuck no," he says. "Proving Lucy wrong was a bonus. She was getting on my nerves."

I think about that for a second. I don't *think* this offends me at all, to be honest. Should it? I got something out of it, too, so who cares? Again, no one here is trying to be in a relationship with the other. I decide that I don't care about any of that except for one thing. "So, has our friendship been fake this entire time?" This would genuinely hurt me. Oliver has been such a support system for me. A true friend. My new friend group has been amazing and super kind, but the kinship I've felt with him has felt more substantial than others. None of my other class-mates have the same fucked-up humor we do, and I don't think I've had a more honest friendship in my life.

"First couple of days, yeah. Obviously, I just wanted to shag you. I am a man, for fuck's sake." He smirks. "But you know I adore you, and if you don't want to do this again, then that's fine." He grimaces and pauses. "I mean, to be honest, it's not. You'd be a *fucking* dimwit because we had fantastic sex. And honestly, I have all these plans now, and you would truly be throwing this away, and you really could use with a bit of casual sex since you're so fucking crazy maybe it will help you relax a bit." He takes a deep breath. "But yeah, you idiot, we would still be mates."

"Huh." I mutter. Am I overcomplicating myself here? If you think about it, it is the perfect setup. No feelings, no commit-ment, great friendship, and no self-consciousness. Pure honesty. "Okay, let's do it."

He smiles broadly and leans over me, caging me between his arms. "Perfect, because I'm ready for round two."

"Hold it!" I press my palm against his chest, trying not to get distracted by the ridges and valleys of his muscles. "We can't just start something up like this without any ground rules! It would be a massive disaster."

He groans and rolls onto his back, staring up at the ceiling. "God, you are so annoying, you know that?" He exhales and rubs his hands down his face. "Fine. What are your rules?" he asks in a mocking tone.

"Would it help if we call them policies? Seeing as we are currently studying policymaking?"

He laughs. "Alright. Let's have your sex policies, then." I snort.

"Alright, before we define our *policies,* we need to discuss the most important part first. When were you last tested?"

He looks at me seriously. "Wow, okay. A bit of a mood killer, eh? But a fair question, I suppose. I did not expect this to be so serious, though." He smiles. "Last month. And I always use a condom. Seriously. Even with Lucy."

I would hope so if you're in an open relationship!

"Okay, good enough for me. Second—"

"Whoa, whoa," he interrupts me, shaking his head. "What about you?"

"What about me?" I raise an eyebrow, challenging him.

"You know what. When was the last time *you* were tested?"

Oh no.

I know I'm an adult, but getting tested is *so annoying.* I already hate going to doctors, so the thought of having to sit in a waiting room in a doctor's office I don't know and then getting checked out is cringy. Also, I'm just plain lazy.

I am winning at this adulting thing, as you can probably tell.

"I don't need to get tested."

"Ha. Nice try. You're getting tested." Oliver points accusingly at me as I frown.

Oliver gets out of bed—naked—and walks over to his desk. You have to admire someone who evidently gives no fucks about walking around completely bare. I see the number of scratch marks I left all over his back and flash back to a particularly delicious part of our romp. It was a bit hard to control myself sometimes. I needed something to hold on to.

I'm brought back to planet Earth when he opens the last drawer on the bottom of his walnut desk and pulls out a roll of chocolate Digestive cookies. "I mean," he says as he stuffs a cookie into his mouth, "you can't be that big of a hypocrite."

I laugh internally at this man who tries to pass himself off as an alpha but has a secret stash of McVitie's Chocolate Digestives in his bedroom. I can just imagine him at work in one of his ridiculously tight three-piece suits, this large man, trying to look serious with a tiny teacup and chocolate cookies in his hand.

"Agreed, I will get tested. But you can't just hide cookies from me. Gimme, gimme!" I say, jumping on the bed on my knees and sticking out my hand toward him. He drops a cookie into my hand, and I take a massive bite out of it. The smooth milk chocolate melts on my tongue, the crumbly texture of the cookie dancing in my mouth—the whole thing an experience. I moan in pleasure, my stomach growling in hunger.

"Okay, next policy," I say as he sits back into bed. "No sleeping with anyone else in the program but me."

"Are you fucking serious?! You can't do that to me!" He looks appalled. "I was so close to getting with Eloise!"

"First off," I start, "Eloise hates you, and you know it. Second, I am not asking you to be exclusive here. You can still sleep with whomever you choose; it just has to be outside of the program. I don't want to have to deal with cattiness or jealousy or whatever." I take a deep breath. "It would just be too weird. What if the other girl gets all weird and competitive? And if I'm being totally honest—and please don't read too much into this —I am far too insecure *not* to get jealous if you're not paying attention to me and are trying to hook up with someone else. You know I can be a little crazy."

"You're an idiot, you know that? How many times have I told you that you don't see yourself? But yes, I accept your *situational* exclusivity policy. On to the next one."

"Okay, but pass me another Digestive, will you?" I take a bite of the cookie and moan. "*God*, why is chocolate so fucking *good*?"

Oliver groans, frustrated. "Can you not make that sound? It's making me want to skip these '*policies*'," he says with a mocking tone, "and go straight to round two."

I roll my eyes at him as I chew. "Next policy: no one else can know about this. This is gonna be like Fight Club. We don't talk about it. No one knows. Our secret."

He dismisses me with a hand. "What? Is this really such a big deal? It was amazing. Are you going to tell me you wouldn't want to tell any of your friends?"

I smack him across the head.

"Ugh! Fine! It's not like anyone would mind, but whatever!"

"Final one. We've already talked about this, but absolutely no cuddling or spooning. We have a no cuddling or spooning policy in this deal, got it?"

He rolls his eyes at me for the millionth time this morning.

"Okay, crazy. You're on." Oliver smiles broadly and sticks out his hand. I shake it.

"Perfect. Round two, or shall we go out to breakfast?"

"Both."

Eleven

IT'S BEEN two days since my Saturday of sex with Oliver, and I am happy to report not much has changed in our friendship. Besides a slight increase in suggestive comments on Oliver's side in our text exchanges (carnal knowledge has made him more creative and graphic), things have been great and have stayed pretty much the same. Apart from the several instances in which he has requested I send him nudes (I haven't), there is no awkwardness whatsoever, making me feel like perhaps this whole thing might not turn out to be a colossal mistake.

Maybe casual sex without feelings is possible with the right person, and all the romcoms have it wrong. I can totally do this. But more importantly than that, I totally want to. It's been a while since I've given into doing whatever I want, especially it being guilt-free. And it feels nice to not have to worry about being judged or anything.

Over the weekend, I thought about how completely mind-blowing Saturday had been. We had sex, ate breakfast, napped, had sex again, ordered Domino's pizza for lunch, which we ate naked in bed while watching Netflix, slept, and had sex one more time.

The whole thing left me sore, that's for sure. But sore in a fantastic way. It was like my body suddenly remembered what sex was like, realized it was better than any sexual experience it had ever had before, and decided it needed it to survive—and a lot of it at that.

It was crazy how fast we got to know each other physically,

and I could already respond to his cues and Oliver to mine without thinking. I don't believe I've ever had that experience with any of my other partners, except for maybe my two exes, and that was after some practice. It was like he could read my mind and knew exactly what to do and how to do it. Oliver didn't need Google Maps to find anything down there, if you know what I mean, and he could always tell what kind of mood I was in at the time.

I hate to think about it and would never admit it out loud, but Oliver's sexual prowess is not to be underestimated.

I could write a full Yelp review of his many talents.

Stamina, creativity, strength, kinkiness, sheer skill.

Six out of five stars. Would recommend.

Which is why I shouldn't be surprised that I haven't even tried to talk myself out of it, like I normally would've. It's exactly the reason why I currently find myself headed out of the school infirmary after my testing appointment. It's not truly fair to have Oliver abide by specific rules but then not have these rules apply to me. He's right, of course—I can't be that big of a hypocrite.

But still. No one likes getting tested for STDs. I'm twenty-two, I know. But it will always be a little bit embarrassing.

The infirmary is located in the main building, right by the cafeteria. This means that anyone seated at the right table while having lunch can see the infirmary entrance. I don't think anyone I know saw me go in, and I pray to God no one sees me come out. I don't want any questions or to have anyone find out who I'm sleeping with at the moment.

I dash out of the waiting room and try to put as many feet as possible between me and the entrance until I hear someone from behind me call my name.

Fuuuuuckkkkk, seriously?

I wince before turning around. I know exactly who it is.

"Josh. Hi…"

"Hey," he says with a huge smile. He's so nice. Why is he

always so nice? "Are you okay? I saw you leaving the infirmary. You're not sick, are you?" he asks with concern.

So sweet.

He's wearing a printed long sleeve t-shirt with *Maui* written on it, highlighting his shoulders.

When did he get broad shoulders?

His jeans are ripped, and his shoes are worn. His dirty-blond hair is ruffled, and he looks rather cute today.

Whoa. Stop. Nope. Nope.

All the sex this weekend is just making me think about more sex.

Calm down, Crazy.

I laugh awkwardly. "No, no. All good. Just a check-up, you know," I lie, feeling guilty.

He furrows his brow, his green eyes expressing concern. "Check-up? Isn't the infirmary supposed to be more for, like, an urgent care thing?"

I can literally never get away with a lie with this man. Can he not let anything slide?

"Um... Sure, sure," I say quickly, trying to sidestep this conversation. "Hey, how about I buy you a beer, huh? Do you have class?" I link my arm through his and drag him in the general direction of the student union pub on campus.

He raises an eyebrow at me, reluctantly dropping the subject.

Here's the thing about Josh: he is hyper-aware of everything, which has made him an incredible friend. It's also become somewhat of a problem for me sometimes because he seems to be tuned in to everything I'm feeling. And his powers have only gotten stronger since game night. I don't like feelings, and knowing someone as sweet and caring as Josh can tell every emotion going through me without me having to speak a single word is—like I've said before—overwhelming. And also a little scary. I don't feel comfortable. And since he's such a good person and can tell that I am not feeling even the slightest like myself, he'll try to talk to me and make me feel better.

I know I'm being ridiculous. I should be ecstatic to have such a good friend who can tell when he's needed and is so supportive, but I can't handle it from him for some reason. It's too much. It's way too much. I'm more of a fan of repressing my emotions.

"Uh, sure, I'll take a beer," he says, walking with me.

Despite the fact that it's only three p.m., the Student Union is already packed when we get there. People in London don't fuck around with their alcohol. I wonder idly how my liver is doing since having moved here.

We walk toward the bar, and I order us two beers.

"Here, I'll get it," he says with a smile.

I shake my head. "No way. I owe you for the immeasurable amount of granola bars I've stolen from you these past couple of months."

He chuckles. "You didn't steal them, Penny. I always bring an extra one for you."

Something in my chest tightens, and try as I might, I can't breathe.

"Or...you know," he quickly corrects himself, furrowing his brow, "anyone else who might need one—in case of emergencies."

I do my best to swallow the knot in my throat, doing my best to breathe deeply, stretching my lungs. A little rattled, I try not to think about how I almost suffered an allergic reaction or something to whatever emotion I almost felt.

"Right, right. Sure," I say, avoiding eye contact.

While we stand there and wait for our beers, the companionable silence has disappeared again, and I'm hit with a wave of sadness and regret. Ever since Stonehenge, our friendship has devolved from something stable into a fucking rollercoaster of emotions.

After what seems like an hour, the bartender hands us our beers, and we miraculously find a free booth to sit at.

"So, why do you look so guilty?" he asks over his beer with an amused look in his eyes.

"Me? Guilty? I don't feel guilty."

Jumpy? Yes. Guilty? No. I have nothing to feel guilty about.

"You totally look guilty. Like you ran over someone's dog." Josh chuckles a little.

"Uhhh..." I debate telling him. I feel like I need to talk to someone about this. Allie doesn't know Oliver, so even though she was extremely happy for me when I came home the night after, I don't think she could fully comprehend the significance of me sleeping with him. Chloe and Jane are phenomenal and two of my closest girlfriends in the program, but I'm not sure how Chloe would react, seeing as she's known Oliver the longest. And I love Jane, but she would tease me for the rest of my life.

Josh is part of my close friend group. He's also close to Oliver. He knows us both well, and it would be nice to talk to someone about this. Also, maybe this could be a way to get back to where things were. It would show Josh that he has nothing to worry about, because I'm not into him. It would probably help with the awkwardness between us, solidifying that Josh and I are just friends, and I don't expect anything from him.

I know I'm breaking one of the rules Oliver and I set, but Josh is a trustworthy guy. It should be fine, right?

"Uh, so I did do something..." I laugh awkwardly.

He smiles, smiling a little. "I know you more than you think."

Yeah, I know, and I honestly don't know how I feel about that.

He flags down a waiter and quickly orders a cheeseburger, giving me a second to organize my thoughts.

"I hope it's okay if I eat. I skipped lunch today and am starving."

I nod absentmindedly, searching for the right words.

Why am I so nervous?

"So, what is it exactly that you did that is making you look like a dog who destroyed its owner's furniture?" He smiles.

I take a deep breath. "Okay, I'll tell you, but you have to promise not to judge. Alright?" I eye him suspiciously, and he nods. "I mean, not that I need your approval or anything, because I am an adult, dammit, and an independent woman, and no one owns me, and I can do whatever I want with my body with whomever I want to do it with, whenever I want to do it, and however many times I want to do it, you know?" I get it out quickly.

"Um, sure," Josh says, taking a sip from his beer, nodding.

"Okay, here's the thing. But you have to promise not to judge or react."

He rolls his eyes at me. Maybe I'm being dramatic. I take a deep breath. Josh is a nice guy and my friend. Of course he'll be supportive. Josh will probably just laugh in disbelief and shake his head. He'll probably make fun of me a bit, but he won't judge. He's chill.

"I kinda maybe slept with Oliver after the pub night thing." I wince, and he stops mid-sip, never breaking eye contact.

He finally puts his glass down and stares down at the table after a few seconds, pressing his lips into a thin line.

"Did he do this to you while you were passed out at his house after the pub?" he asks in a cold tone I've never heard him use before. "Because I will fucking kill him. I knew I shouldn't have let him take you home with him," he snarls.

"No, no!" I shake my hands in front of him, laughing a little at the idea of a showdown between Oliver and Josh. "It was while we were both sober—the morning after. It was completely consensual." I grimace, waiting for his reaction.

He glares at me. "Are you covering for him?" he asks accusingly. His green eyes are intense, his expression full of rage.

"*Jesus,* no, Josh. I thought you were his friend. You know

that even though he can be kind of pervy, it's mostly an act. He would never do anything like that. God, is that really what you think of him?" I ask, a little taken aback. For all his flaws and forwardness, Oliver has never struck me as a man who acts without consent. Setting aside that he genuinely is a good guy, non-consensual sex would also go against his entire ethos. With women, I get the sense that Oliver is way too competitive not to play a fair game to score. He does things right.

It's actually what I like most about him. No bullshit, no games.

"Swear to me you're not covering for him, Penny, because you were really fucking out of it when you left."

Now, I'm angry. I'm mad for Oliver, and I'm mad for myself. This whole protector thing he's had going on lately is starting to piss me off. Does he suddenly think I'm this little girl who needs his protection or to be guarded? Or is he mad because now I'm tainted or something for deciding to have casual, protected sex with a friend?

Maybe, just maybe, a little voice inside me says, *it's because he wishes it would've been him.*

I immediately push the thought out of my head, the anger and frustration washing over me not wanting to entertain it for a second longer.

No matter the reason for his outburst, it is in no way justified.

"You know what, Josh? You're an asshole. What would be so wrong with sleeping with Oliver, anyway? I thought you guys were friends."

"I *am* his friend, Penny. But I'm also *your* friend, and I also know the state in which you left that night, which was really concerning."

I snort derisively at his comment. "I was not in that bad shape, Josh."

He ignores me, and continues. "I am also confused as to why

you would sleep with him the next morning when you don't seem to be the type." His jaw is tight, and he glares at me.

The waiter comes by and drops Josh's burger in front of him, but he doesn't acknowledge it.

"Excuse me? Don't seem to be *what* type?" I lean forward.

"The type of girl who would fall for his shit or do that type of stuff. Some broken woman who feels the need to fill a void with sex with men like him. He's just using you, and he's gonna hurt you, you know."

"Oh my God!" I throw my hands in the air and struggle to scoot out of the booth. There really is no cool way to storm out of a booth bench, is there? "Did you ever think about the possibility that we are both using each other?" I try to keep my voice down; I really do. But it's difficult to do when you want to commit murder.

"What do you mean?"

I glare at him for a second. "Nothing, you ass. I'm over this. I'm leaving. Enjoy your burger," I say over my shoulder as I storm off.

"Penny!" I hear him yell and see a couple of students turn around to look at us, but I couldn't care less.

Twelve

GROWING UP, I was always told no. I was always told that I couldn't do certain things or follow certain paths in life—that there were more *appropriate* paths in life for me, more *suitable* ones for women of my background. I constantly felt stifled and suffocated, put into a specific box when I didn't just want to be different but wanted to see and experiment with multiple boxes. It felt like most of my time on earth was spent swimming upstream, trying to show people that I could achieve anything I wanted, whether they thought I couldn't or shouldn't.

You're too young, too naive, too fat, not strong enough. A girl.

I grew up in a world where my family always supported me and my decisions—to an extent. Nothing besides eventually getting married to the right man was ever expected of me. Someone with money wouldn't be enough. He would have to be from a good family, provide a stable home, and allow me to be a stay-at-home whatever-I-wanted.

Sometimes, I think living a life of affluent leisure would have been great, but I wanted so much more for myself than what was expected. The notion of me achieving anything on my own—a business, a career, anything of substance—was considered *cute.* "She's brilliant, one of the smartest people you'll ever meet," they'd say. But I was meant to be completely useless—a vase, a receptacle, one of those beautiful blue-and-white ginger jars that you put as decoration but have no use for.

I had to be constantly *on,* changing personalities based on what was expected of me in the situation. I was told I had to act a certain way, dress a certain way, and look a certain way to get what I wanted (i.e., what my family wanted for me). If I rebelled, there was hell to pay, whether it was in the form of verbal abuse from my grandmother or in the constant nagging and disappointed passive-aggressive remarks from other family members.

"Why do you always *need* to be different, Penny?"

"It's different for you than for everyone else. You're an immigrant. You have to be the best. You have to work the hardest to fit in." I wasn't allowed to stand out.

The pressure used to get to me, make me crack into a million little pieces. If I gained a little weight, I wouldn't hear the end of it. "You've gained seven pounds since vacation started! No one is ever going to marry you now, Penny!" I would starve myself for weeks or go on brutal purges until you could count my ribs and see my hip bones again, just to silence the opinions of those around me.

Like a wild horse, they wanted to break me. They tried to mold me into what they wanted. So, what did I decide to do after sixteen years of arguing and rebelling and feeling like I would never, ever be good enough for my family unless I lived up to these standards? Standards that were impossible not because they were difficult to achieve but because it wasn't *me*?

I played along. I pretended. I wore what they wanted. I took a lot of psychological hits. I played along with their stupid fucking rules, all as a means of survival until the day I got to graduate high school and go away to college and just be myself for one goddamn minute of my fucking life.

And even then...I couldn't escape my old life. It was still so ingrained in me that I continued holding myself back. I over-corrected in some things, like my wardrobe, and remained stagnant in other areas of my life, like being emotionally shut off. It was like I was lost, suddenly. Or maybe I was a shell of a person, and there was never anyone in there to begin with.

I remember, in my freshman year, my first serious boyfriend

complained about me having a wall of ice up that would slam the brakes on any type of romantic or profound intimate moment we would share or he would *try* to communicate. If he complimented me or said something sweet, I would yell, "*Line!*" and make a joke about him saying something tender just to get laid.

How fucked up is it that I couldn't even hear him say how beautiful I looked without panicking or thinking he was lying because he had an ulterior motive? It was so ingrained in me that I would never be good enough, that I couldn't trust him. If my own family constantly criticized me and thought I wasn't good enough, why would anyone else think I was, for that matter? In the end, I was able to be physically intimate with him, but emotionally opening up had proven to be a massive undertaking.

I hurt him more times than I'd like to admit, so I started making a conscious effort to open myself up more. I began to let him in and tell him more about how my family made me feel like a failure sometimes or how I was feeling a bit lost. I talked about how I was still struggling with my eating disorder and how difficult it was to keep myself from wanting to throw up everything I ate. I thought I could trust this person with my feelings and that I could embrace his own for me.

In the end, I was "too much" I guess, since we ended the relationship once I started opening up about the more difficult things. I suppose he didn't exactly realize what was going on in my life, and that was entirely my fault. I didn't show him my true colors from the get-go, and that wasn't fair. He didn't get to kick the tires before signing up for the relationship, did he?

Though he bailed because he couldn't handle that shit—even though, as a partner, he should have been able to get me help, at least—I never for one second regret that relationship. It taught me to open myself up to someone but always have my guard up and protect myself, something that I had needed to survive my relationship—and ultimate breakup—with Austin.

It reminded me that boundaries and walls were up for a reason.

When I got to London, things changed, though. I felt stronger, more capable of handling emotional terrorism or attacks from others and even myself, at times. I felt like I had the chance to *fucking finally* find out who I was without any outside influence. No one to tell me how to act or what to do or what I should feel. I'm starting from scratch—for real this time.

London had already begun to transform me, and I had made a conscious decision, not so long ago, to continue on this journey of (sorry for sounding so trite here) self-discovery without letting anyone judge me or get in my way.

Penny Márquez is going to (conscientiously and responsibly) do whatever the hell she wants, and she's never been happier.

So, when Josh told me I shouldn't have had casual sex with Oliver, when he judged me and went thermonuclear overprotective, I lost it. Because I've promised myself not to let anyone tell me what to do or who I should be ever again—especially if they aren't even part of my family. They do not get a say in what I do, who I am, or what I want to be.

I choose how to live my goddamn life.

Josh is wrong. I am not like *"one of those girls"*. I'm just me, and I am not broken.

Even if I were, I am not anyone's to fix. I am my own problem, and I make my own choices, and that's fine with me—*even if I fuck up*.

I stand by my decision to be who I want and do whatever I want, including my new friends-with-benefits arrangement.

So, even though Josh and I have become close friends and enjoy spending time together, this is further evidence that my wall always, *always*, ALWAYS need to remain up. I will not fall back into old habits of letting people tell me what is right or wrong just for fear of judgment.

I won't fall back into old habits.

London Penny is already much more relaxed, and fun, and *real* than any other Penny of the past.

Therefore, no matter how many granola bars he's given me or how sweet he's been, if he can't find a way to be supportive, Josh Fox can kindly go fuck himself.

Thirteen

I STORM into the apartment in a huff and slam the door shut. I toe my shoes off by the kitchen table and throw my jacket and bag on the couch, not caring about Allie's—to be fair—very reasonable request to keep common living areas tidy. I'm too mad to give a shit right now, though.

Allie walks out of her bedroom with a confused look on her face. She raises an eyebrow questioningly, and I grunt in response, shaking my head. The concerned look on her face disappears as her eyes flicker to my things thrown around the apartment. Grimacing, I watch as she struggles to control the urge to tidy up without upsetting me.

I've moved in with a neat freak and am the messiest person alive.

"So...I assume something's up?" she asks, picking my coat up carefully and walking it to our coat rack by the front door as casually as possible—though we both know what's really going on in her mind right now. I know that deep down inside, Allie's dying to tell me off for not hanging my coat up.

Not caring one bit, I throw myself—albeit, a bit dramatically —onto the couch, stare up at the ceiling, and take a deep breath. I don't even know where to start.

"Do you think it was dumb of me to sleep with Oliver?" I ask with no preamble.

She walks over to the kitchen table to pick up my shoes and arranges them neatly together by the door before settling by my feet at the end of the couch. A slight irritation begins to build in my chest at this. Making that mess and throwing my stuff around was supposed to have been an outlet for my frustration.

Neat freak.

"I don't know Oliver, so I can't answer that question." She sighs. "But, I mean, you had fun, right? You were safe. He wasn't a dick after. And you said the sex was mind-blowing, right?"

The first thing I did when I got home from my day of sex was tell Allie all about it. Honestly, it had been so fun that I couldn't even go one day without breaking our agreed-upon policy to keep this under wraps. Allie isn't in our program, so I figured it didn't count as breaking the rules. She had been proud of me but wanted to be spared the details, obviously.

"*God*, yes, mind-blowing. It's like he—"

She holds up a hand. "I don't need specifics, girl. I believe you."

We both laugh before I sit up with a groan. "I got in a fight with Josh."

"The granola bar guy?" Allie says in concern, furrowing her brow. When I had told her the story of the first time he gave me a bar, she *obsessed* over it and how cute it was for days. "*That shit's true love right there. I wouldn't share my breakfast with anyone,*" she had said. It was torture.

"He sounds so cute! He takes care of you...always feeding you, and hydrating you, and taking care of you when you're a hungover crazy person, you little hot mess," she says, ruffling my hair lightly. I swat her hand away.

I've told Allie several times about Josh's hero tendencies, and while I've been panicking, feeling overwhelmed, she thinks I'm a horrible person for sometimes feeling overwhelmed by his kindness.

I am fully aware of how much I suck, but I can't help feeling a bit suffocated, can't help the anxiety as it moves over me like fog, clouding everything in my head, paralyzing my lungs.

Sometimes, even just the thought of speaking to him makes my body tense like it's bracing itself for a crash.

I roll my eyes at Allie, swatting her hand away. "I mean, I guess *sometimes* I have been known to be somewhat of a hot mess, but come on! He doesn't 'take care of me'. I don't need anyone to take care of me."

She laughs. "Of *course* you don't, sweetie," she says sarcastically.

Oh my God, does everyone just assume that I am this disaster incapable of surviving without having someone take care of her? Do people just think that I am a lost cause and am in constant need of supervision or something? What kind of impression do I usually make?

"So, what did you do, anyway? To make him mad, I mean."

"*Me?* Why do you just automatically assume that *I* was the one to mess up our friendship? Seriously."

She raises an eyebrow at me.

I sigh again. "Fine. Josh got mad because I slept with Oliver."

"*Aww!*" She clasps her hands to her chest with a hopeful expression on her face. If she were a cartoon, she would have hearts in her eyes. "See? I *told* you he's into you!"

Jesus, what a nightmare.

Men and women *can* be friends and *not* have feelings for each other. It's even possible for them to have *sex* with each other and not have feelings. We've already established this.

I feel my phone vibrate in my pocket, and I peek at the screen to check it. I already have a couple of missed calls and text messages from Josh apologizing and asking to call him back, but the last two I just received are from Oliver.

OLIVER

If I send you a dick pic, will you send me a tit pic? ;)

OLIVER

> Oh, by the way, do you happen to have the notes for the Organizational Management lecture from today? I had to duck out early and didn't catch the last part of class.

I sigh and type a quick reply.

ME

> Please do not ever send me an unsolicited dick pic. I will never, ever send you a tit pic. And yes, I can email you my notes tonight.

OLIVER

Thanks, mate.

See? This is precisely what I mean. Oliver and I are more than capable of maintaining a sexual relationship within our friendship, which means that it should be even easier for Josh and me to be friends since there isn't anything physical going on there.

"He's not into me. And that's not why we got into an argument exactly. He wasn't upset because I slept with Oliver. I got angry at him because he said that I didn't seem like 'the type of girl who would fall for that,' implying I was a slutty bimbo or something. He actually used the word 'broken', as if I were tricked into sleeping with him or something." I shake my head. "So stupid. God forbid women enjoy casual sex as well." I exhale. "Anyway, I just lost it."

Allie scoffs once and shakes her head. "You're either socially inept or in denial."

"I think most people who know me would *definitely* agree with you on the whole 'socially inept' thing. Not sure about the denial part, though. I consider myself to be a very self-aware person."

She laughs hysterically at this and stands. I'm slightly offended by her analysis.

"Listen, Penny," she says, sobering. "I'm sure he didn't mean whatever he said. Your friend just seems to be on the protective side." *Understatement of the century.* "Which is a pretty great thing, when you think about it. It means that he can take care of you at school when you're out of my sight." She winks and smiles as she gives me a little punch on the shoulder.

"I hate you," I tell her as she walks away with a laugh all the way back to her bedroom.

I AM A STRONG, INDEPENDENT WOMAN WHO NEEDS NO MAN.

Not really having resolved *anything* with Allie, I decide to text Chloe and Jane and see whether they're up for a girls' shopping trip as a distraction. Though Oliver and I agreed to not tell anyone about our tryst or our deal, I feel the need to discuss it with my friends, seeing as Josh and Allie turned out to be zero help at all. Somehow, things have spiraled and I need some advice. I don't want to lose a friendship over something so stupid, especially since I just realized that my final project is due at the end of the semester, and we're supposed to work together on it.

Ugh.

Fourteen

CHLOE AND JANE agree to meet me at Harrod's the next day. I explained that I seriously needed to discuss something but didn't provide any details. I want to see their genuine reactions when I tell them I slept with Oliver, so I choose to keep it to myself until I see them in person. This whole thing with Josh is becoming a thorn in my side, and I'm over it. I need advice on how to fix it.

To be honest, his response has left me reeling. I would have never expected that from him, since he's usually such a level-headed guy.

It isn't a secret to anyone that my favorite place in London has become the shoe department at Harrods, so the girls don't find it weird when I ask if we can hang out there and have teatime after. The luxury department store has several places where one can eat after a day of shopping, but my favorite is the little corner on the first floor at La Durée, the perfect place for a tea and shoe-shopping kind of day.

Sighing longingly, I gently put away a pair of beautiful Manolo Blahnik Hangisis that I will never be able to afford back in their box, when Jane interrupts my wistful train of thought.

"So, why are we really here, Penny?" Jane asks, picking up a shoe and flipping it over to check the price on the sticker. Her eyes widen at the four-digit amount, and she quickly puts the shoe back down on the display table as if it has just burned her hand.

"You normally don't invite us into your safe space," she says with a sympathetic smile.

I sigh again and look down at my hands. I mean, I should just tell them in one go. Rip the Band-aid off. Make it as painless as possible since I feel that this whole secrecy thing would never have worked out anyway. Someone would have noticed eventually, right?

"Alright, but you can't judge. I just need advice. I may have done something stupid and upset someone in the process."

"Okay…what was this stupid thing you did?" Chloe asks.

"I may have slept with Oliver," I say, wincing. My body folds inward, bracing itself for impact.

"I thought you said you did '*something*' stupid, not '*someone*' stupid," Jane deadpans.

I groan, running a hand down my face, embarrassed.

"I mean, it isn't that bad, is it? He's a cool guy, and it honestly hasn't changed anything between us. It's been kind of nice," I say with a shrug, smiling sheepishly.

"Um, hold on," Chloe says, raising her hand. "Why did you just say, '*it's been*'? Is this an activity you've repeated and or intend to repeat?"

"Uh…" I say, getting nervous. I don't feel like a repeat of my argument with Josh with my two closest female friends in the program, so I measure my words carefully before responding. I need them. I cannot deal with the craziness without them. And though I still wholeheartedly stand by the fact that it's my life and I get to decide how to live it, I also don't want to be ostracized due to the choices I've made.

"I mean…yes?"

Jane sputters a laugh, and Chloe's jaw drops.

"But…he…*why??*" Chloe widen, while Jane can barely contain her laughter. "How did this even happen? It doesn't make sense. He's always been so…*forward*. And you've always seemed to be so annoyed by it."

I shake my head at them. "I know. I don't know." I sigh. "It's like, yes, I get what you're saying, but...I don't know. Is it weird that I found him so ridiculous that, eventually, it just became kind of...charming?" I shrug. "And I guess I just wanted sex, too. And he was there. And he looked like he'd be good at it. And God, that body."

Jane bursts out laughing, clutching her hand to her chest. "And here we were, trying to set you up with Josh!"

I roll my eyes. "Yeah, thanks for that, by the way. I haven't had the chance to thank you." I glare at her, and she stops laughing immediately.

"Wait, you what?" Chloe looks at Jane accusingly. "Did you set them up?" A hurt look flashes across her eyes.

I shake my head, frustrated. "No. Ugh. Can we focus? It was just sex."

"With Josh?" Chloe asks, her voice increasing a couple of octaves.

"What? *No*. With Oliver. And it was really, really good sex. And I think that, yeah, I intend to continue sleeping with him, to be honest, but that's not really why I asked you guys to come here—I don't think."

I pause, waiting for one of them to pass judgment, but I get nothing.

"Listen, if that's what you want, I don't blame you. Oliver looks like a fab time." Jane smiles supportively.

Chloe just shakes her head and giggles. "It's a bit shocking, isn't it? Never expected you to actually go through with it, but he really is a nice guy. I don't think he would ever intentionally hurt you."

I smile. After months of spending almost every day with these girls, I should've known better. They're not the type to judge me for this type of stuff. We're all grownups here. I guess I didn't realize just how much their opinion mattered to me. I think that, because I had such a bad experience with people from my past, I may have expected them to act the same way my old friends would have.

"Yeah, Oliver is definitely a nice guy, and he's been a good friend since day one, you know?" I smile fondly at the memory of my breakdown behind the pub the first night I met him and how supportive yet realistic he had been. "He isn't the type of guy to feed you any bullshit and I like that. I can trust that."

"So, what's the problem?" Jane asks. "I don't understand. That's all you wanted to tell us?"

"Well, no, not exactly," I start. "I told Josh what had happened." I clear my throat. "I told him that Oliver and I had slept together, and he kind of went mental." I shake my head in frustration, running my fingers through my hair. "At first, he thought Oliver forced himself on me or something, thought Oliver was taking advantage of me while I was drunk. Which made me super angry because he's not that type of guy, you know? After I confirmed that I was fully sober in the morning before we did have sex, Josh got upset and said he was surprised I would do something like that since I didn't 'seem like the type' and that I was 'broken'—kind of. I didn't like the implications of what he said, so then *I* got upset and yelled at him and stormed out of the Student Union." I sigh, catching my breath. "It was all very dramatic. I felt like I was in an episode of *The O.C.*"

Chloe snorts at my comparison. "What a throwback reference!"

I laugh once bleakly and take a beat. "I just need to know whether I overreacted or whether Josh is as big of a dumbass as I feel he is right now."

Chloe and Jane look at each other.

"Have you considered the fact that maybe he was upset and jealous?" Jane asks tentatively. Chloe looks away, biting her lip, blushing.

"I know what it looks like, but it's not that. To be fair, Stonehenge was incredibly awkward, and your little stunt put a slight wedge between us, so thanks again for that. But honestly, things were almost back to normal until yesterday." I groan.

"Also, he's been spending *a lot* of time with Eloise lately, and you know she was all over him. I think they've targeted each other as potential rebounds." I chuckle. Together, we start heading out of the Manolo Blahnik area, saying goodbye once again to the shoes. *See you next time, lovers.* "So, no, I don't think it's a jealousy thing."

We walk toward the elevators, and I press the down button. It's time for part two of *Let's Cheer Penny Up Day*: tea, macaroons, and sandwiches at La Durée.

"I don't know what to do because I *know* I shouldn't apologize because it's my life, and I chose to sleep with Oliver, and I am young and get to do whatever I want in a responsible manner, and feminism, and all of that, but I feel like I should apologize for some reason. Is that weird?"

"Yes," they say at the same time as we cram ourselves into a packed elevator.

I take a deep breath and exhale, exhausted because I feel like I'm getting nowhere. I am no closer to understanding either Josh's reaction or mine to his. I mean, it can't be as simple as jealousy. It can't. I feel a bit guilty, that's for sure. But is it because we're close friends and I didn't tell him? Why do I feel like I owed it to Josh to tell him about what happened?

I know what Chloe, Jane, and Allie think, but I don't think it's about any feelings he may have for me. It's the opposite. I think he believes that I am interested in him—which I'm totally not, by the way—and that's the reason why he's grown a bit more detached lately. On top of all of that, there is the Eloise of it all. They're into each other, aren't they? Myself stomach rolls at the thought, but I push it away.

Who cares if they're together? I don't.

This is so stupid. It shouldn't be bothering me this much.

"You aren't being very helpful here, you know," I tell them.

"He's just a little overprotective in general, love. Not just with you," Chloe says. "It might just be that he was concerned for your well-being, and we are all reading way too much into this. But I don't think you should apologize, necessarily. Just let things cool down a bit."

Nodding, we exit the elevator onto the first floor. "I mean, I'm going to have to let things cool down, anyways. We have that final presentation of the case study to work on together. I'm even supposed to meet him tomorrow to start wrapping the project up."

Sighing, we make it to the hostess's stand at the front of the café. While Jane speaks to her about getting us a table at the mezzanine, I mull over our conversation. There is nothing here for me to do besides give him a chance to apologize. He hasn't stopped texting since it happened, and we still need to meet to at least complete our project.

I'm still pissed, and I might not be in love with my grad school program, but I am not about to let my grades suffer just because of a petty discussion that can—hopefully—easily be solved through a mature conversation and apology. In the end, Josh is a close friend, and I know that deep down he's a good guy. He was just making sure I was safe, is all.

I reach into my purse and dig through it until I find my phone. To give Josh a chance to explain himself in person, I decide to ignore his previous messages (sixteen total) and just type what I want to say, which isn't much:

ME

> Waterloo Library – tomorrow 2:00 pm before our Research Methods class.

His reply come through almost immediately.

JOSH

> YES. Thank you.

Fifteen

I PULL out my phone in the library elevator one more time to double-check the room number Josh said he booked for us to talk in and, hopefully after, work on our project. It's a study pod I've never worked in before on the last floor of the library. I must admit I'm a bit nervous to see him, as I honestly just want to put this behind us. I don't like how much I've missed him. A *lot*.

I've managed to keep myself from reading all the messages he sent between the Student Union incident and when I texted him yesterday. I thought things would get worse if I started reading his apologies and excuses via text. After talking to the girls, I realized just how much I wanted to get past this. Josh has always been a fantastic guy. He overreacted, but then again, so did I. The amount of baggage I carry around on my back every day makes me the teensiest bit sensitive sometimes.

I pause outside the study pod with my hand on the door-knob. Taking a deep breath, I turn it and push the door open. My jaw drops.

"What *is* all of this?" I ask, a bit shellshocked, to both Josh *and* Oliver. "What is happening?"

A printed sign with the words *I'm Sorry* hangs on the wall behind the two men, each letter on one sheet of paper. Every surface of the study pod is covered in snacks. Ruffles, chocolate Digestive cookies, Oreos, Cheetos, kettle chips, Ribenas, Coke, and many granola and health bars. Kind bars, Luna bars, Nature Valley… So many granola and power bars.

I laugh, dropping my bag on the floor, covering my eyes and shaking my head at the ridiculous scene. I close the door behind me and reach for a pack of cookies, holding them between my hands, smiling. I can't believe he did this. He went all out, and although the *I'm Sorry* sign isn't the nicest-looking thing, I can appreciate the effort and thoughtfulness in the gesture.

God, he's so sweet.

My heart squeezes in my chest, and I feel myself blush.

"I told you she'd like it, mate," Oliver says smugly, crossing his feet on the table, leaning back in his chair, hands behind his head, arm muscles on full display—and looking really good, in case you were wondering.

"It was *my* idea, dumbass!" Josh shoves Oliver, who almost falls back. "It was my idea," he repeats back to me. I laugh and take a cold Coke from the table, cracking it open and taking a swig.

Josh stands and spreads his arms out like Vanna White, showing off the loot. "I know you like your snacks, so I thought this would be a nice peace offering." He takes a deep breath before continuing. "I was an ass," he says repentantly, eyes kind. "Not just to you, but to Oliver, too. You were right. So, I apologized to him for assuming he took advantage of you and then convinced him to help me out here as evidence and backup. I also needed help bringing this stuff up here, because it was *a lot*."

He's wearing a button-down, which is odd for him, a significant change from his usual promotional t-shirts and old jeans. His shoulders, though not as broad or muscular as Oliver's, are visible in this outfit. He looks...*good*. Handsome. His face is clean-shaven, and his hair is brushed and styled.

Josh looks cute today.

I grin, ignoring the thought that just popped into my head. "Yeah, it looks like three hundred pounds' worth of snacks! I can't believe you did this."

Did he dress up just to apologize? Or does he have a date after class? Is it with Eloise?

"Well, I know first-hand what happens when you get hangry or when you're hungover." He smiles, and his eyes brighten. "It wasn't that big a deal, though the security guard at the front desk kept eying me suspiciously, as if I was about to throw a birthday party for a five-year-old upstairs."

And just like that, we're good. That's the thing about true friendships. Stupid fights don't get in the way of them for long. Sure, just like any relationship, you need to work on them, but you always fight for those that matter.

"It's true. She does have the eating habits of a child. All Domino's pizza and junk food and biscuits." Oliver scoffs in disapproval, shaking his head.

I walk toward Josh and hug him, leaning my head on his comfy chest. He holds me close, laying his head on mine, and I get a whiff of his comforting melon-grapefruit scent. His hands rub my back up and down, comforting me, reassuring me that he's still here for me. That we're still us, and we're okay.

Suddenly, the past few days seem so stupid. The awkwardness of the Salisbury-Stonehenge trip and the argument at the Student Union sound so trivial. This fight, or discussion, or whatever it was, was never going to hurt us. We've become too good of friends to let something so silly affect our friendship.

I am done listening to everyone else's opinion on where he and I stand, too. The more I speak to my friends, the more they push me to believe that things with Josh are more than either one of us think. They insist it is something else, despite my denying it at every opportunity, and it has caused a strain on my relationship with Josh Fox. I'm not going to risk anyone else's opinion coming between us—or any good friendship I've formed in London so far, for that matter. I close my eyes and thank the universe for not having to lose anyone else—especially not Josh.

Suddenly, I feel the same gut-punch in my stomach that I felt during our trip. I can't breathe. My heart starts beating out of my chest, and I feel like crawling out of my skin.

Too close, too close. He's too close.

No, no, no, no. Stop. Too much.

My eyes fly open, and I push softly against his chest, trying hard to hide my unexpected freak-out. I want to run out of the room and not come back. Forcing a smile, I thank him again for his gifts, avoiding eye contact.

"And you, too, Oliver. For making sure I heard him out," I say, turning to face him. He raises an eyebrow questioningly at me but doesn't press the subject. Josh isn't the only one who knows me well. He can tell something's up.

"You two are both idiots, fighting over something so stupid," he says, running his fingers through his hair.

"Agreed, you are stupid," I say with a tight smile. I take a deep breath, trying to calm my heart rate. Shoving a cookie into my mouth, I push the huge box of bars toward Josh. "You need to take those, though. You need them in case of emergencies, if I'm ever hungry and there's no food around."

He laughs and nods his head. "Fair, fair. I'll keep these, but you can take the rest of the snacks home with you." He smiles down at me, relief clear in his eyes. "I can help take them back to your place after class, too, if you'd like."

Can't. Breathe.

Oliver claps his hands together once, bringing me back. "So, we're good here? Can I go?"

"Yes, thank you." Oliver and Josh say goodbye by giving each other a repressed male version of a standard human hug: a back-slapping man-clasp. These two care about each other more than they know. Who else would've stepped in to fix such a silly fight? I smile at how restrained they seem to be with each other.

"I'm happy for you, buddy. See you guys in class." Oliver heads out, leaving a smiling Josh alone with me in the study pod.

Josh raises his wrist to look at his watch and says, "We

have about forty-five minutes until our next class. Do you want to work on our final project? I think we can honestly hammer it out in a few days and finish it in the next couple of weeks."

I shift uncomfortably from leg to leg, heart racing, suddenly highly aware that we are alone in an enclosed space. "Sure."

What is happening to me???

My breathing speeds, and I can barely hear myself think with how loudly my heart is beating. It's so hard to breathe, it feels like my own skin is on too tight.

"Actually," I say, "I need to check on something super quickly with Oliver for that workshop we're both in together. Would you mind giving us, like, fifteen minutes? Super quick, I promise."

Yup. A quickie. A stress-reliever.

Josh furrows his brow, confused. "Sure. I'll just finish this reading."

"Great! I'm gonna go see if I can catch him before he leaves."

I run out of the room and take a deep breath. I move my head quickly in every direction, looking for him, praying that he hasn't left yet. I find him by a table, emptying the contents of his messenger bag, preparing his workstation.

I walk up behind Oliver and start packing his bag up for him.

"What the bloody hell do you think you're doing?" he whisper-yells. We start attracting attention from frustrated students, a few of which glare in our direction.

"Pack it up. Let's go," I whisper urgently, shoving his folder and pens inside.

He's quiet for a beat as he watches me pack before understanding hits him. "What? *Now*? *Here*?" he asks, disbelief evident on his face.

"Yes, now. That okay with you?" My voice is urgent and low.

I need this now. I don't know why, but I do.

"Fuck, yes." He dumps everything else into his bag in one sweep of his arm, smiling from ear to ear. Oliver grabs me by the hand and drags me through the library stacks and students studying, making me stumble and struggle to keep up, his eagerness building. Subtlety is not one of this man's strengths. He looks back at me as we walk-jog quickly to wherever it is he's taking me, anticipation in his eyes.

We stop in the farthest corner of the library's top floor, in front of the disabled bathroom. The coast is clear. There doesn't seem to be anyone around to see us go in together and blow our cover.

"Now, I know it's a loo, and it's not exactly the most glamorous thing in the world, but it's hardly ever used and—"

"I don't care. We don't have much time, and if it's clean, I don't mind."

I push him against the door and kiss him deeply once, pressing my chest against him.

"Fuck," he breathes. "Perfect." He holds my face with both hands and kisses me, his tongue invading my mouth. Without breaking the kiss, my hand reaches for the handle, and I open the door. Oliver turns us with a laugh-moan, shutting and locking the door behind us.

I can feel him hard and ready as I wrap my arms around his neck, standing on my toes, pulling him closer to me. Walking me backward to push me against the door, his hand tightens in my hair, pulling my head back to adjust the angle. I moan and bite his lip, lust coursing through my veins, my breathing heavy.

God, he feels good.

"Shit, this is incredible." His hands drag down my body,

stopping at my ass. He turns and checks his surroundings. "It's nice and clean. Let's make it dirty."

I snort. "Did you just say that? You're ridiculous. You know that?"

"*Me*? You literally just came running for me to fuck you." He laughs in disbelief.

"Ugh, please don't remind me. Can we not talk? You're ruining this for me. I don't have much time, and you're going to end up killing my lady-boner."

I need you to distract me.

Oliver isn't smiling anymore. He looks just like he did the first morning—eager and ready. "Well, we can't have that, can we?"

He reaches around to the front of my leg, one hand trailing softly up my thigh, under my skirt, all the way to their junction. His fingers add pressure in just the right spot over my underwear, making me gasp at the sudden surge of pleasure. I can feel his smile against my neck as his hand travels back to my ass, and he maneuvers me to the sink, turning me suddenly to face the mirror over it.

I place my hands on the sink, bracing myself, as his arms travel around my waist, holding me tightly to him. I can feel all of him pressing into my back. I close my eyes as he moves my hair over my shoulder, and I lean my head to the opposite side, giving him room to kiss and bite my neck.

He sucks on my neck and lifts my skirt from behind as I moan.

"Stop. No hickeys." I say.

His hands slip over and under my underwear, cupping my ass. "I didn't mind the marks you left on my back," he says, chuckling. Oliver nibbles my ear, and I breathe in sharply as the feeling shoots straight to my belly.

"Yes, but my scratch marks weren't visible to anyone but me. I'm serious. *No. Hickeys.*"

He kisses me once more on the neck and lifts his gaze as we

make eye contact in the mirror. His eyes remain on mine as he slides my underwear over my hips and slowly down my thighs, past my knees.

Oliver bends. "Right leg." I lift my right leg so he can remove the underwear carefully. "Left." I lift my left leg, and suddenly, I'm going commando.

He kisses up my legs, behind my knees, up my thighs, his hands following wherever his lips touch me. I think I'm going to spontaneously combust.

"Condom?" I ask breathlessly.

"Fuck—yes. I have one, I think." He sounds nervous.

"Are you kidding me? How do you not have one?" I'm shaking. I need him. I need him to have a condom. I'm breathing heavily with want, trying to keep it together.

He's rifling through his messenger bag like a maniac. "Why do you just assume that I carry one around with me?"

"Because you're you," I say matter-of-factly.

His panic is palpable, the small bathroom making it difficult to avoid. While he continues his search, I hold on to the sink, trying to talk myself down from getting caught up in the heat of the moment and saying *fuck it* to using protection. At the same time, Oliver kneels on the floor, pants straining at his crotch, desperately taking everything out of his bag in search of one condom.

I roll my eyes at the ceiling and take deep breaths, calming myself down until he yells, "I've got one!" a little too loudly with the biggest smile I've ever seen on his face.

"Shh," I say. "Too loud! We're still in a library."

"Right," he says, pulling me to him again. Oliver kisses me hard, tongue invading my mouth as I reach for his belt and undo it quickly, despite my shaking hands. I'm so filled with need that I tug his jeans and underwear in one go. He springs free and rolls the condom on without breaking our kiss, turning me quickly to face the mirror again once it's secured.

"Like this," he whispers in my ear, one hand raising my skirt from behind, the other rubbing me in the front.

I gasp. He pushes my back down, folding me over, and I close my eyes as he grips my hips and enters me. I moan, and the hand that was working me up now covers my mouth.

"Shh," he whispers urgently. "You're going to get us caught. Eyes open."

"Shit, Oliver," I say under his hand.

"I know, just..." He breathes deeply once as he thrusts in me again. "Just...we need to be quiet, but..." He groans. "Fuck, you feel so good. I won't last long."

I shake my head, his hand dropping. "It doesn't matter. Just get me there. That's all I need."

Nodding, his hand goes back to where it was before and starts rubbing in circular motions. I bite my lip hard to keep from making any noise while he continues a steady rhythm from behind, never taking our eyes off each other in the reflection of the mirror. I tell him not to stop. I tell him it feels so, so good, how hard he feels. I tell him I'm close. And when I come, he comes right after, biting down on my shoulder to muffle his sounds.

"I don't understand something," I say, slipping back into my underwear. My breathing is still a bit ragged, and my hair is a mess, but I need to clean up and get out quickly to get back to my study-buddy.

"What's that?" Oliver asks, fixing his hair in the mirror.

"You seem to care about Josh. But all that time you were trying to set us up, you were still hitting on me and trying to get with me. Didn't you feel a little guilty?"

Inhaling deeply and turning to me, he says, "No, because

you two are not dating, and he has not asked me to stop seeing you. If he ever tells me, 'Ollie, I love you, but you need to stop fucking her because it's affecting our friendship,' then, yeah, I would stop. Bros before hoes, and all of that."

"Huh. So, if any guy just asked you to stop sleeping with someone, you would stop?"

Oliver laughs once. "Absolutely not! It's not my problem if it bothers them. But Josh is a friend, and once both of you admit you have feelings for each other, then we can stop. Until then, I will take full advantage of whatever the hell it is that we're doing." He smiles at me. Rolling my eyes, I shove him playfully and make sure my hair isn't a complete mess.

We open the bathroom door as if we are secret agents, poking our heads out first to check for any people who might have heard us in the act. Once we confirm the coast is clear, we walk out together but go our separate ways. Oliver heads back out of the library toward the café for a pre-class coffee with a salute, and I walk back to the study pod, back to Josh.

I open the door, thinking that I look fine. Josh won't notice anything because I finger-combed my hair, and hopefully, my skin is no longer flushed. But he lifts his gaze as I walk into the room, pauses, and for a brief second, I think I see a flash of unknown emotion in his eyes. I brace myself for his judgment, but instead, he throws his head back in what can only be described as a cackle.

"Seriously?" I ask with a hand on my hip, slightly embarrassed. "It's that obvious?"

"Oh my God, what did you *do*? You could have at least tried to fix yourself up after." He continues to laugh at me and my clearly disheveled appearance.

His laugh is everything.

"I did!" I narrow my eyes at him, checking whether he's disingenuous in his lightheartedness, but I can find no trace of insincerity in his laughter, although it doesn't really seem to reach his eyes. Maybe he really is okay with Oliver and me hooking up? Why is he shifting uncomfortably in his seat, though?

Oh God, it's still weird, isn't it?

Pulling out my makeup bag from my purse, I ask him what the time is. "You have about fifteen minutes to get decent. Five if you're down to get coffee before class. I need one, and we need to pack all these snacks up before we go," he says.

I balk at the sheer quantity of junk food in the room. It seems to have doubled in size when I'm faced with the reality that I have to take all this stuff back home with me. "Yeah, that's gonna be a bit of a problem."

Opening my blush mirror, I see my lips are bright red, and I have beard burn on my face from Oliver's stubble, but there's really nothing I can do about it at this point. If anyone asks, I'll attribute the redness to the cold November air. My hair is still a mess, but that can easily be solved by putting it up in a high bun, which I quickly do. It's only once I'm about to close my blush compact shut that I notice the bruise-like circle on my neck.

"That motherfucker!" I slam the table with my right fist with a little more force than I intended. Josh stares at me with wide eyes. "He gave me a hickey!" I say to Josh by way of explanation.

He laughs and shakes his head. "What is he, fifteen?" His voice a bit tight and restrained.

"I know, right? Jesus." I pull out my concealer and pack it on, doing my best to cover the bruise-like mark and the uncomfortable feeling in my stomach. "I specifically told him not to!"

Josh chuckles again, and I study him closely. There's definitely still some slight tension, but that could just be due to the fact that we only just reconciled. It doesn't have to mean that he's upset or bothered by my arrangement with Oliver.

Right?

I blend the concealer as much as possible, trying to cover the hickey and make it look natural at the same time, but it just looks like I have an ugly birthmark on my neck.

Who the hell ever thought up the hickey? So idiotic.

Are they part of some caveman instinct to mark territory? I feel like it's one step above peeing on someone, to be honest.

"You're really okay with this?" I ask quietly, giving up completely and packing my makeup back into my bag.

He sobers up and stares at me for a bit before responding. "I just want you to be happy." He sounds sincere. "So I'm okay with it. I was just incredibly concerned about you the night of the Jane's boyfriend's concert. You were really drunk, and I was never able to make sure whether you were okay or not." I roll my eyes at him and start packing up the junk food into some Sainsbury's plastic bags. Josh picks up a bag and starts tossing treats into them, helping me pick up.

"I was fine, Josh. Everyone gets drunk from time to time. I admit I went a little overboard, but it happens." I want to scream and tell him it's not his responsibility to take care of me, that he shouldn't feel that burden. That it's *my* responsibility.

He's the complete opposite of Austin. My ex wanted me to handle my own shit because he didn't want to be dragged into it, and here is Josh, this amazing friend who believes that I'm strong and independent but wants to carry all this weight on his shoulders so that I don't have to.

I reach for the *I'm Sorry* sign and gently pull it down from the wall. While Josh's back is to me, I fold it and slip it into one of my notebooks so it doesn't wrinkle, shoving it quickly into my bag. *I* don't even know how to explain to myself the urge I feel to take this with me, so I don't want to have to explain it to him as well.

"Yeah, but I care about you and what happens to you." I stop breathing. "As a friend obviously," he adds quickly, picking up the bars and shoving them into his backpack. "And when you didn't get back to me all weekend, I was a little worried." He looks up and smiles sheepishly at me, running one hand through his hair while the other swings a backpack strap over his shoulder.

"That's sweet," I say, looking over guiltily at him. I remember getting a couple of messages from him over the weekend and thinking I'd get back to him eventually. I guess I never did. I pick up two bags of snacks in each hand and start to walk toward the door. "But ultimately, unnecessary," I say as we exit the study pod, both looking like pack mules.

"Don't worry about the hickey. You can barely see it anymore—from space." He smirks.

I am going to kill Oliver James.

Josh smiles. "I do have to admit that I'm a bit jealous of what you just did, though," he whispers as we walk through the library toward the elevator, and I tense. "It's always been kind of a fantasy to do it in a library."

I sigh in relief. "Don't be too jealous. It was in the bathroom. It wasn't out in the open in the stacks like in the movies." We laugh quietly as we wait for the elevator.

"I thought it was more like that time Rachel Zane and Mike Ross from *Suits* did it in the legal library at the law firm they worked at. That shit was hot."

He watches Suits? *GAH! He's incredible.*

The elevator opens, and we both enter. Sighing at the memory of the steamy scene, I laugh at the fact that the actress who played the paralegal is now the Duchess of Sussex. "I can't believe Rachel Zane is Meghan Markle. How wild is that?"

We walk into class, coffees and bags of snacks in hand. Chloe looks questioningly at me from across the room. "*Apology snacks,*" I mouth with a nod in Josh's direction. She smiles and nods her head. I dig in one of the bags, pull out a bag of Cheetos (her favorite), and toss them in her direction. Chloe catches it with a smile.

"Is that a hickey?" Jane asks loudly next to me, mouth gaping open. My hand flies to my neck, covering up the spot Oliver left on my skin. I don't need to look in the mirror to know where it is. I can fucking *feel* it.

Subtle, Jane.

I want to die.

Ignoring the snickers around me, I take a seat with my head held up high.

"Ooh! I want a snack!" Oliver puts his hands up, hoping I'll send some junk food his way. Does he really think this is okay? I want to smack him in the head. "Me! Me!"

With a smirk, I pull a roll of McVitie's from one of the bags and throw them in the direction of his face with as much force as I can muster. The gods hear my plea because it hits him right in the middle of his forehead.

"Fuck!" Oliver yells, his hand flying to rub the sore spot.

Josh and I burst out laughing.

Perfection.

"You're a fucking bully," Oliver says, tearing into the package of cookies and stuffing one in his mouth. "But fuck me if these aren't the best biscuits."

Sixteen

I ROLL off Oliver a couple of nights after the cookie-throwing incident and lie flat on my back in my bed, staring up at the ceiling. We're quiet as our breathing calms enough to speak. Finally, he rolls onto his side and leans on his elbow, looking down at me. Oliver's hand comes up to my neck, and he rubs what I can only assume is the hickey with his thumb.

"It's fading," he says quietly. "It just looks yellow now."

"Mmmm," I say in response. Pointing at the faint bruise on his forehead from the cookies I threw at him (turns out I have a phenomenal arm and impressive strength), I say, "Yours, too."

He grabs hold of my hip and rolls me into his side, leaning over me to check my back before rolling me over into my original position, laughing and shaking his head.

"What?" I ask self-consciously. "What's wrong?"

He bites his lip, trying to contain his laughter. "Don't hate me, but I think I've marked you again. Scratches this time."

"Oh." I sit up, suddenly feeling the slight burn on my back. "How did I not notice you doing that to me?" I stand and walk to my mirror, twisting to get a better look. Relief courses through my veins as I realize it's not as bad as it could be. "I guess I was a *bit* distracted." I pull on my robe and reach for my brush on the dresser. My sex hair is out of control.

"I think I'm incapable of not marking you." He laughs at my frustrated expression in the mirror, and I roll my eyes. At least no one can see them this time. They're not out and about like the stupid hickey on my neck.

Of course, everyone eventually found out about me and Oliver (it turns out grad school is just high school, only you're older and it's more expensive), and I got so much shit because of it this week.

Josh wouldn't stop making stupid dad jokes ("Hey, Penny. What do you call an evil wizard who gives good hickeys? A neck-romancer."). Michael asked me if I lost a battle with my vacuum cleaner. And Jane kept sending me links for different types of curling irons that were "burn safe".

Ha.

I hate people.

"It's weird," I muse, mostly to myself. "All this fucking scares me a little."

He looks at me quizzically, slightly alarmed. "What? Why?"

I take a deep breath before I respond. "It's stupid. And complicated. But I think I'm starting to lose touch with what it means to *make love*." Oliver gags at the expression.

"Seriously," I go on. "Like, fucking is great. It's been so much fun. But making love is different. More intense, there's more feeling. And I've reached a point where I'm so shut down that I'm scared I'll never feel it again."

"I can make love to you, if you'd like."

I snort at just the thought of Oliver making love to me. "You don't love me that way."

He shrugs. "I could pretend, if that's what you need. I could pretend to be in love with you."

I shake my head and laugh. "You're a good friend, but that sounds like the worst idea that's ever come out of your mouth. And I've heard you say a ton of stupid shit." I take a deep breath. "You can't fake stuff like that."

"I suppose not." He smiles at me.

Oliver leans back in my bed with his arms behind his head and legs crossed at the ankle. I used to think he would lie back in this position because it was how he was most comfortable. After getting to know him, I now realize it's because he *knows* his body looks best like this. His arms are flexed, his chest is puffed and shows off his abs, and crossing his legs tricks you into thinking that he's at ease and completely confident in his body. He'd tell you that of course he is, but I'd stake my life that, deep down, even Oliver isn't that arrogant. He's too smart to be.

"Why are you looking at me like that?" he asks.

See? No one's that secure.

"You're starting to get a cookie pouch, my friend. You're eating too many sweets." He sits up, and for a brief second, I can see a flash of insecurity in his eyes. It makes me want to laugh, but I'm not lying, either. I've been a terrible influence on him. "You're still hot, so don't worry about it. I just notice it because I see you all the time with and without clothes. Just being honest because I care." I shrug my shoulders.

"Pfft," he scoffs. "Besides having pointed it out just now, I don't see you complaining about it."

I crawl back into bed and straddle him. "Nope. Definitely not complaining."

"Well, your ass is getting jiggly. You need to do more squats." He slaps my right butt cheek as if to prove his point.

I snort, but he's not wrong. Regardless, I've never done a squat in my life, and I'm not about to start any time soon.

He bites my neck, tightens his arms around my waist, and looks up at me with pleading eyes. "Can you feed me? Or can we order something?"

I laugh and push off him. "It's one a.m. Nowhere to order from. Get up, put some clothes on, and meet me in the kitchen."

"Can I shower first?" he asks me.

I nod and toss him a clean towel from the basket of fresh laundry on my dresser.

"Want to shower with me?" he asks with a smirk.

I smile and shake my head. "No way," I say. I know he doesn't mean we would *just* shower together. "I'm exhausted and hungry. No more sex tonight."

I walk out of my bedroom, leaving him to his own devices, and head straight to the fridge, checking its contents. And though it's filled with fresh produce and protein, none of it is for us; all of it is Allie's. With a sigh, I pull open the freezer and pull out a box of chicken nuggets I've been saving in case of emergencies. All I have to do is pop them in the over, and we're good. Suddenly starving, I set the over to pre-heat to the correct temperature, and lean against the counter.

I hear the shower start in the bathroom as I look out my window and sigh happily. My apartment is in a pretty off area of East London, but it has a fantastic view of the beautifully illuminated neighborhood of Canary Wharf. I take a mental image of the metropolitan scene and catalog it in my mind so I can carry it with me forever. This might not be where I set roots for the rest of my life, but it feels like London has already become a part of my genetic makeup. It's become a place where I've been able to grow and separate myself from the everyday bullshit of my old life. I think this place has already changed me.

I love this city. I love my apartment. I love the shitty neighborhood I live in. I love the London Underground queues and delays. I love my new friends, even when they give me shit.

I love the new Penny. The real-ass Penny. The give-no-fucks Penny.

I sigh happily at the quiet of the night, nothing but the sound of the shower in the background. You wouldn't get this type of quiet in New York City at this time of night. Even if you went deeper into the busier parts of London, it would still be significantly calmer than New York.

I love you, New York, but London's got you beat there.

Allie is out for the night, which is the only reason why I invited Oliver to sleep over. If she sees him, I know my roommate will somehow find a way to make this into a bigger deal than it actually is, whether it's because he's a *repeat* or just because I'm trying to move on.

She doesn't know that Oliver and I have been sleeping

together before and after class every day this week. And honestly, it's been great, but it's like I've started this thing now, and I can't stop.

The oven beeps suddenly, pulling me out of my reverie, letting me know it's preheated and ready to go. Sighing, I dump the frozen nuggets onto a cookie sheet, spreading them out evenly before sliding them carefully in the ready oven. I check the instructions: seven minutes, flip them over, then another six minutes. I set the timer and lean back against the counter just as a shirtless, wet-haired Oliver walks into the kitchen, wearing nothing but his black underwear.

Damn.

"What are we having?" he asks happily, leaning next to me on the counter. He smells like my body wash.

He's such a happy guy.

"Chicken nuggets," I say, shrugging. "It's the only thing I have." He walks over to the fridge and opens it, looking over his shoulder at me, confused.

"This thing's full! What are you talking about?"

"Roommate," I say by way of explanation.

"That's alright." He smiles, walking slowly toward me. He places one hand on either side of me on the counter. "I happen to *love* chicken nuggets."

I want to say something sarcastic about how he manages to make every sentence out of his mouth sound suggestive, but my thoughts are interrupted when he leans in to kiss me. It starts off slow, seductive. He bites my lip, and my breathing speeds as he slips one hand into my robe to my waist, and my hands grip his shoulders. I moan into his mouth, and he takes that as a sign to press on, slipping one leg in between both of my legs.

Slowly, and without breaking the kiss, he starts pulling on the tie of my robe. He starts to laugh quietly in my mouth, and I know why. "You're thinking about the vintage shop in Notting Hill, aren't you?" I ask with a laugh, recalling the moment with the black cashmere coat, our mouths so close together our lips never lose contact.

"Yes." He smirks. "I wanted to fuck you so bad then. I would have pushed you into the changing room and done it right then and there if I wasn't doing the noble thing of trying to set you up with my friend."

I feel a sudden pang in my stomach as Josh pops into my head. I try to push him out and focus on what's happening, but it's difficult. Luckily, Oliver makes it a little easier by grabbing me by the waist with both hands and hoisting me onto the counter. He settles in between my legs and kisses me so hard it almost hurts. Oliver's right hand slides over my skin inside my robe while his left goes to my right thigh, spreading my legs farther apart.

Oh, yes.

He opens my robe completely, pushing it off my shoulders, kissing down my neck, my chest, my stomach...

I lean back on my hands because I know where he's going, and *yes*, and *oh my God*, and *more*, and *your tongue*, and *please*, and *don't stop*, and—

"What the fuck?!" I sit up as Oliver straightens. The smoke detector in the kitchen has gone off, bringing my orgasm to a screeching halt. It's only then that I notice the smell and fumes in the kitchen.

The chicken nuggets! Fuck my life.

I was so close.

I must not have set the timer properly!

Oliver sighs and quickly reaches for a chair by the kitchen table to stand on under the smoke detector. I hop off the counter and wrap myself up in my robe. What a freaking mood-killer.

He's fiddling with the device, while I pull the chicken nuggets out of the oven when Allie runs out of her bedroom and into the kitchen. She freezes by the door and takes in the scene. Smoke is everywhere, I'm in my robe, and there is a nearly naked man standing on a chair in the middle of the room.

"Oh my God," I say, turning to her.

"What the hell are you *doing*, Penny?" she asks, clearly and fully justifiably annoyed. Allie runs to open the window in the hopes of clearing some of the smoke.

"I am *so* sorry, Allie. I didn't even know you were here!" I take a deep breath. "We were just making food and... I didn't mean to wake you with the smoke detector." I'm shaking my head.

She looks over to Oliver and blushes. "That's not what woke me," she says quietly.

"Oh my God, no." I feel myself blush a deep red, knowing immediately from her expression what she means.

No, no, no, no.

"*Please* tell me you didn't hear... Oh God!" I practically wail as I see her expression change into a grimace, and she shakes her head.

"Please stop. Don't even finish that sentence," she says, barely able to meet my eyes.

KILL ME NOW.

Oliver finally manages to silence the device and jumps down from the chair, pulling me hastily in front of him, his hands on my hips. I'm briefly confused as to why he positions me this way to cover his body, since he's usually so confident about it, until I feel him behind me.

I bury my face in my hands, mortified. "How are you still hard?" I whisper-yell over my shoulder. "This literally can't get any worse. Can you not see what's happening right now?" I ask him as I feel him shake with laughter.

"Oliver, I presume." I look back to Allie and feel Oliver nod behind me. She's avoiding any sort of eye contact with me.

"Nice to meet you," Oliver says, sticking his right hand out from behind me.

Allie looks at his outstretched hand but doesn't shake it.

"I'm sorry. I thought you said you were going out with that Trevor guy again, and I guess I assumed you would be out much later or come home tomorrow," I say. "I've been home for a while. I didn't hear you come back from your date."

Her reply is low, as if she's embarrassed. "Well, he canceled. So..."

"Oh," I reply. "Well, that's okay."

"Just..." she says quietly. "Can you make sure to clean up? Before you go to bed?"

"Yes, absolutely. Go to bed. We've got it covered," I say quickly.

This is awful.

Allie starts walking toward her bedroom but stops. "Can you..." she starts to ask nervously. "Can you also make sure you fully and deeply clean the area where...you guys...I mean, where you were..." We both grimace. "You know. There's a cleaner with bleach under the sink. Don't use the regular one."

Oliver buries his face in my neck, shaking, still failing to contain his laughter. He's not hard anymore, but he's a fucking asshole, so I elbow him in the stomach.

"Yup, yup. I promise. I'll take out the cleaner right now and do it. Yup, you can go to bed now."

She walks into her bedroom and shuts the door. Oliver bursts out laughing, and I turn to slap his stomach.

"Stop it! It's not funny! That was so awkward." I bend over and pull out the ultra-strong cleaner, as requested, and toss it to Oliver. "Start spraying, my friend." He catches it and starts to spray along the counter.

First awkward sex-related encounter with my roommate. It was bound to happen. We'll get over it. I'm sure. Eventually.

It's just a little hard to remember that when I think about the fact that Allie now knows my sex sounds—and that my OCD roommate now has to face the fact that I was doing something sexual on the kitchen counter.

I reach for my phone in the pocket of my robe and open

Instagram while he cleans, stopping dead in my scroll at a picture of Austin.

But it's not posted on his account.

It's posted on my friend Claire's account.

And Austin's arm is around Claire.

And they're both smiling into the camera.

And the caption reads: *This guy, this view, this trip! Perfection!*

…

WHAT.

THE.

FUCK.

Seventeen

MY STOMACH FEELS like it's fallen all the way to China. My heart is racing. I feel cold all over.

I swipe through the pictures.

Because there are more fucking pictures.

A picture of Claire's dad with Austin, holding up fishing rods.

A picture of Claire, her sister, and Austin next to a campfire.

And finally, a fucking picture of Claire and Austin kissing by the fire, holding sticks with marshmallows at the end of them.

I keep staring at the image on my phone until the screen goes black.

"Hey, do you have any more kitchen towels? I think I over-sprayed, and you ran out of this roll."

I am stone. I cannot move. I feel like screaming.

Really, Claire? Fucking, really?

My mind goes straight to Josh. I want to call him and say, *"See, Josh? I was right. People fucking suck."*

"Hey, are you alright? What's wrong?" Oliver turns me to face him, and I can feel myself getting redder and my eyes watering. "Whoa, hey," he says, concern on his face. "It's not a big deal. She'll get over it. Your flatmate will get over it." A tear slips down my cheek, and he brushes it away with his thumb.

"There are more kitchen towels under the sink." I try my hardest to control the volume of my voice. "I need a moment," I say and push him off me, unlocking my phone again.

It's two a.m. here. That means it's nine p.m. in New York. Perfect.

I long-distance call Henry, my childhood friend who also happens to be seeing Claire's sister. It rings several times before picking up.

"Uh, hello?" he asks.

"It's me," I say in a clipped voice. "Penny."

He inhales. He knows why I'm calling.

No one thought to warn me? Seriously?

"So, judging by your reaction, it's true then?" My voice cracks, and I can feel his pity through his silence. I want to tell him I'm angry-crying. I hate that he thinks they are sad tears. But I know that the second I try to explain myself, the flood-gates will open. I can't have that. I can't have that information reaching Claire. Or Austin.

Austin and Claire.

Henry sighs from the other end of the line. "Yes."

"You couldn't have warned me?" I say my voice breaking.

"Come on, Penny. You know I couldn't. Claire is Lauren's sister, and she…she made me promise."

"Made you promise?" Now I'm angry. Oliver looks at me like he's afraid I might implode, and I don't think he is too far off. "Are you kidding me, Henry? I've known you my whole life, and you've been fucking Lauren for what? Five months? Seriously? Are you that whipped already?"

"Hey! Don't talk about her that way," he snaps back. We both take a deep breath, and I pinch the bridge of my nose between two fingers, closing my eyes.

"Listen, I know it's fucked up because you were friends and she's tight with your group, but…I mean, she's not your best friend, you know what I mean? And you left. And I don't even know what else to say." He sounds apologetic, but it's not his apology to give.

I take another deep breath. "How long?"

Henry doesn't like this question, because he doesn't answer. He's too quiet.

"Henry? How long?" I ask again, more forcefully this time.

"Penny, I..." He sighs, and I wait. "I'm pretty sure they had gone out a couple of times before you left for London. And I think Lauren mentioned he broke up with her for a while in September and then they started up again last month."

Another punch to the gut. Another shot of adrenaline coursing through my body.

SERIOUSLY?

This means that he had already started dating her before our last date. This means that when he laughed off my request not to date any of my friends and said he would never do that, he was lying. This means that while I was conflicted about moving on, he was enjoying life, leading me on, playing house with Claire.

Unacceptable.

My rage has now been redirected to the correct person.

And it's not Austin. Or Claire.

It's me.

Because how fucking stupid do I have to be to fall for his shit *AGAIN*?

I thought I had accepted the possibility that he had been lying to me this entire time about it being a temporary breakup, about us not entering an emotional relationship. But here he is, with someone else, *in a relationship*, and I am still surprised.

Jesus Christ, what an idiot.

"Henry, thank you," I say sincerely, calmly. I refuse to let this affect me any longer. I can finally let go of him—for real this time.

"Uh..." He sounds nervous, waiting for the other shoe to drop, waiting for me to yell at him some more. "F-for what?"

"For telling me the truth. Someone had to. I'm glad I wasn't going crazy. I had a feeling something was off."

I think back to all the cyber-stalking I occasionally

performed in the last couple of months. I knew things were off. I knew things were off before I even left New York.

There is silence on the other end of the phone and then a deep breath. "If it helps, she's more into him than he's into her. It's pretty obvious to anyone with two eyes," he says.

I laugh bitterly once. "I'm sure. But not for the reasons you think. I hope that ends well." And I mean it sincerely. I hope he doesn't play her, too. Not because I give a shit about her anymore, because I don't, but because I don't want him to have the satisfaction of getting away with it again. "Thanks, Henry. I have to go now. It's late."

I don't wait for his goodbye before hanging up.

Claire and Austin. Wow.

"Penny?" I turn to look at Oliver, completely forgotten in my apartment. "Are you alright?"

"No." I push him out of the way and walk back into my bedroom.

Ugh. All the *I love yous* that night at dinner. The hand holding.

The fucking dancing.

I think I genuinely hate myself right now.

I open my bedside drawer and pull out the letter he wrote me before I left New York, along with the emergency pack of cigarettes and lighter I hid in the back when I quit smoking weeks ago. I had a feeling I might need these one day.

"You should go home, Oliver," I say, not looking at him. I open the window above my bed and sit on the headrest of my bedframe.

"But...it's past two," he says, confused.

"I'll pay for your Uber if you'd like," I say, but my sentence is muffled by the cigarette I'm holding in between my lips as I try to light it. I take in a deep drag.

God, that feels good.

"I don't *want* to go," he says, taking a seat next to me. "It's late, and I want a sleepover."

I know why he's staying, but he won't say it. He knows I hate being babied.

I shake my head as I pull the letter from the envelope. "Nope, I need you to leave."

"No," he says seriously. "You really don't." He holds my gaze and reaches out for the hand holding the letter. "Talk to me. What is this?" I know him. He won't rest until I tell him, because he's a good friend, and I know he cares.

So, I tell him. I tell him about the Instagram post, and I tell him about the phone call, and I tell him about the fucking letter.

I gaze down at the letter, not really reading it, but some sentences pop out at me:

Penny, I love you. First and foremost, I should say that. I. Love. You.

I don't know if this is something you would have done if we had stayed together, but it's something you need, babe. Something we need.

You need this time to mature, and I need this time to organize myself and figure out how to grow professionally so I can take care of ourselves and our future.

I snort.

I love you?

Something WE need?

Mature?

OUR future?

Wow.

"Can I read it?" he asks.

"Nope." I hold the letter in one hand and the cigarette in another, bringing it to the corner of the piece of paper.

I. Watch. It. Burn.

And I drop it out the window into our building complex's courtyard. Once I've made sure that I haven't burned the whole place down, I put out the cigarette on the windowsill and lie back in bed, staring up at the ceiling.

Oliver lies down next to me, and I can feel him staring. He doesn't say anything, thankfully.

"Oliver?" I close my eyes.

"Yes?"

I take a deep breath. "Please don't make fun of me, but...can we break the no-cuddling policy just for tonight? I think I could really use a hug or something now."

He's like lightning—I'm cuddled up in his chest before I even know it.

"Don't worry, Penny. We'll make an amendment. Cuddling is okay while wearing clothes or during a state of emergency. And I think we meet both rules right now."

And once again, I cry myself quietly to sleep. This time, in a friend's arms.

Eighteen

I ALWAYS GET **massive migraines** the day after I've been crying a lot. The pressure is killer, and my eyes always hurt for a day or two after. It's a nightmare. It's like the universe's way of kicking me when I'm down.

Oh, Penny, you're sad? Let me give you a crippling migraine that will make you basically nonfunctional for the rest of the day.

When I wake up the next morning, alone in bed, it's exactly how I feel. Nonfunctional. Out of office. Not here. Adios. Speak tomorrow when my brain is back to working condition and it's recovered from being *mindfucked* by last night's new information. Claire and Austin together. A couple. Some friend I have. And what a waste of time Austin was.

But I had figured that last one out already.

I stare up at my bedroom ceiling and think about my next move. I refuse to wallow in self-pity. I refuse to cry again over this unholiest of unions, because I realize that most of the grief I've felt is really just about what the breakup means for me and my future. But you know what? The possibilities are endless now. Because I don't have to go back to New York at the end of my master's if I don't want to. And I don't have to stick to the plan I had set in motion for myself.

Endless possibilities.

I could stay in the country after I graduate, move permanently to London, find a job, and carry out my life here. I could marry a British guy and have babies with bad teeth. I could switch from coffee to tea. I could permanently trade Whole Foods for Waitrose.

I could do a lot of things.

Right now, however, I want to stay in bed just a little longer, just enough to rest my eyes some more before having to leave my room and facing the expression on Allie's face. I'm sure that she's already heard what happened through the grapevine by now.

But then I smell the seductive scent of breakfast: eggs, sausage, and the faint hint of maple syrup. My stomach grumbles.

Traitor.

I was hoping to stay in bed all day today, but alas, my stomach has other plans for me.

I get out of bed and check myself in the mirror. Utter shit. Bags under my eyes, hair a mess, face splotchy. Thank God Oliver left already—although, *how rude*. Not even a goodbye? Whatever. I'll text him after I shower.

I walk toward the bathroom but stop dead in my tracks. Allie and Oliver are both seated at the kitchen table, having breakfast.

"Morning, darling. How are we feeling today?" he asks with a smile.

"Super," I say bitterly and confused. I thought he left.

"Well, you look super!" Allie says cheerily, forced smile shining.

I walk toward them and narrow my eyes. "Scrambled eggs with chives? Breakfast sausage? French toast? And..." I sniff the juice in Oliver's glass. "Is this *passion fruit* juice? *Jesus*, you guys must really feel sorry for me. Did you really go all the way to the Caribbean Market this early on a Friday morning for this?" I can't believe them. I'm half-touched, half-annoyed. Am I really that pathetic that they had to go to all this effort to make me feel better?

"I don't know what you're talking about," Allie says innocently.

"When did you even have time to do this? Or plan this?" I ask. They've bonded. I can see it in their expressions. Oliver is easy to like, and once he's in, he's in. And Allie has just discovered Oliver.

"It's half-past noon." Oliver smirks. "We ran into each other this morning on my way to the bathroom, and I properly introduced myself. Then, we got to talking, and we decided to make a special breakfast—for no reason whatsoever," he speaks the last part quickly.

I take the fork in his hand that he's packed with egg and French toast and shove it in my mouth. "Mmmm, well, I appreciate the pity-brunch. It's amazing. Well done. Truly." I laugh and pull up a chair.

"I'll get you your own plate," Oliver says as I pour myself a glass of passion fruit juice.

"This is amazing. Thank you."

Allie finishes the last of her French toast and rises from the table, taking her dishes to the sink and rinsing them before placing them in the dishwasher. She's so efficient. I wish I were the type of person that could rinse a plate or mug after using it and put it immediately in the dishwasher.

I'm not like that. I'm a stacker. I stack plates in the sink like Jenga pieces until there is no more room and I am forced to run the dishwasher.

Another sign that I'm not the best at adulting.

"I have to head out, but I'm glad you enjoyed the breakfast." She kisses the top of my head. "Claire's a bitch. Take a shower."

"Thanks." I smile at her and take another sip of the golden deliciousness that is passion fruit juice. I wait until I hear the door close behind her before I turn to look at Oliver.

"I need you to set me up on a date with someone."

He blinks at me quietly before saying anything. "A date?" he asks hesitantly as he sets a plate of eggs, French toast, and sausage in front of me. "Are you sure you're ready for that?"

Am I ready for that? Who cares whether I'm ready for it or not? I should be, shouldn't I?

"I'm not sure." I shrug my shoulders, replying honestly. "But maybe I just need a palate cleanser. I need to start dating again eventually," I say, taking a huge bite. "It would be like ripping off a Band-aid.

"It's like the pancake theory," I say. Oliver looks quizzically at me, so I explain. "It's like when you're making pancakes. You haven't made them in a while, and the first one always ends up burnt, or deformed, or whatever. But then the second or third are perfectly golden brown and delicious. I need to find myself a first pancake."

"You're insane," he sighs, exasperated. "But why do *I* have to set you up on a date? Can't you use a bloody dating app like any other normal human being?" he asks nervously.

I hate dating apps.

"Dating apps are lame. They've never worked for me. I either get cat-fished or stuck with a weirdo. I need someone with references, someone a friend can vouch for." He snorts. "Come on, please?" I beg and pout. "You know more people in the city than I do—people who aren't in our class. Just set me up with someone. Filter him out. We can double-date with Lucy. Didn't you say she was coming into town today or something?"

"She canceled," he says. "Are you sure about this?"

"Yes," I groan. "Do it."

He shakes his head slowly. "I don't know, Penny. I think this is a mistake. I think you know who I want to set you up with, who everyone wants to see you with." He sighs, and I pretend to not know what he's talking about. "I love you, but I think you're in *massive* denial."

I smile sadly at him. "Can I tell you a secret?" I ask. "I don't think I'm in denial anymore."

Oliver grins in triumph, but it's short-lived. "What's the

problem, then? Why not just ask Josh out if you think you're ready to start seeing other people?" He raises his voice slightly, frustrated at me.

I've been thinking a lot about this.

In a way, Josh would be the perfect guy for me. He's cute and funny and whip-smart. We can spend hours talking about important things like the current state of the world or debate which *Mighty Ducks* movie was the best (*D2*, obviously). And excluding the most recent awkward silences due to an inexplicable pressure in my stomach whenever I'm around him in certain circumstances, we can also spend an entire afternoon in comfortable silence. He always takes care of me, but it's because he *wants* to take care of me. He actually *likes* doing it—even if it annoys me, even if it makes me feel weak sometimes. When he holds me, and I breathe him in, it's *everything* (and yes, it freaks me out).

Josh *knows* me, knows me to the core, and I know him. Being in a relationship would never be boring.

But that's the thing.

It would quickly turn into a relationship. And I don't exactly want one now. I don't think I'm ready to jump into that again.

"Oliver," I start. "Yes, Josh is special. And yes, I do admit that I have feelings for him. But..." I pause. "Josh is the type of guy you marry—not the guy you mess around with."

He starts to interrupt me, but I hold a hand up and stop him.

"You *know* he is, Oliver. You know that. And I'm not ready for that yet. Not just quite yet. I'm not going to ruin that friendship or my shot at happiness over something as capricious as rushing into a relationship I don't exactly want now. Call it... delayed gratification."

Oliver narrows his eyes at me in suspicion. "What if you miss your shot? What if he starts seeing someone else seriously, and he's gone for good? He's a great guy, Penny. He won't be around forever."

I smile, a little nervous. Maybe he knows something I don't?

Is he dating Eloise?? Why have I been unable to figure that relationship out???

Not knowing is driving me crazy.

"I know. And if he finds someone else, then...good for him. I would just hope we could still be friends."

He shakes his head at me. "You're wrong."

Smiling, I pat his hand. "You're such a good friend, you know that? You still champion for him, despite the fact that you know me dating Josh would mean you wouldn't be able to sleep with me anymore."

Oliver snorts. "I know, I'm a saint." I snort. He takes a deep breath. "So, you're sure about tonight?"

I take a bite of sausage before replying, "Absolutely. Set me up."

He rolls his eyes in disgust, and I laugh. He looks at me through narrowed eyes, like he's waiting for me to break. "I'm fine. Really. I just need to move on, and I need that first pancake before I get a good one."

Nineteen

AFTER CAREFUL CONSIDERATION, we agreed that a date right off the bat would be too much pressure for me, so we decided a *"group hang"* was a safer bet. Oliver had plans to go out that same night with his old rugby team from university. By some happy coincidence, his former teammates had been planning this informal rugby team reunion at a local pub, so there were going to be a lot of male prospects for me there, a lot of rebound options—though we've narrowed it down to one guy.

After breakfast, we looked up the Facebook profiles of each of the guys in the event group chat who were single. Like an old-school matchmaker, Oliver talked me through their different personalities while looking at pictures. We even discussed sexual performance wherever he had any piece of information.

"Bachelor number one is called Cameron. Originally from Edinburgh, Cam works in the city for RBS and enjoys doing copious amounts of cocaine."

"Bachelor number two lives with his parents in Surrey, is dumb as a rock, but I've heard has great oral skills."

"Bachelor number three is George. He lives in a massive flat in South Kensington, purchased for him by his rich parents, but he has been said to have a small dick."

And so on.

Things aren't going particularly well with the search, to say the least. It's not until we're reaching the very end while I am lying on my stomach next to him when I type in the name he gives me: Thomas Delancey. Tom.

I sit up, intrigued.

"He's cute." I point to the screen and look over at Oliver to gauge his expression.

"Uh, yes, I suppose he could be," Oliver says hesitantly, quietly.

I look back to the picture of the man in my computer screen. Is he kidding me? Mr. Delancey is definitely cute. *Hot*, even. The picture shows a tall, shirtless man standing in front of a beach. His eyes are almost closed as he side-smirks into the camera against the blinding sun. He isn't big, but he isn't a string bean either. He is tan and has a great body. Tom also has incredible-looking golden locks that fall slightly over his eyes.

I click through his profile pictures and find one with his arm wrapped around an older woman striking a shocking resemblance to him. His mother? Both blond, both shocking-blue eyes, both wearing ugly Christmas sweaters.

"Seriously? Did you see the picture of him at the beach? And the one with his mom? A profile pic with a mother shows signs of a sensitive and nice guy, don't you think?" I ask eagerly.

I think we've found our guy.

Oliver thinks this over, tapping a finger to his lips. "I guess Tom is nice," he says, shrugging. "We're not *particularly* close, but he's close with my friends." He sighs. "But are you planning on sleeping with him, though?"

"If I'm feeling it, then yes." I realize this doesn't sound like the smartest plan, but I feel like the pancake theory is going to work for me here. And who knows, maybe I like this guy enough that he asks me out on a date, and he helps me train with that, too. It's like when you're looking for work. You start by interviewing for your least favorite roles so you have time to polish your resume and interview skills for the ones you really want. "But if he's boring or I'm just not feeling it in general, then no."

Oliver nods his head. "Good, because I've heard from my female friends that he can be quite...*vanilla* in the bedroom, if you know what I mean."

I keep clicking through Tom's pictures and reply to Oliver without looking. "I always know what you mean."

He sighs and scratches his head. "Just keep that in mind. He's supposed to be quite dull in bed. He's not like us." His chest puffs a little.

I snort and turn to look at him. "'*Like us*'? What does that even mean?"

He rolls his eyes at me and gets off the bed, reaching for his sweater on my dresser. "Forget about it."

"No, please, tell me." I laugh. I need to hear him say it. This is incredible.

"You know what I mean," he says, exasperated. "We're... adventurous. Exciting. We fuck in libraries, and you give me hand jobs in class—"

"Whoa! I did *not* give you a hand job in class. It was an over-the—"

"Yes, yes. An over-the-jeans cock rub. I get it," he says, exasperated. "I'm saying he's the type of guy who just does missionary. Getting a woman on all fours is probably his version of *Fifty Shades*. That's it."

Just missionary?

Boring.

He pulls his sweater over his head and starts walking toward the door.

"You're leaving?" I ask. "You haven't really told me much about him!" I need to prep. I'm not planning on this evolving anywhere, but I still don't want to be rejected or feel like a loser. I need any help I can get. I've been out of the game too long.

Oliver smiles at me, one hand on the door frame. "There really isn't much to say. He barely has any personality, but he is a nice guy, I guess. Great rebound potential." He throws me two thumbs up.

He can't leave!

"We need to strategize before tonight! What if he doesn't like me? You need to help me plan my outfit and what I need to say." So much for 'no pressure'.

Oliver laughs at me as I kneel on my bed and pull on his hand. "You'll be fine," he says. "But if you'd like, I can start talking you up now, tell him I'm bringing someone and that she's fantastic."

"Yes, you do that. Please. Tell him how amazing I am. How I'm a goddess!"

He barks a laugh, nods, and pats me on the head before exiting my room on his way out. "Bye, Crazy! See you tonight! And try to keep the desperation down, yeah?" I hear him yell from the doorway.

Ugh.

I look back to Tom's profile picture. He really does look like a good rebound candidate. I just need a nice, sweet guy to flirt with. Maybe take me on a date. Maybe just have random sex with. I want to go out with a decent human being. I just want an easy night, charged with *fun* sexual tension—uncomplicated, stress-free. The kind of tension that causes adrenaline to course through your veins in a good way.

I need tonight to go well, and I need to pick an outfit that reflects just how naturally vibrant and vivacious and uncomplicated I am.

I need to find an outfit that lies.

I link my arm through Oliver's as we walk to The Red Lion, a classic pub a few blocks away from his apartment. It's cold and wet out, and my hair is blowing wildly in every direction. I snuggle more into his side, seeking cover from the cold and biting wind. I'm also seeking emotional support, if I'm being honest. This doesn't technically break my *no cuddling/spooning policy* (even though we broke that last night), but it provides some comfort.

"As much as I enjoy you pushing yourself up against me and using me as a human shield against the cold," Oliver says through gritted teeth, "probably not the best idea for us to walk into the pub arm in arm when you're trying to get with another guy."

I immediately slide my arm out of his as we reach the front door of the pub. "Good point."

I run my hand through my hair and fidget with my coat. Oliver rolls his eyes at me. "For fuck's sake, you're not meeting the fucking Pope. Will you just relax? You're acting completely mental."

"God, I know," I groan, embarrassed. "I'm pathetic, aren't I? I'm just nervous. I haven't done this in a while. I just suddenly have a bad feeling about this whole night. I'm not great at first impressions. I'm not even sure how I made any friends the first night at orientation."

Oliver opens the door to the pub and lets me in first. "Well, I liked you initially because I wanted to sleep with you," he says matter-of-factly, following close behind. "Not sure why everyone else did, to be honest."

Those are not comforting words.

"I don't think I'm gonna sleep with him," I say. "I might hook up, but I thought about it, and I think I need to take things slow—for my sake."

I gave it some thought over the course of the afternoon, and I came to the realization that I had acted rashly. Sleeping with someone in reaction to Austin's new relationship would be stupid and immature—not to mention, it would prove he had more power over me than I am willing to admit. So, I decided earlier today that I was down to flirt a little and have a little fun, but I won't be going home with anyone.

"Good. You would've wasted your time on him anyway. I told you I've heard that he's not great in bed. Just make out a little, if you want. It's not a big deal."

I nod, but this is all starting to sound ridiculous to me.

The warmth of the pub is welcoming against the winter cold. The recognizable smell of hops and oak soothe my soul and calm me. There's no music playing in the background, just the familiar buzz of a crowd and the occasional laughter rising above the usual noise coming from different tables. The lights are dimmed to set the mood.

The clientele at The Red Lion ranges from blue-haired men reliving their glory days to barely legal teens enjoying their first beers. Places like these are the ones that give me hope that maybe we *can* all get along, that maybe differences can be set aside and truces can be made and friendships solidified all over a delicious, bubbly, cold pint of beer.

God, I love pubs.

The real kind, though—not that hybrid mess Jane took us to. This kind. The kind where the tables are ancient, and everything smells like hops. The kind where all you can order by way of food is fish and chips or nuts, and *maybe* a burger. The kind where fruity cocktails aren't allowed—only beer and hard liquors.

I take a deep breath and smile while Oliver takes me by the hand and yells, "Mate!" to a man by a corner table with five other people.

As we approach the table, I realize that they look like the British version of frat boys.

Oh, God.

"Ollie!" they say in unison.

"*Ollie?*" I whisper and laugh in his ear as I slip off my coat. "Oh my God, yes. Thank you, Jesus." I'm gonna give him so much shit for this. I had heard him use it a couple of times when referring to himself, but I thought he was being sarcastic.

Oliver glares at me as we make our way through. "It's my

very macho, rugby team nickname. Don't fucking ruin it for me."

I pretend to zip my lips, pressing them together to avoid laughing. He's being a pal, so I should minimize the teasing—he really doesn't deserve it. I think I'm going to be nice tonight and be his wing-woman.

"Fucking hell, Ollie. Is this the girl you told us you've been shagging?"

On the other hand, maybe he can go fuck himself.

"Uh...hey, guys. This is my *friend*, Penny." I had made sure he emphasized the friend part. I don't want any of his team-mates thinking that just because we came together, we are expected to leave together. "She's my friend from New York I was telling you about." By the looks on their faces, that's not all Oliver has told them about me.

Where are all the women?

I suddenly feel like a gazelle being brought into a lion's den for dinner time. Perhaps this was not such a great idea.

"Evidently," says the gray-eyed man with brown hair as he looks me over, up and down. He's about six-foot-three and built like a quarterback. I look around at the rest of the table, and they're all pretty much the same body type.

Jesus Christ, what are they feeding these guys? Do they all look like this?

I make a mental note to start watching rugby tomorrow.

"Hi," I say with a pathetic wave to the group of men.

"I'm Jonathan. Nice to meet you." He smiles wickedly at me. "I'm Ollie's biggest competitor."

Oh no.

I take in his expression and look around the table at the other guys. He's told them. He hasn't just told them we've slept together; it looks like he gave details. And they all know.

I want to kick Oliver's ass.

"Excuse me," I say to the group of men at the table, smiling my most saccharine smile. I grab Oliver by the arm and take him a few feet away. "What the fuck did you do? They're all undressing me with their eyes!" I whisper-yell.

Oliver winces. "You told me to talk you up! Which I did! Although in retrospect, I probably shouldn't have mentioned a few things about you," he says, grimacing, waiting for me to physically hurt him. I groan, mortified, and then punch him in the arm.

"How much did you tell them?! *What* did you say?" I ask, venom in my voice.

"I may have...touched upon your sexual talents and...appetite."

Oh. My. God.

"Please don't kill me! I was just trying to help. I didn't think they'd all react this way. I just wanted Tom to be intrigued, to pique his interest," he says, words tumbling out quickly.

I'm seething with anger. That's not an excuse.

"You couldn't have at least texted it privately to him? You had to put it in the group chat?" I ask, but I know it was the group-chat version of locker-room talk. And I had given him permission. It just went too far.

He shakes his head. "It wouldn't have been natural. I never talk to Tom. He's so *fucking* boring." Oliver scoffs, disgusted. "Honestly, you're not in for the best night, I don't think. I think you should consider going with someone else. Richard might have a small dick, but he comes from money, and his flat is incredible."

I stare at him for a second, mouth gaping. I cannot believe him. I cannot believe he did this. This is definitely not helpful. I need someone to pick me for my personality, not based on my sexual Yelp review written in a group text by a moron or because of a competition with another guy.

This is an absolute nightmare.

"I'm just going to go. This is humiliating. I don't know anyone, and I already see you dumping me here alone for some other girl." I nod toward the brunette at the bar who hasn't stopped eye-fucking Oliver since we walked through the door.

I exhale. "Mission failed."

He grabs me by the shoulders and bends to make eye contact with me. "Listen, you've absolutely got this. You're hot. You're smart. You're completely insecure, but I believe you have the ability to hide that sometimes. And there will be lots of beer to loosen everyone up and hide people's personality flaws for the night." He shakes me a little. "You can do this. Now, let me properly introduce you to everyone—especially Tom, I guess."

I'm only on my second beer, so I shouldn't feel this drunk, but I do. I'm dizzy, and the pub is blurring a little, making it difficult to stay balanced. Tom is telling me something about his job. He's a photographer, I think? It's hard to focus for some reason, which makes me feel bad. Tom is so nice. He's been so sweet and nice and patient, and he even watched my beer and purse for me when I went to the bathroom earlier.

Oliver was right. Tom doesn't have much of a personality, but that's fine. I tried finding him to thank him for introducing me to a nice guy, but I had the feeling he had disappeared with the brunette from the bar about a half hour ago. Shame. I was hoping he could take me home.

My head spins, and I grip the bar.

"Whoa, hey, are you all right?" Tom asks.

I shake my head slowly, trying not to make it worse. "I need to go home. Do you know where Oliver is? I need him to take me home."

"He's gone, love," Tom says softly, rubbing my back in gentle motions. He smells like hops and oranges. "Let me take you home," he says. "It's not safe out there."

I close my eyes, nod, and lean against the bar as Tom settles the tab. "Is she alright?" I hear the barman ask him.

"Yeah, mate. She's fine. Gonna take her home."

Tom walks me outside, and we wait in the cold. Where's my coat? He wraps an arm around me. "Uber will be here in a sec," he says serenely. His calmness right now is soothing. He's not panicking, so I shouldn't either. "It's here. Let's get in."

"Wait," I say, my eyes flying open. I never gave him my address. Where is he taking me? But I feel myself being taken under somewhere. I don't know where. "Wait, stop..." I try to say, but I can't manage to finish a sentence.

"Shhh, sweetheart. It's alright," he says. "No, she's fine." I think he's talking to the cabby. "Just need to put her in bed." I hear the cabby mutter something in reply but can't understand it. Why is he calling me sweetheart?

But...what does he mean by 'put me in bed'? I never gave him my address. How does he know where to take me? I don't want to go with him. Stop. I need to call Oliver. Something isn't right.

"Where's Oliver?" I manage to ask, feeling myself shake. I'm cold and frightened. My arms and legs feel like Jell-O.

No, no, no.

"He went home, sweetheart. I told you. He left." He rubs my back in gentle motions, but it causes goosebumps to break out all over my skin. "I'm taking you home now."

No, he wouldn't leave me with a sexual predator. Oliver wouldn't leave me if he thought I wasn't safe. Maybe Tom just wants to make sure I don't end up in a ditch somewhere. Maybe I really will be okay.

But then, why is it so hard to speak? And move?

"We're almost home," he says, sitting up. A hand slips over and inside my thighs, gripping me tightly.

The beer.

I went to the bathroom and had him guard my beer.

He put something in it.

Twenty

WHEN I FINALLY MANAGE TO OPEN MY eyes, it's to the shaky movement of Tom carrying me up a flight of stairs. The place is dark and unfamiliar. Heart racing, I realize this isn't my apartment building.

"Where are we?" I manage to ask, my words slurred. "Why are you carrying me?"

"Shhh," he replies as he continues to climb the stairs with me in his arms. My head is weighing on me, and I let it fall over his arm, legs dangling.

Don't pass out, don't pass out. PENNY. DO. NOT. PASS. OUT.

I struggle to keep my eyes open.

We reach the end of the stairs, and he sets me onto my feet, my legs shaky. "Just need to open the door," he says, turning the knob. I try to make a run for it, to at least crawl down the stairs and find a way home somehow. But my legs won't move, and he manages to scoop me up in his arms again before I can try and escape.

Next thing I know, I'm in a bed, and he's undressing me, raising my shirt over my head and kissing down my stomach. I feel like vomiting.

Stop, stop, stop.

I try to find the words to ask him to stop, to leave me alone, but nothing comes out. Panicking, I try my hardest to keep my eyes open because I know the second that I close them, I'll pass out, and he'll be able to do whatever he wants with me. I'm conscious enough to understand that being taken advantage of while blacked out is not something I think I would be able to survive right now. So, I think through my options as best as the fog allows me to.

I'm not strong enough to get him off me. Even if I were completely sober right now, the man is built bigger than he looked in his Facebook pictures. He's much more muscular in real life and seems to have grown even larger since I first met him. Or maybe it's just because he's making me feel so much smaller now...

Tom falls on top of me and gripsmy wrists so hard it hurts— and not in a good way. Not in a fun way. Not in a pain-meets-pleasure way. There's no way I can fight him; here's no way I would even be able to push him off me. He holds me down with his body weight as he kisses my neck and unbuttons my jeans with one hand, caged in, unable to run away.

So, what do you do when there is no option of *fight or flight*? Just accept it?

"Tom," I manage to whisper. I won't cry. I can't cry.

"That's right, baby. Say my name."

I feel the bile rise in my throat. "Tom, please. Stop."

He doesn't. He sits up and pulls my jeans down in one rough movement.

I'm scared.

Don't pass out, Penny. Don't pass out. Hold on a little longer.

"Tom, please. I'm too drunk," I say, although we both know that I'm not drunk. We both know he slipped me something. "I want this, too," I lie through my teeth, doing my best to keep my eyes open and look him in the eye. His expression is frantic, like he needs to get this done now, before he gets caught. "Can you just let me sleep it off a little? I want to remember this. Let me sleep, and then we can have sex," I manage to say. I don't know how I'm even able to talk now, but I thank God or the universe because, even in the dark, I can see him start to consider this. I need to convince him that I want it, too.

And then, once he's asleep, I'll slip out without him noticing. I'll wait until I feel better and run away. I just need to stay awake.

I push my hips up into him, and his eyes roll into the back of his head, and I gag.

I want to die.

"You promise?" he asks, pinning both of my arms down painfully.

"Yes, I promise. Just let me sleep a bit. Half an hour?"

He nods and sits up, removing his shirt. "Alright, lie on your side."

I do as he says and roll over, hoping to God he respects my request. He slides behind me, and his arms come around my waist, hands skating over my body, grabbing at me, squeezing. I feel like throwing up, and it's not from the alcohol. I squeeze my eyes shut and feel a tear slide down my cheek.

Stay awake, stay awake…

But I don't.

I fall asleep and then wake from a sudden pain in between my legs, an ache on my inner thigh. "Ow!" I scream.

"Shhh," he says, his head between my thighs. I'm lying on my back in his bed. When did that happen? Did he roll me over again?

He continues his ministrations down below, holding my hips down, and I stare up at the ceiling. It's evident that I will not get out of this without him getting what he wants. I'm still not strong enough to walk on my own, and he doesn't seem to want to take a break and sleep.

I can succumb to unconsciousness and let him do whatever he wants with me but live the rest of my life without knowing exactly what he did. Or I can stay awake and try to control the situation as much as possible. I can try and fake liking it. I would remember everything, but I think this would give me more peace of mind. If I passed out now, I would forever wonder what he actually did to me, how he violated me. By staying awake, there would be no mystery. I could live with that. I *would* live with that.

"Tom," I say weakly, trying not to cry. "Stop. I want you," I lie.

I hate you. You have already changed me.

"You…what?" he says. He knows what he's doing to me. He knows what he's doing is wrong. He knows he's violating me. I throw up a little in my mouth and swallow it back down. He doesn't notice me gag. I need to convince him that I want it, too. I think that's the best way to avoid him physically hurting me.

"Come here," I say. Shocked, he scrambles quickly over me, reaching for a condom on the nightstand. The best way to get out of this situation is to go through it. Then, he'll leave me alone. And I can go home.

I just want to go home.

He rolls the condom on, and he's inside me, rough and unpleasant. I choke back tears while he digs his fingers into my legs, face in my neck, breathing ragged.

"Come on, tell me how much you like it," he demands.

So, I give him what he wants. I fake it. I moan. I scream. And I cry, but he doesn't see that. I let him think he's pleasuring me, but I won't let him see how he's absolutely devastating and breaking me.

For all the buildup, he thankfully doesn't last long. The guy has no endurance—thank God. Maybe that's why people think he's boring in bed—he usually can't make it past missionary into anything more exciting. Well, I can say with certainty that there wasn't one second during the whole experience where I was bored.

"He's really vanilla."

I laugh internally. What a fucking joke.

He rolls off me and passes out with a smile on his face, never even bothering to take the condom off.

I fall asleep right there, naked, uncovered. And for the second night in a row, I cry myself to sleep.

Twenty-One

TOM IS STILL ASLEEP when I manage to slip away, finding my clothes and purse by his bedroom door. I try not to take too much of his room in—I don't want to add any more information or material to the flashbacks I know I'm bound to experience for the next couple of days.

I make it home—no idea how. I think I ordered an Uber? Whatever he gave me still has me fuzzy when I get to my apartment.

I stand in my doorway, not moving, mind blank.

It's odd. I know exactly what happened, but I still can't believe it. Can't process it.

I sigh, dropping my things on the floor, not giving a shit about leaving a mess. It's dark and almost six a.m. I don't want to wake Allie, but there's no fucking way I'm going to bed without a shower. I can still smell his sweat all over my body.

I turn the shower on, staring at the tile floor cold under my feet, waiting. While the water heats and I undress, I notice my muscles begin to ache and tighten. As the fog of whatever he slipped me begins to fade, I feel pain in certain areas of my body awaken.

With the light on, I examine myself in the mirror.

Holy shit.

My wrists. My wrists are bruised. Actual marks on my wrists from his fingers where he held me down. Scratch marks on my shoulder—when did that happen? Bruises on my hips from him trying to keep me immobile. And finally. And finally.

And finally. I notice something inside my left thigh. A painful red mark. I poke at it and wince.

Fuck, that hurts!

I open my legs to take a better look at it. A bite mark. But not just a bite mark. I very lightly run my fingers over the bruising area and feel the teeth indentations. Still? How is that possible? How hard did he bite me? Hard enough for it to hurt without touching, apparently.

Oh my God.

The reality of what happened slams into me like a freight train. I can't breathe. I feel like I'm asphyxiating. I try to choke back the tears and fail. I start to shake, teeth chattering.

Oh my God.

I let him do that to me.

I let him.

But I had no choice.

Didn't I?

I was scared it would have been worse if I had tried to fight him. I was afraid he'd hurt me even more.

Can what have happened even be called...?

I start bawling and jump quickly into the shower to quiet my sounds.

I let the scalding hot water fall over my body, fall over my skin, wishing more than anything that it could wash away the last ten hours of my life. Wishing it could wash away the memory of the feel of his body on mine. I reach for the soap and start scrubbing away at my shaking body, tears disappearing and combining with the water.

Dirty, dirty, dirty.

Unclean.

I scrub harder and harder. I take the loofah and fill it with body wash. I scrub until my skin burns.

I try to scrub the bite mark on my inner thigh, but it hurts, and the flash of pain makes me gasp. I sob and power through.

I need to get clean. I need to be clean. I need to wash the night away.

Twenty-Two

I'M IN BED. It's noon.

> I'm alone.
>
> Someone take me away.
>
> Please.
>
> I'm numb.
>
> But I'm in pain.
>
> And I'm unclean.
>
> I get up and a shower for the fourth time today.

Twenty-Three

IT TOOK a while to accept that no matter how many times I showered, it would unquestionably *not* erase what had happened last night. So, eventually, I just stopped trying.

At around two p.m, I finally heard Allie leave the apartment. I think she must've assumed I had slept over at Oliver's, because she never checked to see if I had gotten home or not, and for that I was thankful. I wasn't ready to face anyone just yet.

It's late in the afternoon when I eventually leave my bedroom in search of my cell phone and some food. I'm not in the mood for anything, but I think maybe something might make me feel better. In the end, though, I open my fridge and stare into it for a couple of minutes, not seeing its contents. I can feel my emptiness in my stomach, the void—but I can't bring myself to care, to eat. Every time I blink, I can see his head between my legs or feel him touching me, and it makes me gag.

So, food is out of the question, then.

I sigh and head for the couch, sitting down in front of the TV, checking my phone for the first time since last night. Not really sure I want to join civilization again, I unlock the screen and check my notifications.

I have several missed calls and text messages. Hesitating, I consider ignoring them and spending the rest of my life in isolation by myself at home—or at least for the rest of the weekend. But then he wins. And I can't let that happen.

Shit.

Three messages and two missed calls from Josh.

JOSH

Hey, I'm waiting in pod 10. Are you close?

We said today 2 pm, right?

Hey, I just called you. Hope you're ok. LMK if you need anything. I'm headed back home.

I start crying again.

Josh.

Sweet, caring Josh.

We were supposed to finish our project today, and I just disappeared. I completely forgot. And his first instinct wasn't even to get mad for bailing—he was concerned.

I should have listened to Oliver.

I sob, eyes blurring from tears. I apologize for missing our study date and reply back that I'm not feeling well and think I'm contagious. I had to say something to keep him away, or he would show up with chicken soup and comfort food.

The next message is from Oliver from a couple of hours ago.

OLIVER

You're an absolute legend! Tom just told us what happened last night. Have to say, I'm surprised. I thought you didn't want to shag him. So proud of you.

I stare at the phone screen until it goes black. So he told Oliver—or rather, told *them*. Does he mean the entire rugby team's group chat?

And he's proud of me?

Yeah, I'm proud of myself, too. For being a complete and fucking moron. For being an idiot. For putting myself in danger just because I felt like I had something to prove instead of taking it easy and going back into the dating world at my own pace.

Super proud.

I'm so stupid.

I can't breathe. I feel like I'm choking. I sit up in my bed and gasp loudly.

Oh. It was a dream.

No—not a dream. A flashback in a dream.

It's five p.m. on Monday and raining. The pitter-patter of the rain, usually a soothing and calming balm for my soul, has left me feeling unsettled and uncomfortable. The cacophonous sounds of the drops hitting the windows of my apartment have added to the scramble in my brain that Tom's abuse has caused.

I skipped class today. Fuck school, though. I can't even remember why I chose to come here. I don't even remember why I ever thought going to another country, another continent, would be good for me. I can't clearly remember why I ever thought leaving New York would be a good idea.

I do remember Friday night, though. I remember seeing Tom for the first time in person. I remember thinking how cute his blond curls were and how kind his eyes looked. I remember speaking to him most of the night and feeling happy that, although he was in fact a bit boring, he seemed incredibly nice.

And then...I remember the force with which he held my hips down, the darkness in his eyes, and the sharp pain as his teeth sank into my thighs. And the tears start falling again. I thought I had been unconscious for that part. Does that mean I'm going to start remembering more things?

I clutch my head in my hands.

Please, God, no more.

I rub my eyes with the heels of my hands, sore from crying, and then rub my temples with my fingers in a circular motion trying to relieve the sudden blinding migraine.

I swing the covers off me and get out of bed. My body aches. Every movement, every second, for the past three days has been pain. The slightest action causes a flashback to pop into my head and puts me in a tailspin. The smallest wrong movement can make my body ache and remind me of all the places he physically restrained me. Every time something like that happens, I start to cry inconsolably for hours. So, I've been avoiding all human interaction.

Another shower. I need another shower.

I force myself out of bed and walk to the bathroom when I hear a knock on my door.

Odd. Usually whoever wants to come into the building has to be buzzed up.

I pad weakly to the door and peek through the peephole.

Shit.

It's Oliver.

I consider not opening the door. I consider staying in here forever.

I don't want him here. I don't want him to know. I don't want him to blame himself. I want to get past it.

"I know you're there, Penny. I can hear you crying from the other side of the door."

Oh. I didn't even realize I had started again.

"Open the fucking door."

I choke back a sob. "Now's not really a good time, Oliver. Can you come back later?"

He starts pounding hard on my door, and I wince. "Please stop that!" I cover my ears, squeezing my eyes shut.

"Open the fucking door! You've been MIA since Friday night. You didn't even come to class today. Just tell me what's happening. It's not like you to ignore everyone's messages and calls. Did you think no one would notice?"

Honestly, yes.

I take a beat.

"I know you stood Josh up," he says, voice low. "And I know you've been ghosting your girls' group chat all weekend."

It's true. Jane and Chloe kept texting me to meet up, but I had flat out ignored their invitations. Last I'd checked, Jane had sent me a *Where in the world is Carmen San Diego?* meme.

If I don't let Oliver in, he might suspect something is really wrong and press until I crack. If I open the door, maybe I can play it off as a sickness. Maybe I can tell him I have the flu or something, or the whole Austin-dating-Claire thing—which now seems so stupid in comparison.

Perspective is a true force.

"Come on, Penny, please?"

"Are you alone?" I ask.

"Yes," he sighs, exasperated. "Just open the door."

I take a deep breath, bracing myself. I wipe the tears from my eyes and try my best to clean myself up, quickly knotting my hair into a high bun at the top of my head. I'm sure I look like shit.

Oh well.

I open the door to let him in, but Oliver doesn't move. He's gaping at me, eyes wide in disbelief. He's pale, staring, taking me in. I can't even begin to imagine what I look like. I've been crying for three days straight, haven't eaten since Friday afternoon, and my sleep schedule has been fucked.

"What...what happened? Are you alright?"

"I'm super," I say, voice flat. I walk away, leaving him in the doorway, but he still makes no movement to walk into the apartment. It's like he knows something horrible happened, and he's not ready to face it yet. "I was actually just about to shower, so I can't talk for long."

Finally, he walks in and quietly shuts the door behind him. "You're scaring me. What happened?"

I shrug. "Nothing. I just need to take a shower is all."

It takes a Herculean effort to maintain my face as expressionless, to keep myself from breaking down. He knows me so well by now that I don't know how much longer I can hide it, though. I don't want to cry. I don't want to talk about it.

"I'm just feeling a little out of sorts."

"A little out of sorts," he repeats quietly. "You call this *a little* out of sorts? I've never seen you like this."

I've never felt like this.

"You haven't known me very long." I shrug.

We're standing in my foyer. I haven't really invited him into the apartment, but he's made no effort to come in either. He's still doing the mental math, studying me, thinking over the events of the past several days.

"How did you get into the building without me buzzing you up?" I ask accusingly.

"Your building's gate is broken. Anyone can come in, so you should call someone to fix that. Someone might end up hurt."

I snort. Too late.

"When was the last time you ate?" he asks, his eyes narrowed.

I shrug. "Maybe Friday? Not really hungry."

I know what he's thinking. I normally need to be fed every three hours, and I hadn't eaten in three days? To be honest, I'm a little terrified of eating right now. I feel like I'm already spiraling, and I definitely don't want to add a *relapse* to this whole situation.

Because I am desperately craving it. I want the control back. I *need* it. I want to call Domino's and order two pizzas with everything on it, some Coke and cookies, devour it all in under ten minutes, and purge. Cleanse.

I sigh and start walking toward the living room as soon as I realize that Oliver has no plans of leaving my apartment any time soon. I need to sit down. I feel like I'm about to pass out. I sit on my leather couch, crossing my legs, and stare up at him.

"Is this all because of your ex?" he asks, confused. Oliver runs a hand through his hair. "I don't get it. I thought you had an angry reaction to his new relationship, not a depressive one. What happened between Friday night and now?" He looks me over, and I can see the exact moment when the realization hits him. It could have been the mention of Friday night or my completely devastated body language. More than anything, though, I imagine it was the bite mark on my thigh peeking out from under my PJ shorts that caught his eye.

His eyes flash, and he kneels in front of me.

"What the fuck is *that*?" he asks angrily. "What is that, Penny?"

And the dam bursts.

I try to keep it in, but I can't stop the tears from flowing once he points it out. I hang my head in my hands and feel my body shaking, convulsing.

"I don't know, I don't know." I shake my head from side to side. I do know, and he knows I know, and he knows, too.

I feel his arms around me, pressing me into his chest. "What happened?" he asks over and over again. It gets harder and harder to breathe. I'm choking back sobs.

Unclean, unclean, unclean.

I push Oliver off me, jump off the couch and run into the bathroom, locking myself in. I turn the shower on and proceed to cry under the hot water until my breathing calms and my heart rate slows.

I stand in front of the foggy bathroom mirror, examining myself. The bruises have started to fade, but there is still some yellowing around my wrists. The scratch marks have begun to heal, and though I am sore and exhausted, at this point I think it's more from the emotional turmoil and starvation and less about the actual physical trauma my body went through.

That bite mark, though. It hasn't faded. It hasn't budged. It has actually darkened to purple, almost black. A constant reminder of what happened.

And the pain.

God, the pain.

I take a deep breath and curse under my breath. Fuck. No towel. All my towels are wet and in the hamper from the sheer quantity of showers I've taken since Saturday morning. I can't walk out naked and steal one of Allie's because Oliver is out there. And though he's seen me naked on different occasions, this is not something I want him to witness.

But I have no choice.

"Oliver?" I ask through the door. I hear him quickly get up from the couch and run to the bathroom door. I open it, leaving only a crack in between, enough for me to look him in the eye. He looks frantic, guilty, like a man on death row.

He's blaming himself.

Shit.

"Can you get me a towel from Allie's room, please? She should have some clean ones in her closet. I'm out." I'll wash them before she gets back.

"Yes, of course." He rushes into Allie's room and comes back with two fluffy towels. I smile weakly. One for my hair and one for my body. "Thanks," I say, taking both towels in my hands. His eyes fall on my wrists, on the yellowing bruises.

"Can I see?" he asks. "Where he hurt you, I mean."

"Uh...I don't see how that will do anyone any good here," I say.

He closes his eyes. "I need to see it. It's my fault."

I knew he would do this. I knew he would blame himself. "It's definitely not your fault. Don't ever think it's your fault. Just because you introduced me to him does not mean it's your fault."

He still doesn't know the details, and I have no intention of telling him. But after everything he's done for me, I can't let him think that he carries any of the blame here. I owe it to Oliver to give him peace of mind and explain.

I open the door fully and haphazardly wrap one of the towels around me. I tell him. I tell him about how he drugged me. I tell him about how he pretended to care about me with the barman and the cabby, how I thought it was to throw them off because I was clearly too far gone and he was getting handsy. I tell him how I asked Tom to take me home, but he clearly didn't. I tell him about how I fought to stay awake. I tell him how he hurt me and how I decided the best, least-violent course of action was to go with it. Pretend to like it. But I never told him once that I asked for Oliver's help. He didn't deserve that. He held me all throughout the retelling of one of the worst nights of my life, patting my back and reassuring me that everything was going to be okay whenever I had to stop and take a breath.

"It sounds horrible and dark to say, but...how absolutely *pedestrian*. Such a cliché." I sniff and wipe my nose with the back of my hand. "Not that I ever imagined being...you know...before. But really? Roofies? A roofie in my beer? What a prosaic and uninspired way to..." I take a deep breath. "Not that I needed excitement or newness—the violation of my body and spirit was enough, thank you very much. But it annoys me greatly that I am now left feeling positively crushed, unclean, and broken by the most banal way one can be taken advantage of." I humorlessly laugh once. I'm disappointed in myself. It was so simple, and I feel like I wasn't smart enough. I shouldn't have trusted him just because Oliver knew him.

"This isn't funny. Nothing about this is funny," he says angrily.

I sigh deeply and nod. "I know."

"Then how about you stop trying to joke about this? I hate it when you try to add levity to these types of situations."

I raise an eyebrow at him. "What types of situations? Rape? Because in the span of our three-month friendship we've had the misfortune of going through shit like this on a weekly basis?" I say haughtily.

"You know what I mean, Penny. Don't fucking joke about it. And it feels longer than just three months." He takes a deep breath, running a hand through his short hair.

"That's what happens when you see someone almost every day."

"Show me what he did," he says, his hands closed into fists at his sides.

I hesitate for a second but, for some reason, decide to drop my towel, giving him a full-frontal view of my body. He takes in the finger bruises on my hips and my shoulder. He delicately pulls on one of my hands and closely inspects my wrist. He carefully drops my arm to my side and holds my gaze. He's asking for permission, and I know exactly for what. I nod, and he slowly kneels in front of me. I squeeze my eyes shut as he pushes my legs open a little to get a better view. I hear him gasp. Looking down, I see his hands hover over the bruise, trembling in anger. I run my fingers through his hair, and he looks up, torn.

He opens his mouth to say something, but we're interrupted by a knock on the door.

"Perfect timing," he says. I ask him what he means, but he wraps the towel around me and pushes me gently in the direction of my bedroom. "Put some comfortable clothes on, and let me know when you're decent. I'll get the door."

Confused, I walk back into my room and decide to slip into leggings and a hoodie, perfectly covering any and all bruising and marks left over from Friday night's nightmare. As I finish pulling the sweater over my head, I hear his voice.

"I brought the pizza, like you asked. Is she okay? She told me she was sick on Saturday, but I haven't heard from her since."

Josh.

I run out of my bedroom. "You called him? You fucking called him?" I yell angrily. "I don't want to talk about this, Oliver. I don't want to tell anyone. And least of all him!" Josh physically recoils, staring back at me with hurt in his eyes.

"What happened? What did I do?"

"You didn't do anything, mate. I did," Oliver says. "I need you to make sure she eats something and doesn't leave this apartment. I'll be back in a couple of hours." He looks at me angrily. "I have an errand I need to run."

I gasp, comprehension dawning on me. "No. No. *No.* I told you, no." I grab on to his arm with both my hands, pulling him away from the front door with all of my body weight. "I don't need you to *'run any errands'*, and I don't want to make a big deal out of this. It's fine."

Oliver laughs bitterly once. "It's fine? It's fine. She gets date-raped, but 'it's fine'?"

"She *what*?" Josh yells. I keep my eyes on Oliver, though, not wanting to see the expression on Josh's face.

"You had *no right*, Oliver. You had no right to call him here. You have no right to do anything. This is *my* problem. Mine to decide what I want to do—and I want to move on!" I yell.

He runs both his hands through his hair, gritting his teeth. "We need to report this. It's what you're *supposed* to do when something like this happens."

I sigh. Of course I've thought about this—I'm not an idiot. I always thought that if anything like this ever happened to me, I would run straight to the authorities. I never understood those women who stayed quiet. I couldn't fathom how someone could just let this happen to them and not try to get revenge.

But man, do I understand now.

There is literally nothing I want to do less than to press charges, to start a whole process, to have to talk about this for weeks on end to a bunch of strangers, to have to see him, just for it to end with some community service for him, or worse: in nothing.

"Listen," I sigh. "I know it's hard for you to understand, but I don't want to have to revisit this. I admire all the women who are able to come forward when something like this happens to them, but I just don't have it in me. I can't," I start sobbing. "I don't want to deal with this anymore, guys. I don't want to see him. I don't want to speak to him. I don't want anything to do with him. And you fighting with him definitely falls under those categories, because it means I have to worry about you, too." I wipe my eyes with the heels of my hands. "I feel like the whole process would just kill me. *Please*, just let this go," I beg. Oliver lightly bangs his forehead on the door frame a few times, his expression sad.

Oliver pushes off the frame and looks at the floor, quiet. I stare up into Josh's face as he looks back and forth between us.

"Penny…"

"It's fine," I say. "Please, please, please. *Please* let's not add any more drama to the situation by adding violence to the mix."

"But he…he said all these things in our group chat the day after…and he… It's not okay," Oliver says.

"Wait, hold on," Josh says, still holding the pizza. "No. Don't listen to her. Let's go. This isn't right." He hands me the pizza and starts to pull Oliver by his jacket. "Come on. Let's go."

"I swear to God, if you guys go and say something, I will tell everyone that you're making it up." I glare at them both. This is not helping. "You don't understand. I *asked* for it. I felt like I had no choice because I was scared he would hurt me more, but I actually ended up *asking* for it."

"But you were coerced. You just said so yourself. This isn't right," Oliver says.

"I know it's not, but I never have to see him again. And he knows what he did. But you don't have to beat him up."

"I'm about to lose my mind. Can you please tell me exactly

what happened? Because I'm imagining the worst here." Josh looks at me and then to Oliver, expecting answers. I can't tell him. I don't want him to know details. I don't want him to have that image of me.

"Josh..." I shake my head.

"Listen," Oliver interrupts, "I'm gonna take a walk around the block and come back. I need to cool down."

"Oliver, don't!" I shove the pizza box into Josh's arms again and hold on to Oliver's jacket.

"I promise I won't do anything, Penny. I just need to go and clear my head. Take a breather." He opens the door and starts to leave but stops in the middle of the doorway to look at Josh. "Make sure she eats. She hasn't eaten in three days." And with that, he walks away.

He hasn't said anything yet, and I appreciate it. I don't need him pushing, and he knows it. Josh hands me another slice of pepperoni, but I shake my head, suppressing a gag.

"You need to eat. You've only had one slice," he says disapprovingly.

I shake my head again, pushing his hand away. "I'm fine," I assure him. "This is the first time I've eaten in a while. It's plenty of food for me."

To be honest, I'm still a little hungry, but the urge to purge is just too strong right now, and I don't know if I have it in me to resist temptation.

We're on the couch, watching Netflix, and I'm exhausted. Beat. Drained. I think it's the crying. I think the crying tires you out more than anything. I pull the blanket that is folded over the arm of the couch and wrap myself up in it, leaning into Josh. He lays his head to rest over mine.

I breathe him in, and a wave a regret hits me hard in the chest, knocking the wind out of me.

I messed it up. I messed everything up. I should've just asked him out. I should have just grown a pair and done it. But I didn't, and now…and now I don't know.

But now it's too late, because if I wasn't a total mess before, I definitely am now. I'm not good for anyone.

Everything hurts.

Ow.

I inhale deeply, breathing him in again, closing my eyes and letting him comfort me with his silence. In a moment of weakness, I let myself fall asleep in his arms, imagining things had gone a different way.

Twenty-Four

IT'D DEFINITELY BEEN a hell of a week. I needed a mental break from everything. Between Austin's new relationship and the events from Friday, I had never felt so overwhelmed. I decided to email all of my professors, letting them know I was ill and had to take the week off. They weren't particularly happy with me, but then again, I wasn't particularly happy with grad school either.

School was exceptionally uninspiring, and it had become clear with each passing day that deciding to do this master's degree was a mistake. I wasn't learning anything here that I hadn't learned in undergrad or during any of my internship experiences. I thought maybe it would get better, that the courses would become more developed and challenging, and that perhaps, as the weeks passed, the case studies would become less Anglocentric or dated and more worldly and current.

I was wrong.

Time off from classes has helped me gain clarity into one thing: I'm wasting my time and money. I'm basically paying for a line on my resume to increase my appeal to future employers, but I honestly couldn't care less anymore.

I want to go back home and regroup. The idea of moving back to New York doesn't really make me happy—in all honesty, it sounds like taking two steps back—but it feels like my time here has come to an end. I finally realize that there's no escaping bad things, so what's the point in trying?

Luckily, my school offers the option to drop out and receive a refund on most of the tuition paid. I just have to submit the paperwork that I have yet to fill out by December 1st. It's early November, so I'm still good on time, but it's become increasingly difficult for me to gather all the documentation needed without anyone finding out. I don't want anyone to know that I'm planning on leaving, so it's been complicated to do with my friends constantly babysitting me. Once word of *The Incident* got out to Chloe and Jane, a twenty-four-seven watch was put into place. I was never alone.

Ever.

Oliver even spoke to Allie to make sure I was being watched when I was at home and they couldn't be there for me. My friends thought I hadn't noticed their little scheme, but it had become blatantly obvious, a couple of days ago, that they were all waiting for me to crash or implode and were working together to have at least one of them be there when it happened. After our study group, I was packing up my stuff to head back home from the library when I saw Jane and Josh exchange strange glances. Josh cleared his throat and gave her a look. Jane stood with a start and whispered, "Are you leaving?" Standing and gathering her things, she said she would go with me, making an excuse about having to go in the same direction— something about having to pick up something in my neighborhood.

That was a massive red flag.

There's nothing in my neighborhood except for residential buildings, a park, and a vet clinic. With that, Jane had confirmed my suspicions.

I didn't want to be an asshole, but I had to ask her to leave me alone and give me some space. Don't get me wrong, I truly appreciate the time and effort put into this by all of my friends —I'm not an idiot. When I realized that they had started to plan their lives and schedules around me to make sure I was okay and supported in case I had a breakdown, I almost cried. It made it that much more difficult for me to make the decision to drop out of school, because I have never had friends like these. But I've made my decision. I'm definitely ending this and going back home.

It's been a week since the whole Tom thing and the first time I've been alone in the longest time. It's been amazing. I was finally able to re-organize my closet the way I like it (i.e., *not* the Marie Kondo method, just the normal human method) and eat a bunch of cookies alone in bed with no one bothering or judging me. The urge to purge has been strong, but I have managed to suppress and overcome it. I'm close to pulling a Rachel and dancing naked in my apartment in celebration of finally being alone when I decide that I should probably be using this precious time to fill out my drop form. I can't risk people finding out that I'm leaving, and now is the perfect time to do it. So, I order a pizza, some gooey chocolate chip cookies, and a 2-liter bottle of Coke and start prepping my materials when I hear a knock at my door. Closing my computer, I reluctantly get out of bed and walk toward the front door.

I look through the peephole, and the feeling in my gut is back.

Josh.

Ugh. When are they going to fix the stupid building gate?

Last week, before the whole thing with Tom even happened, I had finally admitted to Oliver and, more importantly, to myself what I've been repressing for so long: I have feelings for Josh. Big ones. To the external observer and to Josh, we had resolved our issues after his adorable apology in the library with snacks and junk food and are in a good place—back to being good friends. To me, interacting with Josh has become really difficult.

Yeah, I definitely have feelings. A million of them. I am a mess—my emotions are everywhere. I'm jealous of the time he is spending with Eloise (I mean, are they hooking up or not?). I spend every second of every day angry at myself, regretting never having given us a shot. I am scared nothing will ever happen between us.

But I am also scared something *will* happen between the two of us. I feel like I can admit it to myself that this thing with Oliver—though very, *very* fun—had started in reaction to Josh. I can trace it back to feeling overwhelmed by him, by my interactions with him. Jesus, I mean, I even ran to Oliver so we could have sex a minute after Josh had apologized to me in that cute way.

It was like I was using my friends-with-benefits arrangement to build and solidify a wall between me and Josh. All those charged moments in Salisbury and Stonehenge where I felt like someone was punching me in the stomach, how hard it was to breathe around him sometimes… They all make so much sense now—I didn't have Oliver as an outlet then.

God, I'm such a shitty person.

Not that Oliver gives a shit that I used him, but still.

Anyway, spending time with Josh has been super hard, so when he knocks for the second time, I need to take a deep breath to steady myself and slap on a fake smile before opening the door.

"Hey," he says with a huge smile on his face.

I groan internally.

He looks so cute tonight.

He's smiling his genuine smile tonight, not the pity kind that's been plastered on his and everyone's faces for the past few days. His blond hair is styled in the way I love, which he's learned how to do in the past couple of months. His coat is open, and I can tell he's wearing the blue button-down shirt that makes his eyes pop and shoulders look like home. I know that shirt well. Every time he wears it, I feel like pushing him onto my bed so I can lay my head on his chest and cuddle.

I'm suddenly *extremely* aware of how I must look. My signature at-home outfit is a messy top-knot, leggings, and oversized sweatshirt. And I can't forget mentioning the crumbs covering most of my body! I've been putting in an effort for whenever I leave the apartment, but I seriously cannot be expected to give a shit when I'm indoors, especially if I'm home alone.

If I had known he was coming over, I would have cleaned up a bit. Changed my shirt. Brushed off the crumbs from my clothes and hair. But no, people just show up unannounced nowadays. I know that this thing with Josh is super unlikely, but I mean, give a girl a chance!

"I brought Wagamama," he says, holding up the takeout bag in his hand with a hopeful smile.

"Great." I take it from his hand. "It'll go great with the Domino's I just ordered." He laughs as I push the door open to let him in and walk into the kitchen, Josh behind me.

"Glad to see your appetite is back." He smiles.

My appetite hadn't been the problem—it was what I wanted to do *after* I ate that was the problem. The monster on my back that wanted to make a comeback.

But I'm good now, so I ignore his comment.

"So, is it your turn, then? To babysit me, I mean," I ask as I unload the bags of food onto the kitchen counter.

"Not sure what you mean," he replies, sounding nervous, removing his coat and setting it on the chair by the kitchen table. "I'm here because I happened to be in the area and thought I would stop and say hi."

"Hmm." I open the cupboard and reach for two plates begrudgingly. I had just wanted to pig out and eat my food in bed so I didn't have to do any dishes later. "Is that a fact? You live all the way in Southwark, but you happened to find your-self in my part of town at this time of night?" I pull some forks and knives for us from the cutlery drawer. "You know, that excuse is getting old." I put a hand on my hip and raise an eyebrow at him. "Jane used the same one today."

She means well, though.

He scratches the back of his head and grimaces. "We're that obvious, huh?"

"You think?" I sigh, exasperated. "I know you guys are making sure I'm okay, and I am truly incredibly thankful for it. It really means a lot. But it can be slightly suffocating sometimes. I mean, at least make up better excuses. Chloe came over the other night claiming she had left a baking dish here. *A baking dish*, Josh." He laughs at my expression. "Chloe wouldn't even be able to scramble some eggs, let alone bake a cake!" I shake my head. "Please tell me why I would have a baking dish of hers here." I scoop some rice and chicken katsu onto each plate, covering them in curry sauce. "Just for that, I'm only going to let you have one duck gyoza." I still have a pizza and cookies to eat.

Josh laughs and nods in agreement. "I deserve that."

"At least you brought food. *Some people* just come over and raid my fridge."

"Oliver?" Josh asks with a smile, and I nod.

Oliver and I haven't slept together since before Tom, for obvious reasons. Besides the fact that I was... *you know*, the fact that feelings for Josh and Oliver's guilt, we just aren't feeling it. I've assured him several times that it isn't his fault that Tom is a dick, but it's like he can't let it go.

To be honest, I am actually a bit terrified of what my next sexual experience will look like after what had happened. I know that what happened wasn't my fault, but sometimes it's hard to remember that, and I realize that my next sexual partner is going to have to be very understanding. I know that the next man I choose to sleep with will have to be someone I trust, because I just don't know what to expect.

I've researched a lot about post-rape sex from different discussion boards and articles, and what I've found has not been reassuring. Many women have trouble getting intimate. Some even wait years before getting back on the horse, so to speak. Others have issues orgasming or have lost their libidos altogether. Some women with severe PTSD even get panic attacks.

The next guy I sleep with has a lot cut out for him. Would he leave me if I freaked out? Or would he be understanding and patient?

There is no question about it: the next guy will definitely have to be the right guy. And although Oliver has always made me feel safe, he isn't it.

"How's *he* doing with all of this?" I ask Josh. Oliver and I haven't been able to dive deep into the topic. I think neither of us want to.

He shrugs and pops a plum sauce-dipped gyoza in his mouth. "He feels bad, but you know that." He picks up both of our plates and walks them to the table while I carry the cutlery and some napkins. "I think he told his friend group what happened, which, from what he's told me, has caused some drama. But it is what it is. Tom deserves it."

I don't want to think about Tom anymore. I don't want Oliver to bother with him either.

I sigh and pick at my chicken katsu curry. "It's fine," I say. "Let's not talk about it and just have a chill night."

Josh places his hand on mine, and I look up to meet his gaze. My stomach does the gut-punch thing again. "It's not fine," he says with a sympathetic smile, "but we can still have a chill night and not talk about it." He holds my gaze for several seconds, and my breathing starts to speed. I catch his green eyes flickering to my lips, and I gulp, my heart in my throat.

"Penny—"

There's a knock on my door.

He closes his eyes and hangs his head with a sigh.

"Uh, that'll be my pizza," I say, getting up unsteadily from my chair. I walk toward the door and try to calm my breathing.

I have no idea what that was back there…

Was he gonna kiss me?

The delivery guy shoots me a smile in recognition as soon as I open the door. "Hello again, Penny! Here's your pizza. Same order as always!" He hands me the box of pizza and cookies and the bag with the 2-liter bottle of Coke.

I order Domino's so often that the delivery guy knows my name and order?

So, this is what rock bottom feels like.

I make brief small talk with the guy—Amir—for another minute or so before he leaves to make another delivery. As he just made evident, we interact frequently, and I really don't want to ruin what I have going with him now. I happen to like the fact that I get my orders right and in thirty minutes or less.

I walk back to the kitchen to find Josh staring absentmindedly out the window.

"Hey, can we move this to the couch? Pizza is meant to be eaten in front of the TV. Bring the Wagamama with you."

He picks up our plates and walks them to the living room with me as we rearrange our food set up.

"This certainly is an interesting food combo," he says with a chuckle.

Josh shoves a slice of pizza in his mouth as I check the time on my phone—six p.m. "It's still pretty early. You down for a movie while we eat?" He nods, trying not to laugh at how full his mouth is.

"I'll get my computer. I have a bunch of movies on there that we can play on the TV. How do you feel about a *Godfather* marathon?" I come back from my room and hand my closed laptop to Josh.

He laughs as he takes the computer from my hands. "*The Godfather*? I took you for a chick-flick watcher in times of heartbreak."

"Um, who said I'm heartbroken?" *Ha, yeah, okay, Penny. You're doing great.* "Plus, in times like these, I feel like I need gory action, you know? I don't want to think about *more* heartbreak when I'm already heartbroken."

Josh seems affronted by my statement, but he smirks and says, "*The Godfather* trilogy is full of heartbreak, what are you talking about? You're crazy!" He laughs. "Fredo betraying Michael—his own brother! Connie getting the shit beat out of her every night by her husband, and Sonny's death! And those are just to name a few of the tragedies that happen in the Corleone family! How can you say there's no heartbreak there?"

"Um, Sonny was a hotheaded asshole who got himself killed." Josh gasps at me. "And I didn't say it didn't have heartbreak, just not the heartbreak I'm talking about." I smile.

He gapes at me in mock horror, not knowing what to say.

We burst out in laughter at the ridiculousness of this conversation, and we're back. We're back to that feeling in my stomach, which I can now recognize only happens when he looks at me in a way that makes me think he might feel even a little bit of what I'm feeling too.

His eyes are extra green today, like malachite. I could stare into them all night.

But no. This is neither the time, nor the place. I need my friend tonight, not a guy I like.

I try to bring myself out of this daze and point to my computer in his hands. "Can you do it?" I ask. "I'm so technologically challenged. I never figured out how to set it up so it can play on our TV, but Allie's done it a bunch of times."

He opens my laptop, and we both freeze at the words on my computer screen:

WITHDRAWAL FOR INTERNATIONAL POSTGRADUATE STUDENTS

I want to slam my palm to my forehead for being such an idiot. Neither of us moves for a minute, both staring at the screen. Josh quietly sets the laptop on the coffee table in front of us and says nothing.

"Um…" I reach over and minimize the window. "I'm just gonna open iTunes and… yeah, so just the first two movies, then? The third one obviously isn't as great, and I was thinking

—" I pause and look over at Josh. His elbows are on his knees, forehead resting on his hands. I sigh. "Don't tell anyone, okay? I don't want to make a big deal out of it."

He doesn't move. Instead, he takes a deep breath as if preparing himself for this conversation.

He's so disappointed in me.

He hasn't said anything yet, but I can already tell he's not happy with me.

"Josh," I say again, but he doesn't look at me. "Josh." I pull at his arm this time, making him look at me. "I'm just not learning anything here, you know? It's a waste of money. You and I have discussed this. You even agreed with me the other day, remember? We talked about this. And I don't even know if I want to keep working in politics or non-profits, so it's kind of a waste, no?"

He scoffs. "Come on, Penny. You're not leaving because of the program, and you know it." He takes another deep breath and gets up from the couch, heading for the kitchen where he left his coat.

He's leaving. Fuck.

I follow closely behind, heart beating loudly in my chest. "What's *that* supposed to mean? I just told you why I'm leaving. It makes no sense for me to stay. It's a waste of money!"

He laughs once, bitterly. "Yeah, okay. Whatever you say. But we both know you're running away from what happened to you. And from what you've told me, it's not the first time you've run away from shitty situations," he says with venom laced in his voice. "It's your M.O., apparently."

It's a low blow, and he knows it. His words feel like a slap across the face. They physically hurt.

"That's not…that's not what this is." I shake my head, trying not to cry.

"You *know* it is. Don't fucking lie to me. You're either lying to me or lying to yourself."

I close my eyes, holding my head in my hands, shaking it

side to side. This is why I didn't want to tell anyone. I don't want to talk about this. I can't deal with this. "So what if I am running, Josh?" I throw my hands up. "So what if I am? It was horrible, and I'm honestly so done with everything. I'm *tired*, Josh. And I want to go home."

He rolls his eyes at me. "You wanna go *home* or you wanna *go*? Which is it, Penny? Because I get if you want to go home to your family, if that's where you think you'll get better, get help, and feel supported. But if you want to leave just because you're not happy, it still sounds to me like you're running away." Gone is sweet, supportive Josh Fox. I don't know who this tough-love guy is.

"I want to just not feel this way anymore," I say in a small voice as my tears start to fall.

"You're never going to stop feeling like this until you leave this fucking apartment or talk to someone. You don't want to press charges? You don't want us to kill him? Fine. It's your choice, even if I don't like it. But you need counseling, you don't need to run and hide and make excuses. It's fucking okay to feel how you're feeling. Jesus!" he says angrily, running both hands through his hair. "Just don't go. Finish school. Get your degree. Don't let what he did control your life. I'm here for you. We all are. We can help you find a professional to talk to, if you want."

Up until now, Josh has always been able to understand me and every aspect of my life, but not where *The Incident* is concerned. He's frustrated and tired of bargaining with me. He just doesn't get it. And he never will.

Josh and I stare at each other in silence, his eyes blazing.

He's right, of course. I'm absolutely bailing. I can't handle this anymore. I can't handle the constant reminders of what happened that night in the form of my supportive friends constantly babysitting me or the stupid bitemark bruise on my inner thigh that refuses to fade. I can't handle this program and thinking that I made a massive mistake in picking it. And I really can't handle how big of a mess I feel like right now.

Yes, I want to run away. I admit it.

I want to go back to New York where I don't ever have to tell anyone what happened or have to deal with it, and the worst thing I will have to face are the truly insignificant rumors that people will spread. Because that's the best thing this whole situation has taught me: what I left behind isn't nearly as bad as what I went through here.

"It's not that simple," I say.

He huffs and rolls his eyes at me. "It really fucking is, though."

"Josh, come on," I say again. I catch him just as he's slipping his coat on. "If this is about the final project, I can stay and finish it with you and then go. I have until December to drop out, so you don't have to finish it yourself."

"You think I'm angry that you're leaving *because of the final project*?" he asks, looking at me as if I'm the biggest idiot in the world.

"No, I didn't—I mean, I don't know." I'm starting to hyperventilate. He's really leaving. He picks up his backpack and squares his shoulders before turning for the door. "We're not gonna finish talking about this? You're seriously leaving?"

"What does it matter? You clearly are."

Please, no.

I can't breathe. I knew I was going to eventually have to say goodbye, but I wanted it to be on my terms.

"Josh." His name on my lips is a plea as I follow him to the front door. But he's relentless.

He opens the door angrily and stops before turning around. His glare gives new meaning to the phrase *"If looks could kill"*. He opens his mouth as if to say something but laughs bitterly, shaking his head, changing his mind at the last second.

"*Josh*," I plead as he walks toward the elevators. He shoves his hands in his coat pockets as he shakes his head, ignoring me. "Can we finish talking about this? Can you just please listen?"

The elevator dings, and he hesitates for a second, eyes on the floor. He turns on his heel and walks determinately toward me. He looks tall and intimidating, and his shoulders seem broader as he walks up standing straighter. The indomitable look in his eye right now makes me almost shiver, feeling it in my core. And I know it sounds awful, but I don't think I've ever felt more attracted to anyone in my entire life until this very moment.

Josh opens his backpack and takes out a plain black notebook. Holding it out to me, he says, "I planned on giving this to you as a Christmas present, but... I guess it will be a goodbye gift, then," and walks away without another word or look in my direction.

I watch him enter the elevator and disappear, taking my heart with him.

"Josh," I say weakly again, but he can't hear me now.

I shut the apartment door and lean against it, sliding down all the way to the floor. Dropping the notebook, I hug my knees to my chest and feel my eyes water.

Twenty-Five

I SLIDE the unlit cigarette under my nose, inhaling its sweet, smoky scent. I'm at the park, lying on a blanket in the grass by my building complex. I stare up at the clouds behind my sunglasses, for which I am eternally grateful. I've been crying so much lately that my face looks super scary. The circles under my eyes have gotten so deep and dark I look like a drug addict. Thankfully these massive dark lenses cover half my face, so I can finally go out in public.

I roll onto my stomach and look down at the cigarette in one hand and my hot-pink lighter in the other, vacillating between firing this baby up and falling off the wagon or dealing with my problems without the use of a crutch.

Ugh. I really want to smoke.

Setting aside that moment where I burnt Austin's letter with a lit cigarette, I've been really good about not smoking. Do I really want to screw up all of my progress here? I groan, frustrated, and stuff the lighter in my bag, choosing to take the much more difficult route. I keep the cigarette in my hand, though. Just holding it makes me feel a little better, and after last night's harsh exchange with Josh, I need *something* to comfort me. Because he was absolutely right. If I leave now, it's because I *am* running. And I can't keep being that type of person anymore.

This morning, I made the decision to stay. I plan to give school more of a chance and finish my degree. I also plan to enjoy the time I have left in London with the amazing new friends that I've made so far. I'm here now. I may as well make the most out of this situation.

So what if my Master's degree is not what I expected? At least I have the opportunity to be able to be part of it, and I can make more of an effort to make the most of it. I plan to stop complaining so much and focus on the bright side. I want to become a more positive person.

Or at least try to be...

Yes, the case studies offered were almost all from the World War II era, but there isn't anything wrong with a history lesson, right? I can absolutely handle this and try my hardest to make the best of the situation.

As for *The Incident* with Tom, it had obviously been terrible and life altering, but I'm not going to let an asshole ruin this life experience for me. Up until then, moving to this city had been the best decision I had ever made—and it still can be. I just need to not let the bastard win. I have a massive opportunity in front of me, and I almost let one guy ruin it with a traumatizing experience.

I know I still have a lot to overcome with that in the future, but I think I can handle it for now. I understand what happened to me, and I don't blame myself for it anymore. And I don't blame Oliver either, even though I can still see him struggling with it. *That* is something I will have to fix soon. I can't let him spend another day blaming himself for what Tom did. It's definitely not his cross to bear.

My phone vibrates, and I pull it out of my bag. There's only one person I want to hear from today, and it's definitely not a message from him.

CHLOE

> Friendly reminder that Jane's birthday is tonight! We understand if you don't want to come, but if you do, it starts at 9.

I sigh, so tired of being babied. I realize that I may have given them reason to believe that I wasn't doing particularly well, considering the fact that I skipped class and rarely left my apartment, but that's got to end. It's time to rebuild myself and my relationships, and that starts now. I want to show my friends that I'm okay—or as good as I can be. I would especially like to thank them in person for truly being an incredible group of people and showing immeasurable amounts of support.

I mean, Jane even offered to revisit the shoe department at Harrod's the other day when I know for a fact that that place gives her hives.

And even though I have every intention to be there tonight, I don't want anyone I know to expect seeing me there. I need to talk to Josh, and I don't want him to start avoiding me. Given yesterday's fight, I'm not so sure he wouldn't skip Jane's party as a way to prevent seeing me, which is why I'm vague in my reply.

ME

Of course! I'll think about it.

I stuff my phone in my bag and stop at the notebook Josh handed me last night. It's sticking out of my purse, taunting me, saying, *'Read me! Read me!'* I delicately pull it out and lay it in front of me. I haven't opened it yet, but I think I know what it is. I can just feel it.

Can just feel that it is for me specifically. It isn't a regular old notebook. And it was ready to go in his backpack, which probably meant he was waiting for the perfect time to give it to me.

I twirl the cigarette in my hand nervously and stare down at the basic black cover. It makes me so damn nervous you'd think it had an explosive device attached to it. I know whatever is in here is going to change my relationship with Josh, for better or for worse.

I put the unlit cigarette between my lips and, leaning on my elbows, open the notebook to the first page.

Dear Penny,
I made—

I slam the notebook shut and take a deep breath. I flip through the pages of the notebook and see that each entry he's written begins with the same two words: *Dear* and *Penny.*

Oh no.

I knew it. I knew what it was down to my mother-effing *bones.* I don't know how, but I KNEW IT. I'm not exactly sure what's in these letters, but I am positive that whatever he has handed me will permanently change our relationship forever.

I roll back onto my back and stare up at the sky, running a hand through my hair.

It's a notebook.

Full of letters.

Addressed to me.

It's a notebook full of letters addressed to me.

What does this mean?

I concentrate on taking deep and even breaths as I look up at the clouds, trying to focus on slowing my heart rate. I'm so nervous I don't know what to think. It seems likely that whatever is written here is not hate mail. In fact, I get the feeling that these were written with romantic intent. At least I hope so. Because, *God,* wouldn't that be amazing?

Except it wouldn't, though. Not really. Had he given this to me over a week ago, then maybe. Or had the whole Tom thing never happened, definitely. But if I thought I wasn't in a good place to be with anyone before, I can't stress how unlikely it is that I'm ready for anything serious right now. I mean, I've only *just* been able to admit to myself that I have feelings for him, you know? And I've tried not to have them. I've tried really, really hard. And now I absolutely regret not having been able to just be strong enough to accept and pursue them.

Sure, the idea of being in another relationship had scared me so much that sometimes I felt like I was going into anaphylactic shock, but who knows, maybe I would have been able to overcome that fear. Instead, I chose to take a very immature and self-destructive route. But hey, hindsight is twenty-twenty, right?

Oh, God, what am I supposed to do now?

I'm going to have to see him eventually, right? And whether I read what's in this notebook or not, we're going to have to talk about it and our argument and the fact that I decided to stay in London and finish out my program.

So...fuck it.

I take the cigarette out of my mouth, take a deep breath, and open the notebook to the first letter.

Dear Penny,
I made a note on my computer a few days ago about the twenty-seventh day of us first being introduced. Now, normally, the fact of someone remembering twenty-seven-plus days of knowing someone could be considered to be quite creepy, even a little borderline stalkerish.

I snort, smiling, and continue reading his first letter.

But I have an amazing memory! The fact of the matter is that on the twenty-seventh day of us knowing each other, I couldn't sleep—at all. I had decided then and there that from that day forward, I needed to be more than just friends with you. The friend zone was not somewhere I wanted to be.

Now, this places me in quite a bind, as I obviously do not want our friendship to end, but I also would not be able to live with myself without telling you that, well...I like you. I like you in more than just a let-you-eat-my-granola-bars kind of way.

Don't get me wrong—I love taking care of you. I love that you need me and want me to help. Bringing you food and emotional support whenever you need it feels like a privilege to me. But I confess that I want more.

I came to London to recharge my batteries, and never in my wildest dreams would I have dreamt that I would have found someone as beautiful, charismatic, funny, and caring as you. Maybe you can be a bit misunderstood, but it's because those who don't understand you don't know you. Hell, I don't know you as well as I'd like to, but I think I know who you are underneath all the details that make up a person.

I saw a side of you the night we played

Risk that I am sure not many people in your life have seen. And not a second goes by where I'm not immensely grateful for you lowering your emotional protective barrier and showing it to me.

I like you, Penny. I really, really like you.

And I gotta say, sometimes I think you like me too, but I'm not sure you're ready for that yet. Like today, for example, we spent all day alone together, walking the Salisbury Cathedral and sharing desserts and talking endlessly about absolutely everything and nothing at the same time, like we were together (I absolutely love that you and I both agree the Oxford comma is the shit). But then there'd be these moments where I could tell you were panicked. Where I could tell it was too much for you.

And that's fine, Penny. I know you're not ready, and I would never push you to do anything you didn't want to do. And to be honest, maybe I'm not ready yet, either.

I've almost asked you out so many times, but we always get interrupted. Have you ever noticed? Someone always walks in the room, or one of us gets a text, or whatever. It's almost comical! After the fourth time, I just decided it was fate telling me to wait. So, I'll wait. I'm cool with that.

Anyway, I know that you'll probably never

read this, but, Jesus, I had to get this out of my system.

Yours,

Josh Fox

My heart squeezes in my chest, and it's hard to breathe—but in a good way.

Josh likes me.

He likes me, and he wrote the most amazing letter ever because he proved he *understands* me. He doesn't push. He doesn't ask me to get over it and give him a chance. He gets it. I needed time. Need time? I sigh. I don't even know anymore.

He wrote this first letter the night of the Salisbury-Stonehenge trip. God, I was exhausted that night—and not just from all the walking. The emotional exhaustion from that trip was real. It was like a fucking rollercoaster of emotions.

I think back to our interactions the past few months, looking for clues of his crush. Of course, there were days where I was so scared that he was into me or had feelings for me, but I never allowed myself to think that. I was so scared of losing him I think I was just in denial.

Did it ever really seem like he was about to ask me out? I guess maybe that afternoon in the library, perhaps? I remember he had started to say something but never went back to it once Jane and Oliver came into our study pod. I didn't think anything of it.

Have there really been other moments? I can't believe it. Have I really been so blind?

I take a deep breath, steeling myself for the next letter.

Let's do this.

Dear Penny,

I don't know what's happened between us, but I gotta say, I'm kinda miserable.

I miss you. I miss my best friend.

What happened to us after Salisbury? Where the fuck have you been?

I get that things might have been a bit weird after the trip, but did it really merit you just disappearing? Sure, I still see you in class and when we work together on the project, but you're not really there anymore, are you?

Eloise says that you're probably one of those people who uses people and then discards them when she's bored of them. But I almost told her to shut the hell up, because I know you're not like that.

Right?

Anyway, I don't know if it's something else that's bothering you, or if you're really upset with me about something I said or did, but I wish you'd just fucking talk to me. I'm going out of my Goddamn mind here.

Yours,

J.

I think back to those days following our trip and feel sick to my stomach. I was definitely avoiding him—and I guess, in retrospect, my feelings for him as well. I hadn't realized how much it had affected him or that he would even miss me.

He was hanging out with Eloise so much I thought they were dating, for Christ's sake! When in reality, they probably started hanging out more because I had disappeared from Josh's life a little—or at least wasn't spending nearly as much time together as we usually would.

God, I'm such an idiot.

Dear Penny,

You smiled at me today for the first time in a while. And then you did that thing where you bite your lip and your teeth leave little indentations.

It makes me want to kiss you so bad it fucking hurts.

God, I miss you.

When will you come back to me?

Yours,

JF

The next entry is dated a few days later, and the handwriting is a bit more frantic than the last three, like he can't get the words out fast enough. Was he upset when he wrote this? I roll over onto my back, changing positions, and start the next letter.

Dear Penny,

I'm a fucking asshole.

I'm so, so, so sorry. I can't even tell you how fucking sorry I am. I can't even process what a jerk I was to you.

The things I said, the way I reacted. Please know that was all on me, Penny. And I obviously don't think those things about you. I know this can't excuse what I said or how I reacted, but it was clearly out of jealousy and shock.

I knew you and Oliver had gotten close, but... Jesus. That fucking hurt. And I freaked the fuck out, Penny. I'm so sorry.

Just when things were getting better and back to normal between the two of us, too.

And then the things I said about Oliver weren't fair to him either. He was my friend. Is my friend! God, I need to apologize to him too, even if he wasn't there. The things I said weren't fair to either of you.

I don't know what the hell I was thinking.

I thought he wasn't caring for you the same way I was. I spent all night terrified, making sure you were okay, trying not to be too overbearing. But I'm pretty sure I failed, because I could see it in your eyes.

And then you went home with him, and it was like all my skin was on fire, Penny. I swear. I was half rageful, half scared that you'd end up together.

I knew he was in a relationship, but I didn't know how you felt about him. You spent so much time together, for all I knew you could have had feelings for him. So, I completely overreacted. It was obviously all because I was jealous and not because I was disappointed in you. You're your own person and are allowed to do whatever you want with whomever you want, but in that split second, I was so mad you were with someone other than me.

It was like someone had torn my heart out of my chest and I was bleeding internally.

Or like I was on fire.

Or both?

I don't fucking know anymore, Penny. I don't know what I'm saying.

All I know is that I haven't been able to sleep since then because I can't believe I was such an idiot, such a moron. I had no right to say the things that I did.

I used to lie awake at night, scared that I would lose you as a friend if I ever told you how I felt about you, that you'd run in the opposite direction because you didn't feel the same way or weren't ready for the commitment. It was literally my worst fear to live without you in my life.

Now I know that worst fears can be topped. You leaving me because I love you sounds like a walk in the park over you leaving me because you hate me.

I can't stand it, Penny.

I'm so sorry I hurt you. You have no idea.

I wasn't thinking.

I can't sleep.

I'm so tired.

Please forgive me,

Josh

I frown, remembering that day, how hurtful his reaction to the news of me and Oliver had felt. How he'd made me feel cheap and how angry I was at him. I guess I had to have known on some level that he had feelings for me, because I was definitely nervous to tell him. And *of course* it had been out of jealousy—Josh would never have truly meant those things. He's not that type of guy.

His next letter is short, neat, determined.

Dear Penny,

Having you hate me is unacceptable. I miss my best friend, and I think I found a way to earn your forgiveness. I just need Oliver's first.

Love,

Josh

My breath catches in my throat. It's the first time he uses the word love. I sit up, cross-legged and start on the next letter. It's dated a few weeks ago, days after we reconciled.

Dear Penny,

You forgave me, and now we're back to being friends again.

And I've accepted that that's all we'll ever be.

I can't do this anymore, Penny. I can't keep entertaining thoughts of us being together, of you finally realizing that we care about each other in more than a friendly way.

I'm so scared. I literally lie awake at night, indecisive, wondering whether I'm doing the right thing by not telling you about my feelings for you. Sometimes we have these moments where I think that we could do this, we could be together, but then I see you doing shit like sneaking out of class with Oliver to do God knows what, and I think, 'She's nowhere near ready for anything serious,' and it's just not fair to me. Not that I blame you. I blame myself. I'm doing this to myself.

So, I've decided to let go of you, Penny. I'm done. For my sake.

Please remember, though...no matter how tough, sad, shitty, depressing, or painful life gets, I will always be there for you. Friend Zone or End Zone—though I would prefer to be out of the Friend Zone and into your heart.

You will always have a friend in me.
Your friend,
Josh Fox

My heart feels like it's breaking, tearing. I had noticed him pulling back a bit after that, but I guess I was too wrapped up in Oliver to notice too much—which I guess, subconsciously, is exactly what I was trying to do. I think I've known for a while that I have strong feelings for Josh and have just been doing everything possible not to.

I start crying, tears falling on the pages, ink streaking on the paper.

"Fuck!" I say, dabbing my tears with the sleeve of my sweater, trying to dry Josh's words.

I think I may love him.

God, I don't know.

I've only ever loved one other person, and it never felt like this. Austin never felt like a best friend or confidant. He felt more like a dramatic lover. Ugh, I hate that word, but I guess that's how it felt. I was never one hundred percent myself with him. He made me feel small and insecure, and he criticized so much of who I was and what I liked. But then, when he praised me, I felt like I was ten feet tall, like I could do anything. He had the ability to tear me down and build me right back up in a matter of seconds.

I can clearly see now that it was never a healthy relationship.

Josh, on the other hand, makes me feel like I can fly, but also like I have my feet firmly on the ground at the same time. And I want to be that person for him too.

I love whenever he gives me advice. I love when he comes to *me* for advice. I love arguing with him about important things like Double Stuf Oreos vs. Regular Oreos (Me: if they're the same price and same number of cookies, why wouldn't you get Double Stuf? Him: classic or bust), and he doesn't make me feel like it's small or insignificant.

I can't believe what an idiot I've been. Of course it was all there. Of course I could see it. I was just too scared, too intimidated to do anything about it. It's like he said: I didn't want to ruin it. I didn't want to ruin our relationship and lose him, too. It would have been too much to handle. We need each other, and the thought of willingly doing something that could risk our entire relationship, that could break it, was simply unacceptable.

I hold my head in my hands as I cry. I can hear the children laughing as they play in the park, dogs barking at each other while their owners throw their balls, and what looks like two old friends catching up on the bench by my picnic blanket. I try to focus on one of the dozens of things going on around me to avoid a panic attack.

Breathe in, breathe out. Breathe in, breathe out.

I need to make things right tonight. I need to go home, shower, change, and really think about what happened.

I pack my water bottle and chips in my bag and am about to put the notebook away when a current of wind blows it open. I catch it, and it lands on a page I haven't read, close to the end of the notebook.

It doesn't have a salutation or a date.

Odd.

I don't know what to say except that I want

to beat the shit out of him.

I've never, ever had such strong feelings of hatred toward anyone. Fuck, Penny. I hate him. I hate that he did this to you.

And I hate that you won't let us do anything about it.

Why won't you report it? Or at least let me and Oliver kill him, you know? I realize now that Oliver loves you, too, by the way. Not in the same way that I do, but I know he cares about you.

We both want to beat the shit out of him. We talk about it. We talk about how angry we are, how frustrated. But I can't even imagine what you're actually feeling right now, Penny.

I'm scared for you.

Your light is out, and I can barely see you in there. I keep hoping for you to come back, but what can I expect? It hasn't been that long since it happened. I'm sure you're still in shock. Hell, I'm in shock.

I know you've always been averse to being taken care of, but you didn't seem to mind so much when I would. Now, though, I can see it in your face. You see the heartbreak in your friends' eyes, the guilt plastered all over Oliver, and you hate it. You fucking hate it, and you run from it.

I understand. I understand that it reminds you of what happened, and all you want to do is forget about it and move on.

And I'm trying, Penny, I swear I'm trying for your sake. But fuck, I love you and it's killing me that he hurt you and changed you. You were never a cheerleader-type of light, but you had your own shrewd humor. You still crack jokes, but they're to cover up the pain, and we all notice it.

But I'm never gonna stop trying to protect you, even if it annoys the shit out of you.

So, I'll confess that I've asked everyone to keep an eye on you, make sure you are okay, make sure you never have to be alone. Because I think you haven't processed it yet, Penny. I know you'll hate me for it, but I don't care.

So, sue me. I care about you, and I need to know you're okay.

I know you're not okay, though.

Thomas Delancey. I'll hate him until the day I die.

I wish you'd talk to me.

I miss you.

I love you,

Josh

My chest rips into sobs as I struggle, gasping for breath.

He organized all of my friends into babysitting me. He cares about me. He's been worried about me. But most importantly, he loves me.

And *of course* I love him.

Of course I do.

Because he's amazing and incredible and sweet and kind and strong. And he knows and understands me better than anyone.

What am I doing? I need to talk to him. I need to fix this.

I pick up the notebook and hold it close to my chest as I sling my bag over a shoulder and reach down for the blanket I've been lying on. I basically jog back to my apartment to shower, get ready, and make myself perfect for him, because I've decided that tonight is the night. I'm gonna tell him.

I'm going to tell Josh that I love him too.

I'm smiling like a goofball all the way to my building. I start peeling my clothes off as soon as I'm through the door, honestly not caring whether Allie or anyone catches me, throwing my shoes over my shoulder as I make it to the bathroom. Swinging my shower curtain open, I start jumping in place, turning on the hot water, and practically dancing while I wait for it to heat.

I'm finally going to tell him how I feel. I need to wear something amazing, something that will make him forgive me for being an asshole. Maybe that tight black dress I wore out the other night? I saw him checking out my legs in it. I need to do an awesome job on my makeup, too, but avoid lipstick because it can get everywhere when you kiss, and I plan to do a lot of it once we put all the bad shit behind us.

And then the other shoe drops.

Oh. Wait.

Twenty-Six

I CATCH a look at myself in the mirror and see the bite mark bruise on the inside of my thigh. Again. Still there. Still black-purple. Still a constant reminder of that fucking night. And I start to panic.

It's like a bucket of cold water falls over my head.

What the hell am I even thinking? I'm not ready for any of this. I'm not ready to be anyone's anything right now! I'm a mess. Now that I really think about it, having someone that close to me this soon after it happened is unthinkable. There's no way.

I have to start rebuilding myself first, and it's something I'm going to have to do *on my own*. I know that Josh will take care of me and will want to make sure I'm okay and always safe, but how is that supposed to make me stronger or help me get over this hole I feel I've dug myself and been dug into?

And how is that fair to him? To be with someone who didn't used to be broken but now totally feels like she is. Like Allie said, I'm a walking dumpster fire. No one deserves that—especially not him. Not Josh. He deserves to be with someone as good and kind as he is, who won't ever take advantage of his good heart.

The steam from the shower fills the bathroom and fogs the mirror, giving me my cue that it's time for me to get in, which I do. But I don't shave my legs, and I don't exfoliate. I let the hot water fall on my back for a long time, hoping it helps relax my suddenly tight muscles.

Once I'm out of the shower and I realize it's time to go, I dress well enough so that my friends don't think I'm depressed, but not too well that I'm trying to impress a certain someone. I decide to take an Uber to Jane's birthday because fuck the tube tonight. I deserve a taxi for once, even if it is well over sixty pounds and way out of my budget.

When I get to Jane's, I'm so strung up and tense I feel like I'm about two seconds from getting a back spasm. The place is packed, as I would expect it to be. Jane is such a charismatic and friendly person. I'm not shocked by the number of people that surround and love her.

"Babe!" she yells from across the apartment. Yup, there it is, that look of pity. God, when will they stop doing that?

"Oh my God, happy birthday!" I congratulate and hug her with as much energy and force as I can muster, ignoring The Look.

Let's do this, Penny.

She grabs me by the elbow and pulls me into a corner. "I want to talk to you," she slurs. Definitely drunk already. "I love you so much, you know? I'm so glad you're here and that I met you and we get to spend this year together." Her breath smells like she's had one too many negronis. "I hope you plan on staying in London after graduation as well."

I feel a pang of guilt when she says this. She doesn't know that, until yesterday, I was fully planning on bailing on school, moving back home, and starting from scratch in New York. Not that she would have taken it personally like Josh seemed to take it, I don't think.

"I'm so glad I met you, too. And I think London is the place for me," I say genuinely. Jane is incredible and so much fun, definitely a part of why I decided to stay. "Have you seen Josh?" I ask her as I crane my neck, looking around the apartment for him in every direction. I need to get this sorted. I need to apologize, and we need to clarify what's in the notebook. After much thought, I've decided to pretend like I don't like him and let him down easy. I even have a whole speech prepared: *Josh, I appreciate the beautiful words in the notebook you gifted me, but I need you to know that, despite me caring about you deeply, I do not reciprocate the romantic feelings you have expressed to me here on these sheets of paper.* Yeah, it's going to be amazing to have this conversation with him. Super looking forward to it. Not. But it just has to be done. "I really need to talk to him."

"Oh!" she says excitedly, clapping her hands. "He's over *there*, with *Eloise*." She points toward a corner of the apartment with a slender and perfectly manicured finger, her smile like the Cheshire cat's, wide and wicked.

Oh, no.

I whip my head around and see them in a corner, Eloise's back to the wall and Josh leaning over her, brushing her hair off her face. Her eyes are on his lips, and his are on her bright-red smirk.

Oh my God, they're gonna kiss.

But I guess I've said it aloud, because I vaguely hear Jane say, "I know, right? Eloise's been trying to get with him since forever, but it always seemed like he was more into you. I wonder what happened to make him finally go for it, though."

No, no, no. Look away, Penny. Look away.

But I can't.

And then I see it. And I wish I hadn't. Because, Jesus, I've never felt anything like this.

They're suddenly kissing, and her hands are linked behind his neck, and his finger is hooked into the loop of her jeans while his other arm is wrapped around her waist.

I have to actually look down to check that I'm not bleeding out, because it feels like someone ripped out my heart from my chest and left me to die. I can't breathe. I feel gutted and raw.

Jane clears her throat, and the fog lifts slightly. "Whoops, sorry, what did you say?" I ask, but my voice sounds distant even to my own ears.

"I asked whether you were okay." She shakes my shoulder to get me to look at her.

"I'm fine, Jane." I try to at least remain expressionless, even though I'm about two seconds from wailing and running out of this apartment, jumping in a cab, slipping into my jammies, and calling my best friend, Amir from Domino's, to bring me my usual pizza, cookies, and soda. "Happy birthday," I say.

She frowns and shakes her head. "Darling, you've said that already."

I force a smile. "I know, doll. Just restating the important things tonight." I take a sharp, deep breath. "Listen, I think I'm going to go look for Oliver, given that Josh seems to be busy at the moment. You seen him?"

"Bedroom." I lift my eyebrow at her. *I'm not going in there, buddy.* But she gets what I mean and rolls her eyes at me, "Not like *that*. He was on the phone with someone."

I laugh and kiss her on the cheek. "Alright, crazy girl. I'll see you around. Enjoy your party, and please note that I owe you a gift."

"I'll hold you to that!" she yells as I walk away toward the bedroom, where I find Oliver sitting on the bed on top of a pile of coats.

"Hello, lover," I say in a jokingly seductive voice.

His head whips up to look at me, but I immediately see he's not in a joking mood. "Now's not the time, Penny," he mutters, his brows pulled together in a deep frown.

I sit next to him as he sighs frustratedly. "It's never the fucking time anymore, Oliver. Are we gonna talk about this or not?" We've been avoiding it for far too long, ever since he left my apartment to take a walk the night that he found out what happened. It hasn't been easy on him, I know. But it sure as hell hasn't been easy for me, and I miss him so much.

"I'd really rather not, to be honest." He gets up and starts pacing in front of me, but I reach out and grab hold of his hand to stop him.

"Listen. Jesus, I don't know how many more times I can tell you this. It. Wasn't. Your. Fault."

He looks miserable.

"I just..." He sighs and runs his fingers through his hair. "I know. Logically, I know. But my dick doesn't know that."

I laugh once in shock. "Excuse me, what?" His face turns beet red, something I've only seen happen once to him, and that was during an embarrassing moment for him while having sex. We had just had Mexican food before, and just as he was about to come, he farted the loudest fart I have ever heard in my life (it wasn't the most pleasant smelling, either). I wasn't able to finish because I was laughing so hard, but I don't regret it because it may have been one of the funniest experiences of my life.

"What do you mean *your dick doesn't know*?" I try to contain my laughter because, honestly, what the hell is he talking about? I'm really struggling to stay in control.

He sits back down on the bed, hands on his head, fingers running through his hair. He takes a deep breath, and I pat his back, attempting to be reassuring. He mumbles something I don't understand, and when I shake him a bit too roughly and tell him to spit it out, he screams, "I can't bloody finish! Not since the night I found out! Alright?"

It's dead quiet in the bedroom.

Oliver plays it off like he's super tough, but I know him better than that. I know he's been having a hard time, especially if he hasn't been able to gain relief. "Like, not even alone? By yourself?" I ask in a small voice.

He blows air out his mouth without ever looking at me. "Nope. Nothing."

"Shit," I say, genuinely concerned. This is very out of character for him. "Well, don't you think it's—"

He lifts a hand to shut me up. "You don't need to psychoanalyze me, yeah? I know what this is. But I don't know how to fix it."

"Uh, dumbass," I say, punching him in the shoulder. "Maybe if you had talked to me and would stop avoiding me, you would have been able to save yourself from the torture of not being able to come?" I try to speak in a joking tone, but we both know this is a tough conversation that we should have had a while ago. Not just about Tom but about what we mean to each other. "I love you, you know?" I lean my head on his shoulder and hold his hand. "And I am so fucking thankful to have met you and to have a friend like you." He picks up my hand and kisses it.

"Even if I ruined your life?" he murmurs.

"Are you kidding?" I straighten. "You helped *bring* me back to life!" I grab his chin and make him look at me. His eyes are red, and there are deep dark circles under them. "I was an even bigger mess than I am right now! And here I am, not much has changed except for the fact that I now have the strength to say '*fuck off*' to everyone in my life who has ever drained me of energy and just do my own thing.

"If I hadn't come here to London and the Tom thing would've happened with some other asshole, I'm pretty sure I would not have been able to survive it. You taught me to believe in myself and be strong."

God, we should have done this ages ago. Where have I been?

He looks like a man carrying the weight of the world on his shoulders, and of course his psyche is punishing him, taking away his favorite thing in the world, that thing that is related to what hurt me. He looks like he hasn't slept in weeks. It sounds dumb, but it is this second right here when I realize for the first time that what happened with Thomas Delancey affected more people than just me. Tom violated me, made Oliver question his trust in certain friendships, Josh and my other friends were concerned, and I'm sure if you asked some of the girls, at least one of them would sadly say that it had brought up memories of their own experiences, because statistically speaking, at least one of my friends has probably gone through something similar.

He laughs once. "I *told* you my dick was magic." We both laugh, and I roll my eyes at him. God, it feels good to laugh with him.

"Seriously, though, dude. We're good. We're more than good. We're perfect."

"Good." He kisses my hand again.

"But we're definitely not having sex again," I clarify. I meant it when I said that the next guy I sleep with has to be *the* guy— or at least the right guy for that moment. Not a random person and not a booty call.

"I understand where you're coming from, but I'm available if you change your mind," he says with a wicked gleam in his eyes. Oliver did always have a tendency to be able to bounce back quickly.

"I'm on a *No Casual Sex* policy. Sorry, bro."

Twenty-Seven

AS OLIVER and I leave Jane's bedroom, hand in hand, I see Josh coming out of the bathroom across the hall—alone. An image of Josh and Eloise kissing flashes through my head, and I suddenly feel nauseated. My heart stops and so do my legs. I seem to have forgotten how to walk, because I keep trying to move and nothing happens.

Josh seems to be suffering from the same affliction since he, too, stands still in the middle of the doorway, one foot in the bathroom, the other in the hallway, unmoving. His eyes are wide, gaze locked on mine until it drops to my hands, which are currently intertwined with Oliver's.

This isn't necessarily weird for Oliver and me, as we have a very touchy friendship, but I believe that in the current climate of the Penny-Josh relationship, it might not look great. I mean, the more I think about it, the man just gave me a notebook about twenty-four hours ago, bearing his soul to me, and now I am leaving a room with a guy I've been known to have casual sex with on a regular basis?

And he still doesn't know I'm not leaving.

Josh's eyes narrow into a menacing look. I can tell he's trying to control himself, to not say what he wants to say, but ultimately, he breaks and says, "One last goodbye before she goes, huh?" His words are like daggers, cutting through every inch of my skin, and I wince.

"Pardon?" Oliver says with an edge in his voice, tightening his grip on my hand.

"I'm just saying," Josh says, shrugging. "Did you guys have a final romp before she leaves? A parting of legs and ways?"

I gasp.

What the actual fuck? Who the fuck is this guy?

Also, wasn't he just hooking up with that chick, like, half an hour ago? And we are absolutely nothing to each other. He has no right to talk to me or Oliver that way whatsoever.

Oliver closes his eyes and rubs his forehead with a small, unfriendly smile on his face. "Mate, you're gonna want to take that back."

"Josh..." I say softly, calmly. I'm scared. Neither of them has had a release of their frustrations. Oliver has been wrecked with guilt, and Josh is just pissed off at me. I haven't been able to talk to him all night. He's been too fucking busy in a liplock with Miss Slutty Lipstick. "Josh, I'm not—I mean, we weren't—"

Oliver interrupts me. "You don't need to justify anything to him," he says, which annoys me because I'm trying to calm them both down, and they're just going to end up fighting over a non-issue, all because Josh won't even talk to me.

"I'm just saying, Penny, you could've shown me a bit of respect, I don't fucking know." Josh raises his hands as if I were pointing a gun at him. "But, hey, don't mind me. You can be fucked by whomever you want. I don't get a say in anything here." We've started to garner a crowd. Josh is drunk and loud, and we're quickly becoming the prime entertainment of the party, the main show. "I just have to sit by and watch it all happen while everyone but me gets a turn."

Oliver finally lets go of me and grabs Josh by his shirt collar. He's not that much taller than Josh, but he is definitely broader, more muscular. For a brief second, my stomach churns at the thought of Oliver and Josh getting into a real physical altercation, but Josh doesn't fight him. He's already defeated; he's got no fight in his eyes. Oliver thankfully drags him by the shirt and forces him into the bedroom, away from prying eyes, where

I follow close behind. Josh is pushed down on the bed where he settles into a sitting position at its edge.

I don't know what to say. I don't know who goes first. Do I say something?

Oliver crosses his arms across his chest and looks down at Josh. He doesn't look like someone who wants to beat the crap out of the other guy. He looks like an older brother trying to keep his younger brother calm and in check. I've seen it in real life at home.

"Are you going to apologize to her?" Oliver asks in a grave voice.

Josh doesn't look up. In fact, it looks like he just about found the most interesting spot to look at in the world in Jane's fuzzy white carpet, because nothing's gonna get him to move his gaze from there. Oliver kicks Josh's shoe, signaling that he expects an answer.

Josh still doesn't look up, but he rubs his eye and sniffs. "Did she tell you she's dropping out? That she's moving back to New York?"

Oliver uncrosses his arms and looks at me in shock. "Is that true?"

I sigh. "No," I say to Oliver and kneel in front of Josh. "Josh, *no*. That's what I've been trying to tell you all night, but you've been busy with…other things."

Josh scoffs. "Right, because you haven't," he says with a glance and nod to Oliver.

"Oliver and I needed to have a serious talk as well—one that was not appropriate to have in front of other people. Not that that's any of your business, anyway." I can't just let him get away with what he said. "You had no right to say those things to us, Josh. No right."

"I'm drunk," he says petulantly, looking down again.

"Not good enough, mate," Oliver growls. He looks more grizzly bear than teddy bear tonight.

I look over my shoulder to Oliver, still kneeling in front of

Josh, and ask him to leave us alone so that we can talk. There's so much that needs to be said now.

"Josh," I start. "Let me start off by saying that you were right. I was running away, and it was not the correct way to handle what was going on in my life. I do have to learn how to handle my issues and work them out like a grownup, get help and all of that. So, I've decided to stay, to finish out my degree and graduate. I think that it doesn't necessarily have to be a waste of money. I can, of course, use this degree to my advantage and find a job here in London. Set some roots down, you know? So, I'm done running away. I definitely don't want to go back to New York."

I take a deep breath before continuing.

"Second, your notebook was *beautiful*. I mean it. Every word. Even the *fucks* and the *hells*." I get a smile out of him for that one. "I loved reading every damn word of it," I say with fervor, because it's true. It killed me to read them, but the words in that notebook filled my heart with love and hope until it exploded and reality seeped in.

I pause before continuing, and he senses what I'm going to say next. He drags his fingers through his hair and finally looks up at me again. "But?" he asks.

I take a deep breath to steel myself before saying the words I know will hurt both of us because they're lies. "But I don't feel the same way." *I'm lying, Josh. Tell me I'm lying. Push me, and I'll confess.* "I love you like a friend. I just don't see us together that way." The words come out choked and rough. I don't think I've ever had a harder time getting a sentence out of my mouth.

I hate it.

I hate every second of the last fifteen minutes.

He takes a deep breath and looks out Jane's bedroom window. "It was worth a shot, right? Being with you would've been great." He stares back at me with those beautiful eyes of his, lighter today than usual, green-gold instead of malachite.

"But you're with Eloise now?" I ask.

Please say no. Please say no.

He shrugs. "Not really. She's cute, but whatever."

I sigh, half relieved, half disappointed in him for treating her like a random hookup when she's clearly been after him for a while.

He sighs and dips his head between his shoulders, avoiding eye contact. "I'm so fucking sorry. I was hurt and embarrassed over that stupid notebook. So, I went to Eloise, and it was a mistake. So immature. I stopped it about five seconds later and went to the bathroom to clean that idiotic lipstick off my mouth. What even *is* that? What guy wants to look like a clown after kissing a girl? 'Cause that's what I looked like." He throws his hands up in frustration. "Anyway, I was upset and went looking for you because Jane had mentioned you were around, and then I saw you and Oliver leaving the bedroom together, holding hands, and it just sucked, you know? I was way out of line—again. And a complete and total asshole."

I nod. "You're right. You were a *complete* asshole, Josh."

He nods, and we're quiet for a moment, neither of us looking at the other. My thighs start to burn from the strain, so I change positions and sit cross-legged in front of him by the bed.

"You know," he starts, "I used to think you were just in denial." I swallow the knot in my throat. He laughs gently. "Maybe I was the one in denial."

I reach out and hold one of his hands in both of mine. "It's fine. Please. This doesn't have to change anything between us." My voice breaks, and I'm so close to crying. "We don't have to stop being friends. We can still hang out."

He looks up at me, alarmed. "Stop being friends? Of course not. Jesus. Didn't you get what I said in that damn notebook? The reason I never pushed it was because you are—and have always been—my priority. Having you in my life is my priority. And that still applies here and now. Friends or...you know, *not* friends. I want you in my life any way I can have you."

My heart squeezes in my chest, and I feel like throwing up.

The gut-punch feeling is back, except this time it feels like someone's using my insides as a punching bag, hitting over and over again.

"So, we're good?" he asks. "You're staying? We're still friends? You're not gonna get all weird on me?"

I take a deep breath and try to smile. "Totally. I'm not going anywhere, and we're good." I pat our hands with my free hand, and he helps me up from my sitting position. "I just need a minute," I say as he opens the door and motions for me to go ahead of him. He nods, understanding, and walks out, closing the door behind him.

I throw myself on the bed on top of all the coats.

Jesus.

Never a dull moment in the life of Penny Márquez.

Oliver seems to be in a better place with the whole Tom thing after our talk, which is huge. I wouldn't have been able to stand it if he had kept going on like that, because he doesn't deserve it. Despite *The Incident*, I honestly don't think I've ever felt stronger than I do today—even with the Josh thing.

Falling for him has been eye-opening. It's shown me exactly how wrong Austin and I were for each other and that maybe I was just upset over losing a determined future but not the person himself. The attachment I feel for Josh is incomparable, to be honest. Austin showed me what I didn't deserve out of a relationship, and Josh has shown me what I want in one.

There's no person who understands me as well as he does. He's had me pegged since the beginning—that I liked him but was in denial. He's more aware of me and my feelings than I am myself! But I agree with him. Having each other in our lives is more important than risking losing each other for good over a failed romantic relationship.

The risk is too high.

No Dating Josh. Penny's new policy implementation.

Twenty-Eight

"I SWEAR TO GOD, if Chloe forgets the wine again, I'm gonna murder her," I say, about to have an anxiety attack. "We should've gotten one to drink between the two of us while we cooked today so we could have at least secured our own buzz," I say to Jane as I open the oven door to baste the turkey.

It's been a couple of weeks since her birthday, and things seem to have settled down a bit between Josh and me. We swept the whole notebook thing under the rug and were even able to finish our presentation for Strategic Management early, like we planned. Six weeks ago, I would have thought that would be great, because more time for fun! Right? Except it wasn't, because it's become harder and harder to find ways to see and hang out with him outside of class, and it's left more time open for me to pine over him.

Even though we agreed that "EVERYTHING IS OKAY!" between us and we can move on from this, the reality of the situation is that everything is *not* okay. Spending time with Josh has become this sort of contradiction. When I'm not with him, I crave his company to the point of it hurting. But then when we're together, the pain in my chest and the twisting in my stomach leaves me breathless. Needless to say, I've been a bit miserable, but I know that I'm doing the right thing by him. The last thing Josh needs right now is to get romantically involved with someone as complicated and messy as me. Josh deserves sweet and simple. Until I work more on myself, there's no way I can be good for anyone, let alone him.

Oliver, on the other hand, is still a little pissed at Josh and his overreaction to seeing us both leaving Jane's bedroom at her party. But I suspect it will all go away after a few glasses of wine have been had. I know them both pretty well, and they care too much about each other to let this argument go on any longer. They're a couple of softies.

I've been acting like everything has been freaking peachy up here in PennyLand, and I've been very convincing, actually. The unsolicited visits and the uninspired excuses behind them have come to a full stop. My friends only hang out with me now when they want to and vice versa.

I was able to thank them all in person at Jane's party individually. They were pivotal to my recovery, but after a while, they became a constant reminder, and I just couldn't have that. I needed to find a way to move on with my life. Thankfully, no one took offense, and they understood. As a thank you, I offered to host a Friendsgiving at my apartment, which is why I am currently about to lose my mind.

"There's no way we would've been able to get half the things done for this number of people with a buzz," Jane snorts. "No possible way."

I groan. "I know, but still!" Initially, I was going to keep it to six of my closest friends, but news spread, and I am now hosting a Thanksgiving dinner in my tiny apartment for twenty-two people! I even had to invite the weird guy from the Air Force since he overheard us talking about it after class last week. I couldn't say no to a fellow American!

And then, Allie's jet-setting boyfriend broke up with her and canceled their trip to Gstaad, so that was an extra person added to the dinner. Though, of course I don't really mind because she's obviously amazing, and I mean, it *is* her apartment too, to be fair. I just don't want her to feel awkward around all these people she doesn't know and then get overwhelmed by the mess. I even told her to stay in her room while we set everything up.

Eventually, the whole thing snowballed to a point where it had to be at least part potluck, part cooked by me, and part catered. I am doing the turkey, Josh is picking up the catered sides from Whole Foods, and then other people are bringing additional sides, alcohol, and desserts for after dinner.

Jane had come over earlier to help with the prep and the arrangements, but even with her assistance, I still haven't been able to get dressed for the night. I'm just a sweaty, messy-haired, unmade-up mess trying to cook and organize a dinner for too many people.

I am annoyed, that's for sure. I've never understood how anyone would think it's okay to invite themselves to another person's home. I mean, I understand that Brits don't celebrate Thanksgiving, but it's kind of a big deal to us, and they know it. *"Oh, you're hosting a Thanksgiving dinner. How nice! I'd love to come."* I think most of the non-Americans were kind of fascinated by the idea of being part of a holiday that has essentially turned into an excuse to eat obscene amounts of food all while celebrating a horrific and controversial part of American history. They saw a chance to be a part of it, and they took it.

Ugh.

Jane quickly wipes down the kitchen table and throws a tablecloth over it. I rush over with fancy disposable plastic forks, knives, plates, and glasses and try to arrange the table as prettily as possible. There is no fucking way I'm doing twenty-two people's worth of dishes. Our original plan was to have a sit-down dinner, all smushed together, but the table will now have to be used as a buffet, and dinner will be eaten on the couch, chairs, or standing up.

Deal with it, people.

We both hear the obnoxious buzzer alerting us to the first people to arrive.

"That better be the alcohol," I practically growl. "Can you get that? I need to get dressed," I say, looking down at my pajama bottoms. Jane nods with a grin, and I run into the bedroom to get dressed before someone catches me in my current state of disarray.

I've finally done my hair and makeup and am picking out what to wear when the door to my bedroom swings open, and someone quickly slips in. I practically throw myself into my closet, covering my body with scraps of fabric, and see a smirking Oliver standing by my bed.

"Dude, I am *nude*," I say, aghast. "What are you doing in here?"

He snorts and rolls his eyes. "You're not *nude*—I've definitely seen you in far less. Is that a new lingerie set? I've never seen it on you."

I roll my eyes, wrapping whatever I'm holding tighter to my body, fully aware that he's right, that he has seen me naked more times than I can count. But things are different now. I'm different now.

"I need to speak to you before you go out there," he says gravely.

I sigh, exasperated. "Fine, but can you please turn around so I can get dressed?" Oliver turns to face the closed door while I extricate myself from my closet and search for an outfit to wear tonight. "What do you need to talk to me about?"

I find a mod-inspired black dress with bell sleeves and a pom-pom trim which should go great with my cat-eye makeup and the half-up-half-down subtle bouffant I miraculously managed to execute in under fifteen minutes.

Oliver takes a breath and says, "So, Josh brought Eloise as a date tonight."

My stomach drops all the way to China, and I suddenly feel an immense urge to throw up.

"Huh. Good for him," I try to say as casually as possible. "Zip me up?"

I turn around, back facing Oliver, and watch him over my shoulder as he walks cautiously toward me, as if he's afraid to startle me.

"You're fine with this?" he asks, moving my hair out of the way so it doesn't get caught in the zipper.

I try to remain expressionless, but I can feel myself wincing, hoping Oliver can't see. "Yes. I'm okay with this in the sense that I'm glad that he's moving on." He finishes zipping me up and fastening the hook, so I turn to look at him. "Am I *happy* about who he's with? No. I think he could do way better, but whatever."

He raises an eyebrow at me, skeptical. "What about you? You're not upset because it's not you?"

"I don't want to talk about this. You know how I feel."

"Yes, but he doesn't know how you feel, and you could easily be with him right now if you told him the truth."

"But I don't want to be with him. Jesus, don't you get it?" I'm really upset and annoyed now. "I'm no good for him right now. No good for anyone. I need space and time to process what happened and what my next steps are. I'm not going to half-ass a relationship with him right now. I wouldn't be able to give him what he deserves. I feel like half a person now." I take a deep breath and shake my head, taking a seat on the edge of my bed. Oliver settles right next to me.

"Okay." He wraps an arm around me, and I lean my head on his shoulder. "Alright."

"Thanks," I say. "At least you warned me they are here together. I don't think I would've been able to look unaffected if I saw them making out again—especially not in my own home. Now I'm mentally prepared to endure that horror."

He laughs and smacks my thigh before getting up, but his smile evaporates just as quickly. "Um, your dress. It's, uh, short. A bit too short." He points to my upper thigh, and I look down.

The bite mark on my thigh.

Yup. Still there.

I sigh and try to pull the hem down, but it's no use. This is a real mini-dress and is unable to hide the actual evidence left behind from my night with Thomas Delancey.

"I'll wear tights underneath to cover it up," I mutter and push him out of my bedroom so I can finish getting dressed. Plus, I definitely need a moment to prepare myself for the rest of the night. I can hear the people slowly starting to arrive and the buzz of conversation and the occasional laughter. From what I can smell, the turkey is close to being done, and the sides and appetizers have arrived. Hoping the music has been turned on by Allie and not by someone who took liberties with my sound system, I shake myself off a little and open my door to host my first Thanksgiving dinner.

Twenty-Nine

IF ELOISE EVER MURDERS ME, I doubt anyone tonight would find fault in her doing so. I mean, I fully realize that what Josh and I were doing was kind of wrong. But it's not like we meant to do it. I absolutely meant what I said to Oliver: I have no intention of starting something with Josh—at least not right now. But something weird happened tonight that shook up our friendship and turned us into a partnership of sorts.

I think it's Thanksgiving's fault. I really do.

I mean, I was technically supposed to do all the hosting since it is my place (Allie had been relieved of those duties for obvious reasons, and I'm glad she was since she's spent most of the night flirting with Oliver), but I desperately needed a co-host. Someone who knew how to carve the turkey and defend our American holiday from the ball-busting Brits whenever they criticized us for celebrating a genocide. (which, it totally is —but I like Thanksgiving because it's when I feel closest to my family, and fuck me if I didn't miss them). And I was definitely not going to enlist the help of the psycho Air Force guy.

Anyway, so it organically just spiraled into a weird co-hosting situation. I mean, Josh knows my kitchen in and out since he's been over so many times, we're obviously comfortable with each other, and I guess the adrenaline of having so many people around kind of made us forget that A) he had brought a date, who he had completely ignored for most the night, and B) the whole awkwardness of the love letters and where we currently stood in our friendship.

In all honesty, it's been like playing house, and I really, *really* haven't wanted to stop. I want him to stay after everyone leaves and rub my feet as we break down everything that happened at dinner—who came, what they said, who went home together. I want us to pick at the leftovers late at night in our jammies, cuddled up on the couch. I want to drag ourselves to bed, too full and tired to have sex but still managing to find the energy because we care about each other so much.

But nope. That is definitely not going to happen tonight. So, yeah, I fucked up and let it get to this point because I knew I was never going to get that part after the dinner party—the true intimacy part of the night. That part is for Eloise—if Josh ever realizes that he needs to stop paying attention to me and needs to start paying attention to her tonight, that is.

"I need to talk to you," Oliver says as I start serving the dessert.

"I'm kind of busy," I say, pointing at the pies and the line of people in front of me, waiting for a piece.

With a glance in their direction, Oliver tells the group of people waiting on the pumpkin and pecan that they can serve themselves and promptly pulls me by the elbow into my bedroom.

"Jesus Christ!" I say, pulling my arm from his grip once we are safely locked inside. "What is up with you tonight?"

"Are you going to pursue Josh or not?"

"I'm sorry, am I having a déjà vu episode here or what? Did we not have this conversation, like, *two hours ago*? No. I do not intend to pursue anything with him." I exhale, exasperated. I'm so over this topic I could scream.

"Then what in the bloody hell are you doing out there, Penny? You're ruining this night for him."

"What are you talking about? He's fine! He's been chilling with me all night."

Now it's his turn to be exasperated. Throwing his hands in

the air, he says, "Exactly! Exactly! He's been with *you* all night—not his hot date, not the woman he came with. Which, by the way, I know you're going to hate me for saying this, but I'm so bloody proud of him right now."

I put my hands on my hips and glare at him for that comment, even though I know he's right about the former.

"Fine, I see your point, but he's a grownup, you know? He can make his own decisions. And if he chooses not to spend time with his date, it's his fault, no?" I know I sound like a spoiled, jealous brat but fuck it. He was my friend first.

Oliver shakes his head. "No, because you know he can't say no to you—even if you don't even ask. You have to tell him no. Thank him for all of his help, but tell him that he needs to go back to his date and enjoy the rest of the night."

"But..." I start. I know he's right. I know that Josh would never abandon me in a time of need, and I guess I looked as overwhelmed as I felt over this stupid dinner, and he dropped his date to help me. Even if he is an adult who can make his own decisions, maybe he just doesn't realize that, when it comes to me, he always makes the wrong ones.

"Shit or get off the pot, mate," Oliver says simply.

"Right. Off the pot, then." I take a deep breath and walk out of the room, Oliver in tow.

I search for Josh and find him on pie duty while Eloise sits in a corner, alone with a drink, sulking and staring at him from across the room. No matter how I personally feel about her, it's not cool to be part of something that hurts another woman, you know? It was never my intention to hurt her, and it's something I need to fix this before it escalates.

I walk determinately toward Josh and take the pie cutter from his hands, ignoring the feeling in my stomach as our hands come into contact.

"Hey, why don't you get yourself a plate and go sit with your date. I don't think I've seen you guys together all night."

He sighs as if suddenly remembering. "I know. Poor Elle."

Elle? They're on a pet name basis now?

I swallow the lump in my throat and go on. "Yup, so just go ahead, and take her some pie, too."

He smiles, piles on a massive slice of pecan, grabs two forks, and walks toward Eloise. Her head pops up once she sees him walking toward her, and she smiles broadly, predatorily.

Ugh, I want to cry.

"I'm thankful *foooorrr...*" Chloe taps her finger to her lips, thinking. "...testing out of having to take Quantitative Research Methods and Statistics next semester," she says with a massive smile on her face.

Jane and I groan in unison, and I throw a balled-up napkin at her face. The two classes Chloe's talking about are the most dreaded in the entire program. The department offered the chance to test to opt out of having to take the classes for those who thought they could, but only Chloe was able to qualify.

We're all absolutely jealous of her now.

"What is it you Americans say? Don't hate the player, hate the game?" she says with a smirk.

I snort. "Literally no one says that."

Most of my guests have left already, which I don't mind. Allie went to bed with Oliver's number and a huge smile on her face, so it's just Chloe, Jane, and me.

I like this part of the night. It's more intimate. And I've missed some good girl time.

The turkey has been massacred, and the yams and the string beans have all but disappeared along with the stuffing and scalloped potatoes. And the pecan and pumpkin pies are being polished off as we go around the room and say what we're thankful for.

"What are *you* thankful for then, Penny?" Chloe asks with a smirk.

I glare back at her. To be honest, I have a lot to be thankful for this year. School (with reservations), for one. The fact that I'm able to go to a graduate program abroad is pretty sick. And yeah, it's unfortunate that I'm not able to spend this holiday with my immediate family, but I was able to form a mini-family here and celebrate with them—and the unwelcome extras.

"I'm thankful for *you*, Chloe," I say with a smirk. "Because now I've officially designated you as part of my clean-up crew before you leave."

I really don't mean it since almost everything we used is disposable and compostable. All I need to do is toss the garbage and put the leftovers in containers.

I check the time on my phone. "Actually, guys, it's almost two," I say. "Do you mind if I kick you guys out? I'm exhausted, and I'm sure Jane is, too."

Jane rolls to a sitting position from where she was on her back and agrees. "*YES*. I either go to bed right now, or I'll be up until five. And I have an essay to write tomorrow, so I would rather not be hungover and tired tomorrow."

"Noted," Chloe says, getting to her feet.

Jane and Chloe mercifully depart soon after I reassure them that I do not need any help cleaning up. I think this was the one instance where I was happy to do so, since it gave me a kind of active quiet time. Sure, I don't have the partner I crave or his company to share the post-party breakdown, but I can just as well go through it by myself.

I manage to clean up in under fifteen minutes, tossing everything into garbage bags, not giving a shit about leftovers (don't judge—there were barely any left). I must have broken a record.

Exhausted, I slip into my pajamas, aching for my bed, when my phone rings.

Josh.

I hesitate. Should I pick up? It's a quarter to three. This must be important.

"Are you okay?" I answer.

"Buzz me up. I'm downstairs," he says simply and hangs up.

Okay.

I walk over to the intercom, incredibly confused, and buzz the outside gate open, which was thankfully fixed a couple of days ago. I unlock the top and bottom locks of the door and remove the security chain. The *woosh* of the elevator sounds loudly as it rises to reach my floor and my hands shake in anticipation.

When Josh walks out of the elevator a moment later, brows furrowed, forehead creased, my stomach turns. I know he didn't come back because he left something behind. His eyes meet mine as he walks over to the door with determination, frown deepening. I freeze in the doorway, nervous, but he just pushes by me into my apartment.

I gently close the door, taking my time to lock it, preparing myself to hear whatever it is he came here to say—because I know it won't be easy to hear.

With a shuddering breath, I turn to find him much closer than I expected. I feel the heat of his body radiating over me, the energy of whatever he's been keeping inside electrifying the air around us.

We look at each other in silence for a moment, until he breaks it with a simple, "Hey. I think we need to talk." His voice shakes a little, betraying the composure he tried so hard to keep.

I put my index finger to my lips and mouth, "*Allie.*" He nods in understanding, and we quietly walk over to my room.

I jump a little as the door clicks shut, the knowledge that Josh and I are alone and locked in my bedroom sinking in. Suddenly, I am *extremely* aware of the queen-sized bed located right smack in the middle of the room. A familiar pressure in my chest starts to build, the feeling of complete panic, but excitement flooding my system at the same time, confusing me. As my eyes rake over Josh's body, the white-and-blue floral duvet cover looks more welcoming than it ever has, inviting forbidden fantasies I haven't let myself think about. *Much.*

Despite having spent the entire day cooking and cleaning, feeling more exhausted than I remember being in a long time, I suddenly find myself reenergized. Josh's presence has given me a second wind, for which I am so thankful because I could not have dealt with this in my previous state of fatigue.

"*Soooo...*" I drag the word out, waiting for him to say something.

"Right." Josh nods, bobbing his head, but doesn't say anything else. He looks down to avoid my gaze, he stops at my top, eyes widening briefly before he controls his expression.

At first, I blush because I think he's shocked by my super-lame-but-cute *Aristocats* pajamas covered in white cats (Marie is one of my favorite Disney characters), until I realize I'm not wearing a bra under the white top. Flushing an even deeper red, I cross my arms over my chest as casually as possible.

His cheeks redden, and he groans, closing his eyes, running both hands through his hair. I know him well enough by now to know that something is really bothering him, that he's extremely frustrated and stressed. I mean, obviously—it doesn't take a genius to figure that out. He's here in the middle of the night, so there's that.

"Josh?" I ask. "Listen, it's getting pretty late, so if you're not gonna—"

He blows out a breath. "Stop. I will. Just give me a second to organize my thoughts."

Now I'm just annoyed. You'd figure that when someone decides to make a surprise visit at three in the freaking morning, they'd at least know what the hell they're going to say. I roll my eyes, at a complete loss.

"You and me," he says, pointing back and forth between us. "We need to talk about you and me."

Gut punch. The air is knocked out of me, but I swiftly recover.

"I thought we talked about this already. Why are you bringing this up again?" I can hear it in my voice—the warning, the venom.

Don't do this, Josh. I will shut you down and end this friendship if I have to.

He shakes his head, desperate. "No," he says. "No, no, no. *No.*"

I glare at him. "What do you mean '*no*'? We talked about this, Josh. There is no 'you and me'."

He scoffs. "You're so full of shit, you know that?"

Now I'm pissed.

"Alright, time to go," I say, grabbing him by the shoulders, trying to spin him around and push him out my bedroom door, but he slips away from me.

"No, we're gonna talk about this."

"I don't even know what '*this*' you're talking about," I lie.

"I'm not leaving until you listen to me, because *I know* that I'm not crazy."

I sigh and look out the window at Canary Wharf. I can see the KPMG and Barclays buildings in the distance, which will soon be filled with employees in just a couple of hours, thanks to their miserable working schedules. Miserable as they are, I would trade places with them in a heartbeat just to avoid having this discussion right now.

"So, after I picked up the food before dinner, I went to pick up Eloise, and we hung out at her place for a while—"

I put my face in my hands and groan silently. I really don't want to hear this.

"See? That reaction right there tells me that you're definitely full of shit."

"Can we speed this up? I'm tired and want to go to sleep," I say impatiently. He looks tired, too, but in a different kind of way. In a way that tells me he's done fighting this silent battle with me and the wall I built up. I imagine Josh as Andy Drufresne from *Shawshank Redemption,* trying like hell to dig his way out of the prison cell now known as the *Friend Zone,* only to be told time and time again by me to fuck off.

He sighs loudly, eyes wide. "Goddammit! Just listen to me, alright?" He runs his fingers through his hair again, agitated. "So, I'm at Eloise's, and we're on her couch." *I'm gonna throw up. I swear I'm gonna throw up the ten million pounds of food I just ate all over Josh.* "And her hand is on my thigh, and she's talking, and I'm looking at her lips, and it's obvious we're about to kiss, and all I'm thinking about is how I'm gonna have to figure out a way to clean my lips of her stupid fucking bright-red lipstick without using sandpaper because, Jesus Christ, that shit takes forever to come off. But I felt like I really didn't have a choice because she kept talking and talking and—it sounds awful—but I wasn't really listening, or I was trying not to, because I kept comparing her to you, and that's not fair to anyone—especially not her. So, I pulled back right before our lips touched and told her I didn't want to keep you waiting and that we needed to go to your place immediately because of the food I was in charge of bringing. As you can guess, she didn't take that too well, so my night started off rocky to begin with."

He stops to take a deep breath and looks out the window. "Tonight was our third date, did you know that?"

I gasp a little. I feel like someone just stabbed me.

Excuse me, they've been going out on dates? I thought they had hooked up at Jane's and that was it. I thought this was their first date. Since when have they been actively dating?

"No," I say quietly. "I did not know that."

"Yeah." He nods, his gaze locking on mine. "So, you can imagine Eloise had some expectations on how tonight would go."

I know what a third date means.

Oh no.

"And I think we both know that I didn't exactly live up to them."

He spent all night with me. He barely even looked twice at her all throughout dinner until I told him to go sit with her after Oliver's intervention and she had looked miserable for most of the night.

I don't like her at all, but I know that is mostly out of jealousy. She doesn't deserve to feel like crap. It isn't her fault that she is dating the same guy I am falling for. She and I aren't friends and never have been—it's not the same situation as Claire. *She* is the wronged one here.

I should've known better.

"Oh," I say simply.

"Yes. *Oh.*"

We're quiet for a second. I think neither of us knows exactly what to say. I can feel him building up the confidence to finish what he came to talk about, and I don't want him to stop, but mostly because I need him to finish so that he can leave.

"We got to your place, and it was like...like I couldn't help myself. I saw you stressed and working so hard to make sure everyone was enjoying themselves and looking so fucking beautiful that it knocked the air out of me that I just couldn't help myself. I was drawn to you, like I always am, and I wanted to help you, to be the person you could rely on.

"I expected you to kick me out of the kitchen after a few minutes, but I told myself I would help as much as you let me, which I figured wouldn't be long. You usually freak out from our closeness, something I used to interpret as a negative reaction toward my feelings for you, like you were making sure to draw a line and tell me that you and I weren't on the same page. So, I never expected you to let me stand by your side and work together like that for most of the night."

He pauses.

"But here's the thing I figured out tonight, Penny." He takes a deep breath as my heart is going a million miles a minute. "You were so wrapped up in making everything perfect and so distracted by everyone that you forgot." He takes a step closer to me, and I can smell his signature scent of shampoo and cologne. "You forgot to push me away and make me believe that you only care about me as a friend. You didn't notice how you would touch my arm and shoot me a flirty appreciative look after I took something heavy from your hands and carried it for you. You didn't notice how you jumped in my arms and hugged me when I carved the turkey for everyone. You didn't notice all the smiles and laughs we exchanged. And you certainly didn't notice how you never backed away from *my* smiles, *my* touches, or even *my* embraces."

I flash back to my shared moments with Josh, and I guess we did flirt and touch a lot more than normal. I mean, it was obvious enough that Oliver had to intervene, but I guess not obvious enough to me.

Oh, God. What have I done?

He takes another step toward me, and I realize I should maybe recoil, but my brain seems to be unable to communicate this action to my legs, because they remain unmoving.

"I know it was wrong of me to leave Eloise like that. I am perfectly aware that it was a dick move, but there was no way I was going to give those moments up. No fucking way."

I say nothing, scared to even breathe. *Deny 'til you die*, I try to remember. Don't cave. It's for his own good.

"And then," he continues, "something happened." He runs

his hands through his hair in frustration. "I don't know what or who made you realize what was happening, but you suddenly realized what you were doing." He shakes his head. "Sorry, *doing* isn't the right word—that implies intent or consciousness. But that's the best way I can put it."

I press my lips together, tightening my arms across my chest.

"You told me to walk away, to go back to my date, and I did. I took the win and walked back to my very unhappy date." He half-smiles, staring at me with those gold-green eyes.

I start tapping my foot as he starts walking back and forth in front of my bed.

My bed.

I try to avoid eye contact with it and Josh, looking anywhere else. In doing so, my eye catches my black lace bra hanging on the back of my chair. My eyes widen, and I rush to it when Josh's back is to me, stuffing it under my crossed arms.

"I don't know if you noticed, but we left shortly after."

I manage to shake my head. After I sent Josh away and back to Eloise, I did my very best to ignore them. I honestly didn't realize that they were gone until I caved and started looking for him at around midnight. I was a bit devastated that he had left without saying goodbye. But I didn't want to dwell, didn't want to think about where they were or what they were doing.

"Elle and I grabbed an Uber and went back to her place. Did you know she lives in Chelsea?"

Of course she does. *Of course* she lives in one of the nicest neighborhoods in London. I bet her apartment is all white and modern, and perfectly organized, and she has a cleaning lady, and her fridge is full of organic produce, and she doesn't even need a roommate, and drinks green juices and cleanses, and does yogalates.

The only yogalates I do is wear yoga pants while drinking lattes.

I shake my head to rid myself of the petty thoughts running through my mind, but Josh takes it as an answer to his question.

"Yeah, she lives in Chelsea. So, we're on our way to her place in the Uber, she's snuggled up into my side, and I have my arm around her, and I'm thinking, '*Shit, I'm the worst date ever,*' because everywhere we drive by reminds me of you. And then we pass the Manolo Blahnik store, and I smile because I *know* how much you love those shoes, and I think about how crazy it is that me—a straight dude with absolutely no knowledge of fashion—knows this.

"And then I can tell we're near her house, because she starts sitting up and kissing my neck—"

"You know what?" I stop him. "It's really late, and I think I've heard enough, so you—"

"And she kisses my neck," he continues, ignoring me. I push by him and open the bedroom door. "But I start laughing, Penny. I start laughing because we just drove by *Bluebird*, that place that's always on that stupid reality show that you love so much." I stop and look at him, closing the door again. "Eloise looked up at me and asked what was so funny—naturally, since she was coming on to me and I was laughing hysterically. So, unthinkingly, I told her that something just reminded me of you and made me laugh. I was thinking of you while she was kissing me in a cab two blocks away from her apartment on our third date, and *I told her,*" he says as if in disbelief of himself.

Josh exhales. "I was a dick to her. I know I was. I just didn't realize it at the time." He looks disappointed in himself, because I know him, and I know he's not the type of guy to intentionally hurt someone. I know that, no matter how he feels about me, he probably feels horrible for tonight and how he made Eloise feel. "So even though she pretended to be okay with it when we got to her place, I definitely couldn't."

He stops in front of me again, so close I have to back up against the door. Has Josh always been this tall? I'm sure he must have grown a foot in the last fifteen minutes. Six inches, at least.

"So? What's your point?" I ask.

He sighs. "So, when we got to her place, I told her."

"Told her what, exactly?"

"Told her that I loved you, and I couldn't go out with her anymore."

I inhale sharply as I feel time stand still.

Did he seriously just…?

Josh and I look into each other's eyes, neither of us saying a word for the longest time.

"Oh," I finally say.

"Yeah," he seems to agree.

I shuffle uncomfortably from side to side, arms still crossed in front of my chest, trying not to look at him and failing miserably.

"She was upset, obviously," he continues. Josh looks so calm, not like a man who has just said *I love you* to someone with a high risk of getting rejected. He runs his fingers through his hair and looks down at my lips before continuing. "Rather than just taking the hit and asking me to leave, she said a few choice words." He clears his throat. "None that I didn't deserve, to be honest." He takes a deep breath, as if steeling himself. "She was right about everything, except for one thing." He raises his index finger. "She said that you didn't have feelings for me, that you didn't think of me that way, and that everyone knew it."

I jut my chin out and roll my shoulders back. "I don't," I lie.

Josh smiles sadly and reaches out to place a hand on my cheek, rubbing his thumb back and forth. I try my hardest not to lean in. "See, I think you're lying, Penny."

Don't cry. Don't cry. Don't cry.

He steps closer, putting his other hand on my hip.

"Josh…" I say, my voice breaking. "I don't—"

"It's okay. Stop. It's okay. I finally get it." He's so quiet. "I get it. I get why you don't want anything right now. I know you're freaked out after everything that happened. I finally figured it out. I *know* you."

I start crying, and he pulls me into his arms. "Shh, don't worry. I'm not going to pressure you into anything or ask you to make any decisions. But I just thought you should know that I love you, and I know you have feelings for me, too. And right now, that's enough for me."

I shake my head and push against him, but he doesn't let go. Instead, he moves his hands to my hips, thumbs rubbing the skin under my pajama top. "No, Josh." I look up at him. "It's not enough. That's the whole point. I can't give you what you need right now."

He closes his eyes and leans his forehead to mine. "I know you think that. But it's not about me. It's about you."

I laugh a little. "Did you just basically say, '*It's not me; it's you*'? Because I'm pretty sure the phrase is supposed to be the other way around."

Josh smiles broadly, eyes still closed. "I love that you can make jokes now," he says, chuckling. He takes a deep breath and kisses me on the corner of my mouth with the lightest touch.

My breath hitches.

"So, yeah," Josh says, his lips moving against mine as he speaks. "I just wanted to casually come by at three in the morning on Thanksgiving—or I guess it's the day after Thanksgiving?—to let you know that I love you, and I get why you don't want to be with me right now. That I'm okay with where we are, because I can wait. I can be patient."

It's flutter city all over my body.

What is happening? Is this real?

I close my eyes, feeling his breath all over my face coming out faster now.

He's going to kiss me. Oh my God. I'm not ready for this.

And it's like he reads my mind. He kisses my forehead instead, releases me, and takes a step back.

He's right. He does know me—more than I even suspected.

"Goodnight, Penny," Josh says quietly. He walks around me to open my bedroom door and shows himself out of my apartment, leaving me breathless and immobile as I try to process what just happened.

He loves me. And he says he'll wait.

Thirty

NEW YEAR'S EVE – *New York City*

Hiding in a corner at my family's party, I chug my second glass of champagne.

"You know, you're not supposed to do that until midnight," I hear my brother say from behind me.

I snort and turn to face him, taking another sip. "Don't worry about it, Simón. I'll have another when the ball drops, bro."

"That's not what I meant." He raises a black bushy eyebrow.

Both my brothers look like me, minus the chemically altered hair color (I'm definitely not a natural blonde). But Simón and I are so similar that we could pass for twins. We both have strong eyebrows and our father's square jawline (which I think fits him better than it does me), same dark-brown eyes and slightly toasted skin. We're almost even the same height. There's definitely no questioning that we're related.

I don't know whether that's a good or bad thing, but whatever. There are worse things than looking like Simón.

He leans against the wall next to me and crosses his arms, looking out at the crowd.

"How's therapy going?" he asks.

Simón is the only member of my family who I've told what happened these last few months with Tom and Josh. I called him the day after Thanksgiving, crying, and he found me a counselor to help guide me through recovery. One of his friends is a social worker who offers teleconference sessions, and I was able to secure two a week for the past month. We talk on Mondays and Thursdays, in the afternoon, and she's been amazing at helping me unpack and work through everything that's happened in the past eighteen months.

"Amazing. She's amazing. Thank you." I smile and squeeze his hand. "Camila's been kind of life-changing."

He chuckles. "Yeah, she's great." He sighs, his look far away.

I cock my head at him and smile. "You into her or something?"

He shrugs. "She's outta my league, dude."

I shake my head, taking two glasses of champagne from a waiter's tray. I hand one to Simón and say, "You're an idiot. She freaking idolizes you." I roll my eyes at him as I take a sip. "It's like I can't even bring you up without her swooning."

He smiles. "No shit! Really?" He takes a sip with a goofy smile on his face.

I laugh at his expression and bump him in the shoulder. "Come on, Sim. You should go for it. Seriously. Just don't fuck it up, because I don't want to get a new counselor."

He grimaces. "Then maybe it's not that great of an idea."

"Better to have loved and lost?" I ask with a smile.

It's funny, my brother has always been kind of an unintentional heartbreaker. Not because he's a player, but simply because he's such a good and reserved guy that he hesitates to pursue anyone he likes. I think, if he wanted to, he could get whomever he wanted just by how sweet he is.

Simón laughs at me, eyes crinkling. I've missed him so much.

"You ready to take your own advice?" he asks.

"You mean with Josh?" I raise an eyebrow.

He nods and takes another sip.

I take a deep breath and look down at my phone. There's a text notification from Josh that I haven't opened. Probably a

"*Happy New Year*" text, maybe an "*I miss you*"—he says it often —but I've rarely replied back.

It's been over a month since Josh showed up at my place in the middle of the night and told me he loved me, told me he'd wait until I was ready. But how long is he okay with waiting?

I thought, after our conversation, that things would have been even more painfully awkward, but honestly, it was like every single bit of that tension was gone because all our cards had been laid out on the table. I didn't need to constantly be aware of what I was saying or doing to hide my emotions. We were both aware of the other's feelings and had vowed it wouldn't get in the way of our friendship. And it really hasn't.

Shortly after Thanksgiving, finals started, which meant throwing ourselves into them, unable to place much focus on anything else. Between having to write fifteen-page essays and four-hour tests, I hadn't had the occasion to do anything except grab the occasional coffee break in the library. Truthfully, though, I welcomed the distraction. Even if I barely had time for a social life, let alone a love life.

My friends and I did have a mini-Secret Santa right before we left for break, but that was truly the only time we spent together in a social setting, and we did it the day before I left for New York in the Student Union with Oliver, Jane, and Chloe. I got Chloe a beginner's knitting kit (she's really into crafts), and my Secret Santa got me tickets to a special *Egyptian Mummies* exhibit at the British Museum (of which I was *incredibly* psyched to go to since I have an inkling that I might have been Egyptian royalty in a past life).

We said our goodbyes before leaving for winter break right after we were done with the gift exchanges with promises to stay in touch once he reached California and I went back to New York. It was short and sweet. He held me for a couple of minutes just outside the doors, away from the curious eyes of our friends, where I was able to snuggle into what I have now claimed as my little nook in between his shoulder and neck and inhale his signature scent.

"Camila thinks I'm ready," I say, staring into my glass, swishing its contents around a little.

"Do *you* think you're ready?" Simón asks carefully.

"I *want* to be. Yeah. Maybe I am?" I smile. "Maybe not ready to have sex yet, though."

"Gross," Simón says, grimacing. "Please don't say the word sex."

I laugh at how squeamish my brother is. It's so easy to rile him up.

"Sex, sex, sex, sex," I laugh, and he covers his ears with his hands, mouth twisting as if in pain. "Dude, relax!" I say, pulling on his arms.

"You're disgusting," he says.

"Thanks," I chuckle.

Simón checks his watch. "It's almost midnight. I'm gonna go find Mom. Come with me? I don't want you ringing in the New Year all depressed in a dark corner."

"I'm not depressed, nor will I ring it in in a dark corner. I'll meet you on the balcony. I just need to hit the ladies' room real quick."

He nods and walks away to where my parents and their guests are congregated to better view the fireworks once the clock strikes midnight. We're on the Upper East Side, so we won't really be able to see anything, but my parents have a tradition of making all their guests tie New Year's resolutions onto balloons and then releasing them at midnight. It's sweet and a tradition I actually enjoy, so I really don't want to miss it, but I want to catch Josh before the ball drops.

I sneak into my bedroom and shut the door behind me, opening his message.

JOSH

Hey. Long time no speak. Happy New Year.
Hope you're ringing it in with friends and
family.

ME

> Big party at home and kinda tipsy. HNY to you
> as well.

His reply is immediate.

JOSH

I know you're 3 hours ahead, but no spoilers,
ok?

I snort and bite my lip as I reply, nervous. What I told Simón is true. I think I *am* ready to try things out with Josh for real this time. I just need to find out whether he's still where he was at a month ago. He hasn't said 'I love you' since then, and neither have I. But I want this, and I think I want to lay the groundwork before I see him again in a couple of days.

ME

> LOL. Ok, I promise not to reveal anything.

> I have to go back to this party, but just wanted
> to say hi, wish you HNY, and say that I'm
> looking forward to seeing you again soon.

I can see he's typing and deleting a message over and over again from the three dots that keep appearing and disappearing on the screen. I hear someone call my name—my mother—and I run out of my bedroom. Two minutes to midnight! Maybe Josh's message got delayed due to congested lines.

I'm standing between my mother and Simón when I see the three dots stop completely.

"Ten, nine, eight..." the collective countdown begins.

He's not gonna reply back?

"...seven, six, five..."

Fuck it.

I need to stop being scared of everything and live life.

"...four, three, two..."

ME

> Let's do this. Let's go on a date when we get back.

"...one! HAPPY NEW YEAR!"

I smile and hug my parents first, followed by my brother, when I feel my phone vibrate. I smile, wanting to jump in place just from how giddy I feel right now.

I'm finally going on a date with Josh.

Simón looks at me inquisitively, and I point at my phone, ready to show him Josh's response.

But it's not from Josh...

AUSTIN

> HNY, baby. I miss you. Can we talk?

What?

Thirty-One

MY HANDS SHAKE as I reread the message for the fifth time. Hoping to control the tremor, I squeeze my hands together —but it's useless. My heart beats loudly against my chest as I try to control my breathing.

It's been so long since I've seen him, since I've seen those eyes, since I've been held by him...

God, what would I even say to him? Just, *"Hi"*? How anticlimactic. I've waited for this moment for so long, a simple greeting just doesn't sound right. How are you supposed to greet someone you've had feelings for after not seeing them for a while? Will it be weird?

Of course it will be weird, you idiot. It's not just any old date.

I pull a dress from my closet, hold it up to my body, and groan loudly in frustration at my reflection. Just like the other millions of outfits I've pulled since this afternoon, I hate it immediately and throw it over my shoulder.

"I have nothing to wear!" I stomp my foot like a two-year-old brat and whine to no one in particular.

I pick up my phone and FaceTime Simón. Thankfully, my brother picks up after the first ring.

"What?" he asks, bored.

"I'm freaking the fuck out here," I say, a second away from hyperventilating. "This can change everything. Like, what am I even *doing*?"

Simón snorts. "You're being a bit dramatic here, don't you think? I mean, you *chose* the guy. Just remember why you picked him. It's make-or-break time, kid," he says, taking a bite out of a sandwich, looking as casual as can be.

How does he not understand how important this dinner is tonight?

"Is that...is that a PB and J sandwich? Seriously?" I ask.

"Yeah, Mom made it for me. You jealous?" he asks with a smirk. Here I am, prepping for the most important date of my life (*okay, I'm being a bit dramatic*) and he's just relaxing, eating a sandwich.

"Not particularly at this moment, no. But if you ask me tomorrow, I might be. It's so hard to find peanut butter here." I sigh, appreciating the momentary distraction.

"I'm so nervous, bro."

"Relax," he says, annoyed. "Just be thankful you're not going out with that asshole who texted you on New Year's. Congrats, by the way. I'm so happy for how you handled the whole situation with Austin."

I snort, flipping through my closet in search of the perfect outfit. Blowing off Austin had honestly had been much easier than I thought. Since moving to London, I've actually feared speaking to Austin ever again, assuming the whole experience would shake me to the core. That it would derail all the personal growth I experienced over the past few months.

But when I received his text, though, I felt...nothing.

No. That's a lie. At first, I felt *curiosity*.

Why was he reaching out now? What had happened to Claire? Who the hell did he think he was?

I felt a few things, but none of it fell under or near love—or hatred, for that matter.

I felt nothing but curiosity.

"Yeah, that was a trip," I say with a laugh. "Thanks, by the way. I owe you and Alejandro one."

Austin had wanted to meet up to discuss our relationship, he said. He wanted to talk about getting back together and giving it a second chance—even if it was going to be long-distance. I had ignored his texts all night until he showed up at my parents' door at two in the morning, completely hammered.

"What the hell are you doing here?" I asked him as he stumbled out of the elevator and into my parents' party. I took him by the arm and dragged him into a corner, away from prying eyes. I didn't want him to make a drunken scene in front of everyone.

"I need to talk to you. I think I fucked up," he practically moaned, his hair was a mess, face unshaven, and there were bags under his eyes. He was wearing a tux, but his shirt was untucked, his shoes and pants covered in mud, and there was a tear in his jacket.

What the hell?

"No," I said. "It's fine. You did what you had to do, and now it's time for you to go." I tried dragging him by his overcoat, but he slipped out of it and away from me. I groaned.

"No. I don't want to go. We need to talk. I need to explain myself." He fisted his hand and shook it in the air.

Great. A drunk and belligerent Austin. My favorite.

I sighed and dropped his coat on a nearby chair. "Fine," I said. "Say your piece and get out."

Austin looked around the party and winced at the sight of both my brothers standing in a corner, staring at us from right across the room. Simón was average height and build, but Alejandro, my oldest brother, was six-five and built like a linebacker. Austin was a big guy, but he wasn't drunk enough to forget how easily my brothers could kick him out of here on his ass.

"Can we go to your room and talk?" he asked in cowardice.

I laughed once at the notion of ever having him near any bedroom of mine again. "Just say what you have to say before those guys over there kick you out."

He sighed and ran both his hands through his messy hair. "Okay, okay, but you gotta hear me out." He raised his hands as if to protect himself from an attack. "Promise."

"Jesus, Austin, calm down. I'm not going to shoot you." I rolled my eyes. "Just say what you need to say."

"Right. So, I wanted to say that...uh...first, you look really hot in that dress. Like, your ass is just..." He whistled. I felt my face redden in anger. I was used to being told things like that by Oliver, but *Jesus*, he never sounded so crude. "Wait, no." He shook his head from side to side. "I didn't mean for it to come out that way. Hold on."

Austin closed his eyes and leaned against the wall for balance while he held his head with his right hand. "Fuck, I'm so drunk. This is not coming out the way I wanted it to."

My annoyance was growing exponentially by the second. How was I ever in love with this guy?

"Okay, I got it." He took a deep breath, and I tilted my head toward him, waiting for him to say whatever he needed to say and leave. "I love you, and I fucked up. I should never have dated Claire, but, like, *dude*." He scoffed. "You were just *so much fucking work*, you know what I mean? And then she was just *there* once you were gone. And I thought, '*You know what would be cool? If I dated a regular chick for once*.' But baby," he said, reaching out for my hands, "it's always been you. I need someone crazy like you. You're the only girl that's my equal. That I can respect. That I want to be with. We belong together, baby."

I stared back at him, mouth gaping. I could hear my brothers behind me, laughing their asses off. Did he even hear the words that came out of his mouth just now?

You're the only girl that's my equal. That I can respect?

Who the hell *was* this guy? And what exactly did it say about me that I had dated him? Dear God, was he always such an idiot? It seemed like he had meant to be romantic, but his words lacked substance and were unintentionally insulting to women everywhere. I felt pure joy at the fact that I was able to clearly see Austin for who he really was: a fucking tool.

Despite his arrogance and ineptitude, I felt a little bit sorry for him. He was definitely going to regret coming here tonight once he woke up tomorrow morning.

"Austin," I started to say. "I'm sure that was meant to be very sweet somehow, but I've moved on, and it's time for you to go."

"But I came all the way up here and did the whole big-gesture thing like in those stupid movies you always made me watch," he whined. "Come on, you can't say no now." He reached out for me, and I panicked. My throat started closing up, and I froze.

No, no, no, no.

I pulled away from him as fast as I could. I tried to keep my breathing even, tried to keep anyone from noticing the fact that I had completely freaked out at his touch.

But Simón noticed. He noticed, and he practically flew to my side, grabbing Austin by the arm and pulling him in the direction of the elevator.

"Okay, you're done here, buddy. Goodbye." Alejandro pushed the elevator call button. Between the two of them, they managed to take him down to the main lobby and out the front door. I reported him to the building, and now Austin had been banned for life.

Well, at least there was that.

-

"Don't you have a date to get ready for?" he asks. "You're not going looking like *that*, are you?" He peers at me through the camera with disgust.

I glare at him and groan. "You're an asshole. Bye." I hang up.

I look at myself up and down in the mirror and take stock of myself. My cheeks are flushed, my hair's a mess, and there are dark circles under my eyes. I look like crap.

"Calm down," I tell myself out loud. "It's Josh. *Josh*. Not some scary rando or a crazy ex-boyfriend."

I bite my lip.

Exactly. It's not just anyone. It's *him.*

I realize it's a lot of pressure to put on just one date, but what I told my brother is true. Everything *can* and *will* change after tonight. This date will show us once and for all if we're compatible, if we can have a romantic relationship, if I'm brave enough to overcome everything that's happened.

I'm so scared of losing him for good it almost makes me want to cancel. But our relationship can't survive much longer in the weird limbo it's currently in. Like Simón said, it's make-or-break time. So, tonight is the night.

After I sent Josh the text on New Year's Eve, we agreed to go on a real date as soon as we got back. He had initially suggested we start off slow with a movie and pizza at my place, but I hadn't wanted to. I understood where he was coming from, though. He wanted to give me the advantage of the home base, so to speak. But I didn't want that. I wanted us to go big or go home. "If we're going on a date," I had said, "it has to be *a fucking date.*"

I may have sounded a bit demanding, but he was totally here for it. I could hear the smile in his voice when we spoke on the phone earlier this week and said, *"Hell. Yes.* I like your enthusiasm."

"What's the bloody emergency? Why did you ask me to come over urgently?" Oliver walks into my bedroom an hour later, and I'm *still* in my leggings, picking out an outfit.

"My first date with Josh is in an hour, and I don't know what to wear," I say in despair.

He stares at me for a beat. "Are you kidding me? You made me leave my gym class early for *this*? Couldn't Allie have helped you?"

"She's not here. And to be fair," I say, "it's your own fault for keeping your phone on you while you work out. Also, if you had an iPhone, like most people of our generation, I would've been able to just FaceTime you my outfit options!"

Oliver rolls his eyes and groans, throwing himself onto my bed on his back. He shrugs out of his coat and shakes his head at the ceiling. "I can't believe you made me come all the way over here for this. Now that we no longer have sex, do you see me as one of your female friends? Is that it? In the movie of your life, is this supposed to be a montage of you trying on different outfits?"

I groan in frustration. "Come on, be serious. Help me."

He gets up and helps me sift through several options. I walk him through my short list, but he doesn't approve of any of the outfits. For all his complaining, he seems to be enjoying himself.

"What about that sparkly black thing in there?" He points to a jumpsuit hanging in my closet. "That one looks okay, I think."

"This?" I ask. "You like this one?" I raise an eyebrow and hesitantly hold the black jersey piece with the embellished shoulders to my body in front of the full-length mirror. "You don't think this is too…I don't know. Informal?"

Oliver makes a face. "Hmmm…I don't think so. Add some hot heels and nice makeup, and you've got yourself an outfit."

I look over my shoulder at him in a state of shock. How did he do that?! He just managed to do in two minutes what I hadn't been able to do in two hours—and I'm a girl.

"Go on, try it on then." He takes a seat on my bed and pulls a water bottle from his backpack.

"Um," I say uncomfortably. "Okay, but you need to leave for me to do that."

He stops mid-sip and raises his eyebrows in disbelief. "Seriously?" Oliver's face falls as he sighs deeply, shaking his head. "It's the end of an era, and it's so sad. I'll never be able to see you naked again." He shakes his head and rises from my bed.

I laugh at how dramatic and push him out of my bedroom

to finish trying this look on, but he's right. With the right amount of makeup and the perfect shoes, I've got myself a look.

JOSH

> You good, kid?

My heart flutters in my chest in the back of the Uber on my way to our date, and I bite my lip at the familiar question. Am I good?

I consider making a sarcastic comment or a joke to hide how I'm *really* feeling—nervous, concerned. But he'd see right through that.

ME

> About to go out on a date with this guy, but I'm super nervous.

Understatement of the century.

JOSH

> Don't be. I'm sure he's nervous, too. He's probably so nervous he'll send you a text message as a joke just to make sure you're not standing him up or something.

ME

> Nah, I would never stand this guy up. He means too much to me.

He's unresponsive for a minute as we cross over the London Bridge to the Southbank.

JOSH

Believe me, I'm sure you mean more to him.

I'm sure he got to the restaurant an hour early just to make sure they didn't fuck up the reservation.

I'm sure he couldn't even sleep last night just thinking about what tonight means for the both of you.

I'm sure he's thought of nothing but your smile for the past 12 days.

I feel my heart squeeze in my chest.
God, I love him.

JOSH

See you soon. I hope...

I snort and shake my head.

ME

Josh, I'm not standing you up, you dummy.

Thirty-Two

OH MY GOD, *he's going to think I'm standing him up!*

My first mistake had been to decide to take an Uber for my date. I knew I should have taken the tube since it was cheaper and more efficient, but I wanted the ease of door-to-door service for tonight. I was already so nervous! And then I got stuck in traffic for what felt like hours.

When the Uber driver finally dropped me off, I wasn't just ten minutes late for my date with Josh...I was also at the wrong location.

Turns out, I had entered the incorrect address into the app and now found myself eight blocks away from the actual restaurant.

Oh my God, I'm gonna have to make a run for it.

I look down at my shoes and groan. *Of course* I had to go ahead and pick my highest and spikiest stilettos for tonight. I've suddenly gained full understanding of the term *suicide heels* and wish the universe had chosen another time to teach me this lesson.

I'm going to end up breaking my neck in these heels.

I take a deep breath, push the panic out of my head, stop my internal complaining, and remind myself that there is a very nervous man waiting for me at a nice restaurant, and I can't keep him waiting. So, with the fear of death in the back of my mind, I start what can only be described as a hop-jog down the cobblestoned streets of London, all the way to my date.

I stop to catch my breath just outside the restaurant, bracing my hands on my knees. I can feel a drop of sweat beading on the back of my neck.

Ew. There goes my hair and makeup.

I feel gross and disheveled, but determined, too. Nothing is going to keep me from this tonight. I walk up to the restaurant and catch a glimpse of Josh through the window. I smile and feel my stomach clench.

This is it.

I take a deep breath and open the restaurant door. He turns to look at me and holds my gaze as I step into the warm and welcoming restaurant. Josh looks *incredible*. His hair is perfectly styled the way I like it in a relaxed but neat way. The blue blazer he's wearing emphasizes his already broad shoulders, and the green tie around his neck highlights the malachite tint of his eyes.

Holy fuck.

"Whoa." He takes me in, and I step toward him with a huge smile on my face.

And then I proceed to trip on the welcome mat, twist my ankle, and fall flat on my face.

I can't believe I'm actually crying on a first date.

"I'm fine," I say in between small sobs, trying to calm myself down. "I promise I didn't feel it crack or anything," I lie. The *crrrack* feeling had been very distinct, but I know that if he finds out how much it hurts, he'll use this as an excuse to cancel our first night out.

"Are you sure?" Josh asks, concern visible in his eyes. "Please just let me take you home and we can do this another time. Please?" he begs.

I sniff once and let him and the hostess pull me up.

"I'm fine, I'm fine," I say, wiping my eyes with the heels of my hands, putting all my weight on my left foot. I catch the hostess rolling her eyes at me, but she quickly recovers.

Seriously?

If this had happened in New York, we would have been offered a free dinner by now in order to subdue any thoughts of a lawsuit. Instead, management at this place had barely thought to offer a bag of ice.

I look over at Little Miss Sunshine and say, "I'm fine. You can take us to our table once it's ready, thanks." She forces a smile and nods, motioning with her right hand for us to follow her. Josh wraps an arm around my waist, and I use him as support as I limp all the way to our table.

Once seated, Josh pulls a chair from a nearby table and places it across from me. "Here," he says. "It won't be very comfortable, but if you're not going to let me take you home and reschedule tonight, then you should at least ice it and keep it elevated during dinner."

I blush from embarrassment but accept his compromise. It's not the most ladylike of positions, but I adjust my body accordingly, propping my leg up on a chair under the table—thank God for jumpsuits.

We stay well past finishing our desserts, forgetting completely about the time. It isn't until the hostess tells us the restaurant is shutting down for the night that we notice the hour.

"Oh, wow. It's late." I frown, disappointed. I'm having such a great time. I don't want to leave. I think about inviting him over to my place to keep this date going, but I don't want to give him the wrong idea. I'm not ready to take that step yet, I think.

"How about a walk?" he asks, almost reading my mind as he helps me hobble out of my seat. I look down at my foot and snort. "Uh, right." He scratches his head and chuckles nervously. "A very, very short one? I know it's late, but I'm having a pretty amazing time." He smiles sheepishly, and I see his cheeks blush slightly. I nod. "Can you make it to the South-bank benches?"

I try to control the ridiculous smile on my face by biting my lip, but it doesn't work. It seems to be permanently affixed to my face for the night. "Yeah," I laugh nervously. "I think I can make it with your help."

Josh wraps an arm around my waist, my skin suddenly igniting, my cheeks flushing. We walk out of the restaurant and into the cold January night, the wind biting at my face, and I'm freezing my ass off—but I couldn't care less. The way he holds me so close and so tightly makes me believe he never wants to let go. And I never want him to let go.

We walk down the boardwalk a bit, talking about everything and nothing at the same time. But by the time we reach the National Theatre, I tell Josh I need a break, so we take a seat in one of the benches in front of the building, looking out at the twinkling lights from the buildings across the Thames. I lean into him, breathing in his scent, committing it to memory.

Eventually, we grow quiet. I turn to say something but catch him looking at me, staring down at my lips with a soft smile. Josh brushes some hair away from my face and slowly leans down to kiss me, hesitating just before, giving me time to pull back if I want to. But I don't. Not this time. Instead, I meet him the rest of the way, arms wrapping around his neck, heart beating so loud in my chest I'd be surprised if he couldn't hear it.

I can't breathe—in the best possible way.

It's perfect. The perfect moment.

The kiss is Josh personified. It's everything I love about him. It's warm, comforting, and direct. It's sweet, dependable, and passionate. It's understanding, attentive, and loyal. Most of all, though, it's *hot*. It is need, and hunger, and *way* overdue.

His hands are in my hair, and I moan when he pulls a little. Adrenaline courses through my veins, and our breathing speeds. I claw at his coat, pulling him closer to my body by its collar. I bite his lip, pulling slightly, and he groans, turning the kiss a little desperate. I want to fucking climb him.

Josh pulls my legs onto his lap, swiveling me in my seat so that we're at a more comfortable angle and position as we finally get to taste and hold each other the way we've been wanting to for quite some time, completely and utterly forgetting the fact that we're in a public place.

I scoot even closer to Josh and thank God for the sexual chemistry. I thank God that our connection isn't just emotional. I thank God for the sheer number of inappropriate thoughts running through my mind and all the things I feel like doing to him.

Must remember that we're not in the privacy of our own homes.

All the shit we went through, the stupid arguments, the mistakes, the fights, the crying, the anxiety... After all the good and the bad, we've finally made it. It was all worth it. We're here.

Holy shit, we're here.

I'm still mentally working on separating *Josh the Friend* from *Josh the Love Interest*, but I know with certainty that Josh is *it* for me. I felt it from the second his lips touched mine. The realization hits me like a ton of bricks and takes my breath away, but I don't say anything. There's no need to, because I'm pretty sure Josh feels it, too.

We spend the next hour taking turns talking and making out like teenagers. At a certain point, my teeth start to chatter, and Josh insists on taking me home. "Or I can just put you in an Uber," he says cautiously. "I don't want you to think that I'm expecting something."

I clear my throat. "No, it's fine. I know you know, um, where I'm at with...*that*," I say, feeling my entire body blush at this point. "I just mean we can keep talking there, if you'd like," I offer.

Josh smiles. "I'd like that." It doesn't seem to be a problem to either of us that it's three a.m. "I'll get a car for us."

I feel something electric run through my entire body at the sound of that "*us.*"

I doze off on the way home, snuggled into his side with his arm wrapped around me. He wakes me with a kiss on the top of my head and says, "We're home." I'm too tired to think too much about the fact that I'm inviting him over this late at night and what it means. It's obvious I won't be able to stay up much longer. Should I kick him out? I want him to spend the night, but is that the right thing to do now?

"You sure you want me to come up?" he asks as he helps me out of the car. I nod, and he helps me limp all the way to my apartment. Once inside, we head straight for my bedroom, and I shut the door behind us. I shrug out of my coat and toss it on the foot of my bed, Josh doesn't move an inch from where he stands. He looks unsure and nervous, wiping his hands unconsciously on the front of his pants. "So…" he says awkwardly. "I —I think I'm gonna go," he says, tossing a thumb over his shoulder.

"Josh." I reach out a hand. "Stay." I look into his green eyes, taking his hand. I kick off my shoes and walk backwards, pulling him slowly onto my bed. He's still wearing his coat when he wraps his arms around me and pulls me against his chest. "I'm tired, but I'd like it if you stayed the night." I breathe him in and close my eyes.

This is heaven.

"Yes," he says. "Of course I'll stay," he murmurs. Josh's arms tighten around me, and we proceed to fall asleep fully dressed, over the covers, in each other's arms.

I wake the next morning with a throbbing ankle and Josh's coat draped over me like a blanket. The sight of Josh sleeping next to me fills my chest with so much emotion it makes it hard to breathe. I look at him for a second, taking him in. He's still fully dressed, except for his shoes and coat, which he must have removed in the middle of the night. His dirty-blond hair is a mess, and I smile at his bedhead. He looks so peaceful in the early morning light.

I can't keep the smile off my face. I feel like a creep watching him while he sleeps, but I can't help it. Before I can stop myself, I reach out and brush Josh's hair out of his face. He takes a deep breath and slowly opens his eyes.

"Hey," he says in a low, gravelly voice, stretching a little.

"Morning," I say, and he smiles. Josh reaches out and pulls me to him, his coat sliding off my body, turning me in his arms, his front to my back, our bodies molding perfectly together. The movement feels so familiar, as if we've done it a million times, as if we'll do it a million more, that it leaves me shaken.

He's it.

He nuzzles my neck. "Mmmm, you smell nice," he says in his groggy, sexy voice. I turn my face to look at him, and he kisses me lightly on the lips.

He's everything.

My heart starts to race, and my breathing speeds. I turn to wrap my arms around his neck, and he holds me tighter still, one hand around my waist and another in my hair. He breathes me in. I start kissing up his neck all the way to the corner of his jaw. Josh groans, and I feel him hard against my stomach.

"Penny..." he murmurs. "I think I've reached my limit." He starts to gently push me away with a laugh. "I might spontaneously combust if we don't stop soon." He chuckles sheepishly.

"I don't want to stop." I kiss Josh again, my tongue sliding against his, and I bow my body into his suggestively. I pull away and look him in the eye as understanding dawns on him.

His arm wraps around my lower waist, and he pulls me roughly against him. I push against his chest, and he rolls me on top of him. Straddling his hips, shifting forward slightly, rubbing against his length, and he groans. His hands travel up my back to my zipper, deliberately pulling it slowly down to tease me. I push the fabric off both my shoulders, and he reaches around behind my back to unclasp my bra.

"*Jesus*," he says, closing his eyes, as if collecting himself for a second.

"You want to stop?" I ask nervously, biting my lip.

He answers by pulling me down by the waist and rolling over me, crushing his lips to mine. "Hell no." He rises up on his knees and slides the fabric down my waist, over my hips, and down my legs. He crawls over me, eyes never leaving mine, and he settles in between my legs. Josh kisses me slow and heavy, hands grazing my skin, cupping my breasts. He shifts his hips forward, and I moan, arching into him.

I've imagined the moment Josh and I would be together like this so many times, but the real thing doesn't even come close. I've never felt this way before. With Oliver, it was hunger, but with Josh it's pure *need*. Like I can't get closer to him fast enough. Like I won't be able to keep breathing until we're together. Like I need him to survive. It's like I want him to hurry so we can get there but slow down at the same time so that I can savor him.

He's wearing too many clothes. "Shirt. Off. Now," is all I manage to say in between pants. He obliges and starts unbuttoning from the top, but he's taking too long. I untuck the shirt from his pants and help him unbutton from the bottom. Our hands meet in the middle, and I push his shirt over his shoulders and start kissing his chest, his collarbone, his neck. He pushes me back down by the shoulders and kisses me, his tongue tasting me. My hands travel down his bare chest, scratching lightly, until they reach his belt. I unbuckle it hastily and slip my hand inside, feeling him. He groans and drops his forehead to my shoulder when I make contact. *"Fuck,* Penny," he says, his breathing ragged.

Josh pulls my hands away and unbuttons his pants. I help push them off. His lips meet mine again, but he stops. "Wait, wait." He shakes his head.

"No. No waiting, Josh. I'm so tired of fighting this. Aren't you?" I ask desperately. "Don't you want me?" I ask in a small voice.

"Want you?" Josh looks surprised by the question, like he never expected it to come out of my mouth. "Penny, I've imagined this moment so many times in my head..." He takes a deep breath. "You have *no* idea. I love you, Penny."

My face breaks out into a huge smile.

He loves me.

"I just want you to feel safe. I don't want you to feel pressured in any way, or feel like you *have* to. I mean, we have time, Penny."

I grin broadly, sliding my hands into his hair to pull him back down for a kiss. "I feel completely safe with you, Josh."

He shudders a breath, staring down at me for a beat before quickly helping remove my panties first and his underwear. I reach my hand out, yanking the drawer of my nightstand open, searching for a condom, which I pass to him. Josh quickly tears the foil package open with his teeth and rolls it onto himself.

My hands slide into his hair, and I look into his eyes. Josh's right hand travels slowly down my side, fingertips grazing my skin, barely touching me all the way down. He stops at my left knee and hooks it over his hip, holding it tightly to his body as he slowly enters me. I'm dizzy and breathless, and my chest tightens with emotion. Josh drops his forehead to mine in a groan, and I moan out his name against his mouth. The relief of the feel of him inside me is monumental—like everything is finally right in the world. There is no panic. There is no concern. Josh presses his lips to mine and pulls back slowly then pushes in hard and fast. I gasp.

Josh rolls me over him and sits up so that we're eye to eye, feeling him deeper still. His hands slide down to my hips, holding tight, fingers digging all the way down to my bones. I wrap my arms around his shoulders and press my forehead to his. He pulls me down roughly as he shifts his hips in an upwards movement, and my head snaps back in pleasure with a moan. "Again," I beg, and he repeats the same movement over and over again, creating a jagged rhythm.

He stills. "Penny," he says my name tightly, as if he's trying to hold on. "Look at me," he says. I know he's watching me, but I can't keep my eyes open. It's too much. I close my eyes even tighter and shake my head, pursing my lips, not wanting to say anything. "Open," Josh says in a pant, "I need to see you."

I slowly open my eyes and stare into his. "I love you," he says and kisses me slow and deep as we continue our rhythm. It's so intense, so intimate, it leaves me breathless. I feel my eyes sting, but I manage to control myself. His lips travel down my neck, stopping at my shoulder, and he bites me lightly. One of his hands slides in between our bodies, and he touches me just right, his movements precise.

"*Oh God,*" I groan. "I'm close," I say.

Josh rolls us over, and I'm suddenly on my back again. He hooks my legs over his arms, spreading me wide. He's grinding into me faster, rougher now, and I'm so close. It's right there, it's…

Oh. My. God.

My back arches off the mattress as I start to come. I grab his left hand and hold it tight for support. Josh whispers my name over and over again as a wave of pleasure ripples through my entire body. It feels like it goes on forever. His back goes tense under my fingertips, his body in between my legs. He buries his face in my neck, and I feel him press deep inside me one last time, groaning in relief.

"*Fuck,*" he says in between pants.

"I love you, too, by the way," I whisper after a few seconds of silence as my hands trail up and down his back. He laughs, face still buried in my neck.

"Good." I feel him nod. "That's really good." Josh releases my legs and rolls us on our sides. He crushes my head to his chest, still inside me, kissing the top of my head. I snuggle closer into that nook on his shoulder, breathing him in.

Epilogue

FIVE YEARS *Later*

"I look fat," I say as I struggle to put on my coat. Josh quickly runs to help me slip it on.

"You're not fat," he says automatically (he's had a lot of practice), "you're just pregnant."

It's been six months since I've started showing and six months since we started having this discussion pretty much every day. I almost feel bad for him. *Almost.* He's not the one who has to carry an almost twenty-pound bowling ball in the middle of his body all damn day.

I sigh deeply as he buttons up my coat and helps wrap a scarf around my neck. I hate being babied.

"There," he says with a smile. "Now you're nice and warm."

I pout, and he kisses the tip of my nose with a laugh.

It's the five-year anniversary of our first date, and as we do every year, we're going back to where we finally let our romantic relationship begin. Unfortunately, due to the bun currently being cooked in my oven and my inability to move at a normal human pace, we are currently running late.

Josh hands me my beanie, and I place it on my head. "Maybe we should just stay in," I say with a wicked smile, raising my eyebrows suggestively. "I'll make it worth your while..." Stretching up on my tippy-toes, I kiss him slowly, taking his lower lip into my teeth and tugging lightly.

He softly pushes me away and smiles, shaking his head. "Are you seriously trying to bribe me with sex right now? You just spent the last half hour trying to get dressed, and now you're gonna throw all that effort away?"

"Um, for sex? Absolutely. I can go into labor any second now, and then who knows when the next time we'll be able to do it will be?"

He rolls his eyes at me. "This again."

"Yes. This again."

"But you're just proving my point then, aren't you? This kid is due in ten days. This could be the last time we're alone *for a while*," he says seriously. "Don't you want a nice night out? A walk by the Thames on the Southbank? Make out on our bench?" He grins mischievously, and his green eyes darken at the memory of our first date.

I bite my lip as I remember that night. I remember how terrified I was of messing things up with Josh forever and freaking out over the worst possible outcome. In the end, it was the best—and craziest—date of my life.

Josh pulls me into his arms, and I snuggle into the nook that became permanently mine five years ago. I inhale his signature scent, and he tightens his arms around me.

"Okay, maybe a short dinner." My resolve wavers as Josh kisses me from right under my ear, to my jaw, all the way to my mouth—not an easy task to do when I'm covered in a million layers. "M-maybe just an entrée, you know?"

He removes my scarf and moves my hair to the side, and I angle my head to give him more room to kiss down my neck. His hands slide down my back and squeezes my significantly larger-than-usual ass.

"Mmmm…" he says against my skin. "How about now?"

"I *guess* we could also have some appetizers and spend some time walking around the Southbank." He keeps kissing my neck. "Maybe have some dessert, too." I smile as he bites where my shoulder meets my neck. He always finds a way to make me feel sexy, even when I look like a walrus.

"Nah, I think we should have dessert at home. Naked."

I snort and push him off me.

"Okay." I roll my eyes at him. "You convinced me. Let's go!"

We walk up to the restaurant, hand in hand, and I start laughing.

"What?" He looks at me quizzically.

"Remember how I almost broke my ankle? Jesus, that night was just hilarious. It was just one thing after another with us," I say.

"With *us*? Sorry, but you were the one acting like a crazy person that night," he says, looking both ways before crossing the street with me in tow.

"I was doing mental paperwork!" I say defensively. "I had to recategorize our relationship in my mind. I was distracted." I pout.

He chuckles. "That must have been a lot of mental paperwork, because that was *some* graceful arrival to the date." I slap him on the shoulder in reproach.

"Like it mattered," I say sarcastically. "You know you found me irresistible that night, regardless of my crazy."

He laughs. "Yeah, you were cute. I couldn't get enough of you."

I feel myself blush and smile at him.

We make it to the restaurant just in time for our reservation, and I look around while Josh speaks to the hostess. I'm glad to see that not much has changed except for the upholstery on the chairs. Josh and I don't come here often. We want to keep it a place strictly for special occasions, which means it turns into this sort of time machine every time we eat here.

After dinner, we finish our desserts, pay the check, and head out into the cold January night.

"You feel like walking to our bench?" he asks. "We can take a cab home after." I nod, and we start heading west.

I smile and hold on to his arm as he walks and I waddle on the Southbank boardwalk, staring out at the twinkling city lights across the Thames. It was here where we had our first date, and it was here where, six months later, Josh proposed to me. We tried to "take it slow", but when you know, you know. We didn't wait until we started the rest of our lives, so we married a year later.

Suddenly, I feel Max kicking me hard.

"Oomph!" I say. "This kid is killing me lately."

"He's kicking?" Josh smiles broadly. "I *told* you! I *told* you he's going to be a pro soccer player. He's gonna play for Arsenal, you'll see!"

I laugh at Josh's expression, grab his hand, and place it where I feel the kicking.

"Awesome," he says. "I'm gonna win our bet."

I roll my eyes at him, thinking back to the night we found out I was pregnant.

It was unplanned—a huge shock. But neither of us was disappointed. We were both incredibly happy and, while I hadn't even begun to comprehend the situation or even think about whether the baby was going to be a boy or a girl, Josh was already ten steps ahead of me. His first words to the news had been, "Yes! We're gonna have a pro soccer player in the family!"

It was only after a few months that I started imagining what my kid was going to be like. This child was half mine, and I wasn't exactly the most active person—I did not believe he was ever going to be able to be a professional athlete. So, we made a bet. We had until the kid turned eighteen. Loser takes the winner on a nice trip.

I was confident I was going to win—up until he started kicking. And man, is this kid a kicker. It's like I'm growing the next David Beckham in here!

"Whatever, dude. I'm sure you're wrong," I lie. Josh is definitely gonna win the bet, and it sucks.

"Oliver agrees with me," he says with a smug grin.

I roll my eyes at him. "That's only because he wants one of the twins to marry rich, and he thinks Max will be a rich soccer player."

Oliver and his girlfriend Lucy had twin baby girls last year. They were unplanned, too, and a huge shock, but Caroline and Emily immediately became the apple of Oliver's eyes. They have turned him into an even bigger softie, putting an end to his philandering days. He is so excited that our kids are going to be around the same age and we get to raise them together.

"You're both delusional," I say.

"Why don't you believe in our child, Penny?" he says with a smirk. Josh loves to tease me about this, tries to guilt trip me. "You're such an unsupportive mother. You should just let Max follow his dreams."

"You mean *your* dreams?"

He smiles a goofy side-grin. "Nah, I got all my dreams already."

I snort, wanting to make fun of him but stop myself before I ruin the moment.

I look out at the city in front of me, its bright lights and beautiful buildings filled with such rich history, and laugh.

"What?" he asks.

I shake my head. "Nothing. I just remember when I was younger how crazy the idea of living anywhere other than New York was. Now, I can't imagine living anywhere other than in London with you."

Acknowledgments

Writing a book is never easy. Though I feel like in many ways it gets harder and harder each time, I can also see how much I grow, my writing grows, with each one.

In for a Penny was my first book—and I think you can tell. She was written more for me as a cathartic exercise. A way to process my emotions and my experiences—nothing more. So when I embarked on this journey to "revamp" it, I thought seriously about deep diving into editing it, reworking the characters, editing the plot. But I just couldn't bring myself to do it.

Could I have reworked it into a better book? Yes, I think so. I think that with time I could have improved it far more. But honestly, after considering it, I felt strongly against it.

In for a Penny will remain the same because I don't want to change my past and because I want to see how much I've grown as a writer and a person. So, she did go through some edits—but nothing major.

So thank you for reading it. Thank you for taking a chance on it.

I especially want to thank Melody Jeffries, who made this whole second edition possible. As I've mentioned in the past, none of this would have happened had I not seen the beautiful illustration she posted on her Instagram. Immediately, I felt like it was plucked from my head, from my first date with my husband. The reaction I felt was visceral, bone-deep. It was like a sign.

So I took it and we worked together on the most amazing cover.

So thank you, Melody. You're amazing, and your artwork is amazing, and I can't wait to work on more projects with you.

To my husband, the most amazing, incredibly man in the world. I love you, always. Thank you for never giving up on me, for giving me the time and space I needed, for being patient. I can't imagine my life without you, and I don't ever want to. I love you.

Also by Caroline Frank

Seasons of Love Series (Open-Door Romantic Comedy):

Fall Into You (Book 1)

Shall We Dance? (Book 2)

Standalone Contemporary Romance (Open-Door):

In For a Penny

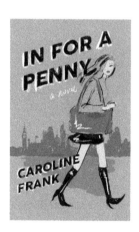

About Caroline

Caroline Frank is a shoe-obsessed indie author. She currently lives in Massachusetts with her husband and two cats, Salem and Señor Kitty—two little dictators.

In For a Penny was inspired by her time in London and is Caroline's first book.

instagram.com/carolinefrankwrites

CPSIA information can be obtained
at www.ICGtesting.com
Printed in the USA
BVHW031303290123
657320BV00002B/25